Praise for the works of Stacy Lynn Miller

Despite Chaos

I honestly do not know what to say! Fantastic story. Everything I've read by Stacy Lynn Miller has been entertaining, engaging and gripping. *Despite Chaos* is yet another amazing story, it's a must book to own in 2022. It's a 5/5. And with a cliffhanger like that... can't wait for that sequel.

-Emma S, *NetGalley*

4.25 Stars. Stacy Lynn ⌐   rite messy, complicated people t   first book in the "Falling Castl   vith Alexandra Castle and Tyler F

-Colleen C., *NetGalley*

This is a well written slow burn romance. There's romance, competition, blackmail, embezzlement and jealously. The story was fast paced, and I enjoyed every minute of it. The love, support and understanding of Tyler's husband was astounding. Hands down a great read and I recommend getting a copy. 4.5 stars.

-Bonnie K., *NetGalley*

Beyond the Smoke

This was really good! This is the third book in Miller's Manhattan Sloane Thriller series and is the best written book of the series. I was caught up in the mystery, it kept me turning the pages, but so did the romance.

-Lex Kent's Reviews, *goodreads*

I loved the first two novels, but I think this one might be the best yet...I've enjoyed all the mystery, excitement, action, and intrigue in the plots of these books, but I've fallen in love with these characters, and want to know what's happening in their lives. This is the mark of an exceptionally talented author.

-Betty H., NetGalley

From the Ashes

I have been looking forward to reading *From the Ashes* by Stacy Lynn Miller since I read her first Manhattan Sloane novel back in April. I fell in love with Sloane, Finn, and all the other characters in this story while reading the first book, and I wanted more, especially since the story didn't completely end with the first novel. I'm happy to say I loved this book as much as the first one.

In this second tale, we find Sloane still struggling with her grief over her wife's death as she also deals with her growing love for Finn. Nothing is ever easy for Sloane and Finn, since the head of the drug cartel they battled in the first book is now looking for revenge, and he's quite willing to target Sloane and Finn's loved ones.

This is an action-packed story with a complex plot. Most of the characters in this book were introduced in the first one, so they are already well developed and we learn more about the different members of the drug cartel and their motivations. This is definitely a character-driven tale, and Ms. Miller has done an excellent job of creating realistic characters, both good and bad.

I enjoyed seeing the romance grow between Sloane and Finn, even with all the obstacles that could come between them. The author did a wonderful job weaving this romance into all the action and suspense in the overall story.

As I mentioned above, this book is the second in the Manhattan Sloane series and takes up where the first novel, *Out of the Flames*, ended. These books really need to be read together and in order to get the most enjoyment out of the story. I highly recommend both novels, though, so get them both. You won't be disappointed.

-Betty H., NetGalley

This was the sequel to this author's very good debut book, *Out of the Flames*.

I enjoyed how the author developed this sequel with realistic problems the characters faced after the loss of loved ones. The author also provided more answers to the car accident that killed Sloane's parents. This was a very emotional moment for those involved. The way it was described, I couldn't help but feel for those characters.

Similar to the previous book, there was a lot of drama when the characters dealt with the cartels. These scenes quickened the pace of the story and allowed for more anxious moments. The secondary characters, both good and bad, increased this story's emotional depth.

Since this was a sequel, I recommend reading the first book to get an overall understanding of the characters and their backgrounds. The author did allow some past events to resurface, but the emotional scenes from the first book were too good not to read and experience.

This book was very engaging with tense moments, emotional breakdowns and recovery, and most of all, tender loving scenes.

-R. Swier, NetGalley

From the Ashes is the sequel to *Out of the Flames* with SFPD Detective Manhattan Sloane and DEA Finn Harper. They're chasing after a Mexican drug cartel that is ultimately responsible for killing Sloane's wife. Sloane and Harper had a connection in high school but they were torn apart after Sloane's parents were killed in a car accident. Then they were thrown together on this case as the drug cartel seeks revenge for the death of one of their own. Miller is a wonderful storyteller and this story had me sitting on the edge of my seat from start to finish. The first book in the series, *Out of the Flames*, was a 5-star read and

From the Ashes is the same as it ducks and weaves and thrills and spills all the way to the end. The chemistry between Sloane and Harper is palpable...Miller certainly knows how to write angst into her characters. This book is a thrill a minute and I can't wait for the next one.

-Lissa G., *NetGalley*

I read Stacy Lynn Miller's debut novel *Out of the Flames* back in May, and couldn't wait to read the sequel to learn what happens to San Francisco police detective Manhattan Sloane and DEA Agent Finn Harper's relationship as well as the drug cartel they were chasing. *From the Ashes* resumes from the point that *Out of the Flames* ended.

The book was fast-paced with quite a few anxious and emotional moments. I don't think that you have to read the first book to enjoy this one, but I recommend it since it is a good story and it will introduce the background and characters in a more complete manner. I'd definitely recommend both books to other readers.

-Michele R., *NetGalley*

Firstly, if you've not read Stacy Lynn Miller's debut novel and first in the series of 'A Manhattan Sloane Thriller'... give it a read. It's called *Out of the Flames* and I can guarantee you will not regret it and be hooked like many of us who are now following her work.

From the Ashes follows on from the first book, you don't really need to read the first BUT PLEASE DO! Its fast-paced action keeps you on your toes and includes romance! What's not to love?

-Emma S., *NetGalley*

This is one amazing follow up to book one. The characters grow very well together, even though there are still mafia issues going on around them. I felt that the plot to resolve all issues was nicely provided. The finish was wonderful, and I feel like there will be a new set of stories (or so I hope) for the main characters to decide on their new adventures.

-Kat W., NetGalley

One of the things that Stacy Lynn Miller is skilled at is breathing life into her characters. Even important secondary characters. They all stand up as themselves, and there's never any difficulty remembering who is who. This is as true for Miller's previous book as this one. In fact, when I read the final passage, my first thought was for the future of a secondary character! Who worries what kind of future the daughter of a criminal will have? Me, apparently.

There is danger here, passion, secrets…all of the things that keep me reading long into the night. But this book wormed its way into me and wouldn't let up. I was quite literally unable to sleep because I was worried about one of the secondary characters—an autistic young man. I had to pick the book back up and finish it just so I knew what happened to him.

Miller wrapped up questions left dangling in the first book that I didn't know I had. There was a satisfying sense of completion and closure, and yet…there is still room for more stories to come from this fictional world. I do hope the author is interested in bringing us more from this made-up world of hers because I'll be among the first in line with my money out.

-Carolyn M., NetGalley

Out of the Flames

This is the debut novel of Stacy Lynn Miller and it's very, very good. The book is a roller coaster of emotion as you ride the highs and lows with Sloane as she navigates her way through her life which is riddled with guilt, self blame, and eventually love. It's easy to connect with all the main characters and sub-characters, most of them are all successful strong women so what's not to love? The story line is really solid.

-Lissa G., NetGalley

If you are looking for a book that is emotional, exciting, hopeful, and entertaining, you came to the right place. There are characters you will love, and characters you will love to hate. And the important thing is that Miller makes you care about them so, yes, you might need the tissues just like I did. I see a lot of potential in Miller and I can't wait to read book two.

-Lex Kent's 2020 Favorites List.
Lex Kent's Reviews, *goodreads*

If you are looking for an adventure novel with mystery, intrigue, romance, and a lot of angst, then look no further.

...I'm really impressed with how well this tale is written. The story itself is excellent, and the characters are well-developed and easy to connect with.

-Betty H., *NetGalley*

BLIND
SUSPICION

More Bella Books by Stacy Lynn Miller

A Manhattan Sloane Thriller
Out of the Flames
From the Ashes
Beyond the Smoke

Falling Castle Series
Despite Chaos

About the Author

A late bloomer, Stacy Lynn Miller took up writing after retiring from the Air Force. Her twenty years of toting a gun and police badge, tinkering with computers, and sleuthing for clues as an investigator form the foundation of her Manhattan Sloane romantic thriller series. She is visually impaired, a proud stroke survivor, mother of two, tech nerd, chocolate lover, and terrible golfer with a hole-in-one. When you can't find her writing, she'll be golfing or drinking wine (sometimes both) with friends and family in Northern California.

For more information about Stacy, visit her website at stacylynnmiller.com. You can also connect with her on Instagram @stacylynnmiller, Twitter @stacylynnmiller, or Facebook @ stacylynnmillerauthor

BLIND
SUSPICION

STACY LYNN MILLER

BELLA
BOOKS
2022

Copyright © 2022 by Stacy Lynn Miller

Bella Books, Inc.
P.O. Box 10543
Tallahassee, FL 32302

All rights reserved. No part of this book may be reproduced or transmitted in any form or by any means, electronic or mechanical, including photocopying, without permission in writing from the publisher.

This is a work of fiction. Names, characters, businesses, places, events and incidents are either the products of the author's imagination or used in a fictitious manner. Any resemblance to actual persons, living or dead, or actual events is purely coincidental. The publisher does not have any control over and does not assume any responsibility for author or third-party websites or their content.

Printed in the United States of America on acid-free paper.

First Edition - 2022

Editor: Medora MacDougall
Cover Designer: Heather Honeywell

ISBN: 978-1-64247-359-9

PUBLISHER'S NOTE

The scanning, uploading, and distribution of this book via the Internet or via any other means without the permission of the publisher is illegal and punishable by law. Please purchase only authorized print or electronic editions, and do not participate in or encourage electronic piracy of copyrighted materials. Your support of the author's rights is appreciated.

Acknowledgment

A special thanks goes to Barbara Gould. If not for her cheerleading and being a card-carrying member of Team Ethan, this book would've never been birthed.

Thank you, Louise, Kristianne, Diane, Sue, and Sabrin. This fantastic crew of beta readers pushes me to be a better writer.

Thank you, Linda and Jessica Hill, for believing in my work and making a dream come true.

Thank you, Medora MacDougall. Her editing magic made this story shine in ways I never thought possible.

Finally, to my family. Thank you for loving me.

Dedication

To Allison Miller
My daughter and co-owner of my heart.
She teaches me every day how special it is to be loved.

CHAPTER ONE

Manhattan, New York, 2007

If not for insubordinate ones, William Castle would have no children at all. First, his oldest, Sydney, had taken off to make wine in Napa with that lowly vintner years ago. Then his nearly thirty-three-year-old twins had betrayed him. He had coerced Alexandra during college to keep her sexual appetites out of the public eye, but she had defied their arrangement twice in recent weeks. Pawing a woman in public at his retirement announcement last month and then the other night at his own San Francisco hotel, of all places. As for Andrew—he had suddenly resigned from the company last month, leaving him without a child he could trust to carry on his legacy.

William had put his retirement on hold, hoping to get to the bottom of his son's hasty departure and entice him back into the business before he would have no other choice but to hand over his empire to a daughter who had proved that she didn't deserve it. Andrew had blamed his leaving on not being named as William's successor, but his failure to look William directly in the eye when he resigned meant that there was more to the story. Meant that the oblique comments Alexandra had made weeks before Andrew's resignation about something being amiss with the books had meat to them.

His desk phone buzzed to Gretchen's soft voice. "Mr. Castle, Ms. Georgia Cushing is here to see you."

Finally, he'd get some answers from the one person ideally suited to ferret out the truth. His gaze drifted to the bookcase to his left and settled on an old, framed photo. He'd assembled the entire staff at the Times Square's front entrance for a ribbon-cutting ceremony thirty-seven years ago. That day marked the first day of business for Castle Resorts and the first day of his and Georgia's secret affair. She was a competent bookkeeper when she first came aboard and had evolved into an indispensable accountant. Though their affair ended decades ago, having Georgia looking into his family's dirty laundry was his best option. She was already part of it and wouldn't dare chance spreading gossip.

"Send her in," William said.

After closing the door, Georgia strode toward William's desk clutching a company folder filled with documents. It had been years since he'd had reason to read her expressions, but he quickly recognized the determined one she was wearing now.

She slammed the folder atop his mahogany desk. "In summary, your son is a thief." The shock value of her one-liner was par for the course. Besides Alexandra and Andrew's mother, Georgia was the only one brave enough to hit William with both barrels, reload, and fire again.

"Please explain." He bit back the bitter taste of her arrogance long enough to get what he needed from her.

"I uncovered what appears to be a significant embezzlement scheme involving duplicate services never performed by V.P. Construction, nor goods received from Suite Hospitality. Both are owned by an individual named Victor Padula. Andrew's signature approved each outlay."

William recognized the name. His son's long-term bookie was associated with last month's shooting at their Times Square hotel. Heat rose in his chest as the picture became clear. His son had involved himself with a gang of ruffians to feed his out-of-control gambling addiction. "How much and for how long?"

Georgia pointed to the folder she'd flung on his desk moments earlier. "A quarter-million dollars since the commencement of the Times Square renovation, but there's an interesting twist."

"What kind of twist?"

"The day after Andrew resigned, Alexandra transferred that same amount from her personal account to the company's general fund."

"What does Alexandra have to do with this?"

"I don't know. I'm not even sure the two are connected. She'd simply marked the transaction as 'repayment.'"

"Have you spoken to either of them?"

"Of course not. You made it quite clear: my job was to audit and report, not make accusations."

"I'm sure the thought never crossed your mind." William straightened his tie and spine to tamp down the storm brewing inside him. Betrayal by one child was bad enough, but it appeared Alexandra had known what Andrew had done and had covered for her thieving brother. That was unforgivable. Her complicity was an act he couldn't overlook, the last straw. "You are to tell no one about what you've found. Since all the money is back in place, I'll handle the matter personally."

"You're going to let them slide, aren't you?" Georgia reloaded for another shot across the bow. "You're blind when it comes to those two."

"What I do with my children is none of your concern because only a Castle can correct a Castle mistake. Am I making myself clear?"

"Perfectly."

William ordered Georgia out, activated the office intercom, and instructed Gretchen to get Robert Stein on the phone. "Tell him it's an emergency."

Minutes later, Gretchen connected Mr. Stein.

"Robert, thank you for returning the call. I need to change my trust, will, and beneficiaries to my business holdings immediately."

"Of course, William. May I ask what this is about?"

William was never one to discuss sensitive topics over the phone, preferring to meet people in person to gauge their responses and ensure a mutual understanding of the issues at hand. This situation called for a patented vague answer, even to a friend of forty-plus years. "Let's say my twins won't be pleased once all is said and done. Can we meet in your office in an hour?"

William disconnected the call, slumped back in his plush leather chair, and wearily regarded the picturesque view of Central Park that had taken him a lifetime to earn. Was it all a wasted effort if he had no child worthy of taking over what he'd built?

"Where did I go wrong?"

He ticked off in his head the things that needed to be done to settle this ugly matter. He'd already checked off one of the to-do items, summoning Alexandra to his office tonight to address the matter of her public disrespect. The rest of the list, though, was long and required special handling. Following a detailed call to his private investigator, he arrived promptly for his meeting at the law firm of Stein, Levy, and Keller.

"May I get you some coffee, Mr. Castle? One sugar, one cream with two English biscuits on the side, right?" asked Laura, Robert's personal assistant.

"Normally I would, but I need to get right down to business today."

Laura escorted him into Robert's stately, masculine office before politely excusing herself and closing the thick oak door behind her. Surprisingly, his Parkinson's-ridden stride seemed steadier than it had been in recent weeks; his mounting anger was likely fueling his surge in energy, he decided.

Robert greeted him with a firm handshake and directed him to sit with him at the two high-back black leather guest chairs. "So, what's this about the twins, William?"

"I've unearthed some alarming information about them. Disturbing enough I've decided that it's time to cut all ties. My will, their trusts, the company, everything."

Robert leaned forward in his chair, placing both elbows on his knees and shifting from lawyer to friend. "I've been your attorney for thirty-seven years. Of course, I will follow any direction you give me regarding your legal matters. However, I've been your friend for longer, and I can't in good conscience do so without first making a very salient point." He gently tapped William's knee with a hand to emphasize his next words. "Will, my friend, if you later change your mind, we can easily undo the legal aspects, but they will surely leave a tangled, emotional mess."

William smoothed the jacket of his custom-tailored, double-breasted, navy blue suit. A gift from Alex, it was his favorite until today. Normally calming, the habit failed to clear the mounting agitation from his tone. This suit would soon find the trash heap. "I appreciate your years of legal counsel, but do not presume to lecture me on dealing with my ungrateful, depraved children." Not since his wife's expected long, drawn-out death had William been this determined to settle his affairs straight away.

"Will, you know me better than that. Now, what is so troubling that it has prompted such a dramatic change?"

"Andrew stole a quarter-million dollars from the company, and Alexandra covered it up by repaying the money. They have disappointed me for the last time."

"Do you want to involve the police and file charges for embezzlement for Andrew's part?" Robert asked.

"I can't have the world knowing I've raised a thief. Castle Resorts has an impeccable reputation, and I won't have him tarnish that. Alexandra covered for him and has defied me for the last time. Her judgment is irrevocably flawed, to the point I no longer trust her. I want to sever all current and future ties with them financially. They get nothing, not one penny more from me." William pounded his fist on the chair's leather arm. "Do you understand? Not a penny more."

"William, I realize this is upsetting, but unless Alexandra altered the financial records it's not as if she committed a crime like Andrew."

Robert's attempt at reason fell on deaf ears. If he only knew the depth of Alexandra's betrayal with that woman, he wouldn't question William's motivation. But that was a humiliation better left buried. Anger far outstripped his disappointment in his twins. He pounded his fist again to emphasize his next point. "No, dammit. It's the same. Both have betrayed me repeatedly. I have given each second and third chances, but they have proven to be incapable of self-control. I will not have them benefit from their immorality."

"There's nothing I can say to change your mind?" Robert pressed.

"Nothing. Make sure everything goes to Sydney." William stood. His oldest may have left the family fold to follow her heart, but she was the only child he'd raised who hadn't betrayed him. Sydney wasn't a thief, nor was she a degenerate as he'd discovered, years after her death, Alex's mother had been.

Robert placed both hands on his knees, pushed himself to a standing position, and walked to his desk. "Very well. This will take some time, but I will have all the documents ready for your signature tomorrow afternoon."

"I would prefer you do it today, but I trust you won't dawdle." William walked out, more frustrated than when he walked in. Explaining his children's scandalous behavior had been more distasteful than expected. He resolved to not rest until he'd cut his ungrateful twins out of his life.

Returning to his waiting town car, William received a call from the private investigator to whom he'd assigned several urgent tasks. "Did you reach him?"

"Yes, Mr. Castle. He'll meet you at the Key Grill in an hour."

"That's fine. Did you locate my son?"

"Yes, but I haven't approached him yet per your instruction. What time shall I tell him to be at your office?"

"Eight o'clock. And have her there at eight thirty." Disconnecting the call, William became more determined to conclude this ugly business as soon as possible. If Robert and his man did their jobs, he could sleep easily by tomorrow night. "Change of plans, David. Drop me at the Key Grill."

"Yes, Mr. Castle." His driver weaved the town car through the light midafternoon city traffic, landing across from the construction mess known as his office building.

The stately Key Grill had been William's favorite place for conducting business for decades; it would serve as the ideal location for his next distasteful task. He may not have been streetwise or familiar with the protocols of calling on a well-connected criminal, but he was a shrewd businessman. And the primary lesson he had learned over the years was that he needed to conduct business on his home turf to get the upper hand. This was business, and he definitely needed leverage.

William expected the stereotypical Hollywood wise guy to show up at his table, decked out in a flashy suit and wearing enough bling to set off metal detectors. He didn't expect the well-dressed, clean-cut compatriot who arrived punctually.

"How may I help you, Mr. Castle?" The man seated himself on the opposite end of William's curved booth. His tone was polite yet cautious.

William pulled out copies of two Castle Resorts invoices from his inside breast pocket, one from V.P. Construction and another from Suite Hospitality, the shell companies Andrew had created to direct payment of his gambling debts. He slid them across the table toward the man he assumed was Victor Padula.

"These are just the tip of the iceberg. A quarter-million dollars siphoned from my company's coffers in all. At this point, I don't care about the money. I only want answers."

Victor stared at William as if he were insane or just plain stupid. "What do you want to know?"

"I know this was my son's doing, a way to pay off his gambling debt to you." Victor's eyes narrowed. "All I want to know is what was my daughter's involvement."

"What's it to you?"

"It's a matter of trust. I demand loyalty from those around me, and right now, I'm not sure if I can trust her."

"You're talking about Alex, right?" William offered a simple nod, and then Victor continued, "She settled his debt."

"What do you mean by settled?"

"We agreed to a final amount to close out his debt and she paid it."

"Did she have anything else to do with this?" William pointed to the papers on the table. "Anything before paying it off?"

Victor answered with a simple "no."

"I think we can both agree that neither one of us wants this information reaching the public's eye, especially those of the authorities." William slid an envelope containing twenty thousand dollars in cash toward him. "Can we consider this matter closed?"

Victor grinned his reply. "Yes."

After the bookie left, William stepped outside, southern winds nipping at his cheeks and signaling that scattered clouds would soon replace the afternoon haze and usher in the forecasted evening spring thunderstorm. He crossed the street to Castle headquarters, his arm muscles turning rigid as he stepped onto the curb. His symptoms had become impossible to hide in public, making the need to settle things and hand everything over to Sydney that much more urgent.

Once through the main entrance, William faced a dozen construction workers, all busy with the extensive remodeling project that had irritated him for months. Whirring power tools, clanking hammers, and a pervasive smell of construction dust disrupted the lobby's usually elegant, professional atmosphere.

He waited with four well-dressed businessmen at the bank of elevators for the next car to arrive. The one standing closest to William broke the customary silence. "How much longer do we have to put up with this mess?"

William would have preferred to ignore the question, but based on the man's head lean the comment was being directed to him. "I believe another month," he said stiffly.

The idiot shook his head. "It's a pain in the ass. Never know from day-to-day which elevator will be working or what stairwell they'll have blocked with their damn plastic sheets."

The arrival of the elevator averted the need to respond—and saved the speaker from possible injury. Given the ire William was feeling today, one more crass comment might have been enough for him to throttle the man—a ruffian response he hadn't considered since his Parkinson's raised its ugly head when Alexandra and Andrew were still at Yale. He sucked in his impatience, waited for the others to enter, and took a position on the other side of the car, creating a two-person buffer between him and the immediate source of his irritation.

The ride up to the twenty-third floor was thankfully silent, giving William time to mentally prepare for what would be a busy evening. At last, the door whooshed open to the jarring reality that would last another month—the incessant buzzing and thumping coming from the adjacent stairwell.

Pushing through the double glass doors leading to his company's office suite, he made his way to the executive wing. At the reception desk guarding his private office, he saw, as expected, Gretchen, his loyal secretary of eighteen years. Garbed in fashionable yet professional attire, her graying blond hair perfectly coifed as usual, she looked up from her computer. Before she could greet him with as much as a smile, he barked, "Grab your pad."

Without delay, Gretchen grabbed her memo pad and pen and stayed on his heels into his office. He had no time to waste. He went directly to the wall safe behind his desk, carefully entered the combination, and opened the thick metal door. He removed a vintage camera and two legal-sized leather document folios, which would drive home his point when he met with his two disgraceful children tonight.

"What a lovely camera, Mr. Castle. Is it a family heirloom?" Gretchen's question, while not overly intrusive, wasted precious time.

"Yes. It was Rebecca's and, at one time, Alexandra's."

"It must be very special to you."

"It is, but it has taken its last photograph."

"Is it broken?"

"No, but the last person who used it is." His stomach turned at the thought that both his wife and daughter had used this exact camera to memorialize their respective sinful exploits—Rebecca with that loathsome Abigail Spencer and Alexandra with that tramp, Kelly Thatcher.

"I'm not quite following."

"Nothing to concern yourself over." He placed the camera on the corner of the desk. "I have one action item for you. I plan on making a dramatic change around here. I need you to schedule a meeting for ten o'clock tomorrow morning with all the executives. Everyone except Alexandra."

Gretchen cocked her head. He long suspected she had a soft spot for his daughter and preferred her management style over his. After tomorrow, that partiality would no longer matter. "Shall I have refreshments available for the meeting?"

"No, that won't be necessary. I don't expect it to take that long."

"Is there anything else, sir?"

"Has Alexandra confirmed my meeting with her tonight?"

"She has. If her flight isn't delayed, she should be here at eight."

Good, William thought. He'd deal with both of them at the same time.

He waited for Gretchen to close the door behind herself before opening the first leather folio. He organized the documents chronicling his daughter's sordid affairs, including the final straw—video stills from the San Francisco resort last night. All the trouble he had gone through to get the camera back had been for naught. He then thumbed through the second folio, which contained years of private investigator reports documenting Andrew's gambling exploits and considerable debt. He added Georgia's audit to them and returned everything to the appropriate folders and then to the safe, along with the camera. He was ready to deal with his ungrateful offspring.

Those two have disappointed me for the last time.

CHAPTER TWO

The moment her plane landed, Alex Castle checked the time on her cell phone. The pilot had made up a portion of the seventy-minute delay in Denver, but not enough for her to make the initial meeting time with her father. She checked her list of voice mail messages, but only one was critical. Gretchen confirmed she'd moved the meeting, but only from eight to nine, not to nine thirty as Alex had requested as a buffer. That meant she had no time for dinner or to change out of her jeans and casual top and into proper business attire. Tired and hungry was not the ideal state to be in to have a meeting with her father, that her sister, Syd, had led her to believe would be contentious, but perhaps an empty stomach was the best way to deal with him when he was in one of his sour moods.

As Richard raced her across the Williamsburg Bridge into Manhattan in the Spencer Foundation town car, outbound cars and a subway train on the upper deck rumbled above. Her reflection in the glass window prompted Alex to pat down her long brown hair, which had become unruly during flight. An intricate pattern of lower deck steel girders fashioned into one giant X after another whizzed in and out of view from the back seat window. It felt more like riding through a tunnel than over a bridge, making Alex wonder how Tyler would react. Twenty hours earlier she had discovered that Tyler had a lifelong fear of bridges, one that had been strong enough to send her in search of a stiff drink before the first time they made love.

Her mind drifted to the earth-shifting connection they had shared the previous night. *Why didn't I say, "I love you" this morning when I had the chance?*

"Ms. Castle?"

Hearing her name pulled Alex from the compunction she was feeling. "I'm sorry, Richard. What was that?"

"Do you need to stop at home first, Ms. Castle?" He glanced into the rearview mirror, briefly locking gazes with her.

"I'm afraid there's no time. Gretchen moved my meeting up a half hour."

"I apologize for the delay, ma'am. I had to take the southern route because of an accident in the midtown tunnel."

"No worries. I'm glad you did. It's such a beautiful evening."

She whispered to herself, "So many bridges." She wondered if Tyler could ever be comfortable living on an island that was home to so many bridges.

We could always use the tunnels. Or maybe I could move to California. Syd would love that. It would make Tyler's divorce from Ethan much easier for her and her daughters. It would also allow Tyler to keep seeing her therapist and continue the progress she'd made in confronting her PTSD from the rape.

Alex knew she was getting ahead of herself, but she couldn't help it. She'd waited so long to follow her heart, and now that she had, nothing could hold her back. Especially not her father. She and Tyler had worked together, by phone, for months on a redesign of the company website, but they had been lovers for less than a full day. She already knew she wanted her in her life every day and night.

Her phone buzzed to a distinctive ringtone. It wasn't the call she would have preferred, but it still elicited a smile. Such things always did from her friend of nearly three decades.

"Hello, Harley."

"Mother said you're coming back to the city tonight. Something about William being on the warpath again. What did you do, Alex?"

"I don't know. All Syd said was that he was madder than when he found out about the Mercedes."

"You mean the time when you took the blame for Andrew taking his new Mercedes out for a joyride and putting a dent in the fender?"

"That's the one."

"Wait. Why did Syd have to tell you? Grumpy Pants didn't call himself?"

"I had my phone off." A memory flashed in Alex's head of her and Tyler curled up between soft sheets; it made her miss the warmth of her body.

"You never have your phone off unless the situation involves a woman. Who was she?"

What was it about the confidants in her life seeing right through her? Syd had made the same assumption when she learned their father hadn't been able to reach Alex on the phone. The only time Alex shut the world off was for a physical escape, but after last night, going communication-silent after business hours would become the rule, not the exception.

"Tyler Falling."

Harley let go of a squeal reminiscent of their carefree junior high school years when all they cared about was Madonna's latest release. "And?"

"Amazing." Alex had spent hours caressing every inch of Tyler, committing to memory every curve, soaking in every sound, and relishing every hitch of her breath. "I'm in love with her, Harley."

"Did you tell her?"

"I'm such an idiot." Alex rubbed a temple with her free hand, wishing she'd handled the missed opportunity differently. "After Tyler told Syd that she loved me, Syd distracted me with my father's summons."

"You *are* an idiot. The woman you've turned hermit over says she loves you and you say nothing?"

"I know. And by the time I realized my horrific mistake, minutes had passed. Any reciprocation at that point would've seemed disingenuous." *Dammit, Syd. Why did you have to mention Father right then?*

"When do you plan to tell her?"

"That depends on my father. I'd love to fly back to California tomorrow, take her in my arms, and show her how much I love her."

"I'm happy for you, Alex."

The town car coasted to a stop. "We're here, Ms. Castle." Richard exited and opened the curbside rear door.

"I hate to cut this short, Harley, but I've arrived at the headquarters building. Can I call you tomorrow?"

"I'll hold you to it. Don't let Grumpy Pants push you back in the closet."

"Not a chance." Alex disconnected the call and slipped her phone into her purse before accepting Richard's helping hand. "Thank you, Richard. I'm not sure how long I'll be, so you should head home. Can you get my bag from the trunk?"

"Mrs. Spencer released me into your care for the evening, miss. I'm happy to stay."

Alex waved him off while he placed her overnight bag on the curb. "I'll be fine. If you're hungry, stop by Margo's at the Times Square hotel and tell them to put the bill on my account."

"Thank you, Ms. Castle. By chance, is Ms. Janay working there tonight?" Richard sheepishly lowered his eyes.

"I believe she is." A cheerfulness filled Alex's chest. She'd never seen Richard's face light up more than it had just now. Her restaurant manager—single, attractive, and uber-smart—would make an excellent match for Richard—tall, broad-shouldered, and a true gentleman. Alex would have to find more excuses to get those two in the same place at the same time. In the meantime… She made a quick call to Margot's as she walked to the building entrance.

As she rode the elevator to the twenty-third floor, Alex contemplated the fact that a month had passed since she'd stayed in her office there past sundown—a dramatic departure from her work habits of the last decade. She'd made many changes after realizing she wanted Tyler more than she wanted the throne of Castle Resorts. The most significant one had been her refusal to continue to conceal her sexual orientation from the public eye.

The hallways were strangely quiet tonight without the construction crews and the presence of the dozens of executives and assistants who tended to the needs of the company's twenty-three resorts around the world. Dropping her suitcase off near Gretchen's desk, she looked toward her father's office. Its custom-carved wood door was open, his unspoken invitation to enter. He was standing near the wall of panoramic windows, staring out at Central Park and the western Manhattan skyline. Bright flashes of lightning streaked through the sky, followed seconds later by loud claps of thunder. The ominous clouds that had followed her into the city had finally opened up and released a pouring rain.

Alex walked up beside her father and joined him in staring at the mounting storm. "Nature's fireworks."

Without breaking his gaze, he replied, "Your mother always saw beauty in everything, even something as violent as a thunderstorm."

"It's one of the best memories I have of her. I remember being at the pier and being frightened when a powerful storm came through. She took me on her lap and explained that lightning was nature's fireworks and that thunder was part of nature's concerto. I must have looked confused because she hugged me, kissed my forehead, and said something like, 'A storm is like a symphony where all the instruments combine to make music. Clouds, lightning, and thunder all combine to make the rain.'"

Recounting that memory tonight gave birth to a moment of clarity: wanting to follow in her father's footsteps had always been a mistake. Her mother's passions were where her heart had laid.

"Mother turned the storm into art for me. Sometimes I wish I would have studied art and made it my life's work."

"Perhaps you should have." William's sharp response signaled the purpose of tonight's meeting had begun. He stepped to his desk and assumed the seat of power Alex had once coveted. Spending last night with Tyler had given Alex much-needed clarity about that as well, however. Even if he handed her the throne, she didn't want it if it meant managing it his way. Unless she could reenvision the company on her terms, he could keep it.

"What does that mean?" she asked.

"It means I wouldn't be in the position now of having to terminate you."

"Terminate me?" She shook her head wryly. "On what grounds? I did everything you asked of me regarding the San Francisco and Times Square remodeling projects."

"The remodels have nothing to do with this."

"Then what is this about?"

"Trust." William snarled. "You've kept secrets from me that impact our business and our family."

"Will you please stop baiting me with cryptic allusions and just come out with it?"

"Andrew." Alex's eyes shot wide open. How much did he know? "I know all about his skimming from the company coffers and why he did it, including his unseemly business with Victor Padula. What I don't understand is why you didn't come to me when you discovered it. Nor why you covered it up."

"I handled it the way I thought best for the family and the company. I confronted him, made him resign, and returned the money. I didn't tell you because I didn't want you to know that your only son was an embezzler. I ensured the accounts balanced to avoid an external audit and media attention."

"All you did was prove that I can't trust you to tell me the truth. Why on earth would you pay off his loan shark when you knew he was stealing from me and, by extension, stealing from you?"

"How do you know about that?"

"You should be painfully aware by now that I keep track of everything my children are up to, Alexandra." His arrow hit her in the heart. He had never told her how he found out about her affair with Kelly Thatcher thirteen years ago at Yale, but once it was clear he had, she had been more careful to hide her personal life.

He raised his chin at her. "How else would I know which of you I could trust to take over the company that took me a lifetime to build? I also know that you made another public spectacle of yourself with that woman last night. I will never trust you again."

So this was how their relationship would end, shattered by the thing that had first fractured it. Alex couldn't take any more. If there was one child who had kept his best interest in mind, it was her. She had deferred to his needs because of his disease and her misguided love for him. Well, not anymore. As far as she was concerned, he could keep his legacy.

"Never mind that I made the company whole again despite my brother's criminal transgressions," she replied with some heat. "Never mind that I kept all of it out of the media. The only thing you can see is that I didn't live up to your lofty expectations. The truth is you still hold it against me that I'm gay, just like my mother. I thought sparing you from the truth about your son was an act of kindness, but I can see now that it was a fool's errand. I won't make that mistake again. You want to terminate me? Fine. I used to love this company, but I love my sanity more. I'll land on my feet, just like Andrew did. Just like Syd did. And live a happy life."

"Well, it won't be on my dime, not ever again. I'm terminating your trust and taking you out of the will."

"A typical William Castle scorched-earth policy. Frankly, I won't miss your money. The only time I ever dipped into the trust fund was to pay off Andrew's loan shark. Money well spent, considering it was yours. I never wanted to rely on your money, and I'm glad I never will. I'm proud that every penny I ever received from Castle Resorts I earned through hard work. You may end up regretting your decision to terminate me. You will never find an executive who will be as loyal to this company or love it as much as I did."

William laughed, shaking his head in unmistakable indignation.

"I don't care what you think because all of that is in the past. It's just sad." Alex straightened her back to deliver her final arrow. "By the way, that woman you say I made a public spectacle over, I'm going to ask her to marry me one day."

William rose from his chair, circled his mahogany desk, and stood face-to-face with Alex, his rage manifested in fiery exhales. "I gave you my love, though you didn't deserve it at times. I gave you every opportunity to follow your dreams, but this will condemn you to an eternity in hell."

Equal in height and temper to her father, Alex stood her ground. "Those were *your* dreams. I am proud of who I am and of whom I love." She lifted her chin with pride and satisfaction. "I'll pack up my office and pick up my things first thing tomorrow morning." She walked out, leaving her arrogant, intransigent father and her suitcase behind. A growing numbness enveloped her. So, this was what being orphaned felt like.

The storm was tailing off an hour later, but another one was clearly on the way. Alex slipped the driver a twenty-dollar bill following the fifty-minute cab ride to Pier 45 on the West Side—the place that calmed her whenever stormy weather loomed. The place her mother had held her on a park bench as thunder and lightning roared overhead. The place where her mother had turned fear into joy and a dark storm into colorful art.

Stepping out of the yellow cab onto the wet pavement, Alex carefully avoided the river of rainwater rushing through the gutter. Her heart thumped, longing for the comfort she once had felt there. The few memories she had of her mother had become jumbled over time, but not the one from this place. She jogged toward the cover of the pavilion one hundred yards down the pier. She silently applauded herself for wearing sensible sneakers with her jeans and for staying in running shape since her track days at Yale. That made the trek fairly easy.

Once there, she ran a hand across the cold concrete bench that had drawn her in like a fish on the end of a line, conjuring up her favorite memory again. "Lightning is nature's fireworks," she whispered for a third time tonight. "I wish you were here, Mommy. Syd said that you always had a way of putting Father in his place. I wish you could do it now. Because I can't help who I love. And neither could you. Why can't he accept me for who I am?"

A lightning bolt zigzagged above the pavilion and lit up the night sky, electrifying the surrounding air, and thunder boomed so hard the vibrations echoed in Alex's chest as if her mother's anger had erupted from the grave.

"At least I have Tyler, Mommy. I never knew that love could feel this wonderful and make me feel so complete. I'm sure you felt the same for Abby." The breeze kissed her cheeks the way her mother used to.

Alex tracked the thinning clouds, a crisp spring night sky peeking through them at irregular intervals. "We might be too old at this point, but I hope Tyler and I have a child together so I can teach her about the thunder and rain. Maybe I can turn everything into art too."

Alex pulled out her cell phone and dialed the person whose voice she most needed to hear. The call connected, but instead of that sweet voice, the line was filled with clanking noises, followed by a string of clear and concise curse words. "T?"

"Babe? I'm sorry, hold on. I was cleaning up after dinner and dropped a mixing bowl. I'm putting you on speaker." A moment later, Tyler asked, "How did your meeting with your father go?"

"It was horrible." The tenseness in Alex's shoulders instantly relaxed at hearing Tyler's concern. "He knows everything about Andrew, including how I covered things up. He even knows that we spent last night together. He used both as an excuse to fire me and take me out of his will."

"I'm so sorry."

"Don't be. I'm done with him. I just need to know that nothing has changed for us."

"Why would you ask such a thing? Of course, nothing has changed."

"Because when you told Syd that you loved me, I didn't say it back."

"You don't have to say it to make it true. I feel it in your every kiss and touch. I see it in your eyes every time you look at me."

"I do have to say it, T, but when I say those words, I want you to be in my arms. When can I see you again?"

As they were getting ready to end the call after agreeing that Alex would fly to Sacramento in a week, Alex heard a faint whimper from the direction of the neighboring bench. It was followed by a series of rapid scrapes against the asphalt. A cautious check revealed a shivering dog beneath the concrete seat. "I gotta go, T. I found a lost dog, and he looks scared."

Alex returned her phone to her front coat pocket and reached for the frightened ball of wet fur. "Hey, fella. It's all right. I won't hurt you." Several minutes of coaxing convinced the thin black and tan German shepherd to crawl from its makeshift shelter. Alex picked it up and held it in her lap. It couldn't have been more than a half-year old and it had no collar or tags. She took a closer look. "Oops! You're no fella. Hi there, girl. Where's your person?"

Another streak of lightning crossed the sky, but this time the thunder rolled in softly like waves against the shoreline. The dog quivered in her lap and buried her nose in an armpit. The pervasive musty scent that wafted up from her convinced Alex her clothes would make their way to the hamper the minute she got home. "It's all right, girl. I'll protect you."

The closest Alex had gotten to having a dog was the runaway mutt that had found its way to the front porch of William's mansion when she was eight. When she had begged her father to keep it, he said he'd never allow a flea-bitten mongrel into his house. For three hours, young Alex had petted and cuddled the shaggy, frightened little thing until Animal Control picked it up. The dog catcher had told her he'd likely end up euthanized. She didn't know then what that word meant, but she'd sensed it wasn't good.

When the dog shifted, looking up with her pleading eyes, Alex knew what she had to do. "It looks like we've both had a sucky day. Let's fix that and get you home."

CHAPTER THREE

Light peeked through the bedroom window and roused Alex from a night of broken sleep. The other side of the bed had been too empty, too cold for her to get settled quickly, and when she finally did, the dog she'd brought home last night had wanted outside. Twice.

A glance at the blanket she'd laid on the floor below the window confirmed the dog had finally fallen asleep. That ended the next moment when her alarm sounded, bringing the dog's head upward to an alert position and Alex's arm flying to shut the damn thing off.

Alex pushed herself up to sit against the headboard and patted a section of mattress between her legs. "Come here, girl." The dog leaped atop the bed. In an instant, a slobbery tongue began a tireless assault on Alex's face. It quickly turned into a nuzzle fest. The fresh scent of baby shampoo teased her nose— the by-product of the late-night bath that had transformed the musty mess she'd found at the pier into the cutest lumbering set of paws in the city.

"All right. All right. Someone must be hungry. I guess I should give you a name. Are you an Ellie? Or are you a Charlie?" Neither name felt right. "I wonder what my California girl would name you?" Tail wags increased tenfold, earning her multiple head rubs. "Is that it? Are you a Cali girl?" A series of lurches and playful growls confirmed it. "All right, Callie, let's take you potty and get you fed."

A bowl of leftover plain pasta and a slice of deli turkey served as breakfast; she'd buy more appropriate dog food after picking up her belongings at the office. Though nothing appeared to have been chewed on overnight, Alex refused to press her luck while she was gone. Her back patio and an open door leading into the unfinished carriage house would have to suffice as a dog pen for the morning.

Alex left out a bowl of water and scratched Callie's ears. "You be a good girl and guard. I'll be back soon."

The taxi pulled to a stop well short of Castle Resorts' offices on Madison Avenue. The driver looked over his shoulder toward Alex. "I'm sorry, miss, but police activity has traffic detoured."

"It's fine. I can walk the rest of the way." After thanking and tipping him, Alex proceeded on foot. The rain clouds that had rolled in overnight had finally cleared, leaving the city smelling fresh. As she got closer, she expected to see the usual plethora of construction vehicles that were connected with the never-ending refurbishing of the building's lobby and stairwells. Instead, several police cruisers, a fire truck, an ambulance, and other city vehicles had blocked the southbound lanes. They might have been there for a fire alarm or gas leak perhaps, but foot traffic was still moving in and out of the building.

Deciding it was safe to go inside, Alex walked straight to the elevators, passing three police officers on her way. The usual clamor of construction was mysteriously absent, making it easy to hear the squawk of a radio, though not audibly enough to decipher what was being said. Though curious, she entered the elevator car and began her ascent to the twenty-third floor. When its doors opened, she expected to hear the usual buzzing of power tools. She was greeted instead by the bustling of several police officers and technicians. They appeared to be dusting surfaces for fingerprints or other evidence.

Worry flooded her. Castle Resorts occupied the entire floor, so something must have happened at her corporate offices. She picked up her pace as she walked toward the reception desk, but a uniformed officer stopped her short of it.

"I'm sorry, miss, but you can't go in. It's a crime scene."

"I'm Alex Castle. I'm the Chief of Operations here." Or at least she had been until last night. "What happened?"

"Wait here, miss. I'll get the lead detective." The officer retreated to the inner offices.

"Detective? Why are there detectives here?" Alex shouted as another officer continued to block her entrance.

Several minutes later, a tall, well-dressed man with close-cropped inky hair emerged from the interior offices' reception area. "Good morning, Ms. Castle. I'm Detective Greg Sterling. Will you follow me?"

Alex nodded without saying a word, knowing somehow that Sterling wouldn't answer her questions until she did as he asked. He led Alex to one of the smaller offices, where Gretchen was sitting in a guest chair. Her eyes were red and puffy, and it was apparent she'd been crying.

Alex's pulse raced. She darted toward Gretchen and knelt on the floor in front of her. She placed her hands on Gretchen's arms. "My God, Gretchen, what happened?"

Gretchen continued to sob. She leaned forward, buried her head in Alex's chest, and cried uncontrollably. Alex wrapped her arms around her and turned her head toward Detective Sterling. "Will you please tell me what happened here?"

Sterling cleared his throat and then said in a flat tone, "Ms. Castle, I'm afraid there was a suspicious death here last night."

"What? Who?" Alex looked back at Gretchen, who continued to cry.

He said, "Your father, William Castle."

Alex half processed what Detective Sterling had said. She looked at Gretchen, who offered a meek, confirming nod.

Given the events of their meeting last night, she'd felt as if she'd already lost her father; his intractability this time had come with a sense of permanence. Though she shouldn't have been, considering the way he'd treated her, she had been numb for hours. With him alive, there had been a chance they could undo their estrangement one day. Now, though...

But there was no going back from what Detective Sterling had just said. Her father was dead. As much as she had hated her father's callousness, she had never hated him or wanted him dead. She felt as if she should cry, but paralysis took over, pinning her knee to the floor and her arms around Gretchen.

Gretchen trembled. "What are we going to do, Ms. Castle?"

Alex forced herself to her feet and paced the room, hands on her hips. The weight that had been lifted from her last night when she was relieved of the Castle legacy returned now in spades. Her father's death had shackled her again. She had to think not only of Syd and Andrew but also of the company. No one on staff was in a position to take the reins. The business soon would be in chaos; thousands would be looking to her for strength and guidance. She had no choice. She would have to step into his shoes, take control, and somehow pull the family together.

As if a switch had been flipped, Alex regained her composure. She straightened her blazer. "You said suspicious death. How?" she asked Sterling.

"We can't say for sure yet, but there appears to be significant head trauma."

"He had Parkinson's. Could he have fallen?"

"We aren't ruling anything out." Sterling gnawed on a well-worn toothpick, staring at her as if assessing Alex's every move and syllable.

"I see." Alex pushed against the waves of emotion that were threatening to crumble her seawall. Despite the sour taste it left in her mouth, she had to be detached like her father. "Have you notified my brother or sister?"

"No, I haven't," Sterling replied.

"I have to call them." Alex pulled her cell phone from her satchel.

"That can wait, ma'am." Sterling reached out a hand in a stopping motion. "I have a few questions if you're up to it."

"All right." Alex's head was spinning, bouncing between her grief and thinking of the people who would be counting on her for calm and leadership—Syd, Andrew, and the entire Castle Resorts executive staff. She hadn't dealt with death since she was five years old and did not know what she needed to get through it or how to get through answering questions about her father's death. The only thing she was up to was falling into Tyler's comforting arms.

"Can you think of any reason someone would break in here?" he asked.

"Not offhand. Other than our computer equipment, we store nothing of value here."

"You don't keep petty cash around?"

"Not here. We keep it at our resort in Times Square. Do you think this was some type of robbery gone bad?"

"We don't know yet. We're considering all angles. Can you think of anyone who would want to hurt your father?"

"He's run this company for thirty-seven years. I'm sure he ruffled a few feathers along the way. But no, I can't think of anyone who would want to hurt him."

"When did you see him last?"

"We had a meeting in his office last night about nine o'clock."

"That seems late to have a meeting. What was it about?"

The hairs on the back of Alex's neck tingled. The subject of last night's meeting was a walking motive for murder. Instinct told her to keep her response vague. "Some business. Some personal."

"Does he usually hold meetings that late?"

"Not particularly."

"How long did your meeting last?"

"I can't be sure, but about fifteen minutes."

"And after that?"

"I went to a park on the West Side near my townhouse to watch the storm. Then I went home."

"All night?"

"That's right." Alex grew leery of Sterling's questions, feeling more like a suspect than a grieving family member.

"Can anyone verify that?"

"No, I was alone. Now, if you don't mind, my father has died. I need to deal with the aftermath, both personal and professional." Sterling's grilling had had one positive effect— it had made her more focused and less emotional. Now she wanted to ask some questions of her own. She sat in the chair next to Gretchen and asked her, "Did you find him?"

Calmer, Gretchen nodded. "He was on the floor in his office. There was so much blood."

"Have you called anyone?"

"Just 911."

"All right. We need to let people know what's happened. I'll call Andrew and Syd. You call the executive board members and have them convene today. We'll have to decide on who will take over as interim CEO until the board can hold a vote."

"I thought—" Gretchen paused when Alex furtively shook her head from side to side. "I understand, Ms. Castle. All the executives are due in for a ten o'clock meeting. I'll gather them in the conference room and wait for you."

Alex felt Sterling staring at her, scrutinizing her every word and movement. His detective antennae clearly were up. Glancing over her shoulder, she saw him jot something in his notepad. He looked up. "This is still an active investigation. I can't have people traipsing through it."

"What was I thinking?" Gretchen said. "I can arrange for a conference room on the twenty-second floor. We've shared office space there in the past."

Sterling slipped his notepad into his inside coat breast pocket. Alex wasn't buying for one minute that he was done questioning her, though. "Ms. Castle, I have a proposition that would greatly accelerate our investigation."

"I'm listening," Alex said. Now her antennae were up.

"As a matter of procedure, we'll need to fingerprint everyone who had regular access to the offices. It's how we eliminate fingerprints we find at the scene. I'd like to have a team outside the conference room to fingerprint everyone. We can be out of your hair in less than an hour."

"I suppose I really don't have a choice in the matter," Alex said. "Now, if you'll excuse us, we need to make notifications."

At Castle Resorts' main reception desk, Gretchen contacted company officers and notified them of police activity in the building and the new location for the meeting. Alex called Syd first, knowing that although it was early in Napa she and John would be up and tending to things at the vineyard. Her calls to Syd's home and cell phone went unanswered, though. Finally she recalled Syd and John had planned to visit their cabin in the Sierra Mountains following the San Francisco resort reopening. That meant they'd be out of cell phone range for several days. That left only Andrew. Ten calls from her cell and company phones went directly to his voice mail.

"Ms. Castle." Gretchen placed a hand on Alex's forearm until she turned to meet her gaze. "Every executive knows to meet downstairs."

"Thank you, Gretchen." Alex patted Gretchen's hand before she pulled away. "You've known me since I was fifteen and you're twenty-five years older than me. It's about time you call me Alex."

"But—"

"No buts, Gretchen. I know my father was formal, but I'm not him."

"It wouldn't be professional."

"Let's compromise. When someone else is around, it's Ms. Castle. When it's just the two of us, it's Alex. Okay?" Alex raised her eyebrow, giving her a "come on now" look.

"Okay, Alex."

Glancing at her watch, Alex calculated she hadn't enough time to search for Andrew before the executives arrived for the emergency meeting but more than enough time to fall apart while waiting for the meeting. Just not here. She excused herself and took the stairs to the twentieth floor, home of the building's fitness center. She removed her clothes in the women's locker room and carefully folded and placed them into her personal locker. She then wrapped herself in a large towel and entered the unoccupied, small sauna room.

From the moment Sterling told her that her father was dead, she had felt truly alone. Her twin brother was a lost cause, and she wasn't as close to her sister as she should've been or wanted to be. She held back the tsunami for as long as she could, but once she let the first tear flow, she couldn't stop. The tears continued to come, one after another. The pain came so hard and fast, she could hardly catch her breath. The hot sauna intensified the sensations, sending the small room into a spin and pushing her to the edge of passing out. She gathered what little strength she had left and burst through the door into the cool air of the locker room.

She stumbled to the narrow wooden bench stretched in front of the row of lockers and collapsed onto it. Before yesterday, she'd have called Harley for the strength to get through this horrible day, but Alex didn't need consoling friendship now. She needed to feel the comfort of the woman she loved. As the room steadied, she adjusted her towel, which was threatening to fall, and whispered, "I need you, Tyler."

Digging through the belongings she'd stuffed in her locker, she located her cell phone and dialed. Despite the three-hour East Coast-West Coast time difference, she needed the calming reassurance from the woman she'd given her heart to. The moment the ringing stopped and the call connected, Alex knew she'd be all right.

"Hey, you. Did you get any sleep last night?" Tyler's voice was groggy but was as soothing as a salve, healing her wounds with each syllable.

"T…" Emotion swelled Alex's throat before she could choke out another word, but her pained tone must have been unmistakable, telling the tale that something was horribly wrong.

"Babe, are you okay?"

Alex cleared her throat at the hard truth. "He's dead, T."

"Who's dead?"

"Father."

"My God. I'm so sorry, Alex. How did he die?" Tyler's voice contained the same shock Alex had felt not an hour ago, and, despite the miles between them, sharing it made her feel as if they were in this together.

"The police are calling it suspicious."

"What happened?"

"I don't know." Tears flowed again, one after another. Her heartbreak turned into relentless sobs.

"I'm here for you, Alex."

"It hurts so bad, T." Alex pressed her free arm against her abdomen, wishing her arm was Tyler's. "I need you to hold me."

"I'm right there with you. Can you feel me?" The strands of Tyler's voice encircled Alex, their sweet tones filling the hollowness that had overpowered her and stemming the agonizing tide.

Alex gathered herself. "I can't reach Syd. She and John are at their cabin in Clio, so I'm flying out to Sacramento today. I don't think I can do this alone, T. Can you pick me up and come with me?"

"Of course, I can. Whatever you need, I'm there for you."

Funny how their roles had flipped overnight, Alex thought. Two nights ago, she had served as Tyler's strength while she traveled the final leg of her journey to overcome the impact of a vicious rape thirteen years earlier—surmounting her aversion to physical intimacy. Their making love had given birth to the real Tyler Falling and had cemented the trust between them.

"Thank you." Alex checked the time on her phone. In thirty-five minutes, news of her father's death would start spreading across Castle Resorts like wildfire. "I have to go. The company will be in chaos if I don't get on top of this right away. I'll send you my flight information as soon as I can." Alex swallowed a growing lump, confident she'd get through today because, in a few hours, she'd be in Tyler's arms. "I don't know what I'd do without you."

"You'll never have to find out."

Alex showered and dressed, slipping back into her business suit and slacks. A glance in a wall mirror at the sinks several feet away revealed a set of red, baggy eyes and a pale complexion—not the professional look she needed to present while addressing the executive board.

Alex sorted through the stash of makeup in her locker and went to the bank of sinks to make herself more presentable. After fixing her hair, she applied foundation and inventoried everything she had to do: find Syd and Andrew, steady the company, make funeral arrangements, get her father's lawyer to activate his estate plans, contact other friends, take care of—. Her breath caught at the thought of Callie. She'd just rescued that loveable furball, who was hungry and afraid of her own shadow. Who could take her while she went into full reaction mode?

She placed her next call to the one other woman who could keep her from going off the rails. After Alex informed her about her father's death and about everything on her plate, Harley Spencer said, "I'll let Mother know what's going on and have your rescue dog brought to the penthouse."

"That will be such a big help."

"You shouldn't be alone today, Alex. I'll come by the office and pick you up after your executive meeting. We'll track down that brother of yours. While we're out, I'll have Sarah pick up some dog supplies. Should I have her take her to a vet and have her checked out and see if she's chipped?"

Alex brought a shaky hand to her forehead. The thought of Harley handing over Callie to someone while she was gone stabbed at her. She had already come to love the way the pup flopped around on her floor and showed her affection with never-ending dog kisses. If Callie had to be returned to an owner, Alex needed to do it herself. Needed to be able to say a proper goodbye.

"Not yet. Let's wait until I get back. I can't thank you enough, Harley."

"We may not share DNA, Alex, but we are sisters all the same. We'll get through this together."

CHAPTER FOUR

Alex entered the alternate conference room where eleven executives had assembled for news that would change the course of Castle Resorts. They had broken into two groups in separate corners, leaving the chairs around the glass conference table empty. A uniformed officer stood near the door, the object of frequent curious glances. Based on the amount of whispering going on, Alex assumed rumors were rampant and alliances were being formed. She walked directly to the head of the table instead of to her traditional seat as second chair, and all conversation in the room came to an abrupt, deafening halt. Detective Sterling assumed a position against the wall where he could observe everyone's reaction, including Alex's, she noticed.

"Good morning, everyone. Please take your seats." Alex waited patiently. "I know you were expecting to meet with my father this morning." A lump formed in Alex's throat as she fought back the enormity of her loss. "Sadly, he passed away overnight." Gasps and low undertones enveloped the room. Alex began again, "I know this comes as a shock—"

"Why are the police here, Ms. Castle?" asked Blake Ward, the interim CFO.

Attempting to look the picture of calm and control, Alex responded in a cool, unemotional voice. "My father was found here this morning, and it appears his death may not be due to natural causes."

Hushed tones filled the room again. Unsure what her father might have told others of his plans to terminate her, Alex cautiously waited for the tension to settle before continuing. The only thing she was sure of was that Gretchen had given no hint that she knew of those plans, but that was no indicator. Gretchen never betrayed her father's confidences.

"Who's going to be CEO?" asked the chief accounting officer, Georgia Cushing.

"I think I speak for all of us when I say that this is indeed shocking," Blake Ward said, shifting his attention to Alex. "You'll, of course, step in as CEO since Mr. Castle already named you as his successor."

Alex felt Detective Sterling's stare scrutinizing every muscle twitch. She looked to Corey Carson, their in-house counsel. "Mr. Carson, what's your take on this?"

Corey removed his glasses, maintaining a grip on them between his fingertips, and rested his elbow on the conference table. "Since Castle Resorts is a privately held company, that decision rests on the board of directors, which consists of yourself, Mr. Blake Ward, and the late Mr. Castle."

Blake scanned the room and was met with ten nods. "I agree with Mr. Carson. You should take the reins, Ms. Castle."

Alex assessed the consensus in the room. "If there are no objections, I'll step in as interim CEO. Mr. Ward and I will appoint an interim chief of operations by Monday. That person will also serve as a company director." Alex paused for several moments, waiting for an objection. With Blake firmly in her camp, she didn't expect to hear one. Not yet. The elbow shoving would happen this weekend when at least a half-dozen executives would likely vie for Alex's and Blake's consideration. "All right then, it's settled. I'll need a status report from every department by noon Monday."

Alex directed her attention to the man who made her feel more like a suspect than anything else. "Detective Sterling, when do you anticipate releasing our offices so we can get back to work?"

"That's hard to say, but I wouldn't plan on the floor being released for four or five days," he said.

Several executives grumbled about how they were supposed to work until then, pressuring Alex to formulate a solution on the fly. "Please, everyone. We can set up alternate workspaces for you and your staff at the Times Square Resort conference center. Most, if not all, of the documents you'll need to access are on the company servers. We can bring in extra computers for your staff to assemble the status reports that Mr. Ward and I need." Alex addressed the company's technology chief, Chase Cotton. "Chase, can you poll everyone and determine what their technology needs are and coordinate with the Times Square IT team?" Receiving an affirmative nod, Alex continued, "I'll have Tim Morris over there set aside conference room and office space starting this afternoon."

After answering a few more questions, Alex finished the meeting by asking the executives to cooperate with the police fully. "Now, before you leave, Detective Sterling needs to fingerprint everyone to eliminate your prints from those he might find in our office suites. Gretchen and I will go first."

Several executives' pinched expressions meant a mutiny was on the horizon. One man asked, "Does he have a warrant?"

Alex stared down the complainer. "My father is dead, and you're worried about a warrant? You have the right to wait until a judge orders you to provide your fingerprints, but I highly recommend you get in line and cooperate if you value your position at Castle Resorts. Do we understand one another?"

The executive stood his ground, meeting Alex's stare. He was testing her authority and her resolve, but Alex wasn't about to back down. Her father had taught her that a genuine leader never showed weakness. The standoff spanned several tense moments before his eye twitched. "Yes." He snatched his folio and notes from the conference table and huffed out to the waiting officers.

"Any other complaints?" Alex directed her sharp question at everyone remaining in the room but expected and received no further insubordination. "All right then, let's get to work."

Alex cornered Detective Sterling once she and Gretchen were fingerprinted. "Detective, I have to leave town for a day or two to tell my sister about our father's passing. If you need anything while I'm gone, Gretchen will know how to reach me."

"Thank you, Ms. Castle. We'll keep you apprised of our findings." Sterling had used a polite tone, but his stiff body language said no one at Castle Resorts was above his suspicion. And that left her with a chill.

Alex walked confidently down the hallway with Gretchen, who was keeping up step for step. She passed along two time-critical tasks. "First, go to Times Square and personally give Tim Morris a heads up about my father and the influx of headquarters staff coming his way this afternoon. Second, draft a memo to all resort managers, detailing my father's sudden passing, the temporary change in leadership, and our plans to appoint a COO early next week."

"I'm on it, Ms. Castle. I'll have it ready for you when you return this afternoon."

"Thank you, Gretch—" Alex stopped in midsentence. Harley Spencer, flawless with her flowing, brown hair and Fifth Avenue fashion finds, was waiting by the elevators. Alex touched Gretchen on the arm. "I have to find my brother. I'll be back as soon as I can. Have Robbie help you in organizing the staff relocation to Times Square. Thanks for everything, Gretchen." Alex gave her a brief hug before walking toward her dearest friend.

Harley closed the distance between them. Without a word, she pulled Alex into a tight embrace, sending the message that Alex wasn't alone in her grief. Her touch wasn't Tyler's, but it comforted her just the same and would be enough until she stepped off the plane in Sacramento later today.

When Alex loosened her hold, Harley said, "Let's go find Andrew."

Minutes later, Alex was staring out the back seat window while Richard inched the Spencer town car around a tour bus that had stopped in front of the St. Regis, and edged his way back into Fifth Avenue southbound traffic. The spotless glass separating Alex from the outside world muffled a whirring siren as the ambulance it belonged to struggled to clear the congestion one block ahead. Alex had so much to do today, but the principal thing on her mind was how to break the news of their father's death to her brother.

Her first hurdle was going to be getting him to see her. After she'd forced him to resign, he had landed on his feet at the Cypress Group, the operator of a growing number of boutique hotels in major urban markets throughout the United States. He was now a direct competitor of Castle Resorts and had an axe to grind. Alex hoped he could put that aside long enough to hear her out.

Harley broke the quiet after Alex had shown her a picture from her phone. "Your dog is heart-melting."

"Which is why I had to bring her home last night."

"Well, she'll be fine until you get back from California. Mother's jet has its regular maintenance this week, but Indra has offered hers. It's waiting at Teterboro. I packed a bag myself and am ready to come with you."

"Thank you, Harley. You're a dear friend, but I called Tyler. She's going with me to Syd's cabin."

"Whatever you need. Richard is ours all day. He'll take us anywhere you need and will drop you at the foot of the jet."

"My pleasure, Ms. Castle." Richard caught her gaze in the rearview mirror and winked.

"Thank you, Richard. Did you say hello to Ms. Janay last night?"

"Yes, I did, ma'am. I'm sure I have you to thank for her dining with me last night. She said that you called and gave her forewarning of my expected arrival."

"Guilty as charged. I hope it was an enjoyable evening."

"It was, ma'am." The lightness in Richard's voice confirmed Alex's earlier supposition. They were a good match.

In minutes, Richard dropped Alex and Harley at the Fred F. French Building, home of the Cypress Group's midtown headquarters. While the two companies were competitors, thanks to Alex's cordial outreach, their relationship was friendly and she had visited their offices occasionally. Each company remained in its lane, with Cypress concentrating on small boutique hotels and Castle focusing on luxury resorts. She wondered how that relationship would change now that Andrew was on staff. But first, she had to get through this weighty task.

When she and Harley reached reception, Alex greeted the young woman behind the desk. "Hi, Quinn."

"Ms. Castle, it's nice to see you again." Quinn scanned the primary appointment calendar on her desk and then looked up with a quizzical expression. "I wasn't expecting you today."

"Actually, I'm here to see my brother. He hasn't been answering my calls. By chance, is he in?"

"I believe so. Let me buzz him."

Alex gently placed a hand on Quinn's arm. "It's vital that I see him today. We haven't been on the best of terms lately, and I'm afraid he'll refuse to see me if you announce that I'm here. I think it's best if I surprise him."

"Ma'am, we usually don't—" Quinn started.

Alex softly squeezed the woman's arm. She was a valiant sentinel with a kind and caring disposition that Alex was counting on. "Please, Quinn. Our father passed away last night. My brother needs to hear it from me, not the local news."

"I'm so sorry for your loss, Ms. Castle." Quinn's eyes moistened with sympathy and darted toward the inner workings of Cypress Group. "He's in room twenty-six-ten. Last door on the left."

After thanking Quinn, Alex led Harley down the hallway. The door was open, a habit Andrew hadn't changed she was grateful to see. His new office appeared uniquely modern but wasn't as lavish as the one he had had at Castle Resorts. Sitting with his back to the door, he was tossing a baseball in the air as he listened half-heartedly to the disembodied voice emanating from the desktop speakerphone. Alex had seen this before. Her brother was bored. His Reggie Jackson autographed fielder's glove was getting a thorough workout today.

She neared the desk, reached out, and snatched the ball in midair from behind him. "Hello, brother."

Andrew nearly fell backward in his chair. "What the fuck?" Once he caught his balance, he turned around, narrowing his eyes. "Hey, Brad, I gotta go." He reached over to his desk and ended the call. "Well, look at what the cat dragged in."

"This isn't the time for your snarky remarks," Harley chided.

"I don't remember inviting you." He stood and sneered at Harley and then Alex. "Or you, for that matter."

"Enough!" Alex rebuked them both and then softened her tone. "I have some sad news, Andrew. Will you sit with me on the couch?" Alex extended her arm in that direction to coax her brother to a spot where they might console one another, but he stood his ground.

The muscles in his jaw tensed. "What do you want, Alex?"

"Fine, we'll do this your way. Father died last night." Alex paused to let the shock sink in. Despite their chilly relationship of late, he was still her twin, and family needed each other at a time like this.

His belligerent expression transformed into a distant, empty stare, a feeling Alex knew all too well. She had no doubt he was numb. "How?" he asked.

"Gretchen found him in his office this morning. The police said he had a head injury."

"Was it his Parkinson's?"

"I don't know, but the police aren't ruling out foul play."

Andrew's stance faltered. He refused Alex's arm when she offered it, dashing her hope of him putting aside his animosity long enough to mourn their loss with her. It felt as if they were no longer family and never would be again. That sense of finality stung Alex nearly as much as losing their father.

"They think he might have been murdered?" The rims of his eyes turned red as they filled with moisture. "Who would do such a thing?"

"I've asked myself the same question a dozen times." She had yet to formulate a single possibility. "The police have cordoned off our offices for their investigation. We'll be working out of the Times Square Resort for the time being. I haven't reached Syd yet, but I know where she and John are for the weekend, so I'm flying out to California after I leave here." Andrew continued to stare into space without uttering a word. "Andrew, are you okay?" Alex touched his arm. He threw off her hand with a wave of unmistakable anger.

"I'll be fine. Do you need me to do anything?"

"Not for now. Syd and I should be at my townhouse by Saturday night. We can all meet there Sunday, early afternoon."

"I'll be there." Andrew nodded his concurrence. "I'm sorry to cut this short, but I have to get back to work."

"Are you sure you're going to be okay?" He could read her so well. She wished she had the ability to do the same with him. Maybe then she'd know what he needed to get through today. As far as she knew, all he had was himself and a few vacuous supermodels on speed dial. She hoped that would be enough.

"As long as I stay busy, I'll be fine," he said.

"That I get." Alex reached out again, and to her surprise, Andrew didn't pull back this time. Tears fell from both sets of identical eyes. A wave of sadness flowed between them, a pain so intense her chest ached. Her throat grew thick, but she pushed out what needed saying. "I love you, Andrew. I hope we can get past this bad blood one day and be a family again."

Andrew stiffened his spine and straightened his tie, a habit he'd picked up from their father, signaling he was done with emotion. "Not likely." He returned to his desk and lifted the handset of his desk phone. "I'll see you on Sunday."

CHAPTER FIVE

Sacramento, California

Alex stayed busy on the six-hour flight to the Sacramento Executive Airport for one reason—to avoid grieving. Reviewing the financial and operational reports Gretchen had given her didn't provide any information beyond what she already knew about the company she'd dedicated a decade of her life to. The files, however, made the hours on Indra's comfortable Gulfstream G200 with the PopCo logo blazoned across the exterior pass a little less painfully. By the time wheels skidded on the runway, though, Alex was mentally and physically exhausted, her only burst of energy coming from the text message she got from Tyler as they taxied to the gate. *I'm here. I see your plane.*

Alex's heart beat faster as the plane slowed to a stop at the loading pad, bringing into view the bustling covered patio of the airport's outdoor café and the woman she couldn't wait to hold. She and Tyler had been riding a roller coaster of emotion the past few months. She had been blackmailed by Kelly and was dealing with her brother's embezzlement and ties to a dangerous bookie. Now she was grappling with her father's death. At the same time, Tyler had been faced with the reappearance of her rapist and fighting to keep him away from the daughter he'd fathered, while coming to grips with her PTSD and emerging sexuality. Oh yeah, and her soon-to-be ex-husband was recovering from the gunshot wound he'd sustained while working for Alex. Their lives, in short, were completely in chaos. Alex was sure, though, that they would find a way to make their relationship work.

Alex's eyes zeroed in on Tyler, who was wearing a bright smile—and tight jeans and a light blue T-shirt, clothes that had never looked so good on anyone else. She'd often wondered what Tyler looked like while they were collaborating long distance on revamping the company website. It had taken months to discover that Tyler was the mystery woman she'd bumped into on the Napa riverfront. Since meeting in person, thanks to Ethan's sleuthing and, remarkably, his encouragement, Tyler had had the same electrifying effect on her every time she saw her.

It was hard to believe that it had been only two days ago that Alex had made love to the beautiful blonde for the first time, a night that changed the trajectory of her life. For the first time, she'd tasted the sweetness of sharing her body and heart as one, and now she refused to settle for anything less. She had learned that life without love was no life at all. She would let nothing keep them apart, not the fact that Tyler was seven years older, not their difference in social and economic status, and not their living on separate coasts. She would bend every which way to make this work.

One of the two pilots exited the flight deck and prepared the cabin for Alex to deplane. "I'll grab your bag for you, Ms. Castle." He handed her a business card and continued, "We'll need at least a three-hour notice for our return flight. Call us when you've finalized your return plans."

"Will do, and thanks for the lift."

"Easier than hitchhiking, ma'am." He winked before opening the exterior door and lowering the stairs. As Alex descended, the heat radiated from the tarmac, screaming for her to ditch her outer coat. The pilot offered his hand as she hit the last step. "Is your ground transportation here?"

"Yes, and I couldn't be in better hands. Thanks again."

Alex picked up her overnight bag and walked toward Tyler's waiting arms. With each step, she counted down the distance in her head. Fifty feet. Forty. Thirty. Twenty. Ten. Five. Without uttering a word, she dropped her bag and purse to the ground and melted into Tyler's embrace. Never had a touch brought such instant relief. Her heart still ached from her loss, but it finally felt whole with Tyler's arms around her. Their breathing synced, with Alex inhaling and exhaling a growing sense of calm. Her weariness turned into drive; she now had the strength she was going to need to get through the rest of the day.

Alex loosened her hold, pulling back enough to stare into the pools of gray that had riveted her from the moment she'd first seen them. They were filled now with ringing concern. She took strength from Tyler's gaze. It said that Tyler would share in her heartache and be a shoulder, distraction, friend, or lover when she needed it.

Tyler's expression steadily transformed from worry into pure love. Alex wanted to say the words she should've said yesterday, but now was not the time for "I love you." Instead, she focused on her looming task. "Let's go find Syd."

Tyler raised up a few inches and gently but passionately kissed Alex's lips. She pulled back and spoke softly, "Let's go."

The drive to Clio took longer than Alex recalled from her previous visit, but the picturesque scenery kept her attention for the nearly three-hour trip. The cityscape had quickly turned into rolling foothills dotted with oaks, maples, and sycamores. The hills gradually transitioned into rocky Sierras lined with tall, rustic pines, and the occasional high meadow, teeming with grasses and low brush, fodder for massive herds of mountain cattle.

The sun had retreated behind the western peaks, leaving just enough weak light to guide Tyler onto the gravel road leading to Syd and John's cabin. She glanced at Alex. "Have you been up here before?"

"Once, right after Syd and John married."

"I feel guilty that I haven't been here before now. John has extended an offer to Ethan and me every year for a decade to come, but between the kids and work, we never made it up."

"Are those two close?" Alex asked. "I know Ethan did some investigative work for John. Beyond that, I don't know much about their relationship."

"They act more like brothers than cousins. They spent every summer together growing up."

"That's wonderful. You'll love their cabin." Alex tried to remember the grounds and cabin from her single visit, fondly recalling the storybook setting. "I think it overlooks a river."

"It must be the Middle Fork. The river runs right through town," Tyler said. "I remember coming up this way as a girl in the winter. This area got a lot more snow than Loomis, so my dad would take me up here along with an old wooden toboggan, and we'd spend hours sliding down a hillside near an intersection of the two major highways. By the end of the day, snow had completely soaked my gloves and shoes. We'd come back home, change out of our wet clothes, warm up by the fire, and drink my mom's hot cocoa."

"It sounds like you had a wonderful childhood growing up here," Alex said, feeling a hint of envy at the mention of Tyler's mother. She'd always wished she had more time with her own, and today brought her loss of her at age five into sharp focus.

"I did. My hometown was lower down the mountain and off the beaten path. We rarely bothered locking our doors at night but were close enough to the suburbs and big city when we needed things. Growing up as an only child in the foothills and watching my parents struggle to keep a roof over our heads, I learned to be resilient and self-reliant. I guess that's how I learned to bury all the bad things and get on with life."

Alex grabbed Tyler's right hand and pulled it up to her lips. She lovingly kissed the back of it. "You're not alone, T. Just as I know I'm not. We have each other."

Keeping her eyes on the road, Tyler caressed Alex's cheek with the just-kissed hand. "Yes, we do."

Tall, young ponderosa and Jeffrey pines lined the access road leading to the cabin. When the gravel widened, Syd and John's mid-twentieth-century log cabin came into view. It looked just as Alex remembered it. John had prepared for wildfire, creating a vertical space between shrubs and trees and a one-hundred-foot horizontal buffer between those flammables and the cabin.

Tyler parked her SUV on a dirt patch next to John's pickup truck. She and Alex stepped out to the intense aroma of pine and the sound of rushing river water. "I miss the smells up here." Tyler closed her eyes and inhaled deeply, a look of pure delight settling onto her face. "So fresh and clean. And it is the Middle Fork. I can hear it."

"Let's go see if Syd is around," Alex said.

Overnight bags in tow, they climbed the three steps to the front door. Alex knocked, but no one answered. She tested the doorknob, but it was locked. "If I remember correctly, they like to walk the trails after dinner." Alex took Tyler by the hand and pulled her along the wraparound split-wood porch. "I know where she hides a key to the back door."

After dropping their bags in the second bedroom, Alex grabbed a bottle of Barnette wine and two glasses from the kitchen and invited Tyler to the back deck. They sat in silence in redwood chairs facing the shallow rocky river and the last bits of sunlight to the west. The day's warmth had given way to an early evening chill, making Alex wish she'd grabbed her sweater before heading outside. The wine and Tyler's company would have to be enough to warm her.

Minutes later, Syd's distinctive laugh echoed from the direction of the river. Two figures appeared on the dirt trail running along its bank. As they neared the cabin, Alex placed her wineglass on the redwood end table and stood at the deck railing.

Syd waved frantically and yelled up to her, "Baby Sis!"

Alex's eyes welled with tears when she heard Syd's voice. She dreaded telling her the news she was about to break. Tyler joined Alex at the railing, caressing her back as she whispered, "You can do this."

Syd walked up the stairs leading up to the deck, with John following closely behind. Eleven years Alex's senior, Syd carried her beauty well. Working the vineyard had toned her body into straight lines and sharp angles. Her rustic mountain clothing made her appear nothing like a Castle—just the way her leaving the family fold had intended.

"What on earth are you two doing here?" She walked up to her sister, arms wide, ready to pull her into a hug, but stopped short. "Alex?"

"Let's sit." Tension instantly swirled in the air. Alex directed everyone to the round wooden dining table in the center of the deck, with Syd sitting between Alex and John. Emotion swelled, but Alex croaked out her next words. "I have sad news, Syd. Father has died."

"Nooo." Syd trembled, prompting John to wrap an arm around her. She grabbed his other hand and squeezed hard as grief etched her face. "Nooo, nooo, nooo."

Alex rubbed Syd's back, and Tyler did the same for Alex. The sisters let their tears flow as they dealt with the pain of losing their last living parent.

Syd's weeping slowed. "How? When?"

"I'm not exactly sure about anything yet. I had a late meeting with him last night, and then Gretchen found him in his office this morning when she came in. It must have happened sometime last night," Alex said.

"What happened?"

"He had some type of trauma to the head."

"He fell." Syd lowered and shook her head in unmistakable despair. "His Parkinson's."

"The police aren't sure and haven't ruled out anything."

"Does Andrew know?"

Alex nodded, recalling the fleeting moment their once shared symbiotic connection had returned in Andrew's office. It had felt good to have it back, if only for a moment. "He wouldn't take any of my calls, so I had to track him down at his new office.

We agreed to meet up at my townhouse on Sunday. You and John can stay in my guest room for as long as you need."

"We'll have to book a flight and—" Syd began.

"No need to, Syd. I have Indra's corporate jet. We can fly out of Sacramento Executive any time we're ready to go."

"I'll need to go home to Napa first and pick up some things." Syd wept again. "I don't even know if I have a black dress."

"We'll get you everything you need, dear." John rubbed Syd's back once more. "We should stay here tonight and drive home first thing in the morning."

They decided Syd would fly back with Alex and Tyler while John tended to the winery until the funeral. Exhausted, Alex and Tyler grabbed some leftovers in Syd's kitchen and welcomed the prospect of going to bed. Sleep was long overdue, but first, Alex needed to wash away the day.

Soon, hot surges of water needled her tired, achy muscles. Seventeen hours ago, she had learned of her father's death, sending her day, her life, into a surreal tailspin. Thanks to Tyler, she had held it together long enough to keep the company going without significant disruption, break the news to Andrew, and track down her sister in a secluded mountain retreat. She doubted she could've accomplished any of that if not for the woman who was waiting for her in the guest room.

Alex briefly considered spending an hour in the vitalizing steam, but she needed Tyler's body against her more than she needed the hot water. She dried off at lightning speed, wrapping a towel around her torso to cross the hallway to her and Tyler's bedroom. As she walked out, John approached from the direction of the kitchen, holding a ceramic mug.

"Oops. Sorry, Alex." He averted his eyes to a nonexistent spot on the wood floor.

"Sorry, John. I wasn't expecting you." Alex tightened the towel, making sure to cover her cleavage. The warmth of embarrassment built in her cheeks. "How's Syd holding up?"

"She's quiet but can't fall asleep." He held up the mug. "I made her a cup of chamomile."

"Her favorite. You're a great husband."

Saying good night, Alex silently pushed open the door to her bedroom. Tyler had showered before her. She was sitting now on the edge of the bed, her profile to the door, rubbing lotion on her left leg. She had yet to dress beyond putting on a delicious cream-colored thong that rode midway up her waist and highlighted her toned, silky hips. Lord, she was perfection on plaid flannel sheets.

Alex scanned further up Tyler's torso and paused at the swell of a breast. Only yesterday morning, she had savored touching every curve of it and relished how Tyler writhed beneath her, craving intimacy as she should—with wild abandon.

Alex's appetite stirred for the woman who had convinced her that being alone was no longer an option. She closed the door and let her towel drop to the floor. Tyler craned her neck in Alex's direction, pausing her routine and devouring Alex with her eyes. Kneeling in front of Tyler, Alex caressed her hips, dragging cream silk as her hands descended smooth thighs. Tyler parted those legs, tossing her head back in anticipation.

Slipping one leg and then the other over her shoulders, Alex paused for a moment. The first time she'd taken Tyler this way it had been for Tyler's gratification, not hers. This time was different. Tonight's purpose was to escape. The first lick, even more appetizing than Alex remembered, earned her a moan she'd waited a day to hear. The second groan pinned Tyler to the mattress. The third had Alex's core clenching uncontrollably. Desperate to exchange her pain for pleasure, she climbed atop Tyler. Soft kisses and exploratory touches morphed into powerful thrusts and uncharacteristic pressure. Tyler kept up until she abruptly broke a deep-tongue kiss.

"Stop!" The fear in her voice forced Alex to halt. "Not like this, Alex."

Alex realized she'd hit one of Tyler's triggers from the rape. She'd sworn to herself that intimacy between them would always be something to cherish, born out of love. But this wasn't love. This was desperation. Ashamed, she rolled off and settled into a sitting position. "I'm so sorry, Tyler."

Tears streamed down her face as she agonized over the thought that she'd hurt Tyler. Tyler pulled her down beside her, instantly conveying forgiveness. Their naked bodies molded together, arms and legs entwined, making it difficult to discern where one body ended and the other began. Alex cried for her father. For her mother. For the lover she'd just frightened. And her lover wept for her pain.

Once Alex's sobs slowed and her breathing returned to normal, Tyler wiped her own eyes and whispered into her ear, "I love you."

Alex stretched to look into Tyler's eyes. She'd never felt closer to a woman nor more moved by one. "I love you, Tyler Falling."

The moment her head rested atop Tyler's breast she fell into a deep sleep. She would dream of her mother and father and their last family trip to the beach, making castles in the sand. She would dream of Tyler and the home they would share, a house by the water where Tyler would always feel safe.

CHAPTER SIX

Warmth from the diffused bands of sunlight flowing through the window tickled Tyler awake. The air was cold, as was the space behind her. She sent an arm searching but discovered only flannel sheets. Tyler threw on some clothes and crossed the hall to brush her teeth and tame her unruly hair. The smell of coffee led her to the kitchen, where a mostly full carafe was sitting in the machine and three mugs lay waiting for her on the countertop. After filling a cup, she slipped out the sliding glass door, joining Alex, who was standing at the deck railing gazing at the rocky river below. Tyler matched her stance, elbows resting on the top rail, hands drawing heat from the cup to counter the cold, dewy air.

Without breaking her stare at the rushing water, swollen from an early spring Sierra thaw, Alex said, "I feel horrible about last night."

Memories of Alex's bronze curves surfaced, rekindling the arousal they'd elicited last night. Tyler had never needed her to taste her more than when Alex had kneeled in front of her. She had never wanted to let go more than when Alex climbed on top of her. But her brazen hunger had been shattered when Alex's passion had turned into a force that took her back thirteen years and to the worst night of her life.

"I'm fine."

Alex placed her drink on the rail, turned toward Tyler, and caressed her arms. She kept her expression stern. "Please don't minimize how I frightened you last night. I saw it in your eyes."

Tyler debated how to balance her emotional needs with Alex's. Her psychologist would warn her against losing ground in her long battle of overcoming the PTSD from the rape, and her reaction last night confirmed she still had work to do. But the most important lesson she had learned from working with Gail Sanders was that she could only become whole through honesty.

She rested her cup next to Alex's and looked deep into her eyes. She felt the love in them, as she had for the past two decades with Ethan. The difference between those circumstances was that Ethan had never spurred in her a desire to express her genuine feelings—but Alex did. "You're right. I wasn't expecting you to be so forceful last night."

Alex averted her eyes, shaking her head in clear regret. "I'm so sorry I broke my promise to you."

"It was a sweet promise, but—"

"No buts, T. You should feel safe with me, especially when we're making love."

"You make me feel safe, but you also make me want to win my battle with PTSD." Tyler grasped the sides of Alex's fleece and pulled her closer until their abdomens collided. The touch sped up both their respirations. "I want sex with you to be sweet and tender *and* hot and erotic. I want to push the envelope with you and break down one limitation after another until they're gone. There might be times when I pull back, but it won't be because I don't feel safe with you." Tyler whispered into Alex's ear, lowering her voice, "Last night was hot as fuck." She pulled back. "You were hurting last night and took it too far, too soon. It's okay. We're going to make mistakes."

Alex tugged their bodies tighter together, her breaths turning into steamy exhales in the mountain air. "Hot as fuck, huh?"

"That tongue of yours is very gifted." Tyler pressed their lips together into a burning kiss, searching for that talented organ. The first stroke sparked a cascading buzz because nothing Alex did could genuinely frighten her.

A loud throat clearing broke the "wow" moment. "Good morning," Syd said.

Tyler turned toward Syd and John, with Alex tightening her arms around her waist and resting her chin atop a shoulder. Tyler felt her cheeks flush with embarrassment at being caught necking.

"Good morning, Syd." Alex's vocal cords vibrated against Tyler's collarbone. "How did you sleep?"

"She tossed and turned for hours, but when she finally fell asleep, she fell hard," John said, answering for her.

"You were emotionally exhausted." Tyler rubbed Syd's arm, hoping her genuine concern would come through and negate the awkwardness Syd might feel at finding her and Alex making out like teenagers. "Alex did the same."

"Maybe some coffee will knock out the cobwebs. Does anyone else want some?" Syd asked.

Tyler and John passed on the offer, but Alex said, "I'd love to." The way Syd rested an arm on Alex's shoulder and Alex wrapped an arm around Syd's waist foreshadowed some needed sister bonding time in the kitchen.

John joined Tyler at the rail. "I'm glad Alex has you right now. Losing your last parent isn't easy."

"Thank you, John." She gave him a tentative smile. "I know this isn't easy for you—Alex and me, I mean. You and Ethan are more like brothers than cousins. I never meant to hurt him, you know."

"I know you didn't. He told me what happened to you in grad school. I didn't know. I'm so sorry." He turned and waited until she met his gaze. "Look, Tyler. Ethan is making peace with this, and given time, he'll be all right. I don't blame you for anything. I wish nothing but the best for you and Alex."

"That means the world to me." Tyler gave John a hug. Her pending divorce had been hard on their girls, but gaining John's approval let her hope that Erin and Bree would soon come to accept things as well.

An hour later, Tyler took the wheel for the long drive back to Sacramento, winding her way down the mountains until she reached the rolling foothills. Soon, a freeway sign signaled the approach of the exit that led to Tyler's hometown. She glanced at the digital clock on the car dashboard and calculated that even after making all the necessary stops, she and Alex would have an extra hour before their scheduled meet-up with Syd. She had plenty of time to bring Alex to her daydreaming spot, a childhood harbor she had yet to share with another living soul.

Tyler reached across the center console and squeezed Alex's hand. "I'd like to make a quick stop and show you something very dear to me. It won't take long."

Alex returned her squeeze. "Anything for you, T."

It had been years since Tyler had driven the back roads of her hometown, but she still knew them like the back of her hand. Coming to a particular twist in the hilly road, she pulled off onto a wide spot on the gravel and parked near the tree line. Grabbing a blanket and two water bottles from the back seat, she said, "We better put on sweaters. Bugs are out this time of day."

A short hike took them to a place where the trees and brush cleared near a slow-moving, rocky stream. She laid out the blanket on the dried grass, sat, and patted the ground in front of her, inviting Alex to sit between her outspread legs. When Alex nestled in between them, Tyler wrapped her arms around her and stared at the water that had given her more than hours of relaxation. It had saved her life.

Tyler cleared her throat and began.

"I started coming here when I was almost fifteen. I didn't have any real friends to hang out with during summers, so I'd load my daypack with a drink and snack and head out in the morning for a hike. One day, I noticed the foot trail we just took and followed it until I came across this stream. I loved it here, so I returned here every day for the entire summer. It became my secret place. I'd dream about kissing boys and even one girl who was the cutest thing I'd ever seen. I conjured up a perfect future with a job I loved, a family I adored, and tons of friends who made me laugh."

Alex pressed Tyler's arms harder against her chest. "I wish I had a place like this growing up."

Tyler took a deep breath. "This is the place I go to in my head when things get really bad. The first time was when Paul raped me. I was never so scared in my life. I had no control over what was happening, so I shut down. I closed my eyes and I found myself here, leaning against that tree over there." Tyler pointed to the oak that had kept her company as a teenager when she dreamt of the life she wanted. "I stayed here, in my head, until it was over."

Alex kissed Tyler's arm. "Would you like a place like this where you can see and hear the water all the time?"

Tyler rested her chin on Alex's shoulder. "One day."

"I'm so sorry about last night," Alex said again.

"That wasn't you. It was your grief." Tyler took in the magnitude of bringing Alex here. Sharing it with someone was long overdue. "You're the first person I've brought to my secret place because this is where I'd go to escape. But now, you're my escape. When I'm happy or sad, I think of you. When I'm afraid, I want to be with you."

Tyler loosened her hold and angled Alex to the side slightly to look into her eyes. She stroked Alex's face. "I loved Ethan for years, but it doesn't compare to how I feel about you. I never knew love could be so all-consuming. I'll never leave your side, Alex." Tyler drew Alex's head closer into a slow, passionate kiss. She let Alex lean her onto the blanket, encouraging her to lie on top of her.

Alex broke the kiss. Her heaving chest and longing eyes spoke more to pure love than a deep physical craving. "I'll never leave your side either."

CHAPTER SEVEN

Manhattan, New York

Arm bent at the elbow, head resting in a palm, and body propped on one side, Tyler studied the astonishing sleeping creature a foot away from her. Considering the three-hour time difference from her California home, she should be sound asleep alongside Alex, but once the sun cut through the window of Alex's bedroom and woke Tyler, she couldn't wait to glimpse the arms that had held her most of the night. How could something so strong be so soft and gentle?

Every aspect of the whirlwind Tyler was riding was a contradiction. How was it that she could spend thirteen years avoiding sex and now couldn't get enough of it? How could she dodge PTSD triggers for years and now welcome the challenge of taking them on as if they were pesky flies needing a colossal swat? How could Alex be so strong and self-assured one minute and fall apart in Tyler's arms the next? Wherever this tornado took her, she welcomed the unknown. Anything was better than living in limbo. Better than living a lie.

I love your body.

Tyler was only beginning to understand the nuances of Alex's physical responses and what each movement and sound meant when they made love. She'd learned that when Alex tossed her head back and released a particular low-pitched moan as Tyler licked behind her left ear, she'd awakened the first pangs of desire. And if Alex repeatedly rocked her hips in a specific rhythmic pattern, that signaled that she'd had enough foreplay and wanted Tyler inside her. And when Alex's mouth fell agape without making a sound and she gave a single powerful hip thrust, that meant she was about to tumble over the edge.

I could stay in bed with you all day.

Like a soldier sneaking up on an enemy position, the woman she'd been lovingly studying caressed Tyler's abdomen with a light feathery touch. That alone would have sent Tyler into uncontrollable laughter in the past. Each touch from Alex, though, felt more sensual than the last and left Tyler wanting more.

"Good morning, sexy." Alex breathed the words with her eyes still closed.

"I used to be very ticklish before I met you."

A sly smile crept over Alex's lips, her eyes popping open. "Really? Where were you ticklish?"

"Lots of places. My stomach for sure."

"What's changed?" Alex continued to draw circles with a fingertip.

"You." Tyler shuddered as Alex's touch lightened, testing her newfound lack of sensitivity. "I want you to touch me everywhere."

Alex inched her mouth closer. "Where else were you ticklish?"

Concentrating was becoming nearly impossible. "The tops of my legs."

Alex ran a hand up the front of Tyler's leg, starting at her knee. Her thumb stopped dangerously close to Tyler's center, sparking a familiar ache. "Still ticklish?"

"God, no." Tyler shifted a leg to give Alex better access.

Alex ignored the invitation. She reversed course, moving down the mattress until her mouth stopped at the exact spot where her thumb had just been. Reaching down, she gently stroked the top of a foot with a single fingertip. "Is this ticklish?"

Tyler replied with a very slow and drawn-out "no." Other than the anticipation of Alex devouring her again, coherent thought had left her. Then, a single fingertip stroked the bottom of her foot. Tyler jerked her leg and broke out into uncontrollable laughter.

Alex laughed with her for several fun-filled moments. "Your feet have yet to fall under my spell."

"But the rest of me has." Tyler rolled in one swift move, pinning Alex beneath her in the middle of the king-sized bed and capturing her lips in a fiery kiss. Hands and hips stoked the heat until the doorbell rang.

Alex pulled back, excitement bubbling in her eyes. "Callie's here!"

In a flash, she squirmed out from under Tyler and darted out of bed. Tyler propped herself up on one elbow and watched her dash about the room, gathering together a mismatched collection of clothes.

Alex rushed back to the bed and gave Tyler a quick kiss. "I can't wait for you to meet her."

After handing Tyler sweatpants and a top, she dressed hurriedly and descended to the main floor. Alex threw the front door open to a brunette clutching an overstuffed bag in one hand and in the other a leash attached to the cutest thing on paws.

"Why didn't you use your key?" Alex asked.

"Because of the woman standing behind you," said the brunette, nodding at Tyler.

"Your thoughtfulness is much appreciated. Callie girl." The moment Alex crouched on both knees, Callie spun on her oversized paws and bounced toward Alex, her tail raising a cloud of leaves on the front stoop. A petting fest from head to dust-maker morphed into a playful mauling.

Syd appeared on the stairs from the lower floor, a steaming coffee mug in hand and a smile on her face. "Father would've never approved."

"Exactly." Alex looked up as the woman stepped into the entry hall, closed the door behind her, and placed the bag of dog supplies on the hardwood floor. "How did she do, Harley?"

"We survived, but Mother's Persian rug did not. It's now several inches shorter."

Alex cupped Callie's face with both hands. "Were you a bad girl?"

"It was my fault, really. I fell asleep on the couch, and by the time I woke, she was rolling in a pile of wool." She grinned.

"Oh, my." Tyler covered her mouth with a hand. That furry thing had likely wolfed down a several-thousand-dollar chew toy.

"Where are my manners? You two haven't officially met, have you?" Alex turned toward Tyler. "Tyler, this is Harley Spencer. Harley, this is Tyler Falling."

"It's such a pleasure." Harley gave Tyler a welcoming hug. "Alex has told me so much about you."

"It's nice to finally meet you, Harley. Likewise."

"You've had an amazing effect on our Alex."

"I concur," Syd said, comfortably crossing her legs as she reclined on the couch nestled along the long wall.

"It's the other way around." Tyler had never spoken truer words. She hadn't been herself since the moment she realized Alex was the mystery woman who had turned her life upside down. Saying that it was a change for the better would be the understatement of the century.

With Callie unable to maintain traction on the wood floor, Alex won the ensuing tug of war with a plush toy. *I need more throw rugs*, she thought. All too soon, the doorbell rang. "That must be Andrew." Alex sighed as she glanced toward the door. The coming meeting between siblings would not be easy.

"I'll take the little rug wrecker down to the kitchen. Yell if you need reinforcements." Harley retrieved Callie and the bag of goodies and disappeared down the stairs to the garden level.

Alex opened the door to her twin, once her mirror image. They used to be so much alike in appearance and character, but she barely recognized him these last two months. Heavy creases on his face spoke to his increasingly bitter life. An unrepentant, desperate thief, he had nearly cost Tyler's husband his life. He appeared hollow, broken from having lost the man whose love he'd spent a lifetime trying to earn but had never received.

"Come in, Andrew." When she let him pass, no words, only the stale scent of whiskey followed, telegraphing he would be in a foul mood.

"Hey, Syd." Andrew greeted his older sister with a warm hug, making it clear that he thought Alex didn't deserve one.

Alex moved next to Tyler and gave her hand a squeeze, drawing from her the strength she'd need to get through this meeting.

Andrew stared Alex up and down. "Quite brave, sleeping with the same dyke now that Father is dead." He shifted his gaze to Tyler. "What's your name again, snowflake?"

"Andrew," Syd chided.

"That's enough!" Alex's protective side roared. She balled her free hand, ready for a fistfight, something she and Andrew hadn't engaged in since they were twelve and she coldcocked him with a right hook for breaking her Madonna *Like a Virgin* CD.

"No, it's okay, Alex." Tyler released her hand and extended it to Andrew. "I'm Tyler, the dyke who's here to stay. And you're Andrew, the conniving homophobe who was shown the door not too long ago."

I love this woman, Alex thought.

"I see you're up to speed." Andrew shook her hand with a sneer.

"Let's put our personal feelings aside for today." Syd raised and lowered her hands in a calming motion. "We're family and need to figure out what needs doing."

"She's not family." Andrew wagged a thumb toward Tyler.

"Tyler *is* my family. She stays." Alex hadn't planned to say those words, but they were true, nonetheless. In two months, Tyler had woven her way so tightly into her life that Alex couldn't conceive of going a day without her. She was her family, and if the laws were different in New York, Alex would make Tyler her wife tomorrow.

After Andrew offered a weak nod, Alex invited everyone to sit. She retrieved a folder from the coffee table, removed a collection of papers, and passed them first to Syd. "Robert's office sent over some documents about Father. It appears he detailed his burial instructions in advance, so I've asked my assistant, Robbie, to spearhead the funeral arrangements."

"Sounds like him, dictating from the grave," Andrew said. "What about the will?"

"Robert's office was vague about that. They said they won't release it just yet. Something about the police investigation."

"That doesn't sound right," Syd said.

Alex weighed how much to reveal about her late-night meeting with their father. Based on her first encounter with Detective Sterling, she already felt like she was a suspect. She trusted Syd and Tyler but not Andrew. *Prudence*, she thought. "I know, Syd, but when I met with Father the evening he died, he said something about needing to change his will. I guess the police have to sort through all of that."

"What do you mean? He hadn't already?" Andrew's Adam's apple bobbed several times, a quirk he displayed only when he was anxious. Alex would have bet her last dollar that he thought he'd dodged a bullet, considering their father knew everything, down to Victor Padula.

"That's a question for Robert," Alex said.

"Well then, it looks like we need to meet with Robert," Syd said. "I'll call his office tomorrow and request a meeting with him in the afternoon. Are we okay with that?"

"Sure, Syd," Alex replied, relieved to share the responsibilities. "It's not how I envisioned spending my birthday, but it needs to be done." The moment she said "my" instead of "our," Alex realized the connection she'd once felt for her twin was gone. It made her loss doubly painful. She was grieving her father and brother.

"I didn't realize your birthday was tomorrow," Tyler said.

"That's right," Syd said. "With everything going on, I didn't consider your birthday. Would you prefer to wait another day?"

"I'm fine with it." Alex turned to her brother. "How about you, Andrew?"

When Andrew didn't respond, Syd gave him a stern look. "Are you okay with tomorrow too?"

"Sure." His pronounced reluctance sent Alex's antennae up. What was he afraid of?

Syd threw her hands in the air, her tone laced with impatience. "Finally. I wish you two would get over whatever has you pissed off at each other."

"Me?" Alex pointed at herself. "It's always him."

"Here we go. Perfect Alex," Andrew quipped.

"Enough. If you can't get over your shit, you need to table it until after the funeral." Syd was serious. This marked the first time she'd used a cuss word in front of Alex for as far back as she could remember. Syd rubbed her temples, her tell that a grueling headache was on the horizon.

Alex and Andrew nodded in agreement. Minutes later, he gave a weak excuse about having to meet someone about a wine contract and said his goodbyes.

"I'm feeling a migraine coming on, Baby Sis." Syd pinched the bridge of her nose. "I'm going to take a pill and lay down."

"I'm sorry, Syd. I'll work at not letting him get under my skin."

On her way upstairs, Syd mumbled, "Uh-huh. That'll be the day."

Long after Syd went upstairs and Harley said goodbye, Alex and Tyler were curled up on the couch on the main floor close to where Callie had staked out a spot on the nearby chair for a lengthy nap. This represented the most activity her living room had seen since Alex moved in nearly a decade ago. If she were honest with herself, this was also the first time she wanted to truly live in her house. Despite all the touches she'd added to it over the years, today was the first time it felt like home. Having her arms wrapped around Tyler had everything to do with the transformation.

"I feel bad," Tyler said. "I didn't get you anything for your birthday."

Alex rubbed her back with both hands. "You're all I need. And Callie."

"At least let me make you a nice dinner tomorrow. I'll have it ready when you return from the lawyer's office."

The doorbell rang.

Alex patted Tyler on the bottom before giving her a quick kiss on the forehead. "Let me get rid of whoever it is so we can resume this."

She opened the door to Detective Sterling, dressed in his tailored dark blue suit and tie, standing next to a dark-haired woman in a black suit with a gold NYPD detective's shield clipped to her belt.

"Sorry to bother you at home, Ms. Castle," he said. "This is my partner, Detective Claudia Diaz. Our investigation is coming along, and we have a few questions for you."

"It's no bother," Alex said even as she worried about what had brought them to her home. "Come in." After she introduced Tyler, Sterling asked if she wanted privacy before he started on his questions.

"Thank you, but I'd prefer she stay if you don't mind."

Sterling offered a polite nod. "Do you have an antique camera called"—he thumbed through his pocket-sized, top-spiral notebook—"a Leica?"

"Yes, I do. Why?" Alex asked.

"Would you mind getting it?"

"What does my camera have to do with my father's death?"

"Someone mentioned seeing one in his office," Sterling said. "I'm just following up."

"It couldn't have been mine. I've never taken it into my father's office."

"Can you get it all the same?"

Alex excused herself, leaving Tyler to keep an eye on the detectives. With each step up the stairs, she was bothered more and more by Sterling's request. What was her father doing with a Leica, and why was Sterling asking her about it? She knew enough about police work to know that detectives never idly asked questions nor did they reveal the real reason for them. Retrieving her camera case from her dresser, she felt more and more that Sterling had her in his crosshairs.

Downstairs, Alex offered Sterling her camera. Before accepting it, he put on a pair of latex gloves he'd pulled from his jacket pocket. Alex's antennae raised to full extension. Now she was sure Sterling was in evidence-collecting mode. "Would you mind taking it out of the case?"

"Alex." Tyler placed a hand on her forearm. "You don't have to say or give him anything without a warrant."

While Alex found Sterling's request troubling, she thought she could wrap this up if she complied. The quicker Sterling eliminated her camera, the quicker he'd be on to actual leads. "It's okay, Tyler. I have nothing to hide." Alex removed the custom leather case and handed the camera to the detective.

Sterling meticulously inspected the camera, focusing on a small dark spot on its side. He asked, "Could this be blood?"

Alex eyed the stain. She racked her brain but couldn't recall why blood would be on her camera. "I'm not sure."

Diaz pulled out a gallon-sized plastic bag from her satchel and placed the camera and the case inside it.

Sterling continued, "Ms. Castle, I have to ask you to come with us for more questioning."

"This really isn't—" Alex started.

"Is she under arrest?" Tyler's question came out sharp.

"No, ma'am, but we need to clear up a few things," Sterling said. "It would go a lot faster at the station."

Tyler stiffened her spine. She pulled Alex aside and whispered so only she could hear, "I have a bad feeling about this, Alex. Living with a cop all these years, I've heard lots of stories about how these things go. You need to go with him, but you need a lawyer with you."

Alex whispered back, "You're scaring me, Tyler."

"You need to understand how serious this is."

"I'm sure everything will be all right." Alex gave Tyler a pat on the hand, trying to reassure her, but the attempt fell flat, for herself as well as Tyler, if she were honest.

"Don't be so sure, Alex. Promise me you won't say a word until that lawyer comes."

Alex looked into Tyler's uneasy, watering eyes. The last time they had appeared this way was after Andrew had frightened her at her father's mansion. Tyler was genuinely afraid for her now. "I promise. Will you look after Callie?"

"Of course."

Alex turned toward Sterling. "Let me call our family lawyer first."

"Would that be Robert Stein?"

"Yes, why?"

"He represented your father and is a potential witness. You need to consider an alternative."

Tyler's bad feeling had transferred itself to Alex. Robert's insights into her father's death were likely related to her father's will and her trust, both of which provided glowing motives for killing him. She glanced at Tyler, who nodded, with a concerned expression. "Let me make other arrangements."

Alex picked up her cell phone from the coffee table and dialed Abby Spencer's personal number.

"Hello, darling," Abby greeted. "How are you holding up?"

"Abby, I don't have much time, but I need your help."

"What do you need?"

"The police are here. They're taking me to the station for questioning about Father's death, but I can't use Robert Stein in this matter. Can your lawyer meet me at"—she quickly queried Sterling about where he was taking her—"at the Nineteenth Precinct?"

CHAPTER EIGHT

Jesse Simmons hadn't stepped into a police station to represent a client she'd never met since the two years she'd spent as a public defender more than a decade ago. Once Kline and Rosen had brought her on as an associate and later a junior partner, the only time she'd clocked in at a precinct had been to bail out one of the firm's trust-fund babies and keep their records clean. It was tiresome and, at times, a loathsome job, but the retainers paid the bills and afforded her a sixteenth-floor condo in Chelsea.

Nevertheless, the Nineteenth was her destination this Sunday. It was an eclectic combination of old and new. Its freshly renovated Art Deco exterior facade and heavy metal and glass doors spoke of cherished history. The main lobby remained untouched, however. There, two dozen hard, dirty, resin chairs lined dank walls that testified to years of neglect. Jesse approached the three-foot-tall wooden room divider that separated the public from the police. At its center sat the desk sergeant whose job was to direct visitors and calm them when pandemonium erupted—a rare occurrence in the affluent Lenox Hill neighborhood.

She queued in the short line behind two men—one in a hard hat and construction crew orange vest and the other in a tailored suit and wingtips. The suit was clearly a fellow lawyer.

Her cell phone chimed to the ringtone reserved for her most valued and demanding client. She fished it from her leather briefcase. "I just arrived at the precinct, Mrs. Spencer."

"I knew I could count on you to respond promptly. Alex Castle is like a daughter to me, and she deserves your full measure." Abigail Spencer's comment, while probably well-meaning, irritated Jesse. Although she had been on Mrs. Spencer's legal team for a decade, she performed her work primarily in the background. Today marked Mrs. Spencer's first request for a criminal defense lawyer, which put Jesse squarely in the batter's box.

"I assure you, Mrs. Spencer, I may not be the face of Kline and Rosen, but I have given nothing less, no matter the client."

"That's all I needed to hear. I know she's in good hands."

Abby disconnected the call as Jesse reached the front of the line. She patiently waited while the desk sergeant dealt with what seemed like an annoying question over the phone. "Look, I don't care who you are. If you want that information, you're gonna have to come down in person." He hung up, looked up, and announced, "Next."

She stepped up, dropping her cell phone into her suit's front pocket and pulling out her identification. "Jesse Simmons, attorney for Alexandra Castle. She's being questioned by Detective Sterling."

The sergeant shoved the visitor's log to the edge of the desk. "You know the drill?"

"Yep." Jesse signed her name and received a laminated visitor's pass. Once through the metal detectors, she negotiated the bustling stairs to the second-floor Homicide Division. When she arrived, her favorite lieutenant, Lieutenant Tony Asher, met her and escorted her down a poorly lit hallway. Humming overhead fluorescents flickered along the trail to the interview room.

"Another spoiled trust-fund baby?" He stopped short of the door, looking ever so handsome in his dark gray suit and thinning, business-cut black hair.

"Not everyone with a trust fund is spoiled."

"If you say so." He winked, adding his trademark dimpled smile. "Is it 'someday' yet?"

"Not yet." Jesse appreciated his persistence and his chiseled appearance, but as tempting as he was, she'd be asking for trouble if she had a drink with an opponent. And, for good or ill, police officers were often adversaries for defense attorneys. Agreeing to "someday" in response to his first flirtation was her way of keeping her options open if they ever found themselves on the same side of the table.

"My shift is over in an hour if you change your mind."

"Someday." Jesse opened the door and walked in. An attractive brunette was sitting on the table's far side, facing two detectives who had their backs to the door. The male detective had just asked something about a camera and the blood on it.

"Are you questioning my client without her attorney present?"

The brunette lifted her head toward Jesse. Even in casual clothes, she appeared polished and imbued with an air of being a "woman in charge." She had to be Abby Spencer's surrogate daughter.

"Not at all," the male detective said. "I'm Detective Sterling. This is Detective Diaz. We're just getting to know one another."

Jesse raised an eyebrow, casting a skeptical glare at Sterling. "I'm going to need some time with my client."

Sterling and Diaz gathered investigative folders from the desk in front of them. Before walking out, Sterling turned and said, "Knock on the window when you're ready."

Jesse gave him an affirmative nod and waited for the door to slam shut. "Ms. Castle, I'm Jesse Simmons, an attorney. Abby Spencer sent me. Are you okay with me representing you today?"

"If Abby trusts you, I do too. So, yes. But please call me Alex." The look of concern on her face was a good sign as was her lack of arrogance. It meant Alex didn't expect special treatment or for the authorities to sweep this under the rug.

"Okay, Alex. Call me Jesse. I understand the detectives want to question you about your father's death. Tell me about the night he was killed and this camera they're interested in."

"I met my father in his office Thursday night at nine o'clock as per his order." The distant look in Alex's eyes and how she bit her lower lip gave Jesse the impression there was something behind her choice of words.

"Order? Not request?"

"He issued summons when he wasn't happy with me. That night he was angry. Furious."

"About?"

"I discovered my brother had been embezzling from the company, repaid the missing funds, and forced him to resign. He has a gambling addiction and got in over his head with a bookie. Father said he knew all about it and that I'd paid back what Andrew took. He said he could no longer trust me." Alex's sudden shift and the way her skin was reddening from the neck up signaled she was angry as well. "But his anger was really about his disgust over my publicly seeing a woman. He fired me and said he planned to cut me off, trust fund and will, both of which I couldn't care less about."

Her client had just outlined motive and opportunity for murdering her father, and based on the initial police report, she had the means. That all added up to one thing—Jesse had her work cut out for her. "How long were you there?"

"I'm not sure, but not more than fifteen or twenty minutes."

"What did you do next?"

"I took a taxi to Pier Forty-Five on the West Side to watch the storm and call my girlfriend, Tyler Falling. I found a stray dog at the pavilion at the end of the pier and walked home with her. I think I got there around ten thirty. I gave the dog a bath, and we went straight to bed. The next morning, I took a taxi back to the office and found the police there."

Jesse jotted down some notes. "Is there anyone besides the cab driver who can corroborate your whereabouts after the meeting that night?"

"I'm afraid not."

"Tell me about this camera Detective Sterling asked about today."

"He asked for it, claiming someone had seen it in my father's office that day. But that must be a mistake because I'd never brought it there," Alex said. "I'd only had it a few months. It was an early birthday gift my sister gave to replace the one I lost years ago when I moved back from Yale."

"And the blood on it?" Jesse asked.

"I have no idea."

"If that blood is your father's, we have a problem. I'm advising you not to say a word to the detectives."

"But I have nothing to hide." Alex rose to her feet, palms flat on the table's edge. Her set jaw and lasered stare were not the usual look of Jesse's wealthy clients who were guilty as hell. "I had nothing to do with my father's death. He had Parkinson's, for God's sake. He could've fallen."

"Sit down, Alex." Jesse waited until she complied. "The Parkinson's is an angle I'm sure the medical examiner will factor into his report. But do you know how many people are sitting in prison because of circumstantial evidence? From what you told me, you had motive, means, and opportunity to commit the murder. And blood evidence might be enough to convince a jury. I'm not comfortable offering them any information until we know what they know. Let me do the talking."

"I didn't do this," Alex said.

"I believe you, but the police can twist facts to support any theory, even if they're not true. Trust me. Don't say a word."

Helpless to do anything more, Alex nodded.

Jesse knocked on the glass window, signaling Detectives Sterling and Diaz to return. After taking their seats, Sterling said, "We have a few questions for Ms. Castle, starting with where she was Thursday night."

Jesse replied for Alex, "She met with her father in his office around nine o'clock, left after about fifteen minutes, and took a cab to Pier Forty-Five along the Hudson. She stayed there for about half an hour before walking home, where she remained the rest of the night."

"It was eighteen minutes, not fifteen. We checked with the cab company. What was the meeting about?" Sterling asked.

Jesse replied, "I've advised my client to exercise her right to remain silent. Unless you plan to arrest her, we'll be leaving."

"Your client could easily clear some things up by answering our questions," Diaz replied.

"Not likely." Jesse closed her notepad, returned it to her briefcase, and stood. "Come on, Alex, we're leaving."

CHAPTER NINE

The weight of the day had set in, making each step on the stairway to the front door of Alex's townhouse seem more difficult to tackle than the one before. A sliver of the sun's final golden streaks sneaked through the taller buildings to the west and warmed the top of the front stoop, welcoming Alex back home. She glanced back at the urban forest awash in an orange glow before opening the door; she still had the sinking sense that this thing with the police was far from over.

The main floor was unoccupied, so Alex descended the interior stairs to the garden floor. She paused at the sliding glass door to take in the heartwarming scene in the courtyard. Syd and Tyler were reclined on the patio loungers there, chatting while sipping red wine and watching her dog chase butterflies in the planter boxes. They appeared as if they had no care in the world, while Alex had the sense her world was about to crash around her. She was confident about her lawyer's skills, but what Jesse said about how facts could be twisted to support any theory worried her. After Sterling hauled her in for questioning, Alex was sure she'd become their prime suspect. The only person who had a better motive to want her father dead was Andrew, but not on her worst day could she bring herself to point the police in his direction.

She shook off her fears, slid the door open, and approached Syd and Tyler. "There you are."

Tyler placed her wineglass on the table, walked up to Alex without saying a word, and gave her a lingering, passionate kiss. One muscle after another relaxed, the day's tension falling to the brick pavers beneath Alex's feet.

After ten seconds turned into twenty, and then thirty, Syd cleared her throat. "Hello. Still here." Alex refused to break the kiss and waved off Syd's teasing. "Oh, hell no, Baby Sis. Holster those lips and tell me what happened with the police today." Syd's tone was good-humored, but Alex knew her sister well. Her intent was serious.

Tyler pulled back. "Better?"

"Much." Her mind more focused, Alex turned her attention to her sister, letting a lopsided grin form. "That's twice I've heard you cuss today. The last time you swore was when you thought I wrecked Father's Mercedes."

"Wait. That wasn't you?" Syd's eyes widened in surprise.

"It was Andrew," Alex said. Callie jumped up on her back legs, greeting her with a two-paw doggie hug and earning herself a healthy rub behind the ears.

"You're always covering for that young man."

"You don't know the half of it. But enough of our wayward brother." Alex stood, redirecting her attention to Syd. "Nothing happened with the police. Abby's lawyer showed up, and she advised me not to say anything, so they had to let me go."

"Tyler said they took the camera I gave you. What was that about?" Syd asked.

"I don't know, but they found blood on it."

"They can't seriously think you had something to do with Father's death?"

"I definitely got that vibe from them."

"Well, we can ask Robert Stein what he's heard tomorrow afternoon." Syd glanced at Tyler. "I'm sorry, but he said the meeting is for family only."

"I understand, Syd." Callie lunged at Tyler, her front paws landing on her waist. "I'll keep an eye on this little gal."

"I wish you could be there with me, T." Alex let out an enormous yawn, the hours of waiting and then being in the hot seat taking their toll.

"You must be exhausted." Tyler gently lowered Callie's paws to the ground before rubbing the small of Alex's back. "How about you take a nap?"

"I could use a shower first. Spending hours in a police station, feeling like a suspect, made my skin crawl."

The bathroom's clean lines and the elegant contrast of dark brown granite against white Shaker-style cabinets were inviting, but they did nothing to buoy Alex's sagging mood. She turned on one of the two wall-mounted sprayers, carefully adjusting the temperature. After stripping off the stink of her day, she closed the glass door behind her and let the warm, steady stream gently beat her tired muscles into submission.

Soon, the shower door opened. Alex felt Tyler's hunger the moment the rush of cool air tickled her skin from shoulder to calf. Slender, familiar arms wrapped around her torso, pulling their bodies together. Tyler had correctly anticipated Alex's needs without a syllable being exchanged. Skin to skin, sexual energy flowed between them as water cascaded from one limb to the next. Alex threw her head back against Tyler's shoulder, considering what a waste of luxury this space had been. She had squandered thirteen years of her life, deferring to her father's wishes by refusing to bring her one-night stands home. It was a shame, really. Her shower built for two should've fulfilled fantasies with the same frequency as it had sparked them. On the other hand, she was christening it with the only woman who mattered. And if her instincts about their connection were correct, the only memories she'd have of this space would be ones of her with Tyler.

Tyler clutched her breasts, making at least one of those fantasies become a reality. Alex shifted to turn around, but Tyler tightened her hold, signaling who would be in charge. "What do you want?" Tyler rasped.

No matter how Alex responded, Tyler had already satisfied her deepest desire. Tyler's husky voice heralded her growing confidence with intimacy, which suggested that her PTSD from the rape was waning. "You choose," Alex gasped.

Tyler slowly trailed one hand down Alex's abdomen, gliding past her pelvic bone to the top of her mound. A lengthy pause confirmed she'd mastered the art of the tease. Gentle squeezes encouraged Alex to spread her legs and throw an arm over Tyler's shoulder. Each stroke erased one terrible memory after another until the day became history.

CHAPTER TEN

Precisely eight years had passed since Alex was last in Stein, Levy, and Keller's plush offices. That day was also her birthday, her twenty-fifth. That was when she'd sworn to herself to never rely on her father's money. She feared then, rightly, that signing papers to accept access to the revocable trust fund he'd set up for her would eventually come with strings too cumbersome to bear. The ones she'd already accepted regarding her sexuality, done out of her love for him, were heavy enough. But none of that mattered today. William was dead, and the woman Alex loved was at home, preparing a birthday meal for her.

While waiting in the reception area, Alex scanned the files Gretchen had messengered over on the top three Chief Operation Officer candidates she and Blake Ward would select from later today. She glanced to her left, where Syd sat thumbing through a magazine without really reading it. To her right, Andrew nervously bit his fingernails, bobbing a knee up and down.

Laura, Robert's assistant, stepped in from the hallway and approached the Castle group. "Are you sure I can't get any of you something to drink?"

Her well-intentioned offer received three clipped responses.

"Nope."

"I'm fine."

"No, thank you."

Laura walked to her desk when the phone buzzed. Following a few mumblings, she announced to the group, "Mr. Stein is ready to see you." She led them to his office.

Robert stood from his leather chair and rounded his desk. "Sydney, it's been quite a long time. I'm so sorry for your loss." He shook her hand.

"I'm sorry for your loss as well. I know how close you and Father were," Syd replied.

Robert refocused his attention. "Alexandra. Andrew. I'm sorry for your loss." He shook each of their hands before gesturing toward the dark leather couch and guest chairs. "Please sit. We have much to talk about."

Robert retrieved a folder from his desk and then joined Syd, Alex, and Andrew in the seating area. "Before we begin, I feel it my obligation to inform you that the police questioned me regarding your father. Though it is unclear whether attorney-client privilege survives after death, I felt it my obligation not to disclose the content of our conversations. I was, however, compelled to tell them that your father and I met the afternoon before he died to discuss some legal matters."

"Thank you, Robert," Syd said. "We appreciate your honesty."

He acknowledged with a graceful nod. "Let's discuss your father's estate. First, his Upper East Side home goes to Alexandra." Robert paused as if gauging each heir's reaction. Alex made a concerted effort to not react, while Syd offered a half-smile and Andrew rolled his eyes.

"Next, the trust funds. Each trust fund remains in effect and will receive an immediate ten-million-dollar distribution. For all other assets, including all owned shares of Castle Resorts, the three of you are equal beneficiaries."

Alex prided herself on her ability to read people when it came to business. Most had a tell when they were hiding something—a hard swallow, a twitch, a shift of the eyes, or a sudden head shift. But Robert was always the same—calm, collected, and not a single movement out of character. His finely honed poker face made it impossible to tell whether he knew about her father's plan to disinherit her.

Alex was lost in thought, straining to gauge Robert, when Syd placed a hand on her knee and called her name. "I'm sorry, Robert, you were saying?"

"I was asking about the funeral. I trust you're seeing to the plans per your father's instructions," Robert inquired.

"Yes, of course. It's set for Friday at Green-Wood. My assistant assures me it will follow my father's wishes to the letter," Alex said.

The grin plastered on Andrew's face faded long enough for him to ask, "How much is my share?"

"Andrew!" Syd chided.

"What? I want to know how much the old man left behind."

"This isn't the time to be such a gold digger," Syd rebuked.

Andrew shrugged off her censure and asked Robert again, "How much?"

Robert glanced back and forth between the three siblings before reviewing his notes. "At current market value, minus his home, we value the remainder of his estate at approximately one billion, three hundred million."

Andrew's smile returned. "That's four hundred thirty-three and change for each of us. Not a bad haul." Alex shook her head. His aptitude for numbers and quickness at math abetted his greed. Or was it desperation? Knowing her brother, it was both.

Syd threw her hands in the air. "For heaven's sake."

Alex sat out the ensuing sibling argument and kept her eye on Robert. His gaze shifted between the three of them as if sizing them up. At first, Alex thought he was wondering who would be the first to contest the will. But when his eyes narrowed, she was convinced he was sizing them up as suspects, wondering which among them had killed his lifelong friend.

CHAPTER ELEVEN

Alex stepped through the door of her townhouse, holding it open for Syd, who was two steps behind. Dropping her purse on the entryway table, she was greeted by an enticing aroma. Was that rosemary? Or maybe thyme? Garlic. There was definitely garlic. The mixture drew her further in and had her mouth already watering for a taste.

"My house never smells this good when I cook," Alex said.

"That's because you don't know how to cook. You know how to heat things up," Syd said, turning toward the stairs leading to the bedroom, not the path toward the kitchen downstairs.

"Aren't you joining us for dinner?" Alex asked.

Syd stopped. "Oh, I'll be enjoying Tyler's culinary masterpiece, only upstairs. She texted ahead and set up a plate for me in my room so you two can have a private birthday dinner downstairs."

"She did all of that for me?"

Syd's expression softened the way it had two months ago in Napa when she told Alex it was time for her to stop living a lie for their father's sake. "I won't say that I was happy to learn of you and Tyler last week. Ethan is such a good man."

"Yes, he is." Alex lowered her gaze. She hated to think of Ethan back in Sacramento, still healing from the wounds he sustained while working on a case for her and heartbroken over his crumbling marriage to Tyler.

"But Ethan has filled in the particulars, and if he's okay with it, then I am too. I've witnessed the effect she has on you, and I can honestly say I've never seen you more content."

Alex's heart swelled. "Tyler is the one, Syd." She'd never been more sure of anything in her life. "She's the one I've been waiting for."

"I can see that, but are you the one for her?"

"I can only speak to what I feel when I'm with her, but yes, my heart tells me that we're meant for each other."

"Then go." Syd shooed Alex away with her hands. "Your woman has gone to great lengths to make your birthday special despite Father's passing."

Syd's approval left only one final obstacle to hurdle before she would consider her and Tyler's relationship on the right track—gaining the acceptance of Tyler's daughters. That would likely take much more effort and on multiple levels, however. Only time would tell.

Alex followed the aroma down the stairs to her kitchen, where a sink full of dirty pans provided evidence of Tyler's hard work. Some of those pans hadn't been used in years.

An amber glow from the courtyard patio revealed a storybook-esque romantic setting with a linen tablecloth and napkins, candles, and lush greenery in the background. Her breath caught at the sight of Tyler sitting at the immaculately set table; she was wearing the V-neck, navy blue sheath she had worn on their first date. It was a dress capable of sparking desire then and was doubly so now that she knew what treasures lay beneath it. Alex felt woefully underdressed in a business suit, but she quickly decided changing clothes was unnecessary, a waste of precious minutes.

When she slid the glass door open, Tyler's smile drew her closer. She rose from the table and greeted her with a brief yet passionate kiss that erased every bad memory of the last two days with lawyers.

"I hope you like pork chops," Tyler said.

"I love pork chops. The house smelled amazing when Syd and I walked in."

"Good." Tyler pulled out a chair for Alex. "Now sit, birthday girl. Prepare for an evening of pampering."

"Not before I tell you how delicious everything looks, including you." Her brother may have considered Tyler pedestrian compared to the other women Alex had shown an interest in, but he couldn't have been more wrong. Tyler's slightly fuller body and faint laugh lines made her even more desirable in Alex's eyes. They were proof that Tyler had lived a full life and hadn't fallen prey to the idea that "0" was a size, like Andrew's regular catches had.

Alex gave her another kiss before sitting. The meal looked like something her top chef at Margo's would have prepared. It tasted like it too. After she took her final bite and wiped the corners of her mouth with her napkin, she reached across the table for Tyler's hand. Their conversation during dinner had remained light, touching on the future of Callie, who was upstairs with Syd, and on the source of Tyler's cooking skills— her mother. But Alex's birthday was nearly over and so was Tyler's visit, she feared. Tyler had promised to return for the funeral, but Alex wasn't ready for an empty bed. Not yet.

"Please stay the week until the funeral, T. I don't know how I'll get through the days ahead without you to come home to. Especially tomorrow. I plan to take Callie to the vet to see if she's chipped. I don't think I could bear giving her up if she has one."

Tyler grasped Alex's hand. "I'd be happy to go with you tomorrow. And as far as the rest of the week, Ethan has already offered to stay with the girls until he moves into his new place in a few weeks. Maddie is also onboard with me working remotely on our design projects at Creative Juices. I just have to give them a return date."

Of course, Tyler would have anticipated Alex's need. Every day they'd spent together had brought them closer, made their bond stronger. Their connection was undeniable. "Sunday then?"

CHAPTER TWELVE

In the next hour, Green-Wood Cemetery in Brooklyn would become William Castle's final resting place, where he would soon join Alex's mother. His choice to be buried alongside her was the ultimate act of hypocrisy, proving to Alex that the words she'd said to him the night he died were long overdue. William had spent more years hating his wife than loving her. Discovering years after her death that Rebecca had had an affair with Abby, he had used the last decade to take out his anger on Alex. But in true William Castle form, public appearance was more important than the truth, even after death. Legacy mattered more to him than authenticity. He was a pompous, bitter man, undeserving of Alex's respect, which was why Alex refused to speak today.

Walking into the historic, gothic chapel, Alex pushed aside her outrage and recalled the story her father told her once when they visited her mother's grave on her birthday. He had said that not long after they married her mother had fallen in love with Green-Wood while visiting the cemetery to take in the history of its thousands of interred Civil War heroes. The limestone chapel had particularly captivated her. As her father had told it, she had snapped roll after roll of pictures, trying to capture the structure's beauty that day. She had told him, when she knew the end was near, "I want you to hold my funeral at Green-Wood and to have us buried there together. The rolling hills are simply beautiful, don't you think?" By the end of this day, he would keep his promise and lie next to her for eternity.

Inside the chapel that her mother loved, a massive golden crown-shaped chandelier hung from the ornate central dome, illuminating a cavernous interior highlighted by magnificent stained-glass windows along the perimeter. One hundred of New York's elite, all dressed in dark designer suits and dresses, filled the pews to celebrate William's life. Among them were several Fortune 500 and Castle Resorts competitor CEOs, New York City's deputy mayor, and many friends and business associates. Filling out the front row beside Alex and Tyler were Alex's surrogate mother, Abby Spencer, with her partner, Indra, Alex's best friend, Harley Spencer, Alex's siblings, Andrew and Syd, and Syd's husband, John.

The funeral had William's fingerprints all over it, including which pastor would preside, which scriptures would be read, and which songs would be sung. The only thing William had left to chance was who would speak and give tribute—one small nugget of humility.

Pastor Hastings opened the service with a brief prayer of healing and hope. He segued into Psalm 23, "The Lord is my shepherd; I shall not want..." He next read from John 14, "Let not your hearts be troubled..." and then played a recorded spiritual version of "Amazing Grace."

Several late-arriving mourners entered through the rear of the chapel. Seeing that every seat was filled, they took positions along the left wall. Two caught Alex's attention—Detectives Sterling and Diaz. The pastor then opened the service up for tributes. The deputy mayor spoke first, talking about a close friendship with William for decades brought about through their common interest in landmark preservation, followed by a fellow CEO, who spoke on William's many years of community service and business acumen. Then Robert Stein stepped to the podium.

"Deputy Mayor Simmons, Sydney, Andrew, and Alexandra Castle, distinguished guests, and friends. Today we say goodbye to the youngest and last surviving child of Harold and Ruth Castle. Most of the city will remember their son William as a successful businessman. But those of us who loved him and ache at his passing knew William by the other titles he held: father, son, and husband. I knew him as classmate, client, mentor, and, like so many others in the city where he lived and worked for sixty-nine years, I called him friend.

"William Castle was the baby of the family, but he became its bedrock when he lost his parents in a tragic accident when he was a young man just out of Yale. Despite his pain and loss, he was a relentless dreamer. He bought a single hotel with his family fortune and grew it into a global presence with a collection of the finest resorts in the world.

"I first met William Castle at Yale, not through academics, athletics, or a mutual interest. We met because our girlfriends at the time happened to be roommates. We hit it off instantly. It didn't take long for me to get a glimpse of the type of mettle that made the man. First, understand the times in which we lived in the late 1950s. It was the dawn of the civil rights movement, and racial tensions were high. At Yale, we lived in a bubble where race was not at the forefront. We thought nothing about becoming friends—a young Jewish man from Brooklyn and an equally young man from Manhattan with Mediterranean roots. His skin tone was only noticeable after weeks in the sun, but when it was in full view, there was no mistaking that he was 'other' than of northern European stock.

"The first time we ventured outside that bubble, we found ourselves out of gas in a small town in rural Massachusetts. After a three-mile walk for gas, we stopped for food at an equally small diner. We instantly attracted the attention of the locals, and it became clear we weren't welcome. We ordered our food to go and were waiting when two rather large men approached us and said something like, 'You're not from around here, are you?' and 'I think you're in the wrong place.' I wanted to leave, but William insisted on waiting on the food we'd paid for. One of them crowed at my friend and asked, 'Are you dumb, boy?' William then went into a philosophical diatribe on the differences between dumbness and stupidity, leaving the two brutes speechless. He diffused the situation just long enough for our food to arrive and for us to bid them a good day. I even heard one say in return, 'Have a good day too.' That was when I knew William Castle could talk his way out of anything and dazzle anyone who stood before him.

"While the relationships with our respective college love interests were short-lived, our friendship was not. I am proud to say it lasted decades. We remained steadfast friends through every trial with loved ones, misfortune in business, and challenges with a cruel disease, even when my counsel to him was not well-received."

Robert glanced toward Detective Sterling at the side of the chapel, paused, and then stared directly at Alex and Andrew for several intense beats before continuing, "William Castle was taken from us all too early. At last, he is with his parents, sisters, and beautiful wife, all of whom were called to heaven too early. May his killer be brought to swift justice."

Murmurs broke out among the mourners. Heads shifted left and right as the accusation that William Castle's death wasn't an accident but something more sinister caught fire. Alex peeked at her siblings. Syd squirmed in her seat, clearly uncomfortable with the allegation, but Andrew remained curiously steady and unfazed.

"May God bless William Castle, and may he rest in eternal peace."

Alex tore her gaze from Robert to Sterling, who pulled his cell phone from his suit pocket and read something from it. The icy stare he sent her way afterward sent chills down Alex's spine, making her feel like prey. Sterling returned the phone to his pocket, and he and Diaz left the chapel.

After six more friends and colleagues spoke words of praise, Pastor Hastings invited Syd to come forward to speak on behalf of the Castle children.

"I'd like to thank everyone for coming today. Our family is grateful for your sympathy and kind words. Knowing our father was so widely loved is a comfort. He carried himself as a polished, professional businessman to the world, but we knew him as Father. He was an imperfect man, but what he did, he did out of love.

"Few people knew this, but our father was a very smooth dancer. When I was a little girl, he'd dance with my mother and me almost every evening before putting me to bed. When Alex and Andrew came along, he continued that tradition by dancing with them and his beloved Rebecca every night until she passed away."

Andrew looked curiously at Alex and whispered, "Do you remember that?"

Alex racked her brain, unable to recall more than flashes. "I don't know, maybe."

"Sadly, after she died, I never saw him dance again. So, if you'll indulge me, I'd like to sing a song that I believe captures how I remember my father and what Alex, Andrew, and I are feeling right now."

Organ music played, and Syd sang the lyrics to "Dance with My Father." When she sang the lines, "Spin me around till I fell asleep. Then up the stairs, he would carry me…" a vague memory of the Platters' song, "Only You" flashed in Alex's mind, the song her father listened to every day in his study after her mother died. She remembered the music playing, William spinning her around the living room floor, and her mother, brother, and sister smiling and laughing while they danced. She squeezed Tyler's hand, a warm feeling rushing over her. Tears blurred her vision while she stared at Syd, listening intently to the song.

"I remember," Alex whispered. "He danced with me. He danced with all of us." She glanced toward Andrew. Similar tears had filled his eyes.

Syd finished with the lines, "If I could get another chance… How I'd love, love, love to dance with my father again."

The moment Syd ended, tears cascaded from Alex and Andrew's eyes. They'd joined hands, and, if only for that minute, Alex felt their connection as strong as it had been when they were kids. She was sure he too remembered those long-forgotten, fun-filled dances and had flashes of their father smiling and laughing. Alex wished she could be more like Syd and remember William as the once happy, carefree father who used to dance with the freedom of butterflies. *Maybe one day*, she thought.

"Father," Alex said softly before burying her face in her hands. Tyler wrapped her arms around her, nuzzling Alex's head with hers. She said her final goodbye to a father she'd loathed for a day but had loved all her life. It was time now to move on with the woman who had her heart.

CHAPTER THIRTEEN

Sterling rolled into the Nineteenth Precinct squad room with Diaz by his side. Their lieutenant waved them over. "My office."

Sterling had a strong distaste for his boss's cramped, cluttered office. It had been the site where he'd received several ass chewings from its previous occupant for occasionally cutting corners.

Lieutenant Asher retreated behind a large 1970's era metal desk laden with file folders, loose stacks of paper, and an NYPD coffee mug that hadn't seen soap in months. Clipboards, flyers, and news clippings lined the unevenly painted walls over his shoulders, adding to the chaos. He plopped in his rolling metal chair—the resulting heavy squeak signaling its age.

"Where are you with the Castle case? I'm getting heat from the mayor's office to make an arrest."

"DNA just came back on the blood on the camera," Sterling answered. "It's a match for the vic."

"Do you still like the daughter for this?" Asher asked.

"It's adding up." Sterling's gut told him that Alex Castle didn't fit the profile of a killer, but at this point he had no other suspect that checked all the boxes. "The M.E. says the blow to the head was too severe to result from a simple fall against the desk. He ruled out an accidental fall, so someone had to have pushed him. He also puts the time of death between seven and ten p.m. The daughter had a nine o'clock meeting with him in his office, and the vic's secretary confirmed the daughter was his only appointment on the calendar that evening."

"Are we sure no one else came in after her?"

"There's no way to tell for sure. The building is under construction, and plastic sheeting or scaffolding obscured most of the security cameras."

"What else ties her to the scene?"

"The secretary said he had his daughter's vintage camera in his office the afternoon of the murder, but it was missing the next morning. The secretary identified the camera as looking exactly like the one I retrieved from the daughter. Test results show the blood on it is a match to the vic."

"Do you have a theory for a motive?"

"Her brother tells us their father was a huge homophobe," Diaz said.

So was the little prick himself, Sterling wanted to add, but he held his tongue on that aspect. "Let's not forget the brother had motive too. We found a cache of documents in the vic's safe detailing how he embezzled a quarter mil from the company."

"I agree they both had a beef with their father, but we can only place Alex at the scene. She had the missing camera with his blood on it." Diaz waved her hands in the air. "What else do you need? A signed confession? We have witnesses saying the vic blew a gasket after he saw Alex pawing a woman in public."

"That confirms what the deputy mayor told me," Asher said. "Any evidence that the old man knew?"

Diaz continued, "Besides the stack of documents in the safe, confirming the brother's theory, his computer had a copy of security footage from the resort in San Francisco from the night before he was killed. It shows his daughter in a lip-lock with a woman at the hotel bar. His secretary also told us he was about to make"—Diaz used finger quotes—"'a dramatic change in the company' and had called a meeting the following day of all the executives except his daughter. His body was found hours before the meeting. That all tells me he knew."

"How do you think it went down?"

"We think the old man called her in. He fired her over her public relationship. They had it out. She shoved him, and he fell and hit his head. She grabbed the camera and left."

"All right, take it to the ADA and see what he says. I'd like to make an arrest by the end of the day."

"You got it, boss." Sterling replaced his toothpick to counter the bitter taste in his mouth. This rush to judgment didn't feel right, but what choice did he have? The evidence added up and powerful politicians were breathing down his boss's neck. Sure, the arrest was justified, but he couldn't shake the thought they'd missed something.

CHAPTER FOURTEEN

Following Syd's moving song, Alex rose and invited the funeral attendees to a reception at the Upper East Side mansion she'd be inheriting from her father. Town car after town car dropped off one mourner after another. Caterers efficiently worked each occupied room, serving finger food and drinks to the guests. A buffet table in the main room, where William had handed Alex the reins of Castle Resorts just a month earlier, offered guests more substantial food to eat.

Alex drifted from room to room, greeting guest after guest. Most were congregated by their association with her father—Castle Resorts, landmark preservation buffs, Yale alumni, and so on. Some shared fond memories of William while others made no effort to pretend that making connections and conducting business was their primary reason for attending. At least her and Blake's appointment of the interim COO earlier this week had tempered several of Castle Resorts executives from launching into a full out election campaign.

Alex worked her way back to the packed main room, where everyone important to her had gathered near the black marble fireplace along the north wall. Like a magnet to metal, the most enchanting creature in the room drew her eyes. Tyler's every line and curve had become her kryptonite; she was unable to resist them whenever she was in her orbit. Then their gazes met. How could eyes that alluring be so comforting as well? Chatter became white noise, and motion on the periphery became indecipherable. Alex didn't need to cross the room to feel their connection. It was in her bones.

A hand briefly fell softly on her arm. Alex turned. Indra Kapoor was beautiful and polished in a black long-sleeved Armani jersey dress that hit right at the knee. Its gracefully twisted fabric was gathered inches above her left breast, creating a fitted silhouette. No other Fortune 500 CEO looked as stunning.

"It was a lovely service, Alex. Other than at his retirement celebration, I hadn't met William outside of charity events, but based on what little I knew of him, I'm sure he would've been pleased."

A very diplomatic statement. Indra was intimately aware of the tension between Abby and her father and how it had bled into Alex's life, but her graciousness clearly wouldn't allow her to speak of it today.

"I'd love to take credit, but other than the speeches, every aspect was of his own doing. He planned every detail in advance." Alex gave Indra's hand a gentle squeeze. "But I'd like to thank you for the use of your jet. It made the heavy task of telling my sister of our father's death much easier."

"You're like a daughter to my sweet Abby. Of course, I'd help. But after our mutual adventure in cornering that scallywag who was nipping at your feet last month, I'd like to think that we've become friends."

"We have, but I must say all that business with those awful photos seems now like it happened ages ago." Alex considered herself lucky. Kelly Thatcher's shakedown might have turned Alex's life upside down if not for Indra's help.

"Well, I was glad to be rid of Mr. Castor. The insider trading that he and Ms. Thatcher engaged in provided the perfect excuse. But I have to thank you. Your reaching out for my help brought Abby and me together again. I can't thank you enough for that." Indra gestured toward the room's centerpiece fireplace and Alex's loved ones. "I see things have worked out for you as well."

"I've waited my entire life for a woman like her." Alex briefly returned a gaze from Tyler, whose heart-stopping smile had turned grief into joy and pain into pleasure merely by being cast in her direction.

"I know exactly what you mean." The corners of Indra's lips slowly turned upward as she met Abby's gaze. Decades of love flowed between them. It was a look Alex envisioned experiencing herself thirty years from now. "Let's return to our lovely ladies."

Returning to the fireplace, Alex clasped Tyler's hand and entwined their fingers. Indra did the same with Abby.

"We were just discussing Syd's moving tribute." Abby kissed the back of Indra's hand. "I never took William as one to cut a rug."

"He was a different man before Rebecca died," Syd replied.

"I wish I had known that man," Alex said.

"That's the only thing we still have in common." Andrew's acerbic quip cut Alex to the quick, reminding her that she'd lost him too.

A server approached Alex and whispered into her ear. "Police detectives are at the door, ma'am. They're asking for you."

A sinking feeling formed in Alex's stomach; the timing of their visit seemed intentional. If Sterling planned to make a public spectacle out of questioning her again, though, she wouldn't give him the opportunity. "Please show them to the study. I'll be right there." After the server left, she announced to their small group, "The police have more questions. I'll be right back."

"You're not going to meet with them alone, are you?" Concern rightly cut through Abby's question. Alex was sure the visit would not be friendly, but she was today's host and had little choice but to deal with them quickly.

"I'm sure it will be fine," Alex said.

"I'm going with you." The force behind Tyler's words left no room for argument, but arguing was the last thing she wanted. She preferred Tyler by her side now and always.

"Me too." Syd appeared ready to wrestle Alex to the ground if she disagreed, a feat more likely than not.

"Have at, sister." Andrew smirked. "Chats with the cops rarely go well."

Sliding the heavy double doors open, Alex invited Tyler and Syd to enter her father's study before closing the doors behind her. She met Detective Sterling's unreadable stare, which sent a chill through her. Goose bumps raised on her arms. "Detectives, what can I do for you?"

Sterling stepped forward, pulling his handcuffs from his waistband. "You need to come with us. We have a warrant for your arrest in the death of William Castle."

"You've got to be kidding me. We just buried our father." Syd stepped forward to block the detectives.

"Don't make this harder than it has to be, ma'am." Diaz pressed a palm against Syd's chest, bringing her to a stop.

"For heaven's sake, there's no way my sister had anything to do with this," Syd said.

"Look, ma'am, we're just doing our jobs," Diaz said.

Alex turned toward Tyler, who was straining not to shed the tears gathering in her eyes. She raised a hand, ran her fingers down Tyler's cheek, and traced her jawline before placing an index finger over Tyler's lips to quiet her before she spoke. "I'll be fine. Have Abby call Jesse." She then leaned in, intending to give Tyler a loving kiss, only for Diaz to pull her back before she could.

"Come on, let's go." Sterling cuffed her hands behind her back. "You have the right to remain silent..."

CHAPTER FIFTEEN

When Alex walked into the Nineteenth Precinct this time, she felt suffocated. She'd never imagined herself being dragged into a police station in handcuffs, but here she was, no longer a suspect but the accused. When Sterling tugged her by the elbow, she stepped up to the intake desk. "One for first-degree manslaughter," he said before slapping a completed NYPD form on the desk.

A busty uniformed officer scanned the form before looking up. Her domineering once-over gave Alex the heebie-jeebies, confirming that she had, indeed, lost her freedom. "Against the wall."

Sterling left without a single word.

Alex fell in line with four other cuffed women. She gave the one to her right, the only one who didn't look scary, a small smile to acknowledge that they were all in this together. The woman wasn't that dissimilar from her—tall, tanned skin, dark hair, and an athletic frame. If not for the tight, revealing blouse and skirt and yellow boots that reached nearly to her knees, this one, with her strong jawline and cheekbones, could've been mistaken for her sister. The one next in line, dressed in a tatty blue cocktail dress, was brooding in her smeared mascara. The other two—dressed in layers of oversized pants, sweatshirts, and filthy jackets—appeared to be in the throes of drug highs.

A second female officer called the arrestees forward one by one and confiscated and inventoried their belongings. When it was Alex's turn, she barked, "Step up to the line. Empty your pockets and place the contents on the desk."

Still clad in the black Christian Dior sheath dress she'd worn for the funeral, Alex patted her sides. "I'm afraid I don't have any pockets."

The officer drilled Alex with her eyes, eliciting a hard swallow. "Remove your jewelry and anything in your hair, including hairpins, bands, or barrettes. Then place them on the desk."

"Barrettes? What is this, kindergarten?" Alex regretted her nervous retort the moment it slipped from her big mouth. Her hand shook as she removed her earrings and necklace.

The officer scowled, looking scarier than her father had when he first confronted her about being gay. Alex swallowed even harder.

"I don't want any lip, Barbie. Do as you're told."

"I'm sorry. I'm really nervous. I've never done this before."

"I wouldn't let your cellmates know you're a virgin here. They'll smell blood and circle you like a pack of dogs." The officer wrote Alex's name, date of birth, and contact information on an official manila envelope and placed her jewelry inside it.

"I won't." *This shit just got real.* Alex felt the walls closing in. She could be tough in the boardroom, but was she tough enough to handle the Star Wars barroom crowd likely waiting for her here?

"Anything else on your person you don't want the dogs to steal?"

"No." Alex decided her best and safest course of action going forward was to limit her responses to a simple "yes" or "no."

Following an intrusive pat-down that reached her crotch—thirty humiliating seconds that Alex would rather forget—the officer herded her to the next station.

"Step up to the line and extend your right hand." A male officer placed Alex's fingers one by one on the black and white scanner and then her palms. This device was much larger than the handheld one detectives had used at her office building to fingerprint her and her employees and much more colorful. A bright green light lit up each time, capturing every swirl and ridgeline on her fingertips and hands. When he finished, he pointed to a bank of phones on the far wall. "You can make your call, Barbie."

Alex rolled her eyes at her new moniker and approached the cleanest-looking phone. Until now, she'd been too wrapped up in her own ordeal to consider how worried Tyler must be. As she dialed, every ounce of her own anxiety manifested in a temple-throbbing headache.

Tyler answered on the first ring. "Alex?" Her thready voice told of hours of worry.

"I'm all right, T." Alex dug deep to remain calm. "Did Abby call Jesse?"

"She did. Jesse will meet you at Central Booking." Tyler cleared her throat. She was putting on a good front, but Alex recognized the strain in her voice. "Have they told you anything about how long this will take? Jesse said it could take up to twenty-four hours."

"Twenty-four hours? All they've said so far is 'step up to the line,' and they've taken to calling me Barbie."

"Barbie, huh?" Tyler's voice dropped its edge. Alex's distraction had worked. "Well, you do have that perfect body and legs that go forever. They're to die for."

"One minute, Barbie," a voice bellowed from behind Alex.

Alex acknowledged the summons with a jut of her chin. "Tyler, I don't have much time. How's our dog?"

"Ours, huh?"

"Yeah. I think Callie likes you more than me since we took her to the vet."

"That was a great day, learning she wasn't chipped."

Alex glanced at the male officer whose toe-tapping warned her to wrap it up. "I gotta go, T. I love you."

"I love you too. Watch your back in there, babe."

"Let's go, Barbie," the officer ordered.

He ushered Alex and the four other women down a long, dark corridor lined with tattered posters and various warning signs. After they passed through a large metal door, the rancid smell of urine hit her like a nuclear blast, pushing her toward the edge of vomiting. The escort officer walked her and the others past two large cells, each holding six to eight women of different ages, colors, and, based on their appearances, of various reputes. He stopped at the third of five cells, this one unoccupied, and waved toward a small glass window along the far wall. A loud buzz sounded, and he opened the barred door. "All right, ladies, home sweet home."

Once the officer uncuffed them, the five filed into the filthy cell. Then the door slammed shut, cementing the fact that Alex's freedom was in the past. Furnishings consisted of one long wooden bench, an open, very public, metal jailhouse toilet, and a scattering of dead flies and roaches, cigarette butts, McDonald's wrappers, and what appeared to be the remnants of a religious pamphlet. Alex was not about to pick it up to investigate, but written at the top was "What Do You Want from Life?"

She took a seat on one end of the bench while the woman in boots sat on the other end. A street person relieved herself in the toilet while the other two paced the cell's perimeter. Alex kept to herself, trying to blend in with her cellmates, but that was impossible. The others were dressed to pick up a John or score an eight-ball of meth, as a booking officer had described it, but Alex was decked out in Christian Dior and Prada.

In the first half hour, officers emptied the first holding cell of its occupants and refilled it with newcomers. In the next, officers did the same with the second cell. That movement cued one of the tweaker types in her cell, a term the officer had used to refer to the other drug addict-looking person, to step toward Alex and scan her up and down. "I bet Barbie here ain't shit without all that uptown makeup."

If that was her attempt to establish the cell's pecking order, tweaker number one had another think coming. Alex stood face-to-face, giving her a boardroom stare. "Don't let these Prada shoes fool you. I eat trolls like you for lunch."

The others in the cell let out a collective, "Ooooohhhh."

The tweaker placed her hands on her hips, begging for a fight, but Alex stood her ground, staring her down. After a noticeable pause, Boots pushed herself from the other end of the bench. "I'll be damned. Barbie here has some G.I. Joe balls." Laughter broke out, breaking the tension. Boots cracked a smile. "You're all right, Barbie."

Alex responded with a smile of her own. "Good to know I've got friends in low places."

Laughter filled the cell again. They sat quietly for the next two hours until the officer unlocked the door and ordered them out. "All right, ladies, your limo has arrived."

Alex wasn't sure where she was going, but she knew not to disclose that tidbit to the others; she kept her mouth shut. Tyler had said that Jesse would meet her at Central Booking; she hoped that was their destination and that her opportunity to post bail would come much sooner than within twenty-four hours.

Officers cuffed and herded the five, now relatively cordial cellmates, into a staging area, where they re-cuffed them, hand to hand to one another, in what the officers called a daisy chain. Loaded into the back of a police cargo van, which was curiously devoid of seats and therefore seat belts, the women sat on the cold metal floor. The trip down Franklin D. Roosevelt Drive to Central Booking was excessively bumpy, bouncing the cellmates up and down like corn popping on the stovetop. When the van swerved into what felt like a swooping highway exit, everyone in the rear cabin was forced to one side, toppling into each other. A cacophony of "fuck" and "shit" rang out from the back. If Alex were a gambler like Andrew, she'd bet her last dollar that the driver intentionally had hit every pothole along the way.

The van finally came to a stop. The building signage declared that they had arrived at Central Booking: "The Tombs," according to local lore. Still chained together, Alex and her fellow road-beaten passengers quickstepped it inside, where again the pervasive stench of urine hung in the air. Alex's eyes widened as they approached a horseshoe-shaped collection of holding cells filled with hundreds of men. Her heart hammered at the thought of being locked up next to a cell full of thugs, each of them capable of overpowering her. Much to her relief, an officer marched her group past the men and up a ramp to the next floor, which apparently held the female intake area.

The room's battleship gray floor had a series of painted black lines designating where the prisoners should stand so they could be herded like cattle. Posters of sports stars, both old and new, covered the powder blue walls. *How ironic*, Alex thought. *Andrew would like it here.*

A female guard, the one who looked to be in charge, announced, "First stop: strip-search." A second female guard ordered the five prisoners to stand on a particular black line on the floor, strip and place their clothes in one of the TSA-type buckets sitting atop the eight-foot-long table in front of them. The Central Booking veterans disrobed and stood facing the guards in all their glory, their arms at their sides. Alex undressed and turned, covering herself the best she could with her hands and arms.

The lead guard glanced at Alex's file and pulled a sticky note from the front flap. She appeared to read it before returning it to its home. "This isn't playtime, Barbie. Hands and arms at your sides."

Her nickname had definitely stuck. Alex lowered her arms before quipping, "It's refreshing to know the lines of communication are working well here."

"Zip it, Barbie," the lead guard snapped back when the other prisoners laughed. But this was no laughing matter. This was serious. Alex had been arrested and thrown in jail for a crime she didn't commit. And unless Jesse was damn good at her job, Alex might never see daylight again.

While one guard searched the carefully placed clothing, another inspected the prisoners with a flashlight, presumably searching for weapons and contraband. When she came to Alex, Alex towered over her by six inches.

The guard inspected Alex's hands, arms, feet, legs, and torso before ordering, "Open your mouth."

Alex complied, but the guard struggled without success to see into her mouth. The other prisoners laughed. The lead guard glared. "You wanna push the twenty-four-hour window? Keep laughing." The group instantly quieted. "Barbie, bend down before we chop those stilts off."

Alex bent at the knees until her mouth was more accessible to the guard.

"Move your tongue to the left. To the right. Now up." The guard stepped back and ordered, "Turn around, bend over, spread your legs, and grab your ankles." Moments after Alex complied, she said. "Grab your ass cheeks and spread 'em. Wider. Grab your labia and spread 'em."

Alex had faced being arrested with her chin held high, but this was beyond the pale. The pat-down at the precinct had been humiliating enough, but this was downright dehumanizing. She felt violated. She focused her thoughts on Tyler and holding her in their bed. Funny how they'd only been a couple for a week, but Alex already considered that whatever was hers was Tyler's.

"She's clean."

"Get dressed. Then return to the line," the lead guard barked.

After dressing, they all lined up for the next station—booking photo, according to the sign. A guard at the desk there directed each prisoner to step up to the line and asked, "Name?" He grabbed the corresponding file, entered something into a computer terminal, pressed a button that activated a bright flash, and said, "Next." The rote, mechanical nature of the process was disturbing.

Alex paid attention to the others ahead of her, who were robotically obeying without as much as a forced grin. But when it was her turn, she remembered the mugshot of Paris Hilton, taken with her signature head tilt, following a DUI arrest. It had gone viral last year.

She stepped up, pulled her hair back behind her right ear, smiled as if posing for the media frenzy at the Met, and replied, "Alexandra Castle." Now, that was how to pose for a publicly available booking photo. Belatedly, she wondered if her lawyer would agree.

Their next stop was at bail screening, where a sign on the wall behind this station read "Criminal Justice Agency." A lone clerk who looked sick of his work was sitting behind the desk. He recited the same spiel to each prisoner. "The following questions will determine your suitability for bail. We will provide your responses to the District Attorney's Office and the court prior to your arraignment. Your responses are completely voluntary."

Alex simply responded with, "Okay."

As best as Alex could determine, the series of questions was aimed at gauging her ties to the community. The question about whether she had a home phone number, however, baffled her. The clerk only asked if she had one, not what it was. How in the hell did that determine her suitability for bail? Nevertheless, she answered each question.

"Next," the clerk bellowed.

Last stop: Medical Screening.

The now-tight group of five shuffled toward a stainless-steel counter. At the speed of a sloth, a guard there painstakingly logged each prisoner into the computer system as a guest of Central Booking. He then instructed each to "step to the right," where an emergency medical technician sat at the ready. Behind the EMT's shoulder hung a poster that read at the top, "Think TB!" Alex was reluctant to read beyond that heading and discover what other contagious or communicable diseases might be in store for her. After answering a set of questions about injuries and health issues, the gang of five moved into the holding pen area—seven cages designed to contain no more than fourteen occupants according to the signage.

The guards ushered them into a cell. It already had nine occupants, so adding them put the space at its capacity. The Central Booking veterans rushed to claim spots on the concrete floor, leaving floor space at a premium. The wooden benches along each of the three walls had very few occupants on the other hand. Slow to catch on, Alex found herself relegated to sitting on a hard bench for what promised to be a long, hot, and disagreeable night.

Alex ran her fingers through her hair and cradled her head, mentally recapping her day. It had started with her father's funeral at Green-Wood. It had continued at the mansion for the reception and ended with this nightmare incarceration. Not having eaten at the reception, she was now beyond hungry, bordering on queasy. Adding to her dismal state was the sign inside the cell titled "What to Expect" that specified breakfast wouldn't be served until two o'clock in the morning. Reading further, Alex noted that criminal arraignments were only held until one o'clock in the morning. If her internal clock was working, it was already after eleven. Based on the number of people ahead of her, she held little hope that she would be in court before then and resigned herself to bedding down in the cell for the night.

Sleep was now her primary focus. She tried to stretch out on the bench, but it was too narrow for her to get into a reasonably comfortable position. The interior temperature was nearing an oppressive level as well, which intensified the inescapable urine smell and body odor. Thankfully, her bench space was several feet away from the overflowing jailhouse toilet.

Following an hour of shifting and tossing and turning, a voice called out from the floor, "Barbie, get your plastic ass down here. You'll never get to sleep up there." Boots shoved two cellmates over despite their grumbling and patted a section of the floor next to her. "Barbie? Are you coming or what?"

Still in her Prada shoes, Alex gingerly stepped over three women to get to the newly opened spot. She removed her shoes and held them in her hand before sitting on the dingy floor. "Thanks." She looked around, noting how the other women were using their shoes as pillows. She followed suit, laying her head on top of her heels. While the floor was definitely more comfortable than the bench, the shoes left a lot to be desired. The sides of the stiff soles pressed painfully into her ear and cheek, but it was better than the alternative—the floor.

"Fucking Prada. Next time I'm arrested, I'm wearing Nikes."

Boots chuckled. "Are you thinking about racking up frequent NYPD flyer miles?"

"Not if I can help it." Alex repositioned her arms and legs, trying to find a morsel of comfort, but in the process accidentally kicked the large, grouchy woman lying behind her.

"Watch it, bitch." The woman shoved Alex hard, knocking her into Boots.

"Whoa. Sorry. I didn't mean to hit you," Alex apologized.

The filthy woman raised her upper body off the floor. "Look, Princess Barbie, you may be used to spreading out wherever you please, but that shit don't work in here."

"What the fuck? I said I was sorry." Fatigue drove Alex's sharp retort.

"Oh boy," Boots said in a low voice.

The angry woman grabbed Alex's arm and growled, "What did you say, bitch?"

Alex pulled her arm back, but the woman's hold was too strong. Her grip tightened, fingernails digging into her skin through her dress fabric. For the first time during this ordeal, Alex feared for her life.

Suddenly, Boots reached over Alex and shoved the woman's head against the floor, giving her a menacing look. "You got a problem? Barbie is with me. You fuck with her, you fuck with me. Trust me, you don't want a piece of this."

The woman grunted a few times before sullenly returning to her sleeping position.

Alex turned to look Boots in the eye. They both propped their heads up in a palm, arm bent at the elbow. "Thanks. I appreciate the help."

"I didn't want to deal with a ruckus. The guards tend to lose your paperwork for hours if they have to come in here to break up a fight."

"Good to know. I'll try to keep my stilts to myself in the future."

Boots chuckled. "You're all right, Barbie."

"The name's Alex."

"I'm Destiny."

Now it was Alex's turn to chuckle. "Is that your street name or your real name?"

"Real name. My mother said she thought I was destined for something good when she held me for the first time. But lately, it seems I'm destined to keep dancing the clubs until my tits fall off—unless I don't get a hold of my temper with handsy patrons."

Alex laughed at the image of body parts falling to the stage floor. "How long have you been in the business?"

"Since I was nineteen, so sixteen years."

"Sixteen years? I never knew someone in your business stayed in it for that long."

"Most don't. They end up offering extras and catch something or overdose on drugs."

"How did you last so long?"

"Besides no drugs and no extras, ever? I'm a trained dancer. I did ballet when I was little, before money got tight. I work on my craft and develop a new routine every week to keep the regulars flocking in."

"Is it profitable?"

"I do okay." Destiny shrugged. "I own a condo in Brooklyn. It's not much, but it's mine. I also put a bunch away every month for retirement. Between that and Social Security, I should be all right."

"You plan on doing this until you're sixty-five?"

Destiny laughed. "Not unless I keep getting arrested. It adds to the overhead. I figure I've got another three or four years of socking it away before I can pay off the condo and hang up the feathers. Then I'll get an accounting gig and live off of that until I start collecting Social Security."

"You're an accountant?"

"I graduate from Baruch College with a bachelor's degree this month."

"Let me get this straight. You're an exotic dancer who's put herself through accounting school, nearly paid off a condo, and saved up enough for retirement. You amaze me, Destiny."

"Thanks." Destiny's grin contained unmistakable self-satisfaction. "Let's get some sleep. I can't wait for the two o'clock Rice Krispies."

The lights went out, and Alex finally understood how The Tombs got its nickname. Without windows, the sense that the walls were closing in was overpowering and suffocating.

CHAPTER SIXTEEN

The clamor of prisoners shuffling in and out of neighboring cells had divided Alex's few precious hours of sleep into half-hour stretches. But during each period, she had dreamed of Tyler. It was the same every time. Reclining on a patio lounger, she had Tyler in her arms and they were both staring off into the watery distance. The setting sun had skimmed the horizon and cast a hypnotic orange glow on the gentle ocean waves. No words needed exchanging, only touches. It was the perfect moment in time, one she would move heaven and earth to re-create in real life.

At two o'clock sharp, or so Alex assumed, lights turned on, illuminating the overcrowded collection of cells and the sources of the foul smells that had assaulted her all evening. Cell by cell, clerks made rounds, delivering breakfast.

Alex and Destiny lined up at the cell door for their morning feeding. Destiny recommended, "Don't trust the milk. Sometimes they let it sit out for hours. You'll be puking or crapping for hours."

"Got it." Alex selected two mini boxes of Rice Krispies and two kindergarten-sized cartons of fruit punch before returning to the bench with Destiny.

Her meth-type cellmates pounded down their cereal like it was cocaine. Conversely, Destiny, experienced at Central Booking cuisine, carefully tore off the box top, opened the interior plastic bag, and poured small bits of cereal into her mouth. She washed down each bite with small sips of punch.

Why not? Alex shrugged and followed Destiny's example. Strangely, the combination wasn't half bad, reminding her of her elementary school days, when handfuls of Captain Crunch served as an afternoon snack.

Hours passed, provoking the fear that she'd have to endure another meal in this place. Finally, officers chained Alex and her fellow cellmates together in a line, affixing waist and arm restraints. Alex remained right behind Destiny. The mini-chain gang lumbered through a maze of narrow corridors, creating a cacophony of clanking metal. Officers brought them to another holding area smelling of urine, but with two added features: daylight and enough bench space for everyone to sit. Sunbeams struggled to break through the wire mesh that covered clouded glass. Nonetheless, it was sweet, sweet daylight. Thankfully, they were allowed to wait unchained.

More hours passed with Alex and Destiny sticking together like junior high school friends on a field trip. They passed the time mostly in silence, with only occasional murmurs to one another about their more interesting or annoying cellmates. Every fifteen minutes or so, a guard shouted out a name, prompting someone to stand and follow the guard out the barred door.

"Alexandra Castle," the guard shouted.

Alex patted Destiny on her knee. "That's me. I wish you luck."

"You too, Barbie," Destiny replied with a wink.

Alex stood and took a few steps toward the bellowing guard, but stopped. She turned around. "Destiny, if you ever want to get out of the game earlier and get an honest-to-goodness accounting gig with great benefits, stop by the Castle Resorts in Times Square and ask for Alex Castle."

"You work there?"

"I own it and twenty-two other hotels. If you want a job, it's yours."

Destiny's jaw dropped. "I'll be damned. Barbie has herself a bunch of dream houses. I might just take you up on that."

"Castle!" the guard shouted again.

Alex gave Destiny a wink. "Gotta go."

An officer placed Alex back in shackles and led her down another hallway and into a narrow room. A long counter there divided the room down the center. There were five evenly spaced chairs on each side of the counter. Plexiglass windows separated the stations from one another and from the other side of the counter. The guard parked Alex in the only chair that was empty. To her relief, she saw Jesse staring back at her through the smudged window.

Alex placed her cuffed hands on the counter. "Thank fucking God."

"I know this has been quite the ordeal, Alex, but we don't have much time," Jesse said. "Your arraignment will start in about thirty minutes."

Finally, someone established a time frame, putting Alex more at ease. "First, how is Tyler?"

"She's fine. She, Abby, Harley, and Syd all send their love. They all will be at the arraignment." Jesse paused when Alex sighed. She appreciated and relied on the support of everyone important to her, but she hated the idea of them seeing her chained like a criminal, especially Tyler. "I have a copy of the complaint and a summary of the evidence the police have compiled against you. It's circumstantial at best. Here's what's going to happen: an ADA, assistant district attorney, will read the charges. He'll either ask the judge for remand or high bail. I'll argue against remand. You're a classic case for bail. I'll try to get it set as low as possible. Once that's decided, the ADA will refer your case to the grand jury."

"Do you think I'll be released today?"

"I'm confident that you will. The DA is charging you with manslaughter in the first degree, a class B felony with a sentence of five to twenty-five years. The court usually offers bail."

"Twenty-five years?" Alex yelped, earning the attention of the guards in the room.

"Alex, calm down or they'll take you back to the pen, and we'll do this all over again tomorrow."

Alex sheepishly looked at the glaring guards and lifted her hands in a surrendering fashion. "I'm sorry, Jesse. I'm calm."

"You've drawn a pretty reasonable judge. Barring unforeseen circumstances, you should be out on bail this afternoon."

Alex sighed in half-relief, half-dread. "That's not very reassuring. What if I don't get bail?"

"They will transport you to Rikers Island. You'll stay there until your court date."

"Fuck, Jesse. How did this happen?"

"I'll get you through this, Alex. When you get into the courtroom, stand straight and don't say a word. Let me do the talking. Got it?"

"Got it," Alex retorted.

"Alex." Jesse's expression turned from professional to one of concern. "I know this is hard, but I promise I'll pull out every stop and cash in every favor I can to get you out of here and clear your name. Do you trust me?"

"I do trust you, and I appreciate everything you're doing. I just want out of here. I need a shower, a change of clothes, sleep, and to get back to Tyler."

"Well then, let's go make that happen." Jesse looked over her shoulder and shouted, "Guard, we're done here." She turned back to Alex and lowered her voice. "I'll see you soon."

The guard returned Alex to the holding cell and removed the shackles. Alex looked for Destiny and located her in the spot where she'd left her. The moment Alex sat down beside her, a guard yelled, "Destiny Scott."

Destiny patted Alex on the knee. "That's me. I wish you luck."

"Destiny, I mean it about that job offer. I hope you take me up on it."

Destiny smiled as she stood. "See you around, Barbie."

Moments after Destiny left, the guard called Alex's name again. A police officer led her through a red door marked "Exit" and into the first of two wood and glass booths that looked into the courtroom. He directed her to the first open spot on the bench. "Sit."

Wood barriers divided the courtroom into four distinct areas. Alex and the other female defendants sat in one of them, plexiglass separating them from the rest of the room. The front housed a raised platform with the traditional judge's bench and a desk for the clerk-recorder. The middle section seemed to be set apart for the defendants, their lawyers, police officers, and various administrators. The rear of the courtroom appeared to be open to the public.

Once Alex orientated herself with the room layout, she scanned the sea of people and spotted Jesse in the middle section with her nose buried in a stack of documents. Checking further back, she found the group of people there to support her. Tyler and Syd sat next to each other in one row, with Abby and Harley seated together immediately behind them.

Alex locked eyes with Tyler. She ached to hold her and reassure her that she was all right. Or as all right as one could expect to be after spending the night in jail with exotic dancers, hookers, and drug addicts. Alex forced a smile. Tyler returned it, her eyes saying, "I love you."

Alex directed her eyes next to Syd and then to Abby and Harley, giving each an appreciative nod. For the next fifteen minutes, she watched a multitude of prisoners and lawyers filter in and out of the middle section. The rapid pace of the arraignment process was an impressive display of organized chaos.

A police officer inside the booth announced, "Castle, you're up next. Step to the door."

When Alex stood, Tyler and Syd shifted taller on the bench. Alex stepped out of the booth and made her way toward Jesse, keeping her stare on Tyler for as long as she could. She took her position next to Jesse, reminding herself to stand tall and remain silent.

"Docket number eight-six-nine-zero-four. People versus Alexandra Rose Castle. Manslaughter in the first degree," the court clerk sang out.

"Your Honor, Jesse Simmons for the defense. We waive formal reading of the complaint."

"Very well, how does your client plead, Ms. Simmons?" the judge asked as he reviewed the docket folder.

"Not guilty, Your Honor."

"So entered. People on bail?"

The assistant district attorney straightened his tie after placing a folder on the podium in front of him. "Your Honor, the defendant is accused of the vicious, heinous crime of killing her father, a respected member of the community. She and her family have significant means and have business holdings in countries where the United States has no extradition treaty. The People ask for remand."

Alex forced herself to remain calm.

Jesse responded, "Your Honor, remand is an overreach in this case. Ms. Castle is a well-respected member of the community. She is a business owner and benefactor of many charitable organizations in the city. She has no history of violence or criminal behavior. Has deep ties to the community, having lived here all her life, as evidenced by several family members and lifelong friends in attendance today. She does not pose a flight risk and wants nothing more than to clear her good name in front of this court. The defense requests bail."

The judge thumbed through the docket file the court clerk had provided. "ADA Marshall, I agree with the defense. Remand is an overreach. However, Ms. Simmons, your client has means and is facing a serious charge. To say that she poses no flight risk is simply an understatement. What amount of bail would the People consider?"

"Considering her and her family's vast resources, the People ask for twenty-five million dollars."

Twenty-five million? What kind of sick power play was this? Even with her father's trust fund injection, Alex didn't have that kind of money sitting around. It would take time to gather it up, and that meant more time behind bars. Her temples throbbed at the thought of being caged again.

"Ms. Simmons?" the judge queried.

"Twenty-five million constitutes a considerable hardship and would require that my client mortgage her home, which would unreasonably delay her release. We offer five hundred thousand dollars in cash."

The judge reviewed more of the file. His expression remained unchanged and challenging to read. "Five hundred thousand seems insufficient. Bail is set at five million dollars." The judge hit his gavel twice, signaling that the arraignment was over.

Jesse leaned over and whispered into Alex's ear, "Abby is prepared to have a cashier's check here within the hour. You'll have to go back to the holding cell for now, but you should be released in about two hours. I'll be there to sign you out."

Words eluded Alex, but she nodded her acknowledgment. She had only seconds for the realization to soak in that she'd be free before lunch before a police officer grabbed her by the arm and directed her back toward the holding booth. She kept her eyes on Tyler again for as long as she could. The courtroom door slammed shut, but the image of Tyler remained in her head. *Two hours*, she thought. She had to hold on for two more godawful hours.

The officer led her to a different room. The moment the handcuffs came off, Alex let her guard down. Her throat swelled at the prospect that her freedom would soon return. She should've been elated, but the possibility of twenty-five more years behind bars still loomed. She couldn't bear the thought of being separated from Tyler for that long. She slumped on the wood bench, her vision blurred by emerging tears as she focused on a growing fear. Jesse had kept her word and gotten her out of jail today, but was she a good enough lawyer to keep Alex out of prison?

The wheels of the justice system moved exceedingly slow in Alex's opinion, but, as Jesse estimated, two hours later an officer announced she was free to go. She walked past the glass door guarding a small control room and glimpsed herself for the first time since her ordeal had begun. Her long brown hair, madly tussled from sleeping on the hard concrete floor, had seen better days, and her beautiful black funeral dress was smudged and wrinkled. Christian Dior or not, after spending a night in jail in it, she'd rather burn the damn dress than wear it again.

Walking through the steel jailhouse door felt like it must have to Dorothy when the tornado dropped her in Oz. As soon as Tyler and the others came into view, her surroundings shifted from black and white to vibrant color and her mood shifted from despair to joy.

"You look like crap, Baby Sis." Syd gave Alex a bone-crushing bear hug.

"It's good to see you too, Syd." She gave her a smile and a squeeze. "I'd like to see what you look like after spending the night in jail."

"You look as beautiful as ever, darling." Abby kissed Alex on both cheeks. Her wrinkled forehead, though, betrayed her hours of worry.

"I can't thank you enough for posting my bail so fast. I'll pay back every penny."

"Money well spent." Abby's soft caress on both arms sent the message that the money didn't matter.

Alex returned her attention to Tyler. As they had in the courtroom, Tyler's eyes held her in a warm embrace. Jesse had better be as good as Abby thought she was because she knew she couldn't survive one more day without this breathtaking angel. Alex closed the distance between them until she felt Tyler's steamy exhale. Their nearness breathed energy into Alex's weary body, enough to whisper, "Hi." The same word they had said to each other the day they literally crossed paths and collided with each other in Napa. The day that changed the trajectory of their hollow lives.

"Hi." Tyler's whispery tone indicated she and Alex were on the same page. That a day without each other was one day too many. She grazed Alex's cheek with a fingertip, Alex matching her caress.

"Alex, I hate to break up this Hallmark scene, but I have a concern about what happened in court." Jesse's statement jolted Alex back to reality. Whatever had Jesse concerned at this early stage couldn't be a good sign.

"What is it?" Alex tore her gaze from Tyler to focus it on Jesse.

"The amount of bail requested was beyond excessive. The DA's office must be getting pressure on this case."

"From who?" Syd asked.

"I don't know, but it must be high up. William had some pretty influential friends. My father was one of them."

The hairs on the back of Alex's neck tingled in recognition of a twist that could play against her. "Ah. I didn't make the connection. Your father is Deputy Mayor Patrick Simmons."

"You should've disclosed your degree of association with William before I recommended you take on Alex's case." Abby narrowed her eyes in a fashion she reserved for very few people, most of whom didn't survive her scrutiny without paying a high price.

"I assure you, Mrs. Spencer, and you, Alex"—Jesse's gaze shifted between the two—"my father's friendship with William will in no way influence the way I defend you. I take my oath seriously and place the needs of my client above all else. But if you're not comfortable with my representation, I can recommend several fine defense lawyers."

Alex's instinct was to trust Jesse. Anyone who could impress Abigail Spencer for years had to be the cream of the crop. "Tell me why I should believe you."

Jesse looked Alex straight in the eye. The crease between her brows deepened, underscoring her determination. "Four years ago, my father disowned my younger brother when he came out. He can't accept Jake for who he is, and I can't accept my father for the same reason. I lost all respect for him the day he kicked Jake out."

A kindred spirit of sorts. Alex believed her. "I trust you, Jesse. I want you to defend me."

"All right then. If the mayor's office is pressuring the DA, we have our work cut out for us. It won't be enough to poke holes in their evidence. We'll need to come up with alternative theories and suspects."

"How do we do that?" Syd asked. "Father had business associates, not enemies. No one wanted him dead."

Alex rubbed her temple at the headaches coming her way. If, as Alex believed, William had confronted Andrew about the embezzlement and the circumstances behind him leaving the company on the same night he confronted Alex, Andrew had every reason to want their father dead. Several hundred million reasons. She had never considered her brother violent, but if pushed with the same force with which their father had pushed her out of his life, Andrew could've been angry enough to push back. If Jesse was right and they needed alternative theories, everything Andrew had done would have to come out, and Syd would learn how far he had fallen. "Can we table this until tomorrow? I'm exhausted."

"Absolutely," Jesse said. "I can come to your townhouse, say around eleven tomorrow morning? We need to nail down our strategy as soon as possible."

"That's perfect." Alex turned her attention to Tyler and whispered into her ear, "That gives us all night together."

After Jesse excused herself, Alex glided her lips over Tyler's. The thought of those lips had kept her spirits up for the last twenty hours, and now they felt like heaven against hers. She pressed deeper. Never had a kiss felt so reassuring, so healing. It confirmed what she already knew in her heart. Tyler was the one she was meant to spend the rest of her life with.

Breaking the kiss, Alex smiled her certainty. "Let's go home, T."

CHAPTER SEVENTEEN

The sunrise she saw, even blocked by a mountain of steel and concrete, standing at a bedroom window, was more enchanting than a Monet, but it was failing to erase the dread that had settled in Alex's gut like a tumor, eating away her courage. She'd been humiliated, stripped, and had every orifice examined during the twenty short hours she'd spent behind bars. She had been forced to pee and crap in front of the entire lot. Someone was pressuring the police and the DA for a conviction. That pissed her off. She was also facing the possibility of twenty-five years of the same indignities, and that terrified her.

Alex lifted her stare from the window and glanced over her shoulder, confirming that Tyler was still sleeping soundly in the bed behind her. She was flooded with memories of the previous two nights. They could not have been more different. Making love to Tyler last night had put following black painted lines and being shackled like an animal in the past. How could she survive the next quarter-century without feeling that unconditional love and unquestioning support every day? Maybe it was the fear of having all of this stripped away, but Alex wanted to spin a cocoon, close off the outside world, and wake up next to Tyler every day. That thought gave special meaning to the final words she'd said to her father.

She whispered to herself, "I *will* marry you one day, T."

Tyler shifted her legs, rustling the sheets covering her. Diffused morning light highlighted the curves of her face, casting an angelic glow. Her eyes fluttered open and a smile instantly appeared. "You're up early."

Alex returned her smile. She let the silk panels of her pale blue robe whisk open with every poised stride toward the bed. "Are you hungry, T?"

A devilish grin stretched to Tyler's eyes. "Do you have any Rice Krispies and fruit punch?"

Alex adored Tyler's playfulness. She kissed her, thinking again that once this mess was behind them, a diamond ring was in Tyler's future.

Half an hour later, the smell of bacon lured Alex and Tyler to the garden floor. Syd was working her magic at the stove while Callie faithfully stood guard nearby in the event of spills. After Alex said, "Good morning," Callie cut her greeting short and resumed her position at Syd's feet. "I thought for sure we'd beat you up today."

"Uh-huh," Syd mumbled.

Alex cocked her head. Syd's "uh-huhs" typically packed a bigger punch. "Okay, I'll bite. What does uh-huh mean this time?"

"It means you need thicker walls."

Tyler's cheeks grew redder by the second. Even with Alex, she refused eye contact, opting to busy herself by filling a glass with juice from the refrigerator. Alex kissed her on the cheek and whispered into her ear, "You bring out the animal in me," earning a wry grin. Comfortable that Tyler was at ease, Alex snatched a piece of bacon from a plate on the island counter. "Duly noted, Syd."

Syd pointed a pancake-batter-encrusted spatula toward the unwrapped morning newspapers sitting on the island. "You need to check the *Times* and the *Wall Street Journal*, Baby Sis."

Alex flipped open the *Times*, but she hadn't gotten past the headline before John walked in. "I see you girls are done with your morning cardio."

Tyler spat orange juice on the counter while Alex failed miserably to hide her pride as she thumbed through the newspaper. "Didn't take them long." She ruffled the paper, her mood changing for the worse on a dime. She read aloud, "Alexandra Castle, newly crowned CEO of Castle Resorts, a collection of two dozen luxury resorts around the world, was arrested and arraigned in Manhattan yesterday on a charge of manslaughter in the first degree. She is accused of killing her father, William Castle, who died of head trauma in his corporate offices early last Friday morning. Sources close to the Castle family say that a shake-up in Castle Resorts leadership was expected before Mr. Castle's death, information that ultimately led to Ms. Castle's arrest. NYPD Detective Greg Sterling, who's heading the investigation into Mr. Castle's death, would only say, 'We are confident we've uncovered sufficient evidence to bring in a guilty verdict and a killer to justice.'"

Alex slammed the paper on the counter. "Nothing like being tried in the media."

"You made the local TV news too." John dropped his bombshell with a smile as if Alex had won the lottery rather than entered a quagmire.

"Fucking great."

"I liked the picture they had of you." Alex narrowed one eye and lasered it at him. He shrugged. "What? You took a great booking photo."

Heat built in Alex's cheeks. Her life had been turned into a salacious tabloid headline to sell papers, and John was praising the damn picture that labeled her a killer.

Tyler positioned herself between Alex's legs, blocking her view of John. Alex tried bobbing her head left and right to stare him down, but Tyler placed her arms around her neck and stared into her eyes. "Look at me, babe." Alex stopped and joined Tyler's stare. "Remember what we talked about last night? Count to ten." Tyler leaned in and whispered in Alex's ear, "And think of the things I'm going to do to you tonight."

Alex's frustration morphed into a suggestive stare. She pulled Tyler closer. "I'm holding you to that."

"All right, lovebirds. Let's eat before all this food gets cold." Syd placed the last of the food on the center island. "John has a flight to catch this afternoon."

"You're not going with him?" Alex asked. "Don't you have a winery to run?"

"Are you nuts? John can handle things. Wild horses couldn't drag me away right now. I want to find out who killed Father as much as you do. Unless you're kicking me out, I'm staying until this is over."

"Of course, I'm not kicking you out. It's just—"

"Just nothing. I'm staying, and that's it." Syd placed both hands on her hips, leaving no room for argument.

After they saw John off, Jesse arrived for their strategy meeting. The first topic was the bad press. The way Jesse was rubbing her forehead suggested that the media attention wasn't helping Alex's defense. "The line about the expected shake-up at Castle Resorts caught my eye, though," Jesse said. "The story attributes that to 'a source close to the family,' not the police. Only a couple of people would have known about that. My questions to you are, who would talk to the press and why?"

"Do you think whoever is pointing the finger at Alex had something to do with Father's death?" Syd's question pumped tension into the kitchen. Someone Alex knew and trusted for years may have killed her father or, at the very least, was trying to frame her for his murder.

"I wouldn't rule it out," Jesse replied. "In the meantime, Alex, let's not attract the sharks. You need to keep a low profile and stay out of the public eye as much as possible." She pulled out a newspaper magazine insert and opened it to a picture of Alex and Tyler kissing in the courthouse corridor. "You also made the *Post*'s *Page Six* magazine. They're already speculating about your relationship with Tyler and how William may have reacted to it."

"I won't hide, and I won't put either of us back in the closet." Alex grasped Tyler's hand, pulling it to the top of her thigh.

"Babe, I don't think she's asking you to hide." Tyler gave her hand a squeeze. "She's just recommending we don't fuel the fire, and I have to agree with her."

"But, T—"

Tyler placed an index finger over Alex's lips. "This isn't what your father demanded of you. I'm willing to do whatever it takes for as long as it takes to clear you of these charges. If staying out of the public eye for a while helps, then I'm all for it."

Alex had spent thirteen years being painstakingly discreet, and it had gotten her nothing. It wasn't worth it, but neither was arguing with Tyler. "All right, T, but I'm not happy about it."

"Thank you, Tyler," Jesse said. "I'm learning just how stubborn Alex can be."

Alex gave Jesse a forced smile and asked, "So, what's next?"

"If your case takes the normal path, the ADA can take up to six months to refer it to the grand jury, but his performance in court yesterday tells me he'll likely fast-track it. It could be as early as Friday."

"That quick?" Alex's anger bubbled to the surface again. Someone in a position of power had blindly suspected her of murder and was railroading her into a quick conviction. Before Jesse could answer, Alex's cell phone rang. She looked at the caller ID. "I'm sorry, but I have to take this."

Alex opened her phone. "Gretchen, what couldn't wait until Monday?"

"I'm sorry to bother you, Alex, but I just received an email report from Tim Morris from Times Square that I think you should know about right away. He says that room cancelations spiked tenfold overnight and that he's already lost two major conferences since your arrest hit the news."

"Thank you, Gretchen. Keep me posted via email until I get into the office tomorrow. Also, loop in the interim COO, Legal, and the chief of marketing. We'll have to put out some fires tomorrow."

"Will do. Oh, and Alex, I'm glad you're out. We all know these charges are simply hogwash."

"Thanks, Gretchen. I appreciate the vote of confidence." Alex wrapped up her call and returned her attention to Jesse.

"Sorry about that, but news of my arrest is already impacting Castle Resorts. Cancelations are on the rise, which I expected. It looks like I have a lot of hand-holding to do if we don't want to lose exclusive contracts with our high-end vendors and partners. And with these media leaks, I don't know who I can trust."

Syd rubbed her cheek, her tell she was conjuring up a solution to Alex's heavy plate. "I have an idea, Baby Sis. It's been a while since I've worked at Castle Resorts, but I still know most of the players and how things work. If you're open to it, I can head up your crisis management team and start putting out fires. And the best part, I'll be in a position to ferret out the disloyal cuss who opened their mouth to the media."

A light went on in Alex's head. She weighed the benefits of having Syd in front of this. From a PR perspective, having Syd as the company's frontwoman was ideal. Her presence would lend confidence to employees, vendors, and customers. "I have a better idea. My remaining at the wheel is giving the press too much red meat, which is scaring off customers and vendors. I think you should be interim CEO until I'm cleared of these charges."

"CEO? I'm not ready for that."

"Oh, please." Alex waved off the absurd comment. "Father groomed you to take over the company well before he started doing that with me. You're the only one I can trust. Please say yes. I'm sure Blake and the new COO would be relieved to have the media off their backs for a while."

Syd let out a long, breathy sigh. "All right, but this is only temporary."

Alex clutched Tyler's hand, sensing she agreed this was the right thing to do. "Thank you, Syd. It would be a relief knowing you're there."

"I got your back, Baby Sis." Syd gave Alex a reassuring pat on the shoulder.

"Good. That's settled," Jesse said. "Let's talk strategy. For the DA to prove guilt, they need to show beyond a reasonable doubt that you had motive, means, and opportunity to commit the crime. In addition, they have to link you to the crime scene.

Let's break that down. In the charge sheet, the ADA outlined just enough evidence that lent credence to all four points."

Syd, Alex, and Tyler all leaned forward, giving Jesse their complete attention.

"First, means. The medical examiner's report states your father died from a penetrating head injury. Crime scene forensics showed he most likely hit his head against the corner of his desk with an amount of force not associated with a simple fall. That eliminates a defense based on an accidental fall due to your father's Parkinson's."

"So, someone apparently pushed him hard, causing him to hit his head." Alex blinked at the uncomfortable truth. His dying from a heart attack or an accident was terrible enough, but no matter how she had felt about her father, his being shoved to his death was evil.

"Right. Second is opportunity. According to Gretchen, you were William's only scheduled appointment that evening, and in your interviews with Detective Sterling, you and I told him you met your father around nine. The M.E. puts the time of death between seven and ten, so there's no getting around that fact."

"But somebody could have come in after me."

Jesse raised an index finger and continued, "Hold that thought. I'll circle back to opportunity in a minute. The third point is motive. In Gretchen's statement, she said that your father told her he planned to announce a big change, and you were the only executive not invited to the meeting scheduled for the following day. The implication is that he was firing you, which we know to be true. This leads to the question of why he would fire you. The police retrieved a portfolio documenting your past relationships with women and a video from your father's office computer showing you and Tyler at the San Francisco resort in an intimate encounter. My father also provided a statement about an incident he witnessed once between William and Abby Spencer. He claimed they argued over her sexuality and yours, lending credence to the theory that he fired you because of your relationship with Tyler, which we also know is true."

"It doesn't surprise me that Father had a video of Tyler and me. He was that controlling." Alex hoped he got an eyeful. "But I'm curious about this argument with Abby. When was it?"

Jesse reviewed her notes. "At your father's home on the night he announced you as his successor."

"Abby never said anything."

Syd shook her head. "Sometimes, I can't believe the things he did. Why didn't you tell me?"

"It's all right, Syd. At first, I was angry when he fired me, but after I talked to Tyler, I was relieved that I wouldn't be under his controlling thumb anymore." Alex spoke no truer words.

"I don't want you repeating that to anyone else. It will just go to further prove motive," Jesse counseled. "And that goes for you two also," she said, pointing to Syd and Tyler.

"I would never repeat anything my sister tells me in confidence," Syd said.

"That goes without saying, Syd." Alex squeezed Tyler's hand and looked Jesse in the eye. "I trust these two completely."

"Okay, ladies. Finally, the ADA has to tie you to the scene of the crime. That's where the camera comes into play. It had your father's blood on it. In Gretchen's statement, she said that the day William was killed, he had a camera on his desk that looked exactly like the one Detective Sterling retrieved from your townhouse."

"That's impossible. That camera has been in my possession ever since Syd gave it to me two months ago."

"Then there are only two explanations. Either Gretchen was lying, or there must be two cameras," Jesse suggested. "That doesn't explain about the blood on your camera, though."

Alex let out an exasperated sigh. "I can't believe Gretchen would lie about something this important."

"I tend to agree with you, but at this point, we can't rule out anything," Jesse countered. "The ADA is playing hardball. My guess is someone powerful is pressuring them for a conviction. I'm afraid it won't be enough to just poke holes in the state's evidence. I think our best course of action is to find alternative suspects with motives, find the other camera if it exists, and most importantly, find out who else may have been at your father's office that night."

"So, what's your plan to do that?" Tyler asked.

"We need a detective of our own. Unfortunately, my regular investigator is unavailable, but she's given me the names of some extremely qualified investigators who can do the job," Jesse replied.

"This is my freedom we're talking about, Jesse. I don't want to put it in the hands of an unknown."

"We have little choice here, Alex. My firm doesn't use anyone else."

When Tyler leaned back in the chair with an unreadable look on her face, Alex grew concerned. "Tyler? What is it?"

"I have an idea, but I'm not sure if you'll agree to it," Tyler said.

"I'm open to anything."

"Ethan."

Pangs of guilt speared Alex in the heart. She genuinely liked Ethan and had tremendous respect for him. At Syd's suggestion, she'd hired him to help her when Kelly had blackmailed her with photos of their college affair. He'd helped her when she suspected Andrew was embezzling money from the company. He even confronted a scoundrel of a bookie to help settle Andrew's debts. But most of all, she carried the guilt that he had ended up taking a bullet over those damn photos. He'd given so much to her, and she had repaid him by stealing his wife. She couldn't ask anything more of him.

"I couldn't, Tyler. He's barely recovered. I can't ask him to drop everything to help the woman who almost got him killed."

Jesse asked, "Who's Ethan?"

Syd replied, saving Tyler from an awkward answer. "He's my husband's cousin and Tyler's soon-to-be ex-husband. She left him for Alex. He's a top-notch detective who helped Alex a few times and was almost killed in the process."

"Ooohhh." Jesse leaned back in her chair, seemingly confounded by the soap opera-like account.

"Yes, you can, Alex," Tyler said. "He doesn't blame you for anything and certainly not for what Victor's goon did."

"Victor?" Jesse asked.

Alex shifted in her seat toward her sister, dreading what she was about to say. *Better Syd hear everything from me now, though, and not at trial.*

"It's about time you knew everything, Syd. Victor Padula is Andrew's bookie. Andrew got into him deep and started embezzling from the company to the tune of a quarter-million dollars." Syd sucked in a startled breath. "I confronted him, told him to pay it back, and to decline the CFO position. Instead of doing as I said, he got the bright idea to force my hand by buying Kelly's blackmail photos. To do so, he borrowed two million dollars from Victor. I beat him to the punch with Kelly, leaving him with a hefty debt. With Ethan's help, I paid off his mark for pennies on the dollar, repaid the money he took from the company from my personal funds, and forced Andrew out. That's when one of Victor's guards tried to recover Kelly's photos and shot Ethan, but Ethan shot and killed him. My guess is that Victor was trying to recoup more of his money."

Jesse mouthed a stunned "Wow."

Syd rubbed her brow three, four, and five times after learning how much of a headache their brother had been for Alex. "Ethan explained the shooting as having to do with Kelly's photos but mentioned nothing about Andrew. I can't believe how far gone he is. Did Father know?"

"Yes, he did. He told me that night. He fired me partly because he found out I covered up Andrew's embezzlement. He said he couldn't trust me anymore. I hate to say this, Syd, but if Father planned to cut me from the will and close my trust fund, I'm sure he planned the same for Andrew. He had good reason to want Father dead."

Syd buried her face in her hands. "Dear Lord."

Tyler placed her hands over Alex's. "Babe, you need the best, and we both know you won't find anyone better or anyone who will have your back like Ethan will."

Syd looked up. "She's right. You're up against the clock, and he knows where all the skeletons are."

They were both right. Alex offered a reluctant nod, confirming as much.

"Tell me about Ethan," Jesse said. "Is he licensed to investigate in New York?"

"Yes," Tyler said. "He's licensed in fifteen states as a private investigator, including New York. He's also a newly retired Sacramento police detective and has good contacts in the NYPD that he can leverage."

"We'll need him to start as soon as possible," Jesse said.

Alex took a deep breath, swallowing her guilty conscience, picked up her phone, and dialed Ethan's number.

After four rings, he answered. "Alex? Is Tyler okay?" Of course, his first worry would surround the woman he obviously still loved. That complicated, indisputable fact gnawed at her.

"Hi, Ethan. Tyler's fine."

"Good. You had me scared for a minute."

"Ethan, I have no right to ask after what happened and everything you've done for me, but I need your help." His silence was deafening and signaled she may have asked too much. "Ethan?"

"I'm here, Alex. What exactly do you need?" The tension in his voice could stop a raging bull in a full charge.

"I knew this was a bad idea."

"No, Alex. Look, it's me, not you. I really want to help you if I can." Ethan's tone shifted on a dime, softening into the friendliness Alex had hoped to receive. It not coming at *hello*, though, meant she had some repair work ahead of her. "What do you need? Does this have to do with Andrew?"

"No, it doesn't. I guess you haven't seen the news or read today's business journal."

"No, why?"

"I was arrested and charged with manslaughter in my father's death."

"What! Are they nuts?"

"I'd like to think so. I have one of the city's best defense lawyers." Alex winked at Jesse. "She's come up with a sound defense strategy, but it requires the services of a talented investigator. Her gal is unavailable and—"

"Say no more, Alex. When do you need me?"

"As soon as you can get here." Alex mouthed to the others, "He's coming."

Syd and Tyler simultaneously exhaled sighs of relief.

"Erin can take care of herself, but I'll have to make arrangements for Bree. I'll try to get there tomorrow. Tuesday at the latest."

"I always seem to say this to you, but I can't thank you enough, Ethan."

"Be sure to tell me that when you get my bill."

"You're worth every penny. I'm sure I will." Alex finished her call, more confident that the truth would come out. There was only one uncertainty: how would Ethan take seeing her and Tyler together?

CHAPTER EIGHTEEN

Sacramento, California

"I'm happy for her," Ethan repeated, hoping it would be enough to fill the void Tyler had left behind. "Happy."

When he answered Alex's unexpected call, he'd thought the worst. His heart had lurched. Love was still there, but not the kind that could breathe life into a failed marriage. No matter how hard Tyler had tried to convince him otherwise, it *was* his fault. At least partially. He should've recognized his wife's pain and insisted on getting her the help she needed years ago. Maybe then, Tyler would've woken up in his bed this morning and not Alex Castle's.

Despite the early hour, he considered pouring himself a shot of tequila to drown his sorrows, but he needed to shut down this little pity party before it got out of hand. After all, he'd pushed Tyler toward Alex because he couldn't spark in her the passion that Alex could. He threw off his regrets, stuffed them in a lockbox, and concentrated his attention on the work to be done.

He arranged for Bree to stay with Tyler's business partner, Maddie, for the week and booked a red-eye flight to LaGuardia.

He intentionally left informing Erin for last. She'd taken his and Tyler's imminent divorce the hardest. He could blame her reaction on her being a teenager, but that wouldn't be fair. Having grown up in a family split by divorce, he understood how difficult that could be on the children.

"Erin," he yelled up the stairs and waited for a muffled reply. "Can you come down for a minute?"

Within seconds, Erin thumped downstairs and plopped down in her usual chair at the kitchen table next to Ethan. "What's up, Dad?"

"Your mom is fine, but I need to be in New York tomorrow. Bree can stay at Maddie's for the week, so you're off the hook for babysitting."

"What's wrong? Did that woman dump Mom already? Serves her right." Erin's tongue was extra sharp this morning, which meant Ethan would have to exercise considerable patience.

"No, Erin, their relationship is just fine." Ethan bit back the twinge of emotion in his throat, bolting again the shaky lock securing his bundles of regret. "But Alex needs my help on a case."

"I don't understand why you're helping her. She's the reason you and Mom are getting a divorce and the reason you were shot."

Ethan sighed. Erin always wore her heart on her sleeve and spoke her mind no matter the topic, and Alex had become her hot-button issue. "I know you're frustrated about the changes our family is going through, and I know us not telling you all the reasons for them hasn't helped matters. I hope one day your mother and I will tell you everything because I know for a fact that you wouldn't be upset at Mom's new relationship." He fixed her with a serious look. "Now, about Alex. She was a client of mine long before she and Mom were an item, and I consider her a friend. She's not to blame for our divorce, and she's not to blame for me being shot. She's in trouble and needs my help again. Do you think I should turn away a friend in need, especially one your mother loves?"

Erin's eyes glistened with pooling tears. "No, Dad, you shouldn't." The firm line her lips meant were set in showed she still had deep-seated reservations, but he hoped his example of acceptance was getting through.

After she returned to her room, he opened the email Alex's lawyer had sent and studied the DA's charge sheet. The usual items—crime scene photos, witness statements, and lab results—built a *prima facie* case, but what interested him the most was what the DA had failed to include in his outline of the state's case. New York City had become Surveillance Camera Central since 9/11. It struck Ethan as odd that the DA hadn't included a single source of security footage from the crime scene or the surrounding area, particularly since it was located in a bustling, high-end part of town.

The DA provided only one video actually, which Jesse had categorized as "Motive." Digital tags identified the clip as unedited security footage from Castle Resort San Francisco two nights before William's secretary discovered his body. Ethan knew all too well the importance of that night and location and what it had marked for Tyler. Watching the clip would be torture for him, but for his own peace of mind, he needed to be sure he'd done the right thing. That his sacrifice had made her happy.

Ethan clicked on the file, instantly spotting on the hotel bar stool the woman whose blond hair and toned body he'd admired for decades. *God, she looked beautiful.* Her neck rubbing and toe-tapping meant she was nervous, and the cocktail she was sipping looked more potent than red wine, her usual stress reliever. He gave a rueful chuckle. *Driving the bridge into San Francisco must've made her a nervous wreck.* When she turned, holding her cell phone, he didn't have to guess who would appear on screen. Their fiery kiss brought tears to his eyes. Not since before the rape had Tyler kissed him remotely like that. If he were brutally honest with himself, he never had elicited that much passion from her, not even on their wedding night.

His cell phone rang, the unique ringtone telling him his wife still had a sixth sense about him. She always seemed to know when he needed to hear her voice. He stopped the video, cleared the emotion from his throat, and squared his shoulders, casting off the last shreds of doubt before answering her call. "Tyler, how are you holding up?"

"I'm scared for her, Ethan."

"Rightly so. The DA's evidence may be thin, but it's compelling."

"Please tell me you can help her." Ethan recognized the genuine fear in Tyler's voice, even after hearing it only twice before—once in the emergency room following the rape and once at the creek after her rapist came back into her life. The thought of losing Alex had clearly shaken her to her core, which meant his sacrifice hadn't been wasted. She loved Alex, and that was all he wanted for her—a chance to find passion. Now he needed to roll up his sleeves and make sure she didn't lose it.

"I can, and I will," he said, meaning every word. "Tell Alex not to worry. I'll be on the case in the morning."

When he hung up, their goodbye felt different. It contained a sense of finality that was long overdue, but one that verified that they'd always be a part of each other. He slipped his phone into his pocket and whispered, "Goodbye, Tyler."

CHAPTER NINETEEN

Manhattan, New York

As he stepped off the plane at LaGuardia early the next morning, Ethan made a mental note to always book a red-eye when possible. The absence of crying babies was a rare treat, allowing the engine hum to lull him into a light sleep for most of the six-hour flight. He was rested enough to get right to work. Instead of going to the hotel or Alex's home where he'd likely run into Tyler—something he'd like to stave off for as long as possible—he opted to go straight to the crime scene.

As soon as the taxi let him off in front of the Madison Avenue offices, memories of the last time he'd walked into this building six weeks ago came flooding back. He'd helped Alex deal with Andrew's bookie and with Kelly Thatcher and her blackmail scheme. On the same day he'd handed Tyler over to Alex, revealing to her that the mystery woman she'd also hired him to find was his wife of eighteen years and the graphic artist who was revamping the Castle Resorts website. That was the hardest thing he'd ever done, but he also regarded it as his finest moment. Tyler was now free to truly live.

He shook off the past and let his cop instincts kick in, and he began observing every detail of the area and neighboring businesses. The last time he'd visited, the construction vehicles that had lined a side street and alley were still next to the building. Crew members still bustled in and out of the front entrance today, though some sat idle near the elevators. The buzz of power tools flowed from the nearby open stairwell door. He peeked inside. Workers had covered the walls with sheets of plastic, floor to ceiling, for as far as he could see, something he couldn't recall being there before. Its presence posed a giant complication for security surveillance.

The camera mounted behind a small, tinted glass window above the elevator control panel was barely noticeable. It wouldn't fool a professional criminal, but an amateur would probably never notice it. When he arrived on the twenty-third floor, he checked again for cameras but noted none. He introduced himself to the receptionist, who escorted him to Gretchen's desk. Following another round of introductions, the receptionist returned to the front and he and Gretchen retreated into William's office, agreeing on the use of first names. Ethan studied the room, taking pictures of the layout and objects and making notes of stains, smudges, and anything out of the ordinary.

"I appreciate your time today, Gretchen." Ethan paused his inspection of the bookshelves near the room's entrance to assess her body language. It had changed the moment she stepped into the office. Her tight posture and fidgeting suggested she was nervous—a reasonable reaction, considering she'd discovered William's body there.

"I'm happy to be of assistance. Anything to help Ms. Castle."

"That's good to hear because I'm here to help her too. First, I have a question about the building construction. The last time I was here, the stairwells weren't under construction. How long has the plastic sheeting been up?"

"At least a month."

"So it was up the evening Mr. Castle was killed?" Ethan moved toward the room's stately desk. The tape outline of William's body was still on the carpet next to it, as well as a large bloodstain near the markings for his head. The corner edge of the desk appeared smudged, likely blood from William's fall.

"Yes, it was."

"I'm curious. Why doesn't the floor have security cameras?"

"Mr. Castle was adamant about his privacy at the headquarters."

Interesting, Ethan thought. Cameras were everywhere in the company's resorts, yet nowhere here. "I read the statement you gave the police." Ethan paused when Gretchen's expression suddenly turned sad.

"I feel horrible that Ms. Castle may have been arrested based on what I told them."

"You should never feel bad about telling the truth. Was it the truth, Gretchen?"

"Of course it was." Gretchen's raised voice meant Ethan had hit a nerve, but he retained a skeptical expression, scrutinizing her reaction. According to Alex, she was very loyal to William, and since she was the one who found the body, he couldn't rule her out as a suspect. She could be lying for any number of reasons, but he couldn't tell yet.

"Let's start with Mr. Castle's week before he was killed. Did he have any unusual visitors or phone calls?"

"None that come to mind, but he got upset after he met with Georgia Cushing, the chief accounting officer, the day before he died. After she left, he asked me to reach Robert Stein, his personal lawyer. So I did, and not long after he talked with him, Mr. Castle left the office for several hours."

"Did he say why he left?"

"No, and I never questioned Mr. Castle's movements or motives."

"You're a very loyal assistant." But, loyal or not, the question remained—was she lying? "What happened after he returned?"

"He asked me to schedule a meeting of all the company executives, except Ms. Castle, for the following day at ten o'clock to announce a dramatic change. He didn't elaborate, and I didn't ask. He also asked if Ms. Castle had confirmed her appointment with him for eight that evening."

"Eight? Not nine?" The time didn't match the notes Alex's lawyer had sent him yesterday.

"She called me when her connecting flight was delayed in Denver and asked me to reschedule it for nine thirty, but Mr. Castle insisted she show at nine. He didn't explain his insistence other than telling me that Ms. Castle would report to him on his schedule, not hers."

The way Alex had talked about her father, that sounded like something he would do.

"I understand you saw him with a camera," Ethan said.

"Yes. When he instructed me to schedule the executive meeting for the following day, he opened his wall safe and pulled out two leather folios and a vintage camera."

"The police inventoried the folios but not the camera. That means it wasn't there when the police arrived. Had you seen the camera before?" Ethan glanced at the safe. Its door was open and other than being covered in fingerprinting dust, it appeared in pristine condition, suggesting it had been left open and not broken into or forced open by the police.

"No, I hadn't, but I tried to lighten his mood by asking about it. He said it once belonged to his wife and then to Ms. Castle after his wife passed away. He mentioned that it wasn't broken but that it had taken its last picture. And then he said something about the last person to use it being broken. And no, he didn't elaborate, nor did I press the matter."

"Did he say anything else?"

"No."

After asking about other meetings and when she left for the day, Ethan had one last question. "The next morning, when you returned, was the camera in his office?"

"No, I didn't see it."

"All right then, I'd like a copy of Mr. Castle's calendar for the last year and a complete list of his business and personal contacts, along with any files he may have been working on."

"I can give you what I have, but the police took Mr. Castle's computer."

"You're networked here, right?"

"Of course."

"Then I'd like to talk to your IT manager."

Ethan looked over the rest of the Castle Resorts headquarters offices, including Alex's and Cushing's. Nothing stood out except that in Cushing's office she had the same framed photo on her desk as one he'd seen in William's office. It featured a ribbon-cutting ceremony from decades ago with a group of people standing behind William. Closer inspection revealed a young woman in the crowd of mostly men. She was standing nearest to him and staring at him and not at the camera like everyone else. *Could this woman be Cushing?* he wondered.

Ethan then met with their IT director. He learned that company computers and security footage from each of the twenty-three resorts automatically backed up to the server at headquarters in near real-time. After retrieving a DVD copy of the latest backup of William's hard drive, Ethan went to the building's security office in the basement. Initially, the guard on duty hesitated to provide him with what he wanted, but a crisp one-hundred-dollar bill persuaded him to burn a DVD of the building's security tapes from the night William was killed. Considering the ongoing construction, he didn't expect it would readily provide helpful information, but thoroughness was his trademark.

The only task remaining was to inspect every avenue of entrance to the building for anything out of the ordinary. That included the stairwells. Thankfully, the gunshot wound he sustained to his leg a month ago during his last visit had healed nicely, and a rigorous course of physical therapy had him in top shape. A slow and steady climb from the basement to the twenty-eighth floor would test that theory. By the time he reached the roof, another five stories up from the Castle Resorts headquarters, his thighs and calves were burning but not as much as he expected. Unfortunately, his methodical search yielded nothing of interest.

The trip down the second stairwell was much easier on Ethan's leg, but like its sister stairwell, it was a criminal's dream. Its walls had been encased in plastic sheeting, obscuring the security cameras. As Ethan passed the third floor, he saw that one of the sheets had been partially torn and piled in the stairwell's corner. Unfortunately, it had been replaced with a fresh sheet. He lifted the crumpled plastic and found a matchbook. He photographed it and, putting on a rubber glove retrieved from his breast pocket, he picked it up and turned it over. The front cover read "Arthur's Alley Sports Bar and Grill."

"My, my, my. What do we have here? You don't look like you've been here very long." After taking another photo, he placed the matchbook in a small plastic bag and stuffed it into his coat pocket for safekeeping. This find had Ethan hopeful; Arthur's Alley was the favorite hangout of Andrew and his bookie, Victor Padula. It might have been dropped by someone else, of course, but when it came to murder, he didn't believe in coincidence.

The rest of the building's stairwell, entrances, and alleys yielded no further clues, leaving his least desired task—going to see Alex and possibly Tyler. The idea of his wife being happy with someone else was one thing, but the prospect of seeing her kiss Alex in a way she never did with him was harder to swallow than he expected. So instead of calling, he texted Alex to set up a meeting, tossing out choices—her place or her lawyer's office. He was elated when Alex opted for the latter.

Traveling by subway, Ethan stopped at Sabrett's, the first hot dog stand on his route, for a footlong. Considering his upcoming meeting, he opted for a tiny bit of mustard, forgoing onion and anything else that might leave a lasting odor. Eating it on the fly, Ethan arrived at the Midtown law offices of Kline and Rosen without a single yellow stain on the navy-blue tie he'd bought to match his favorite suit. A receptionist in a dark suit occupied the reception desk. A single silver stud on his left earlobe served as his only visible display of individuality in his otherwise crisp appearance of conformity. "May I help you, sir?"

"Ethan Falling to see Jesse Simmons."

"She's finishing up with another client. If you care to take a seat"—the young man gestured toward the immaculate seating area with tufted, rich burgundy leather chairs—"I'll let her know you're here."

Ethan sat. His attention drifted to the collection of coffee table books, each perfectly aligned in rows on the knee-high marble-topped table. One caught his eye, *Golf Courses of the World: 365 Days* by Robert Sidorsky. He thumbed through the myriad pictures featuring spectacular scenery from well-known golf courses and hidden gems from around the world.

"He's somewhat of a legend around here," an unfamiliar voice offered, breaking the silence in the waiting room.

Ethan looked up. The woman was beautiful, for sure, but it was the way she carried herself, confident and professional yet understated, that held his interest. "Excuse me?"

"Robert Sidorsky. He's a successful New York City lawyer who's written about the world's golf courses in the *Times* for over a decade. His book came out two years ago."

"Ahh, nice second gig." Ethan returned the book to its proper position on the table. "Do you golf?"

"I do, but I wish I had more time for it." She extended her hand. "You must be Mr. Falling. I'm Jesse Simmons."

He accepted her hand. "Please, call me Ethan."

"Call me Jesse." Her gaze drifted up and down, from his head to his toes. At forty-two and still in good shape, Ethan was no stranger to the occasional woman paying him attention, but since the day he'd laid eyes on Tyler, he had never given it another thought. Doing so now felt woefully foreign, but it also cemented the end of an eighteen-year marriage and a twenty-two-year partnership.

"We're still waiting on Alex"—she gestured toward her left—"but we can wait for her in my office." Jesse led him down a brightly lit hallway lined with a fine carpet, sculptures, and oil paintings fit for the likes of Bill Gates. Apparently, Ethan had stumbled into the one-percent world.

Jesse's average-sized office with unassuming feminine touches was a contradiction of the ornate corridor. Flowers, paintings, and various knickknacks lent it a homey, personal feel, not one of elegance or ostentation. The only visible luxury was the view of the Manhattan skyline.

Ethan gazed at the concrete jungle from seventeen floors up and whistled. "Nice view."

She joined him at the window. "It's my daily reminder that I'm just one of the one and a half million people who make this island home."

"Potential clients?"

"Perhaps, but I prefer to think of them as shipmates. We all lead different lives, bound by common shores, all hoping to move in the same direction."

"And what direction is that?"

"In search of something better. For some, a better life or a better world. For others, it could be something as simple as a better night's sleep or a better cup of coffee. But our one common human thread is the quest for betterment."

"I never thought of it that way." Talk about a good first impression. In five minutes, Jesse had captured Ethan's interest and impressed the hell out of him. *I'm going to enjoy working this case*, he thought.

A knock on the open office door drew his attention from the cityscape. Alex stepped through. "Sorry, I'm late, but traffic was heavier than expected."

Ethan instantly turned into a mixed bag of emotions. He honestly liked and respected Alex, but at the same time, he was jealous of the way she could make Tyler happy when he couldn't. It wasn't manly ego but love for the woman with whom he'd spent more than half his life. He tucked away his broken heart and turned to greet his shipmate, as Jesse would categorize her.

"Alex, it's good to see you." Ethan gave her a brief yet welcoming hug.

"It's good seeing you on your feet again." Alex's genuine smile added to the friendly embrace, making it impossible to hate her. "If anyone could overcome an attack as vicious as the one Victor's man unleashed, it's you."

On the other hand, not hating Alex didn't mean he wanted to prolong this meeting and his emotional awkwardness. "We should get started. I've already found some leads."

"Of course, you have," Alex said. "I knew I could count on you."

Jesse sat at her desk, and Ethan and Alex took a seat in the guest chairs.

"First"—Ethan directed his attention to Jesse—"the evidence you sent me last night was convincing but thin. Either the DA is holding back their best stuff or they've shot their entire wad. Have they responded to your motion for discovery yet?"

"They have. My assistant picked it up after breakfast today and is digitizing everything. We'll have a thumb drive ready for you before you leave today."

"Good. I've already been to the corporate office. I went over Gretchen's statement with her. She provided some interesting details that weren't in her original statement."

"Anything contradictory?" Jesse's expression brightened at the first glimmer of something she could use to poke holes in the DA's case.

"No, but she did shed some light on a critical piece of evidence." Ethan turned his attention to Alex. "Tell me about the camera."

"Syd gave it to me for my birthday two months ago when I first told her about my problem with Kelly."

"Kelly? The blackmailer?" Jesse asked. "What did she have on you anyway?"

"She was my girlfriend for one semester at Yale. It ended badly. Two months ago, she resurfaced with compromising photos of us and blackmailed me into giving her a do-nothing job at Castle Resorts. Ethan dug up evidence of insider trading between her and a former boyfriend, so we counter-blackmailed. That's when we think she tried to sell the pictures to Andrew."

Jesse shifted uneasily in her chair. "I applaud your creativity, but let's keep your strongarm tactics to ourselves, shall we?"

Ethan let a grin build, still proud of his handiwork. "Let's circle back to the camera. So, the one the police took from you was Syd's present?"

"Yes, why."

"Gretchen told me today that according to your father, the camera he had in his office the day he was killed belonged to your mother and that she had passed it down to you."

Alex jerked her head back. Her narrowed eyes confirmed that he'd caught her off guard. "That's impossible," she said in a firm tone. "I lost that camera during a move from Yale. Syd bought one for my birthday to replace the one I'd lost. It was the same model but not the same production year."

"What years were they?" Jesse asked.

"My mother's was a 1957, and the one Syd gave me was a 1965 model."

Jesse jotted a few notes. "This is good, Alex. Really good."

"After I talked to Gretchen, I searched the remaining Castle offices and common areas in the building." Ethan removed a plastic bag from his coat pocket and handed it to Alex. "Does the name on that matchbook ring a bell?"

Alex inspected the printed logo, her eyebrows arching instantly. "Victor?"

"Or Andrew," he replied.

"Care to clue me in here?" Jesse asked.

Alex looked more closely at the matchbook before responding. "Arthur's Alley is the sports bar where Ethan and I met Andrew's bookie. It's his headquarters of sorts."

Ethan pointed to the bag. "I found it in one of the building's stairwells that's under construction. It looked like it hadn't been there very long. It could belong to one of the construction workers, of course, but..." He shrugged.

"This is excellent work, Ethan," Jesse said. "Between the possibility of there being two cameras and two other suspects with motive and opportunity, we're off to a splendid start." Jesse gave him a smile packed with more than professional satisfaction, making her personal interest in him abundantly clear.

"Two suspects? I can believe that Victor was involved." Alex shook her head. "But I hate to think that Andrew had anything to do with Father's death."

"We have to explore every avenue," Ethan said. Despite how uncomfortable this made Alex, experience told him that most people were killed by someone they knew, either by family or friends. "We need to run this down."

"I have to agree," Jesse said.

"I know you're right, but I don't have to like it." Alex slumped in her chair with a mixed expression of disappointment and resignation. Ethan didn't enjoy upsetting her, but it had to be done. "I want to be there when you talk to Andrew and Victor."

"That is not a good idea, Alex," Jesse said.

"Victor doesn't scare me," Alex said.

"I still—" Jesse's desk phone buzzed. She lifted the receiver and held up an index finger, signaling for Alex to hold that thought. "Yes? Good, bring it in." She turned to Alex and Ethan after hanging up. "The discovery documents are ready. Circling back, I still don't think it's a good idea."

"I'm going, and that's it." Alex stiffened her spine, leaving no room for argument. Ethan expected nothing less.

A young woman knocked on the door before walking in. "Here are the files you asked for, Ms. Simmons." She handed Jesse a small computer thumb drive.

Ethan's attention sailed to Jesse's left hand. Other than during an investigation to gauge a suspect or witness, he'd never intentionally scanned a woman's ring finger and never before had he hoped to find it empty. He wasn't disappointed by what he saw.

"Thanks, Sally. That's all for now." Jesse waited for her to leave before offering the drive to Ethan.

"Great, more homework." Ethan let his hand linger when their fingers grazed. The touch felt pleasing, yet oddly wrong, convincing him he still had a way to go before he could move on in his personal life. He dug deep and focused on his job. "I also picked up copies of the Madison Avenue building security tapes for the night of William's death, along with a copy of his hard drive from the company server. I'll send copies to your assistant once I review it tonight."

"You work fast." Jesse's single raised eyebrow corroborated that Ethan had just scored some points.

"I'm just doing my job. Alex deserves my undivided attention."

"Just doing your job, my ass," Alex said. "Ethan is a decorated detective, but you'd never hear him admit to it. He's the very best."

"I'm discovering that," Jesse said. "I'm not used to detectives working at breakneck speed. I have a feeling I'll be playing catch-up for the duration of the case, and that will only slow down building our defense."

"Why don't you join me tonight while I pour over the new evidence? It would save a lot of time." Ethan threw the offer out there without thinking. The moment it hung in the air, he realized he didn't want to take it back, which was entirely out of character. Was he this bold when it came to women? Or was he forcing it?

Before he could crack the code, Jesse replied, "I'd love to."

"Great," Alex said. "A suite is waiting for you. I've instructed the staff to keep the kitchen open for you twenty-four-seven. Just charge your meals to the room as my guest."

"Thanks, Alex. That will make things easier." Ethan turned to Jesse. "I'm in desperate need of a shower first. Why don't you come over"—Ethan glanced at his watch—"around five? We can order room service and get started on our homework."

"It's a date." Jesse instantly froze. She may have regretted her choice of words, but Ethan didn't.

CHAPTER TWENTY

Ethan stood under the pulsating stream of hot water for an extra ten minutes to get mentally organized. Steam built as he ticked off a to-do list for Alex's case: discovery documents, videos, computer backup, calendar, contacts, and fingerprints. He inhaled a deep, cleansing breath as he dealt with the underlying meaning of taking on this job. Alex's future, and by extension Tyler's, hung in the balance. The pressure was on to get this one right and fast.

Dried off and standing in front of the hotel room closet clad only in knit gray boxer briefs, he inventoried his limited selection of clothing. Maybe it was all in his head, but the borderline flirtatious interaction he'd had with Jesse made him wish he'd put more thought into wardrobe before leaving California. It had been years, decades really, since he'd concerned himself with such things, but his two-each option of long-sleeve shirts, casual golf shirts, neutral slacks, suit jackets, jeans, and athletic wear now seemed inadequate in terms of presentation. *Slacks? Too dressy.* Though they'd be inside, shorts seemed too casual.

Jeans were the perfect compromise, especially once he'd topped them off with a pressed, gray, two-toned golf shirt. *One can never go wrong with golf attire. Besides, she golfs.*

He returned to the bathroom to double-check his hair, an uncharacteristically vain effort. "Geez, I feel like a teenager." He glanced down at the bottle of aftershave cologne he'd packed and quietly asked himself, "Should I?"

"Focus, Falling. This isn't a real date." Nevertheless, he applied a single splash to be on the safe side.

Ethan set up his laptop and pulled out the files on Alex's case from his satchel. As he spread out the collection of documents and pictures on the couch and coffee table, he realized this method wasn't going to suit his needs. Hands on his hips, he surveyed the mess. "I need a murder board."

He picked up the room phone and called the front desk. "Yeah, hey. I'm Ethan Falling, a guest of Alex Castle."

"Yes, Mr. Falling. We have instructions to get you anything you need twenty-four-seven."

"Great. I have an odd request. Do you have one of those portable magnetic whiteboards? The kind on wheels?"

"I believe we have some in our conference rooms. Shall I have one brought up to your suite?"

"Please. And can you bring up a bunch of those little magnets, a roll of Scotch tape, and a couple of dry-erase markers in a variety of colors?"

"Of course, Mr. Falling. I'll send up everything immediately."

Within fifteen minutes, two hotel staff members arrived to deliver the requested items.

"Come on in." Ethan held the door open and gestured toward the wall opposite the couches. "Put the board in front of the fireplace. I don't plan on using it."

"That's a shame. I love a warm fire." Jesse extended an arm to stop the door from closing before following the hotel clerks inside.

She was early and didn't give Ethan a chance to be a gentleman. He darted toward the door to hold it open for her. "Jesse, sorry. I didn't realize you were there." The clerks finished setting up the items, prompting Ethan to slip each a twenty-dollar bill as they left.

"What's all this?" Jesse asked.

"We need a place to work the case, so welcome to my squad room. This"—he proudly tacked a picture of William Castle to the whiteboard with a round magnet—"is my murder board."

"You love your job, don't you?" Jesse half-stifled a laugh at Ethan's enthusiasm.

"Always have," he said. "I was twelve when I knew I wanted to be a police officer. My cousin and I spent the summer playing cops and robbers, and I had to be the cop every time." Heat flushed the tips of Ethan's ears. He'd never volunteered that story to anyone outside of family. "I don't know why I told you that."

"I admire a person who knows what they want in life. It typically makes them the best at what they do."

Ethan took in a deep breath. He'd dodged a bullet there.

"Plus, the image of you running around with a plastic badge and cap gun is kind of cute," she added a wink.

Check that thought—achievement unlocked: sounding like a fool. And in record time. Ethan hooked his thumbs inside his waistband at the belt buckle. "Now that I've made a complete ass of myself, how about dinner?"

After they ordered from the room service menu, Jesse set up her laptop on the small dining table next to Ethan's. "We should probably review the discovery material first. Then we can outline their case and develop a plan of attack."

"I was thinking the same thing."

They spent nearly an hour analyzing the DA's evidence, pausing only to accept room service and quickly eat. In the third hour, Ethan called the front desk and requested a color printer. Ten minutes later, the clerks who had delivered the whiteboard arrived with the printer. Alex wasn't kidding when she said her staff was on-call to meet his every need.

The muscular clerk with dark hair and a big grin set up the printer on the desk near the windows. "I brought an all-in-one just in case you need to scan or fax anything, and all the cables you might need."

After the clerk left, Ethan printed a dozen digital pictures and documents he'd collected earlier in the day and tacked them to the whiteboard. He and Jesse identified, categorized, cataloged, and placed each item into a timeline. When they finished, they stood in front of the whiteboard, admiring their work.

"This would have taken me days to go through and organize," Jesse said.

Ethan glanced at her and matched her smile. "We do make a good team." When their eyes met, he held her gaze for an extra beat, thinking, *Maybe*. Was he ready for "maybe," though? *Focus*, he chided himself. He turned toward the whiteboard. "Let's talk strategy."

He grabbed a dry-erase marker and circled five points on the timeline, starting about an hour before Alex arrived and ending an hour after she departed. His primary frustration centered on the stairwells under construction and the plastic sheeting that had obscured security cameras from the basement to the top floor. Video of shadowy figures going up and down the stairs near the Castle Resorts' floor at those times led him to believe someone else could have been in the Castle Resort offices before and after Alex. "These are our focal points."

"Wait," Jesse said. "What about the woman in the elevator at seven thirty having a heated discussion with William? The police couldn't identify her because a scarf hid her face."

"She never got off the elevator with him, just rode it right back down to the lobby. I don't think she's a suspect, but we should follow up. I'll have Alex look at her picture. Maybe she knows her," Ethan said.

Jesse studied the timeline and pointed to the ones Ethan had circled. "Why these shadows and not the others?"

"The building has cameras, pointed at the door, in the stairwells on every even-numbered floor. Castle Resorts is on the twenty-third floor, between the cameras on twenty-two and twenty-four. Twice, shadowy figures going up appeared on the twenty-second floor but didn't show up on the twenty-fourth, meaning they had to stop either on twenty-two or twenty-three.

Same thing, going down. Three times shadows first appeared on twenty-two, which meant they had to start on twenty-two or twenty-three.

"Nice catch."

"Unfortunately, the building has a twenty-four-hour gym on the twentieth floor, and a lot of the guests use the stairs for exercise. These shadows might end up being nothing."

"How do you plan to eliminate them?"

Ethan scratched his chin, thinking through possibilities but discarding them as quickly as they popped into his head. None would lend credibility to the theory that someone else entered the office after Alex left. He finally settled on a long shot. "The time stamps on the surveillance tapes give me a starting point. If I can get my hands on video from the surrounding businesses or from traffic cams, those tapes might show me the faces of those coming and going. Perhaps a few Benjamins can shake loose some video. You can subpoena the rest. I'll visit Alex first thing in the morning and ask her about the woman in the lobby. Then I'll canvass the neighborhood and get you a list of businesses."

"The more I work with you, Ethan, the more I'm impressed," Jesse said.

Impressing her hadn't been on his agenda, but maybe it should've been. For the first time since he was twenty years old, he let himself enjoy the praise of a woman who wasn't Tyler.

"You really know how to work a crime scene and fill in the blanks. Maybe after this case is over, I can convince you to stay in New York. You'd be in high demand here."

"Maybe." The idea of starting over in New York was more appealing than doing it in Sacramento, where the life he had for two decades no longer existed. Besides, Erin would be in New Haven, and he'd bet his last dollar that Tyler would soon make a new life right here. Maybe then he'd be ready for "maybe."

"I'll take maybe. Now, what about Andrew and Victor?" Jesse asked.

"I know where I can reach Victor." This was one meeting Ethan was looking forward to. Despite their suspicions, the NYPD never had connected Victor to the shooting at the Times

Square Resort when Ethan had killed the Padula bodyguard who put a bullet in his leg. Cornering that wise guy was top on his list. "I'll check with Alex for an address on Andrew." Ethan grabbed his bottle of water and took a long swig. He looked over the board one more time, searching for more leads. "I'd hoped to get more from William's computer files, but he was old school and worked primarily with hard copies, all of which the police took. Was there anything helpful from the folios?"

"No. It was all dirt digging on Alex and the women in her past and Andrew and his gambling and embezzlement but provided nothing we didn't already know." Jesse flopped down on the couch and continued to study the board. "I think the key to this case is the camera. If Alex's 1965 camera was never in the building, much less at the crime scene, how did William's blood get on it? And if it was the 1957 one Gretchen saw, where is it?"

"That is the sixty-four-thousand-dollar question. We need to press Alex about the blood." Ethan fell onto the couch next to Jesse. "We find that second camera and we find the killer. I still think we can get a lead or two from William's calendar, but I'm too punchy to focus."

"It can wait until tomorrow," Jesse said.

They sat in silence. It was closing in on midnight. Ethan needed to sleep, but he didn't want to make the first move to call it a night. "Can I get you anything else to eat or drink?"

Jesse took her time responding, as if she were measuring Ethan's sluggishness rather than weighing options. Then there it was. Her downturned lips suggested she wanted to stay as much as he wanted her to, just not yet. "We should call it a night."

A part of Ethan was thankful she decided for him. Okay, a huge part. "Maybe" wasn't in the cards tonight. "You're right." Ethan walked Jesse to the door without a doubt that saying good night was the right choice. "Sleep well, Jesse."

CHAPTER TWENTY-ONE

Daybreak had come, but Alex had barely slept. Her mind had churned all night on the charges she faced and their impact on her personal life and her business one. Cancellations at the resorts had soared with no end in sight. On the personal side, though, there were two bright spots in her otherwise dismal week: the loveable thing sleeping on the dog bed near the window and the loving woman sleeping in the bed next to her.

A week of sharing a bed with Tyler had taught Alex an important lesson: their bodies regulated temperature differently. While Alex enjoyed wrapping herself in the blankets, Tyler alternated between stealing and kicking off the covers. Alex much preferred the latter, which exposed her barely dressed, delicious body. Perhaps their seven-year age difference was the culprit; at forty, menopause was right around the corner for Tyler.

The house furnace kicked on, and Tyler kicked the blankets again, this time pulling them off Alex too. She considered pulling the sheets back up, but when Tyler rolled from her stomach onto her side, she discarded the idea as foolish. She spooned Tyler instead and whispered, "You're warm."

"You're cold." Tyler pulled Alex's arms tighter around her. "You tossed most of the night."

"I have a lot on my mind." Alex's skin tingled where their bodies touched, pulling her mind from business to pleasure. "And having you half-naked next to me all night didn't help matters." The moment Alex slipped a hand down Tyler's thigh, the shower door in the next-door guest room slammed shut, the noise rocketing Callie from the floor to the middle of the bed, separating them. "Dammit, girl. You have the worst timing."

Tyler lifted her head. "I have news for you. Dogs are like little kids. She's going to have the worst timing for the next ten years."

Alex rolled and rubbed the German shepherd behind the ear, earning a welcoming slobbery kiss. It was a ritual Alex quickly had come to love and would miss if the unthinkable happened.

"Hey, T." Alex paused for Tyler to look her in the eye, fighting the sinking feeling in her gut. "If I have to go to prison, promise me you'll take care of Callie. She loves you."

Tyler's gaze embraced Alex like a warm blanket. "Of course I will. I love her too. But it won't come to that."

"You're right, T." Tyler was putting on a good front, she saw, though she was fighting back tears just as Alex was. But if ignoring the elephant in the room was Tyler's way of coping, then so be it. Rising from the bed to throw on a T-shirt and a pair of sweats, she forced a smile. "I'll let her out and get the paper if you start the coffee for all of us."

"Deal."

Down on the main floor, Tyler kissed Alex before peeling off to the kitchen on the lower level. Alex headed out the front door with Callie in the lead. Furry paws lumbered down the stoop, landing on the small patch of dirt, shrubs, and flowers along the front of her townhouse. Alex shivered in the chilly spring air, wishing she'd put on more than flip-flops and the light jacket she'd grabbed by the front door. She bent to pick up the papers on the bottom step, but a man's hand appeared, beating her to it.

"Let me." Ethan handed her the *Times* and *Journal*.

"I wasn't expecting to see you so soon," Alex said. "Is this a good or a bad sign?"

"Too early to tell, but I need to talk to you about a few things." Callie finished her business and jumped on Ethan, putting her front paws on his chest. It was a bothersome habit Alex would have to break her of. He rubbed her ears in a well-practiced fashion. "Who do we have here?"

"This is Callie. I found her at the pier the night my father was killed."

"Well, she's beautiful. I bet she's drawn to Tyler," Ethan said.

"How did you know?"

"We had a German shepherd years ago. That fella was completely attached to her, and she was to him. She was devastated when he died."

"You never got another?"

"Tyler refused. She said that Shadow broke the mold."

"She never said anything." No wonder Tyler had teared up earlier. Alex's request had opened up old wounds.

Ethan gave Callie another scratch behind the ears. "It seems our Tyler is still holding back," he said, not looking at her.

"Yes, it does." Tyler had reassured Alex that she'd be there not only for her, but for Callie. Why hadn't she mentioned Shadow? Clearly, she was more focused on Alex's needs than her own. It was a troubling response, one that Alex would have to keep an eye on. She shivered again and gestured over her shoulder. "Let's go inside."

The aromas of fresh coffee and toasted sourdough filled the stairwell leading to the kitchen. Callie led the way down.

"Look who I found." Alex settled her gaze on Tyler, who was sitting on a stool at the granite-top island.

Tyler turned, her smile dropping the instant she saw Ethan. Alex shifted to gauge his reaction. The last time she'd seen Tyler and Ethan together was in his hospital room after Victor's man had shot him. That night, having previously shared just two toe-curling, steamy kisses, Alex and Tyler had only the promise of becoming lovers. Ethan couldn't mistake how their relationship had progressed at this point.

His Adam's apple bobbed hard before he said, "Good morning, Tyler. You're looking well."

"Ethan? What are you doing here so early?" When Tyler rose and gave him a hug, his eyes slammed shut. Despite the brave front he'd put on for Alex's benefit yesterday, he clearly was still hurting. Alex's heart went out to him.

"Some things have come up since last night." He snatched a strawberry from a bowl atop the island and popped it into his mouth. Alex took it as his way of distracting himself from the awkwardness he was clearly experiencing.

"You look tired. Which means you haven't had your morning caffeine." Tyler filled and handed him a steaming mug. "Coffee?"

"You know me so well," Ethan said.

"Ethan," Syd's voice boomed from the stairs. She gave him one of her signature bear hugs. "I'm so relieved that you dropped everything to help Alex."

"Glad to help."

Tyler poured an extra cup of coffee for Syd. "Here you go, Syd. I know you have a big day ahead of you helping Alex."

Ethan squinted.

"I volunteered to put out fires at Castle Resorts and act as interim CEO," Syd said. "Starting with a meeting of the executives this morning."

"Ah, damage control," Ethan said.

"We prefer the term 'crisis management.' It sounds more professional." Syd winked. "What brings you here this early?"

"Three things." Ethan directed his attention to Alex. "We should visit Victor tonight at Arthur's. Can you get us in to see your brother before that?"

Alex nodded her reassurance. "I can set it up after Syd and I meet with the executives this morning."

"Thanks. I also need you to look at this security footage still from the night of your father's death." He handed her a printout. "Do you recognize the woman he's arguing with?"

Alex inspected the photo Ethan handed her. At first glance, the person's profile was challenging to identify; a scarf hid their hair and face. The long coat, feminine slacks, and heels led her to believe it was a woman, though. The perfect posture could indicate it was a younger woman or one who came from an upbringing that stressed such things. Age was impossible to guess with the person's hands covered by gloves.

She looked at the photo more closely, this time focusing on the scarf. Its design and colors looked familiar, and a second glance at the shoes confirmed her suspicion. Of course, she'd seen that scarf before—because she'd bought it. "What time was this taken?" she asked.

"Seven thirty."

"That was before I arrived. Why is this important?"

"I need to identify everyone who may have been on the twenty-third floor that night, and she was. Even though the elevator video shows that she never left the car and returned to the main floor before you arrived, with the building under construction I can't rule out that she didn't return."

"I'm sorry, Ethan, it's hard to tell. Can I keep this?" Alex could count on one hand the number of people she trusted implicitly and in whose hands she would willingly put her life. Unfortunately, one of them was in that photograph. She needed to find out why before she said anything.

"Sure. Let me know if anything rings a bell."

CHAPTER TWENTY-TWO

When Alex and Syd arrived at Castle Resorts headquarters, Alex excused herself for a moment of privacy. Sitting atop the lid of the toilet in her office bathroom, she nervously tapped her phone on a knee for several minutes. Then, unable to bring herself to leap to conclusions, she finally dialed.

"What?" The groggy voice from the other end meant Alex had called too early, but she needed answers.

"I know it's early, but I need to ask you a question."

"Are the chickens even up yet?"

"It's roosters, and yes, they've been up for hours." Alex's stomach knotted, but she had to ask. "Do you still have that scarf I gave you for Christmas?"

"You call me at an ungodly hour because you're still angry I wasn't enamored with your present?"

"Will you just answer the damn question? Do you still have it?"

"Someone hasn't had her morning caffeine."

"Dammit, Harley." Afraid of the answer, Alex rubbed her throbbing temple and repeated her question. "Do you have it or not?"

"I'm sorry, Alex. I know you're stressed. No, I don't have it. I gave it to Mother."

"Go back to sleep." Alex hung up, more relieved than not. The woman in the photo wasn't Harley, but Abby. With her bad knees, she couldn't use the stairs. So the only questions left were these: Why was Abby arguing with her father that night? And why hadn't she mentioned it before now?

"Are you done in there? Our meeting starts in five minutes," Syd nagged Alex through the bathroom door.

Alex pulled the door open. "Someone's a little anxious."

"Can you blame me? Grapes never need inspiring."

"You'll do just fine. Everyone who will be in that room knows and respects you." Alex inspected Syd from head to toe. She still rocked a tailored business suit like no one's business, and the hour she spent yesterday at Alex's stylist in preparation for this meeting had transformed her from grape grower to Wall Street dragon slayer.

"I hope you're right, Baby Sis."

Alex walked into the conference room with her sister and role model by her side and filled with an overwhelming sense of confidence. Today's game plan: instill calm in the company, gauge alliances, and find the leak. Whoever had leaked confidential company information to the media had to go. Like their father, neither sister would tolerate disloyalty.

Alex and Syd sat silently at the head of the conference table, sizing up each executive as they entered the room. Some offered their support to Alex, not believing the charges against her. Others seemed noncommittal yet surprised at seeing Syd and acted cordial toward her. Those were the ones Syd would have to keep an eye on. As the seats around the table filled, the topic of the murmur was clear as glass—the company's future was at stake now that the news of Alex's weekend arrest was going viral.

"Thank you for coming, everyone." Alex kicked off the most uncomfortable meeting she'd chaired in her life. "I know all of you are well aware of the events of the weekend. While I can't discuss any specifics of pending legal matters, I can assure you that I am innocent of the charges and we are mounting a robust defense. Until I am exonerated, my sister, Sydney Barnette, will step in as interim CEO and occupy my office. I'll step away from the business until this is resolved."

As planned, the sisters carefully surveyed everyone's response. As expected, the news had relieved some and shocked some. Curiously, three appeared unmoved. Knowing her sister, Alex guessed Syd already had her eye on them.

As their father had done hundreds of times before to address the room, Syd stood, projecting strength and confidence. "Each of you at this table has been with Castle Resorts for years. You know me and my experience with this company. My father had a unique way of running the business. He kept things close to the vest."

In the Castle family, that was code for legacy. First and foremost, William had been concerned about building a lasting heritage for the Castle name, a perspective Alex had understood but never bought into.

"I am not my father," Syd continued. "I will base my decisions on what is best for Castle Resorts, not the Castle family. Until we stop the bleeding, I expect daily reports from each department. Ms. Winstead, I'd like to meet you and your public relations staff this afternoon. We need to release an official statement by noon today."

After fielding a handful of questions, Alex and Syd adjourned to Alex's office, both unwilling to enter their father's office. Once had been enough for Alex, but this decision did confirm one salient point—Syd might rescue the company, but Alex had no desire to carry on her father's legacy after it was back on an even keel.

While she was packing up her personal items to make room for Syd, Alex's mind drifted to the meeting. "Any suspicions as to who's the leak?"

"I've narrowed it down to three," Syd replied without hesitation.

Alex let out a frustrated sigh. "Me too. I thought I could trust everyone in that room."

"You let me handle this, Baby Sis. I'll plug the leaks and right the ship." Syd's confidence was contagious.

When Syd walked Alex out, Gretchen raised an index finger, signaling she had a message. "Ms. Castle, Times Square passed along a personal note for you."

Alex read the message, an insistent smile forming. "I'll be damned." Syd shot her a look of *What?* "Just someone looking for a job." Alex folded the paper and placed it in her purse. "You got things from here? I need to keep my word and handle this one myself. If that's okay with you since you're the boss at the moment."

"It's not Kelly Thatcher slithering her way back into your life, is it?"

"Hell no." Alex grimaced at the thought. "You made me throw up a little in my mouth. It's just someone I owe a huge favor to. Trust me, she's worth it."

Syd chuckled, "All right, Baby Sis. Go keep your word."

Alex kissed Syd on the cheek, and they parted ways. Keeping her promise would have to wait a few hours, she decided. She had a more urgent meeting to tend to first. She pulled her phone from her coat pocket and dialed. "Hi, Ethan. Are you ready to talk to that brother of mine?"

"I'm in the area but need to pick up surveillance video from nearby businesses. Give me an hour."

CHAPTER TWENTY-THREE

Other than the receptionist typing away at her computer terminal while fielding an incoming call, the waiting room of Cypress Group was quiet and unoccupied. When the call ended, Alex approached her desk with Ethan at her side. "Good afternoon, Quinn. Thank you for helping me again."

Quinn's lip biting hinted the conflict she was feeling. "This is highly irregular, but I really like you, Ms. Castle. As you requested on the phone earlier, I've cleared his calendar to make sure no one will disturb you."

Alex gave her a grateful smile. "Thank you, Quinn. This is important, and we both know how my brother can be."

"Please don't tell him I let you back. I got in trouble last time I let you through."

"Mum's the word. Just tell them you were in the bathroom. But, if anything blows back at you, I'll be happy to offer you a position at Castle Resorts," Alex said with a calm, reassuring voice.

Quinn, still biting her lip, turned her attention back to the incessant phone.

As Alex and Ethan began to make their way to the back offices, Ethan placed a hand on her arm, stopping her. He spoke softly. "Does your brother own a motorcycle?"

"Yes, why?"

Someone entered the hallway from two doors down, forcing Ethan to speak even more quietly. "A gut instinct. I acquired some surveillance video from the jewelry store across the street from your office building."

"I know that place. Kaplan Jewelers."

"It shows a motorcycle roaring out of the building at eight twenty that night." He glanced toward Andrew's office door, which was slightly ajar. "Follow my lead on this, okay?"

Alex opened the door without knocking, discovering her brother asleep on the couch in his white, long-sleeved, button-down shirt and dark gray slacks. Ethan raised an index finger in a "shhh" manner, gesturing for Alex to close the door behind them and watch Andrew while he snooped.

Circling the executive desk, Ethan shifted Andrew's old baseball mitt to one side before flipping through the desktop contents—various papers, folders, and a leather-bound personal organizer. He waved Alex over and pointed to an entry in the calendar the evening William was killed. Several handwritten notes documented Andrew making some phone calls, and eight p.m. had been circled, but nothing more written.

When Andrew stirred, Ethan and Alex came back around the desk. Ethan hovered over Andrew until he finally opened his eyes with a start.

"What the—"

Ethan peeked at Alex and then returned his stare at Andrew. "You know, Alex, for twins, I think you're much prettier. Though he has a bit of a feminine vibe to him. Maybe if he let his hair grow out a little."

Andrew sat up straight. "You can leave now."

"You should get better security around here. We just walked right in with no one at the front desk." Alex was sure Ethan slipped that in so Quinn wouldn't catch heat for today. "You never know who might walk in and catch you sleeping or doing anything else you might do behind closed doors when you're alone."

"Leave or I'm calling the cops." Andrew popped to his feet.

"Alex, I bet he doesn't know about the video."

"Yes, it was quite helpful." Alex followed Ethan's lead, trusting his gut instinct.

"What video?" Andrew took the bait.

"It's amazing what videos pop up when you throw enough money around. I know you were there that night. You must not have caught much traffic on your motorcycle." Whatever Ethan was leading up to, Alex didn't like it. She didn't want to believe her brother was a killer. "You were right on time for your eight o'clock meeting, despite the rain."

Andrew formed a fist. Experience told Alex he was on the defensive. "I didn't kill him if that's what you're thinking."

"Of course, I don't think that." Alex honeyed her tone to put her brother at ease. "Neither one of us could've killed him. He was our father, for God's sake, and I saw him alive after you left. All we want to know is what you and Father talked about that night."

"And why should I tell you anything after you kicked me out of the company?"

"Because you don't know what the cops found in your father's office. If you don't tell us what we want to know"—equal to Andrew in height, Ethan stepped forward, staring him down, toe to toe—"I'll personally turn over every piece of evidence we've collected to the police, documenting that you embezzled a quarter mil from the company you allegedly love so much."

Andrew appeared visibly shaken and looked toward Alex to confirm Ethan's threat, which, as much as it pained her, she gave. Her brother swallowed hard. "Father had his P.I. track me down and ordered me to his office that night. When I got there…"

* * *

Two Thursdays ago, eight p.m.
To his surprise, the attempt to burn off his frustration by running the stairs instead of using the elevator left Andrew

only slightly winded. When he stepped onto the twenty-third floor, he patted himself on the back for staying in running shape and at a level that rivaled his years on the Yale track team. The endorphin rush had kicked in, laying waste to the burn in his quads.

Flashes of lightning through the hallway windows lit the corridor as he entered Castle Resorts' corporate headquarters, setting an ominous tone for this meeting with his heartless, manipulative father. The late-night summons meant one thing—Alex had finally betrayed him.

He passed by his old office, choking on memories of the many fruitless years he'd spent there trying to please a man who couldn't be pleased. He'd failed to live up to expectations, but surprisingly, in the end it had been Alex, not his father, who forced him out of the family business, the last possible avenue via which he might possibly earn his father's love.

Andrew's resentment returned with a vengeance. Sure, skimming from the company coffers had been a stupid idea, but he didn't deserve to be exiled to Siberia for it. He entered his father's office—the seat of power that he'd spent a lifetime coveting. Sadly, deep down, he still did so. If on the off chance William welcomed him with open arms tonight, he decided, he would accept it without as much as a blink and fight Alex for what was rightly his. This bold resolve only lasted until his gaze met his father's. The fury that had filled his eyes the day Andrew had resigned was still there. If anything, it had been magnified, confirming his choice of wardrobe for the meeting had been appropriate.

"Prompt, if not presentable." William's tone contained his trademark condescension.

Andrew specifically selected his wardrobe—jeans, tennis shoes, and a leather riding jacket thrown over a ratty white T-shirt—for his father's benefit. He was done looking the part of a Castle and done trying to impress a man whose standards he could never meet. "Nice to see you too, Father."

"Sit," William ordered.

Andrew complied, plopping down insolently in the first guest chair immediately opposite William's executive desk. He crossed one leg at the ankle atop the knee of the other. "I don't like being summoned by your lackeys, Father."

"If you had availed yourself to me, I wouldn't have resorted to sending my lackey." William appeared steadier than the last time Andrew had seen him. Perhaps medication was controlling his Parkinson's better.

"Can we just get this over with?" Andrew said, an extra bite to his words.

"I have a question first. Exactly how stupid do you think I am?"

"That's a loaded question." Andrew grinned his delight at his quip. That was the closest he'd ever come to standing up to his father.

"Did you not think that I wouldn't find out what you had done?"

"What are you talking about?"

"Rebecca would be ashamed to know that her son had grown up to be a thief."

Andrew kept his mouth shut but refused to back down with his eyes. He had feared the day that his father would find out about his ill-advised scheme and the consequences he'd have to face as a result. He was relieved, actually, that that day had come at last. He could finally stop running.

"I had held hope that you had some true Castle mettle and would fix your gambling problem while at Yale, but you failed." Andrew struggled to remain steely-eyed, his resolve to remain silent rapidly waning. William continued, "You instead deepened your debt to that horrid fellow, Mr. Padula, and siphoned company funds to feed your addiction."

Andrew had one burning question. "When did Alex tell you?"

"Her hands are not clean in this, and I can no longer trust her either, but she kept your dirty little secret. Lord only knows why."

"I'll be damned. She didn't tell you?" His father's haughty head jerk told Andrew that she hadn't. "At least Alex kept her word."

"Her word means nothing to me anymore, and neither does yours. You both are depraved, lost souls."

Andrew snorted. "Oh man, you don't know how long I've waited for you to finally lose those rose-colored glasses and see Alex for what she really is. You found out, I guess, about Kelly Thatcher blackmailing her way into Castle Resorts and the pictures of those two doing the nasty?"

"What I see is that the two of you really are two peas in a pod. You kept your sister's dirty little secret even though you know homosexuality is an abomination."

"I am nothing like her, or you, for that matter. I could care less about who she sleeps with. All I cared about was that it would upset you. But, trust me, if she hadn't forced my hand after finding out what I'd done, I would have spilled the beans about Kelly and those photos weeks ago."

"Each of you should have been honest with me about the other. But you weren't. Both of you are immoral and untrustworthy."

"You raised us. I guess you reap what you sow."

"What is that supposed to mean?"

"Oh please, I spent enough time around Accounting to learn that you and Georgia were a thing back in the day when you were married to Syd's mother. You're a hypocrite, plain and simple."

"Yes, well." He sniffed. "I learned from my mistakes and corrected my errant ways. No one can say the same about you or your sister. Both of you seem compelled to feed at the trough of depravity."

Andrew laughed again. "So, you know Alex is still eating pussy? Oh, this is rich."

"Watch your tongue. There is no call for such crassness."

Andrew continued to laugh.

"Enough!" William shouted. Andrew buttoned up but still reveled in his father's misery. "You think this is a joke? We'll see who has the last laugh. As of tomorrow, I am cutting you off. You are forever barred from returning to Castle Resorts. I am terminating whatever is left of your trust fund, and you are out of the will."

"I expected nothing less from you. It really doesn't matter to me, because I've been living without your money since I left. I'll be fine. Are you at least doing the same to Alex?"

"That is none of your business. Your mother would have been ashamed of you both. I'm glad she's not alive to see any of this."

"I wish you would've died," Andrew grated, "and not her. Maybe then I would've turned out differently." He had often speculated what kind of man he'd be if his mother hadn't died. He doubted he would've spent decades idolizing a man who didn't deserve it. "But that didn't happen. Instead I was stuck with you as a role model."

"Enough of your insolence. You are no longer my son."

"Well, it's perfect symmetry because you've never been a real father. I hope you die a sad and lonely man."

Andrew stormed out of the office and down the stairwell, trying again to burn off his heightened frustration.

* * *

"I had similar words with him that night," Alex said, "but I'm surprised you thought I'd tattle on you like a little schoolgirl."

"After you forced me out, nothing you'd say or do was out of the realm of possibilities." Andrew's sharp words had their intended effect—they cut Alex to the quick. Then, his expression softened a fraction. "But I was not totally surprised to learn that you hadn't." He shook his head. "I lived most of my life disappointing Father, and that night was no different. I finally understood that you did me a big favor by forcing me out and getting me out from under his thumb. I had no other choice but to get a job on my own. So when he cut me off that night, I didn't give a shit."

Those words gave Alex hope that her brother wasn't as lost as she once thought. That once all this mess was cleared up and the stars aligned correctly, they might reconcile and be a family again.

"Let's say we believe you," Ethan said. "Where did you go next?"

"To Arthur's to give Victor a heads up, but he gave me the impression that he already knew Father was on to us."

"When you were in William's office, was there anything out of the ordinary on his desk?" Ethan asked.

"Like what?"

"An old camera? A Leica?"

"You mean Mother's old Leica? No, I haven't seen that since the old man had me swipe it from Alex's stuff when we moved back from Yale. He couldn't wait to get his hands on it."

"He did what?" The tips of Alex's ears burned. She balled her fists. All thought of eventually reconciling flew out the window. "And you went along with it?"

"What can I say? He bought me a car to get it back without you knowing."

"I loved that camera." Alex grabbed him by the tie with one hand and wound up for a crushing blow with the other. What he'd done was unforgiveable.

The moment she flung her fist forward, Ethan blocked it with a forearm. "Whoa, Alex. You're on bail. The last thing you want is to give the judge a reason to revoke it." He refused to break eye contact with her until she lowered her arm and took a step back. "I've got this," he said to her before directing his next comment to Andrew. "Did your father ever tell you why he wanted it?"

"No, but I suspected it had something to do with Kelly Thatcher." Andrew shifted his gaze to Alex. "I'm sorry. You know how he could be."

Understanding her father's and brother's behavior and excusing it were two different matters. As far as Alex was concerned, forgiveness was a long way off.

"I think I've heard enough," Ethan said. "You better watch your back with Victor. His bosses might consider you and him a liability since your father's death, and they may decide to clean house." He signaled to Alex that it was time to leave.

In the elevator down to the lobby level, Alex fumed, processing everything Andrew had said. As furious as she was about the camera, she still couldn't consider her brother capable of murder. "As much as he burns me right now, I believe him."

"I do, too. Andrew is a gambler and a thief, but he doesn't come across to me as the violent type. Besides, I don't think he had the balls to stand up to William. Do you know who your father's P.I. was?"

"I wish I did," Alex said. "He might know who else met my father that night. At least we now know there was a second camera."

"We find it, we find the killer," Ethan said.

"That will be like trying to find a needle in a haystack." Alex focused on her last shred of hope to clear herself. "But my money is on Victor."

"Mine too."

CHAPTER TWENTY-FOUR

Alex stepped up to the host station at Margo's, the main restaurant at Castle Resorts Times Square, fully prepared to keep her promise. The host clad in a groomsman-gray tuxedo glowed with recognition. "Good afternoon, Ms. Castle. I've already shown your party to your usual table."

"Thank you, Max." She glanced at the seating chart. "How are reservations?"

Max's expression grew long. "Down by half, ma'am."

She patted him on the hand. "Don't worry. Business will pick up again." Or so she hoped. The renovation of this place had given it a unique dining ambiance and earned it a five-star rating in the *Times* last month. If Syd couldn't work her magic, all that money and effort would've been for naught.

When her table came into view, Alex hardly recognized Destiny Scott. She'd traded in her tight clothes, knee-high yellow boots, and overly done-up hair. Her dark blue blazer, pale blue button-down, conservative makeup, and perfectly straight black hair cut into an A-line bob would turn every head in the boardroom.

Destiny stood the moment their eyes met. Her matching pencil skirt and sensible pumps completed the transformation from streetwise to Wall Street. She extended her hand. "Thank you for meeting with me, Alex."

"What happened to Barbie?" Alex winked as they shook hands.

"Sorry about that."

"No worries. The name grew on me." Alex made a show of eyeing Destiny up and down. "You look amazing."

"Thank you. I believe in looking the part, whether dancing or analyzing spreadsheets." Once they were seated, the server dropped off menus at the table. "What do you recommend?"

"You can't go wrong with anything here, but I'm partial to the Caesar wrap for a light meal."

"Beats the hell out of Rice Krispies and fruit punch." Destiny winked.

"That it does." Alex placed their orders with the server and had him refill their waters. She raised her glass. "Here's to making Rice Krispies a thing of the past." They clinked glasses. "I hope your call today means you're ready to take me up on the job offer."

"It does. That is if you're still willing to take a chance on an exotic dancer." Destiny squared her shoulders, appearing as confident as ever, making Alex's decision an easy one.

"On an exotic dancer? No. On a smart, incredibly motivated businesswoman? Yes. You impress me, Destiny. I know people with every advantage in life who haven't accomplished half of what you have. I'd be a fool to not bring you into the Castle Resort family."

Destiny's tanned cheeks blushed. "Thank you, Alex."

"So, is accounting your dream job or do you have something else in mind?"

"I've always had a head for numbers. For example, I was curious about Castle Resorts' last quarter. Have you been doing a lot of renovations?"

"Yes, we have. How did you know?"

Destiny leaned forward, resting an elbow on the table with a glint in her eye. "Your net income was down from last year, yet adjusted earnings were up considerably. That tells me your depreciation took a hit, which means an influx of new assets. Since the number of hotels has remained steady at twenty-three, major improvements are the likely explanation."

"I'm impressed. With a mind as sharp as yours, I should find you a position in finance."

They chatted about more minor things throughout their meal and left the table with Alex promising to start Destiny in her new career first thing the next day. In the sparsely populated lobby, loud voices caught their attention before Alex could hug her new friend goodbye. She focused on the arguing pair at the entrance to the bar, instantly recognizing both parties. Jesse was holding her own with her father, her body language demonstrating a refusal to give ground.

"Excuse me, Destiny, but it appears I might have to rescue my lawyer."

Destiny's expression contained a tinge of disgust. "He's your lawyer?"

"No, she is." Alex stepped toward Jesse when their voices grew louder.

"Listen, Dad." Jesse propped both hands on her hips, staring him straight in the eye. "She's my client, and I'm giving her the best defense possible."

"For heaven's sake, Jesse. She killed one of my dearest friends."

"Allegedly. The People's case is weak and circumstantial at best. It has holes big enough to drive an eighteen-wheeler through. And spare me the dearest friend bit. You loved his donations for landmark preservation in the city. You're angry because the money spigot has stopped because he's dead."

"Do you really think I'm that shallow? William and I developed a close friendship over the years over our common interest. Of course, I'm upset over his death. And we'll see about that weak case when I have the DA turn up the heat again."

"Are you threatening my client?"

"No. I'm promising to bring the full weight of the justice system down on her."

Destiny maintained her distance while Alex hastened toward them. "I think you should take this somewhere more private," Alex said in a hushed tone.

Jesse's father stared at Alex, his eyes piercing her like well-sharpened knives. "I think not."

Alex stood her ground. "Then I'm asking you to leave, Deputy Mayor Simmons." She glanced over to a security guard standing at the main entrance and snapped her fingers at him. The guard scurried over. "This is my place of business, and I have the right to refuse service to anyone who's causing a disturbance. Please leave before I have you escorted from the premises."

The deputy mayor scanned his surroundings and the dozen gawkers. He straightened his shoulders in the same smug fashion her father used to. "Good day." He smoothed his jacket, his attention focused on Jesse. "We'll finish this at Sunday dinner." On the way out, he pulled out his cell phone. "Adam...yes...I have a problem I need you to handle personally."

Once the deputy mayor was out of sight, Alex turned toward Jesse, hands on her hips. She wouldn't have been surprised to see flames and smoke pouring from her mouth and nose. "So, *he's* the one pressuring the police and DA"

"It appears so." Jesse sighed regretfully.

Before Alex could light the lobby on fire, Destiny tapped her on the shoulder. "I'm sorry, Alex, but I really must be going."

Alex shook off the disturbing awareness of having a face put to the one railroading her and focused her attention on Destiny. "Of course. I'll let Tim Morris know to expect you first thing tomorrow."

"If you don't mind, I've remembered a few loose ends I need to wrap up before I start. It shouldn't take me more than a day."

"Thursday then." Alex pivoted. "Where are my manners? Jesse, this is my friend, Destiny Scott, our newest financial analyst. Destiny, this is Jesse Simmons, the wonderful lawyer who's going to get these false charges against me dropped."

Shaking hands with Jesse, Destiny asked, "That windbag was your father?"

"So my mother tells me," Jesse said. "I'm sure I'll get an earful on at dinner on Sunday."

"I hate to meet and run, but I should be going. It was a pleasure, Jesse." Destiny gave Alex a light hug. "I'll catch up with you after I acclimate to the position."

After Destiny walked out, Jesse looked the way Alex felt—flustered by the public spectacle. Ethan approached through the main entrance. He looked from Alex to Jesse. "What did I miss?"

Jesse sighed. "I don't know about you, Alex, but I could use a drink."

Not missing a beat, Alex linked arms with Jesse. "Come on, Ethan. We need to throw back a few."

Without a hint of hesitation, Ethan gestured toward the bar. "Lead the way, ladies."

Once inside the sleek, modern bar, Jesse took point and plopped down like a ton of bricks at an out-of-the-way table. "Anyone up for tequila?"

Within seconds of Alex sitting down, a server was at her side, ready to take her order. "In that case…" Alex directed her attention to the server. "Chad, bring my private stock of tequila, would you?"

"Coming right up, Ms. Castle."

Ethan remained silent while Alex and Jesse went on a simultaneous rant. "Can you believe that man?" "I'll never hear the end of it." "What's up his ass?" "If he thinks he can bully me, he's got another think coming."

Minutes later, Chad returned with three glasses and a black walnut box on a silver serving platter. He carefully placed a glass in front of each person at the table before opening the container, revealing a suede-lined interior cradling an elegant crystal bottle with etched labeling.

Jesse whistled her approval. "Wow, this *is* the good stuff."

"That looks more like bourbon than tequila." Ethan inspected the most expensive bottle of liquor in Alex's private stock—one she had cherished but which no longer held meaning.

While the server poured the first round, Alex explained, "It's Gran Patrón Burdeos, named after the vintage Bordeaux barrels in which it was racked. It's triple-distilled and aged for a minimum of twelve months to achieve its smooth, full-bodied taste and rich, dark amber hue."

"Who knew?" Ethan shrugged.

"My father. He sent it to me as a gift after he told me I'd be his successor." Alex inspected the filled glass. Her fascination with it had disappeared entirely. "He made sure I knew every nuance about it so I'd be properly impressed."

Ethan raised his glass. "Well, he's dead. So here's to beautiful women and expensive booze."

"Hear, hear," Alex said.

"I can drink to that," Jesse said.

All three downed their shots. Each marked their appreciation for the silky libation with "Damn, that's good." "Smooth." And a single moan.

"All right, ladies, care to clue me in? Why are we drinking the good stuff?" Ethan pressed.

"My father." Jesse held out her glass, a request for a refill which Alex obliged.

"Who is?" Ethan probed.

"Besides an ass?" Jesse bantered

"That would help," Ethan replied. Alex finished pouring the second round, watching these two and their body language. *They're so much alike. Definitely a spark there.*

"He was William Castle's best friend, is deputy mayor of the city, and is the one pressuring the NYPD and the DA for a quick conviction."

"Yep, an ass." Ethan raised his glass again, and the two women mirrored him. "Here's to kickin' some ass."

"Hear, hear," from Alex, and another "I can definitely drink to that," from Jesse. They sipped their shots.

"Jesse, Alex and I met with her brother today." Ethan returned his glass to the table. "Andrew was there that night, but before Alex arrived. I need to get security footage from other stores on the street to confirm his story."

"More importantly, my brother confirmed that there is a second camera. He said that my father had him steal the original one, my mother's, from me after graduation."

"What a piece of work, both of them." Jesse scowled. "But unless we find it, all I can do is argue about its existence." Her cell phone buzzed. She glanced at the caller ID. "It's my assistant. I have to take this." She swiped the screen. "Yes, Sally…What did he say…? You've got to be kidding…Clear my calendar. This will be my only case until then." Jesse's temple rubbing was not a good sign, but Alex waited patiently until she finished the call.

"Not good news, I take it," Alex asked.

"It appears my father has been on the stick already. The DA just set your grand jury for Thursday."

By all rights, Alex should've panicked at the news. She had only two days before the DA would present her case and she'd possibly have a felony indictment hanging over her head. But her future was out of her hands. She had to trust the two people sitting at this table enough to do their jobs. She sighed, grabbed the bottle of Gran Patrón, and poured a third round.

Ethan, on the other hand, slumped back in his chair, rubbed his face with both hands, and muttered, "Shit."

"No worries." Alex put on the same excellent front she was sure Ethan had done earlier in her kitchen with Tyler. She patted his hand. "With you and Jesse in my corner, I can't lose."

Jesse sighed with a note of concern. "I'm not worried about the grand jury. The DA has total control over that process. It's no joke that he could indict a ham sandwich if he wanted to because the threshold to indict is extremely low. However, I am concerned about which judge we might draw for Superior Court arraignment. My father's reach is pretty deep in this city, and I'm worried you may lose your bail until trial, which could be months."

Alex swallowed hard at the thought of going back to jail, but she kept her cool and picked up her glass. "Like Ethan said, here's to kickin' some ass."

Ethan followed with, "And beautiful women."

Jesse added, "And expensive booze." They downed their drinks.

Alex slammed her glass on the table. "What's next on the agenda, team?"

"Victor Padula, but I should sleep off the tequila a bit first," Ethan said.

"I'm coming with you," Jesse insisted.

Ethan leaned forward and suggestively asked, "To sleep it off or talk to Victor?" Their interaction spoke volumes to Alex. These two would definitely end up being more than colleagues.

Jesse leaned in and slowed her next words. "Which would you prefer?"

Yep, these two are so going to hook up.

Ethan locked gazes with Jesse. The doubt Alex could see on his face took this beyond the typical bar pickup and clearly went to thoughts of what might be satisfied by saying yes. It spoke to a heart that still needed healing. He straightened his tie and stood. "I hate to drink and run, but I have some work to get done before we corner Victor. I'll meet you two at Arthur's Alley around eight tonight." He gave Alex a friendly peck on the cheek and took off toward the elevators.

Alex drilled Jesse with her eyes. She was a mystery beyond being single and forty and having a reputation as a top-notch lawyer. Was she married to the job, or did no one stay long enough to interest her? Did she treat lovers like takeout? Devour them for one night and then throw them out with the next day's trash? She shook her head in embarrassment. Who was she kidding? She was projecting. That's what she'd done for years out of deference to her father. Ethan would soon discover what the deal was with Jesse. Just in case, though…

"You know he's going through a divorce and is in a very vulnerable state."

Jesse cocked her head to one side as if sizing up Alex's statement. "Normally, I wouldn't pry, but since he and I comprise your legal team, I need to know if there's a volcano waiting to erupt. Is he okay with you shagging his wife?"

Jesse's crass question made Alex's relationship with Tyler seem dirty and superficial. It was anything but, and Alex took more offense for Tyler than herself. She sharpened her stare to make her next point crystal clear. "Tread lightly, Jesse. You have no idea what Tyler has been through nor how it's impacted her family. Ethan is a good man and has earned saint status. If you hurt him—"

Jesse raised a hand in a stopping motion. "First, I apologize for overstepping. Let's attribute it to the tequila. Second, I don't do one-night stands and have no intention of becoming his rebound. I genuinely like Ethan. Hurting him is the last thing I want."

"I'm glad you understand."

"You're my client, Alex. My primary duty is to you. If you have a problem with the possibility of Ethan and me, I'll apply the brakes."

"That's not my decision to make."

"Then what do you want, Alex?"

"For Ethan to be happy. He's earned it ten times over."

"Then I think we're on the same page."

CHAPTER TWENTY-FIVE

One shot too many, Ethan silently chided himself. Never dating a client was a cardinal rule in P.I. work, and his flirting with Jesse was the closest he'd ever come to mixing pleasure with business. Though who could blame him? He was divorcing. They were both on the young side, and any warm-blooded man or woman would classify her as cute as a button. But, beautiful or not, his client came first, and he had to remain smarter than his hormones. *No more drinking around Jesse until this case is over.*

Fortified by his newfound resolve, Ethan stepped out of the taxi below the gaudy yellow neon sign at Arthur's Alley, a sign bright enough to attract every moth on the island. The last time he was here, he had handed a lowlife bookie a cashier's check for a half-million dollars. The same bookie who'd sent a thug to look for Kelly's photos. The thug who'd shot Ethan in the damn leg and that he'd had to kill. Self-defense or not, taking someone's life was an awful thing.

He focused on the task ahead, reminding himself to keep it about business tonight. Victor Padula was a dangerous man and well-connected, with ties to organized crime in the city. The last thing Ethan needed to do tonight was to stir a hornet's nest. Again. *Well, maybe just a little stirring.*

He'd arrived early enough to do some scouting as he waited for Alex and Jesse. After taking a stroll up and down the block, he took a position several feet to the left of the entrance of Arthur's Alley, he searched for two things—signs of law enforcement surveillance, which could help his investigation, or signs of other mobsters, which could complicate it. What he found made it abundantly clear they should change their plans for the evening.

He tried calling Alex, but his call went to voice mail. Moments later, Jesse stepped onto the curb after exiting a taxi, looking ever so captivating in jeans and a leather jacket. "Sorry, I'm late. Tequila."

Her traffic-stopping smile made her tardiness of two minutes easy to forgive. "I should be the one apologizing for wasting your time."

"How's that?" she asked.

"See that flower delivery van across the street?" Ethan gestured a thumb in that direction. "Either the FBI or the NYPD are unimaginative."

"I'm not following."

"I checked it out earlier. It's a surveillance van, and it appears they've been there a while."

"How can you tell?"

"First, there's no flower shop on the block. The van shouldn't be here longer than it takes to make a delivery. Then there's the pile of cigarette butts outside the sliding door. They've been there for days, likely weeks." Ethan chuckled at the ineptitude. "My guess is that Victor Padula hit their radar after I was shot at Times Square. There's no way he got into Castle Resorts headquarters without being followed."

"So what now?" she asked.

"Talking to him would be a colossal waste of time. I'll check with my NYPD contact tomorrow. He should be able to rule Victor in or out as a suspect and even confirm Andrew's alibi about coming here." When Jesse shivered in the cold night air, he opened Arthur's weighty glass door. "Let's head inside and wait for Alex."

Ethan approached the host station and requested a table for three. The host led them through a hundred patrons cheering on the games and races of all sorts that were being displayed on large-screen televisions dispersed along each wall. The crowd clamored in waves, the sounds electrifying the well-lit dining room.

When the server came over, Ethan said to Jesse, "Their nachos are pretty good. Split?"

"Sure, why not?" She looked at the server and added, "And two waters."

Ethan's lack of experience with women in the last quarter-century made the wait awkward. He spent the first minute fumbling with the table condiments and the next adjusting his position on the wooden chair.

"This hot and cold thing really isn't my thing." Jesse's bold icebreaker virtually cut Ethan off at the knees. He felt like a bumbling teenager, unsure how to make the first move. But was that even a good idea? *Maybe*, he thought again.

"I don't mean to lead you on, but I'm rusty at this attraction thing," he said.

"So, you *are* attracted to me." Jesse cocked an eyebrow, clearly pleased that she'd cornered him into a near admission.

"I'd have to be blind if I weren't." His reflexive dodge meant that "rusty" was an understatement.

"You didn't answer the question."

Ethan leaned forward, enjoying her directness. "All right, counselor. Yes, I'm attracted to you."

"Yet you backpedaled at the hotel earlier."

"Like I said. I'm rusty."

"Rusty or gun shy?" She cocked the same eyebrow. If this was a preview of how she cross-examined witnesses on the stand, he had no doubt Alex wouldn't spend one more day behind bars.

"Nothing like cutting to the heart of the matter."

"Let me make this easy on you. I'm attracted to you," Jesse said without blinking an eye. "I'm divorced and well past the age of playing games. Alex gave me the third degree earlier and filled me in on the essentials. I know you are going through a divorce and that Alex's girlfriend is your soon-to-be ex-wife. She didn't elaborate on the details, other than she thinks you're a saint. She left me with the impression that if I broke your heart I'd have to answer to her."

"She did, huh?" Why was Alex so hard to hate? Every time he turned around, she did something that made him like her even more. She may have laid the groundwork for him needing to move on, but the greatest gift she gave him was making Tyler happier than he ever could.

"Alex has a powerful mama bear instinct." Jesse stirred the ice cubes in her water with a straw, perhaps her nervous tell. He got the impression that Alex made her more anxious than he did.

"When it comes to family, you bet I do." Alex slipped into the seat next to Ethan's right, giving him a rub on the shoulder as she passed.

"Did you get my voice mail about tonight?" Ethan rose briefly from his chair until Alex sat in hers, marveling at their convoluted family connection. Alex was his soon-to-be ex-wife's partner and his cousin's wife's sister. Both standings might seem distant to most, but he got the impression that Alex felt they were much closer. He did too.

"Sorry, I had my phone on silent," Alex said.

He explained about Victor's babysitters across the street. "I'm sorry, Alex. I feel like I'm failing you. You're depending on me to build an alternate theory in two days, and it looks like I've bungled it."

"We've had a long day. Let's regroup at your suite tomorrow." Alex's gentle rub to his forearm and her soft expression told him she still had faith in him. It was a level of blind trust Ethan felt he hadn't earned, but he appreciated it nonetheless.

"You're right." He blew out a long sigh. He was tired and was thin on leads. A good night's sleep would give him the focus he needed. His phone buzzed to a familiar, unique ringtone. "Tyler, is everything okay?"

"I got a call from Maddie about Erin. She's fine, but we need to talk." Worry cut through Tyler's voice. "Can you come over?"

"Alex and I will be right there."

Twenty minutes later, Alex led Ethan up the front stoop of her West Village townhouse. She pulled out her keys as she reached the top. "I hope nothing is seriously wrong with Erin."

"I'm sure it's just teenage stuff." Ethan downplayed his concern that the pending divorce had prompted his oldest to act out. "Just teenage stuff" was more of a hope than a certainty.

The moment Alex swung the door open, Callie barked and her claws scrabbled across the wood floor. The barking instantly stopped when Alex turned the corner and rubbed behind her pointy ears. "Hey, girl, settle down."

Tyler rose from the couch, her eyes on Ethan. "Thanks for coming over." Her expression gave the impression that whatever had happened to Erin had her concerned but not rattled.

"Anything for the girls," he said.

"I'll take Callie outside and give you two some privacy." Alex pecked Tyler on the cheek and then followed the sound of thumping paws down the interior stairs to the kitchen floor.

"You look tired." Tyler rubbed Ethan's forearm. "Can I get you anything to drink?"

"No, thanks. I'm fine." If Ethan wasn't one hundred percent sure that things were over between him and Tyler, he was now. She seemed right at home, offering him a drink. Deep down, he was happy for her, but it still stung. He gestured toward the couch. Once seated, the twenty-two years they'd spent as a couple made it easy for him to recognize the disappointment in Tyler's eyes. "What did she do?"

"Maddie surprised Erin with a homemade dinner tonight, and she said our house looked as if a bomb went off in it. And she thinks she smelled marijuana. I'm sure if we called the neighbors, they'd confirm she threw a blowout party last night."

Ethan snickered, recalling his own teenage years. "Do you know how many parties I threw when I was younger? I doubt the weed was hers, but we can have a talk with her."

"Aren't you concerned?"

"She's just blowing off steam. Both her parents are out of town, and we sent her little sister off to a friend. We essentially dumped a teenager's wet dream into her lap."

Tyler grimaced, covering her ears with her hands. "I don't want to think about our daughter having a wet dream."

Ethan rolled back on the couch, letting loose a full belly laugh. Tyler joined him. When the laughter died down, a comfortable silence replaced it. Ethan reached for Tyler's hand, which she accepted.

"Our girls are growing up," she said.

Ethan squeezed her hand tighter. "Yes, they are." He refused to fight it any longer and let tears brim his eyes. "I already miss the idea of being there every day for them."

Tyler shifted, turning toward him and releasing his hand. "I never meant to hurt you."

"I know you didn't, which makes this even harder." He sat up, hard realities bubbling to the surface. "I know you and Alex are getting closer, but have you thought about what comes next? Assuming she's cleared of the charges, it's not as if she can pack up her headquarters and move to Sacramento."

"I don't know, Ethan. It's impossible to focus on anything beyond the grand jury." Tyler ran a hand through her hair, her sign of frustration.

"Tell me this. Do you love each other?" Tyler's lip-biting nod told Ethan everything he needed to know. A devastating picture of his family's future suddenly took shape. Tyler would soon relocate, likely bringing Bree with her. Erin would move to Yale this summer, leaving him with nothing but the mortgage in Sacramento. He leaned forward, elbows on his knees, sucking in the gut punch. "Phew, this is harder than I thought it would be."

"We're still a family." Tyler rubbed his back in gentle circles, a touch that had always reassured him that no matter what went wrong, they had each other. That no longer held true, though.

He held Tyler's gaze, wishing for the way things used to be before the rape had irrevocably changed her. For a time when they had their entire lives still ahead of them. "I'm trying hard to believe that."

Tyler cupped Ethan's jaw in her hands. "Listen to me, Ethan Falling. We are a family, and I will always love you. Those things will never change."

"I love you, Tyler." Ethan pressed their foreheads together, hoping to hide his tears from her, but her closeness hastened them. She pulled back, using her thumbs to dry the tears that were refusing to stop. She then paused, radiating an enduring love, one that deserved one last kiss. He pressed their lips together, letting it linger longer than it should have, but neither of them fought it. The kiss wasn't one of passion but of love and respect, sealing the family bond that they would always have.

Tyler caressed Ethan's cheek before breaking the kiss. "You should be going." Movement to her left caught her eye. She turned to see Callie romping on the floor and Alex standing at the top of the stairs with tears rolling down her cheeks.

"Alex." Tyler rose to her feet.

Alex raised a hand in a stopping motion when Tyler took several unsteady steps toward her. "I can't do this, Tyler. You two obviously still have some things to figure out." She snatched up her purse from the entry table and left, taking Tyler's hope of a future together with her.

CHAPTER TWENTY-SIX

Numbed to her core, Alex latched onto the iron rail to steady her trip down the stoop. She hurried to the bottom step, refusing to stop when Tyler yelled her name from the front door. Stumbling to the sidewalk, she hailed a passing taxi.

"Where to?" the plump, stubble-faced cabbie barked.

"Just drive." Alex hadn't thought beyond putting distance between her and the heartbreak at the top of those stairs. Three city blocks worth of images of Tyler and Ethan and the love flowing between them gripped her tighter and tighter until she couldn't breathe. She'd been in love once before and been dumped for a man. That pain Kelly had caused her had broken her for years, and facing that it had happened again was beyond her capacity.

She rolled down the window to counter the suffocating, pine-freshener scent of the cabin. Crisp spring night air filled her lungs as deafening wails of a passing ambulance jolted her back to the present. Passing East Side street signs confirmed she'd been in a daze longer than she thought she had.

"Anywhere in particular, miss?" the driver asked again.

Only one location came to mind. "Upper East Side," she said in a firm tone before specifying the address.

Despite coming here regularly, it had been years since Alex had come without giving forewarning. But even if no one was there, she needed to be in the only other place where she felt at home. Keying in her personal code, she rode the elevator to the penthouse. Stepping inside the entry hall, she bypassed the unoccupied living room and entered the kitchen.

"Sarah." Alex waited for the Spencer housekeeper to turn around from her work of wrangling dirty dishes at the sink. "Is Harley here?"

"I'm sorry, Ms. Castle, but she's out for the evening." Sarah's eyes narrowed in apparent concern. "Are you all right, miss? Can I get you anything?"

"No, thank you. I'll be on my way." Of course, Harley would be out. Nocturnal by nature, she was likely at a trendy cocktail cathedral, chatting up a blonde or redhead with legs that went for days. Unsure where to go next, Alex pivoted to walk out.

"Sarah, I'm turning in for the—" Abby stopped in midstride. "Alex, what brings you out this time of night?"

"I needed to see Harley, but I should've called ahead."

"That woman doesn't know the meaning of a quiet night at home." Abby placed her teacup on the kitchen island before rubbing Alex's arms. "You look upset, dear." When Alex's lips trembled at the thought of having lost Tyler, Abby wrapped an arm around her shoulder, setting off an avalanche of sobs. "Let's go into the library."

Tears blurred her steps down the hallway. She'd had too much loss in her life recently—first the estrangement with Andrew, then the death of her father, and now Tyler. However, the juxtaposition of those last two events hurt most. She'd wasted a lifetime loving a man who didn't deserve it, and at the same time, she'd waited a lifetime for a woman who did. Now, she'd lost both with nothing to show for it.

The minute she stepped into the library, its warmth consoled her. This was her favorite room in the world, not for its dark cherrywood accents or luxurious furnishings, but for the memories it evoked. This was the last place where she'd played and giggled with her mother. And following her mother's death, this was the place where Abby made her feel like she had another mother in her.

Alex sat at the end of the cream leather couch, staring at the orange glow from the fireplace. Flickering flames had thoroughly burned the logs, leaving a mixed pile of ash and charred wood. She felt just as burned, with nothing in her life left untouched by heartache or grief or doubt.

Abby handed her a glass of red wine before sitting beside her. "Talk to me, dear."

"I've lost her, Abby." Alex paused when Abby squeezed a hand. "But what hurts the most is that I probably never had her."

"Why would you think that about Tyler?"

"She still loves Ethan, and he still loves her. I heard them say as much to each other. Then"—Alex placed the wineglass on the end table then and buried her face in her hands—"they kissed."

"I'm so sorry you're hurting." Abby paused for several beats. "But…"

When she didn't continue, Alex looked up, her broken heart gravitating toward any glimmer of hope. "But what?"

"You didn't see her after the police took you away. She was frantic, unable to eat or sleep. The poor thing told me a bit about her past. Trust me when I say you had her. Tyler loves you, of that, I am sure. But letting go of a marriage, especially one as long as hers, is never easy. They share children and a lifetime of memories. And making it more difficult is the fact that neither of them is at fault for the breakup. I'm sure she will always love him, but not the way she loves you."

"I want to believe that, but the kiss makes me think otherwise."

"I agree the kiss is concerning, but before you give up on the love of your life, I suggest you first find out what it meant to her."

"I know you're right, but I have so much going on right now, Abby. I feel if I don't receive the explanation I need, it might break me. I can't take it, at least not tonight."

"Then stay the night. Get your bearings." Abby slung an arm over her shoulder when Alex slumped back on the couch, staring into the fire. "Tomorrow, you can get answers."

"I think I *will* stay." Buoyed by Abby's silent comfort and support, Alex decided she needed to resolve one nagging doubt. "May I ask you something, Abby?"

"Of course. Anything."

"Do you have the Christmas present I gave to Harley?"

"The beautiful Hermes scarf? My daughter's lack of taste is my gain."

Alex shifted on the couch to look Abby in the eyes again. "Ethan showed me a picture of a woman arguing with Father in the lobby of his building not long before his death. The police aren't interested in her because she left after that, but Ethan considers her a possible witness or a suspect. Her face was obscured but she was wearing a scarf. One just like Harley's scarf. Why didn't you tell me you were there that night?"

Abby released a long breathy sigh. "I could say it was because you had so much on your plate after your father was killed, but the truth is that I felt guilty because I made things worse between you and him."

"What do you mean? What were you two arguing about?" Alex asked.

"You. I was defending you."

"Against what? Did you know what he had planned?"

"Not exactly, but I'd pieced it together after a call from Gretchen. I've known that woman for eighteen years, and not once had she betrayed your father's confidence. But she chose sides that day; she was concerned about you. She told me of William's visit to Robert's office and the short-notice meeting of the company officers he'd called to implement some big change."

"Gretchen called you? But why?" Alex was stunned. The closest Gretchen ever had come to telegraphing her father's private business to Alex was a silent nod or concerned facial expression. Something her father had said to her must have given her great concern.

"Yes, dear. You weren't there to defend yourself, but she knew I would do it on your behalf. So, I went to your father's office to plead your case, but my history with your mother set him off. He said so many vile things about you and me, getting more and more worked up. I'm so sorry that I made things worse for you."

"Gretchen is full of surprises. I'll have to thank her, but Father had made up his mind. There was nothing you could've said or done to make it better or worse for me, but thank you for trying."

CHAPTER TWENTY-SEVEN

Slobbery, wet dog kisses woke Tyler to a jolting reality—Alex's side of the bed was cold and empty. The soft light of sunrise filling the window signaled that she had been gone all night, making her heart sink lower than it had the moment Alex ran out after that stupid kiss. Tyler rubbed Callie behind the ear to make her stop licking her long enough to check her cell phone. Alex hadn't answered even one of Tyler's half-dozen calls and text messages. She shook off the pain she felt; she was done crying. Before her head hit the pillow last night, she decided that the only thing she could do was to trust in the love she felt from Alex. Trust that she'd come back to hear her out.

A persistent wagging tail signaled that more sleep would have to wait. Tyler scratched Callie again behind both ears. "Do you need to go potty, girl?" Callie sprang from the bed.

Outside in Alex's courtyard garden in the chilly dawn air, Tyler clutched her sweater. Watching Callie sniff every plant and bush, she mentally inventoried what she wanted to say to Alex when she finally returned. Tyler could tell her that the kiss was merely a final goodbye, of course, and meant nothing more, but that wouldn't be the whole truth. It had also been a confirmation that the life she and Ethan had built still held meaning.

She decided that Alex should know the most profound truth about last night—that no kiss she and Ethan ever shared came close to the way Alex could curl her toes. Before they'd pressed their lips together for the first time six weeks ago, Tyler had never imagined a single kiss could simultaneously fulfill every fantasy she had and spark new ones. Every touch from Alex made her feel desired and, most importantly, safe. As hard as Ethan had tried and as much as Tyler had wanted it to be so, that was something he could never do for her.

"She'll come back."

Tyler glanced over her shoulder in the voice's direction. Syd was gripping a heavy cardigan tight around her torso.

"But will she believe me?" Merely posing the question pained Tyler.

"Kissing your ex in Alex's home wasn't your finest moment, but after you explained it to me, I can understand it. I'm sure Alex will too."

"I hope so."

"Give her time." Syd maneuvered herself into a patio chair. "She's been in love only once before and was badly burned by it. She'll figure out eventually that you're nothing like that hussy, Kelly Thatcher, and will come running back to you."

"Well, I'm not sure if I can wait that long." Tyler hadn't considered the Kelly angle. Kelly had left Alex for a man, and Tyler realized now that Alex likely feared that she had done the same. Perhaps waiting for Alex to come to her senses wasn't the right tack. "Where do you think Alex might be?"

"My guess is that she spent the night in the owner's suite."

"Of course. Do you mind feeding Callie? I need to find Alex."

Armed with the owner's suite room number and a burst of can't-wait certitude, Tyler kissed Syd on the cheek and hailed the first passing taxi. Her confidence steadily built through each traffic light until the cabbie pulled up to the curb of Castle Resorts Times Square. Tyler hadn't planned past duplicating their first kiss to convince Alex that she was in love with only her, but that would have to be enough.

Tyler stood at the door of the suite, summoning the courage to face the consequences if her spur-of-the-moment plan didn't work. The lonesome bed she'd slept in last night was a chilling reminder she had nothing more to lose. Tyler knocked and waited. After a minute, when no one answered, she knocked again and tried the door handle, this time not caring if she acted the fool. "Alex," she said loudly into the door. "I know you're hurt, but you have to know that you're the only one I love and want to kiss. I'll stay here for as long as it takes to convince you that you're the one I want to grow old with."

"Excuse me, miss." Glancing over her shoulder toward the voice, Tyler discovered a jolly-looking housekeeper with the cutest round glasses and dimpled cheeks. The woman brought her cleaning cart to a stop near the door, which seemed to be locked tighter than Fort Knox. "May I help you?" the housekeeper asked.

"I need to speak to Alex Castle. Do you know if she's in there?"

"I'm sorry, miss, but I can't give out the information."

Tyler wasn't about to walk away empty-handed, not without giving it her all. A boldness, likely ill-advised, swelled in her. She glanced at the woman's name tag. "Shayna, have you ever met someone that you knew you were meant to be together with from the first hello?" Tyler didn't wait for a response. "Well, that's how it was for Alex and me. From the moment I first saw her, she turned my life upside down. And now, because of a stupid kiss goodbye from a man I'd spent twenty-two years with, raising two beautiful girls, I may lose her."

The housekeeper looked down both ends of the hallway as if searching for a means of escape. Tyler couldn't blame her. She'd just bared her broken heart to a stranger, and based on the maid's reticent posture, she had likely come across as a nutcase.

"You must think I'm crazy, and I am. Crazy in love with Alex Castle. But she thinks I'm still in love with my ex-husband, and that couldn't be further from the truth. I need her to know that it was all a misunderstanding. I need her to come home, back to our bed, so I can show her how much I love her."

"You make it sound like a fairytale."

"It is, and all I'm asking for is a chance to make things right."

The woman scanned the hallway again. Finally, she leaned in as if she was about to reveal the riddle of the Sphinx. "I'm not supposed to give out information, but I can tell you that Ms. Castle didn't spend the night here. The owner's suite hasn't been used in months."

Those words punctured Tyler's hope. She slumped against the door, feeling the weight of last night's misstep anew. "Thank you, Shayna. I appreciate the information."

Tyler retraced her steps toward the elevator, her legs feeling ten times heavier than when she'd arrived and her heart thumping hollowly in her chest. When her phone buzzed to an incoming text message, she swiped the phone open, hands shaking, hoping to see Alex's name, only to be dropped to earth with the force of a two-ton anvil. Ethan had sent a friendly reminder. *Who is picking up Erin at LaGuardia on Friday? Her tour of Yale is this Saturday.*

"Dammit." Tyler felt like the worst mother in the world. She'd been so wrapped up in Alex's grief and legal problems and their burgeoning love affair that she'd forgotten about the most important trip of her daughter's life. She rubbed her temples. "I'm a horrible mom."

She'd started the morning with an abundance of optimism and determination, but so far virtually every facet of her life was turning out to be a bust. Until Alex reappeared, she needed to repair those things she could, starting with a face-to-face.

Six floors down, Tyler knocked on the door. It swung open moments later. "Wow," Ethan said. "That was quick, but you didn't have to come over. A text would've been enough."

He appeared well-rested after last night's debacle. He'd ditched his casual golf attire for his favorite dark blue dress pants, white button-down shirt, and navy blue and white dotted jacquard tie—Tyler's favorite combination on him. *He must want to make an impression today*, she thought.

"I know, but I was upstairs looking for Alex when you texted. May I come in?"

"Sure." He let her step into the living area of the elegant suite. "Alex never came home last night?"

"No, she didn't." Tyler sat on the couch, resisting the powerful urge to fall apart.

"I'm so sorry, Tyler. It was wrong to kiss you. I didn't mean to mess things up with you and Alex."

"You were hurting. I wouldn't have let you kiss me if I didn't know what it meant to you. So don't apologize for saying goodbye." She briefly rested a hand atop his. "I may have to do some repair work, but Alex and I will be fine once she's had time to think."

"If there's anything I can do to patch things up, please let me know."

"Enough about Alex. Let's talk about Erin. I know you're busy with the case, so I'm happy to pick her up if we can't go to the airport together. Is the plan still for her to stay in the suite with you?"

Ethan nodded. "That's why Alex set me up with a two-bedroom suite. But I was thinking. Why don't we fly Bree out too? You could use a little time with both your girls."

"I think you're right as usual. I do miss them." Tyler paused for a few moments, considering the implication of Erin and Alex being in the same room together. "You know Erin hates Alex."

"I don't think she hates her. She just blames her for our divorce. I tried to set her straight before I left."

"You're a great dad, you know that?"

A knock on the door sounded. As Ethan walked to answer it, he said in a playful tone, "Yes, I am." He pulled the door open. Jesse was smartly dressed, looking very lawyerly and juggling a small bag in one hand and a tray of two drinks in the other.

"Please tell me that's coffee," Ethan said with a level of glee in his voice Tyler hadn't heard in a while.

"And scones." Jesse proudly displayed the bag of goodies. When Ethan gestured for her to enter, she took two steps before stopping and stiffening. "Tyler? Good morning." She placed the food and drink on the coffee table and redirected her attention to Ethan. "I can see you weren't expecting me this early. Why don't I wait for you downstairs in the lobby?"

If Tyler read Jesse's expression correctly, she wasn't merely acting polite. She was disappointed. And Ethan's nervous thumbing of the belt around his waist solved the mystery of whom he had intended to impress today. Surprisingly, the idea of these two as a couple made Tyler happy.

"No need to go, Jesse. I was just leaving. I can't thank you enough for everything you're doing to help Alex. She means the world to me, as does Ethan. You take good care of him, now." Tyler gave Jesse a sly wink and grabbed her purse.

"Let me walk you out." Ethan followed Tyler to the door. "I'll make the arrangements for both girls to take the red-eye here, arriving Friday morning."

"Thank you, Ethan. I can't wait to see them."

"Now, go find Alex. You two belong together."

"I will." Tyler leaned in and gave Ethan a quick peck on the cheek. She glanced back toward Jesse, who still appeared uncomfortable. "I think she has the wrong impression about what happened here. You better go explain things."

Ethan formed the kind of smile that said he was genuinely happy. "I'm glad things aren't weird between us anymore. I consider you to be my best friend."

"Me too." Tyler gave him one more peck on the cheek. "Go get her, tiger."

Playing matchmaker had reenergized Tyler. Walking down the hallway, she formulated the bones of Plan B to get Alex back. She dialed her cell phone. "Syd, Alex wasn't there. I need your help."

"I don't know, Tyler. This is between you and Alex."

"And I respect your reluctance, but she might answer a call from you. All I need is for you to ask her to meet me at the resort. But before you do that, can you talk to the hotel manager and…"

CHAPTER TWENTY-EIGHT

The clanging melody of UB40's "Red Red Wine" jolted Alex out of a deep sleep, bringing into focus some of last night's poor choices—too much of said wine and too much silliness with ringtones after Harley returned home. Harley's playfulness, though, had worked its magic and lifted Alex from her funk, erasing any lingering doubts she had about Tyler.

Temples throbbing, Alex blindly patted the top of the nightstand until a hand hit her cell phone. She flipped it open and put it to her ear. "What, Syd?"

"Do you think you've tortured Tyler enough?"

Alex rolled onto her back, hoping to find the proper position to ease her mild hangover. "Did she tell you what happened?"

"She did."

"So you know why I was upset."

"I do."

"I hate it when you do that."

"Do what?"

"Answer me in two-word sentences."

"You disappoint me."

"Three words. That's progress."

"Will you stop that?" Syd's edgy tone meant their teasing was over. "Tyler was worried sick about you all night. She wants to talk."

"I didn't mean to worry her, but I needed time to think. I'll talk to her in the morning."

"It is morning."

"What?" Alex sprung her eyes open. Sunlight confirmed she was the worst girlfriend ever. She jumped out of bed, adrenaline winning the hangover battle. "What time is it?"

"Almost nine."

"Shit. Tyler must be frantic." Alex held the phone to her chin and slipped on her jeans. "I'm coming home now."

"Don't bother."

"No, no, no, no, no. She must think I hate her." Alex's heart hammered with regret. She questioned every decision she'd made since seeing that ghastly kiss, from leaving to not calling to drinking an entire bottle of Barnette's best. She could blame it on her inexperience in love, but that wasn't why she walked away. She was afraid to hear the truth, unable to take on any more disappointment. Abby and Harley had knocked some sense into her, but Alex had foolishly let Harley drag her into acting like drunk college kids. Unwinding like that was needed after the events of the last few days, but she should have taxied home and trusted that Tyler's explanation would have been what she needed to hear. Now she was too late. Tyler was gone.

Alex threw the phone down and jammed a shirt over her head before snatching it again. "I have to find her, Syd. Did she fly back to Sacramento?"

"She didn't."

"You're torturing me with two-word responses. Where the hell is she?"

"Your hotel."

"Finally, two helpful words." Alex slipped on a sneaker and then the other. "I'm on my way."

"Hold your horses, Baby Sis."

"Did she go back to Ethan?"

"Will you stop jumping to the worst conclusions? Tyler's been desperate to see you since the moment you walked out. She wants to meet you in the ballroom."

An unshakable grin formed on Alex's lips. Every muscle relaxed as the weight of her stupidity lifted. "Thank you, Syd."

Following the slowest cab ride of her life, Alex flew through the automated sliding glass doors of Castle Resort, past the lobby, and down the recently renovated corridor leading to the conference rooms. She came to a screeching halt at the ballroom door, pausing to catch her breath and gather her thoughts. She'd never been in a situation like this before and was unsure of an approach.

Business was so much easier. Alex instinctively knew what to do in every situation at work by following the two simple tenets her father had passed down to her—showing weakness was a death knell and showing compassion was to be reserved for garnering future leverage. But Tyler was not a competitor over whom she needed to gain the upper hand. Tyler was instead her lover, her partner, and, if Alex could someday persuade her, her future wife.

She tentatively pushed the door open, deciding to follow her heart. The silver- and gold-accented ballroom lights were dimly lit, casting a romantic glow. The slow beat of Van Morrison's "Someone Like You" was playing over the room's sound system—just as it had been during their first kiss. The lyrics conveyed that Alex wasn't the only one whose soul-searching had led her here, hoping to find someone who could make all her choices worthwhile. That Tyler, too, had carried a heavy load, hoping for someone like Alex to come into her life.

Tyler was in the center of the dance floor, standing beneath the grand chandelier. Jeans and a blue camp shirt had never looked more beautiful. The fatalistic fears and imaginary worries of the previous night faded into the woodwork the moment Tyler smiled. Without the weight of doubt, Alex glided toward Tyler, her heart stuttering with anticipation. Tyler reeled her in with each delicious curve, making each step effortless.

Alex drew close, stopping when the warmth of Tyler's breath mixed with hers. The love in her eyes spoke all the words that needed saying. They said that Tyler was hers, last night, now, and always. That once Tyler loved, she loved forever. That nothing, except Alex's own boneheadedness, could tear them apart.

Alex had nearly destroyed everything they'd built with her insecurities, but Tyler's eyes rebuilt it now, brick by brick. Alex cupped Tyler's cheeks with both hands, kicking herself for ever doubting this woman. For thinking that Tyler's love wasn't strong enough to withstand the pull of history and familiarity.

The reason that brought them to the ballroom no longer mattered. But the fact that Tyler chose this place in which to make her grand gesture did. This was the place Alex had selected for their first magical kiss. It was where they began and where they would begin again.

Alex whispered the one word that encompassed her relief, love, gratitude, and trust. "T." She pressed their lips together, leaving yesterday behind. No regret, only love.

Tyler's body trembled. Quivering lips and sharp, rapid intakes of air conveyed her unnecessary apology. There was nothing to forgive. Alex understood now and trusted that last night had been Tyler and Ethan's final goodbye. That this kiss, reaching deep inside her, was between soulmates.

Alex broke the kiss but didn't pull back. "Shhhhh." She kissed Tyler again, this time deeper, with the same passion that had filled their very first kiss. Her hands dropped to Tyler's torso, pulling her closer until she felt her drumming heartbeat. Tyler matched every caress, touch, and squeeze. Moans replaced tremors when Alex sent her tongue searching to begin a slow, sensual dance with Tyler's.

Nothing mattered except how Tyler made Alex feel loved and wanted. Not Ethan. Not her thieving brother. Not her father's death. Not the downward spiral of Castle Resorts. And not the charges hanging over her head. Alex could survive all of that ten times over with Tyler by her side.

Alex broke their second kiss. So many words needed saying, but before Alex could get out a single syllable, Tyler placed an index finger over her lips and tugged on Alex's hand, leading her out the double doors into the bright hallway lights. Silently, Tyler guided Alex toward the lobby, stopping at the bank of elevators. When the door swooshed open, Tyler pressed twenty on her way to the back of the car. That meant only one destination.

When the door closed, Alex and Tyler were alone again. Alone except for the control panel camera, that is. Alex leaned Tyler against the wall panel, positioning herself between Tyler and the intrusive lens. Placing a palm on either side of her head and pressing a knee between her legs, Alex fed on their silence, preferring to let her eyes say the words that were screaming to come out. Needing to do so didn't feel like a constraint. In fact, it felt downright sexy.

Hot as fuck.

Instead of listening to her lips, which were aching for another kiss, Alex raised her knee a fraction, eliciting the reaction she wanted. Tyler's eyes closed, her lips parted, and her chest rose as she took a slow, deep breath. They continued the ride up in silence, with Alex lifting and lowering her knee in an unhurried rhythm. Never had she been so brazen in public and her place of business, but she didn't care. In fact, it was about damn time.

When the elevator bounced to a stop, Alex stepped back, a sexual tsunami cresting between them. She grabbed Tyler's hand and led her to the owner's suite door. Tyler stopped Alex when she'd raised her free hand to enter the security code on the panel above the handle. She pulled a key card from her back pocket, inserted it into the slot, and pushed the door open. Soft music, dim lights, and a glowing fireplace created the picture of romance. Unquestionably, Tyler's grand gesture had many layers.

Romantic as hell.

Steps inside, champagne and orange juice were on ice atop the bar. *She thought of everything.* Tyler approached the bar and lifted the champagne, but Alex rested a hand atop hers and gave her a firm negative headshake before she could pour. Beside the fact that she was nursing a mild hangover from last night, Alex wanted a clear head for what Tyler had in store and for all the things she wanted to do to her.

Tyler returned the bottle to the bar before wrapping an arm around Alex's waist and jutting her chin toward the bedroom.

Alex let a smile gradually form and gestured for her to lead the way. No matter what came next, if this was the way Tyler made up after every argument or misunderstanding, Alex might have to feign a squabble every now and again.

The bed had been turned down, and the lights were set to the same romantic level as those in the main room. The absence of rose petals on the bed was a relief. Besides bordering on cheesy, they'd only get in the way.

Surprisingly, Alex's heartbeat was remaining steady. With sex a foregone conclusion the moment she stepped through the ballroom door, everything up to this point was about seduction. And Tyler had charmed her with the magical equivalent of Paris in the spring.

At the foot of the bed, Alex removed Tyler's camp shirt and jeans, and Tyler obliged by doing the same to her thin T-shirt and slacks. It took only one night of fearing she'd never again know the smoothness or sweet taste of Tyler's skin for it to acquire a more irresistible allure than it had yesterday. Alex slowly ran her hands down each of Tyler's arms, starting from the shoulders. Her fingertips glided as if stroking the world's finest velvet, but Tyler's skin was much more desirable. Anyone in the world could possess the precious fabric, but every one of the curves and lines standing before Alex existed only for her. Of that she was sure now and would never doubt again.

Disposing of their remaining garments, Alex guided Tyler to the bed and laid her body atop hers. Skin to skin. Gazes locked. Alex's heart and body belonged to the woman beneath her. For the next hour, without exchanging a single word, Alex showed the depth of her love for Tyler, and Tyler did the same. By the time Alex lay sated with Tyler in her arms, she was more sure than ever that they would face whatever the world threw at them, hand in hand, and grow old together. Until a court of law decided her future, however, commitments would have to wait.

Tyler squeezed Alex's arms tighter around her. "I love only you, Alex."

"I feel it in my bones." Alex released her hold and nudged Tyler to shift until they faced each other. "I've let myself love only once before, and that ended in disaster. Then, last night, when I thought I'd lost you to Ethan, the hurt I'd felt before came flooding back. I now know you're nothing like her."

"I'll never hurt you like that." The disappointment in Tyler's eyes spoke the truth behind her words.

"I want to take you somewhere special." Alex snuggled a little closer.

"Can you leave while you're on bail?"

"Jesse said I have no restrictions, but Abby's beach house is in-state. It's been special to me since I was a little girl. If everything goes well after the grand jury tomorrow, we can leave right after the hearing. Please say yes."

"I'd love to, but my girls fly out on Friday morning."

"The house has plenty of rooms. I'm sure Abby would love it if we filled it with family for a long weekend."

"That would mean Ethan popping by too. Erin has her orientation at Yale this Saturday."

Alex entwined her legs with Tyler's and snuggled closer. "Yale would only be two hours away by car ferry. Please believe me when I say that Ethan is welcome too. He is your family, and I trust both of you."

"Thank you." Tyler's smile meant all was forgiven and that their trust had been restored.

"Has Erin found a sponsor to tour her around campus?"

"Not yet. The orientation letter said if she didn't line one up herself, the school would assign one."

"Nonsense. She'll have four alumni at her disposal. Harley, Abby, and Indra all have to be up there to dedicate a new art building, and Harley detests all the stuffy handshaking at those events. So touring Erin around would be a welcome distraction. I'm sure she would do it. But if you think it wouldn't be too awkward, I'd love to be Erin's sponsor."

"This could turn out to be a great weekend." Tyler snuggled even closer.

Alex hugged her tightly. "I hope so, T. I hope so."

CHAPTER TWENTY-NINE

Ethan and Jesse worked for hours in the hotel suite, painstakingly reviewing surveillance video from the office building and the jewelry store across the street. He'd hoped to find something, anything beyond Andrew on a motorcycle, that would give them another lead. Unfortunately, the only thing he'd discovered was that he was too old for sitting on a couch staring at a computer screen for hours without a break. His legs felt like he'd jammed himself into a Yugo for a cross-country drive. Even worse, his vision was blurred more than it had been the night of his bachelor party.

Time was running out. The New York City Grand Jury, notorious for rubberstamping whatever the DA laid at their feet, would meet the following day. An indictment wasn't Ethan's primary concern, but, like for Jesse, the required bail hearing that followed an indictment was. Someone with powerful influence in the city, likely Jesse's father, was pulling strings to make life as difficult for Alex as possible.

"This is getting us nowhere." Ethan's best two suspects, Andrew and Victor, were likely dead ends, which meant he was losing the race against the clock to keep Alex out of jail. He slammed his laptop shut and snapped up to a standing position, groaning and limping his way to the linen-covered dining table-for-two that room service had wheeled in not long after Jesse had arrived. The half-eaten pancakes sitting beside half-empty glasses of orange juice had long since lost their appeal. "Think, Falling, think," he chastised himself.

"Don't be so hard on yourself. You've done so much in just two days. You've already established that Andrew was there and that there are two cameras."

"But there are still two shadowy figures in the east stairwell after Alex left that I can't account for." Ethan paced around the room, unable to see any more straws of hope to grab onto. "The building gets too much foot traffic with that damn gym. I'll be tracking down potential leads for weeks."

"At a minimum, we have plenty to throw at the DA's case to cast reasonable doubt when this goes to trial."

"I'm trying to ensure that her case never gets that far. Alex can't spend another day in jail. It would break her."

"Alex's a strong woman."

Ethan stopped pacing. There was more at stake than Alex Castle. "Not her. Tyler."

Jesse's face went slack. Her deep sigh meant Ethan had blown it. *Falling, you idiot!* The record needed to be set straight, so he sat on the couch next to her. "Jesse, Tyler may be my soon-to-be ex-wife, but she's also my best friend. You have no idea what she's been through, and I can't stand seeing her hurt again."

"It's obvious you still love her."

"Of course, I love her, but not as a wife or a lover. We're family. We've shared our lives for over twenty years and are raising two incredible girls together. We'll always be connected." Jesse's long, hard swallow meant he had some convincing to do yet. "But we don't make each other happy the way couples should. Alex does that in a way for her that I never could."

"Did she ever make you happy like that?"

"A long time ago, but then something happened to her, and she changed. I loved her, so I just accepted it. It was only last month that she came to terms with what happened and we both realized we were much better off as parents and friends than husband and wife."

"Are you comfortable telling me what happened to her?"

Now it was Ethan's turn to swallow hard. He choked on the unchangeable fact that he'd failed Tyler. He had been so wrapped up in his job of protecting others that he'd forgotten the most important job of all—protecting his wife and family. He should have been more observant, more vigilant regarding someone he loved.

His voice cracked. "She was brutally raped." He paused when Jesse closed her eyes and stiffened her lips at the unthinkable. "I should have recognized that Tyler hadn't fully dealt with the trauma. But once she met Alex, everything changed. She saw a therapist and finally accepted that she was no longer attracted to men, including me. I'm actually grateful that Alex came along. Tyler deserves to be happy. That's one of the reasons I refuse to give up on this case. I'd never forgive myself if I missed something that could clear Alex."

Jesse placed a hand on Ethan's. "I'm so sorry you and Tyler had to go through that. You're an amazing man, Ethan Falling." The look in her eyes begged for more closeness.

Forget professionalism. Forget his raw heart. Ethan slowly leaned forward, inching his lips closer and closer to hers. She did the same. His heart pounded. Tyler was the only woman he'd kissed since college. *Do I even remember how to do this?*

Ethan hovered, their lips inches apart. Before the question of his readiness was answered, though, his cell phone rang on the nearby coffee table. He slowly pulled back, thankful for the opportunity to regroup. He smiled and whispered, "I better get that."

"Yeah," Jesse whispered. She gradually withdrew before falling back to her seat.

Ethan flipped his phone open and brought it to his ear without breaking eye contact with Jesse. "Falling."

"Ethan, it's Jimmy. I got what you asked for. Can you meet me at the Blue Star Diner in an hour?"

"Sure thing, Jimmy. I appreciate you getting back to me so fast." Ethan wrapped up his call, slipping the phone into his suit pocket. "My NYPD contact has the FBI report of the surveillance at Arthur's Alley." He handed Jesse the room service menu. "Order lunch for yourself while I'm gone. I'm not sure how long I'll be." A break was exactly what he needed to clear his head and figure out if he was ready to finally move on.

Ethan entered the Blue Star Diner, the place that NYPD lieutenant Jimmy Stoval had suggested they meet. Their three-year-long friendship had begun when a Manhattan drug case had led Jimmy to Sacramento. They had paired up to turn a key witness, convincing him to testify and bring down one of New York's largest heroin trafficking rings. It had earned Jimmy a sweet promotion. Ethan hoped that bar on his uniform collar and the extra money in his paycheck meant all the favors he'd been asking of Jimmy since meeting Alex Castle hadn't put an end to that friendship.

Ethan felt right at home in the diner among the men and women in blue and plainclothes detectives. Located one block from the Nineteenth Precinct, the Blue Star was a quintessential 1970's-era New York diner. Out front a faded dark blue awning hung over a wall of plate-glass windows; the interior was just as formulaic. A glass case filled with desserts sat beside the front register, a long counter and stools guarded the kitchen, and a black and white checkerboard floor led to a wall of tiny, worn booths with torn vinyl seats.

Arriving early was Ethan's trademark. He took a seat at the counter, where two neighboring stools sat empty. He scanned the lunch menu and ordered a burger and soda.

A moment after he dug into his food, Jimmy plopped down on the stool next to him, giving the server behind the counter a quick nod. "This is becoming a habit. You California slugs can't do your own legwork anymore?"

"Every now and then, we have to throw you New Yorkers a bone." Ethan gave his friend a firm handshake. "Good to see you, Jimmy."

"Glad to see you walking again, buddy."

"You and me both."

Jimmy scanned the nearby crowd as if sizing up who was within earshot. He lowered his voice. "Word has it that some heavy hitters have a hard-on to convict Alex Castle. If they find out I had a hand in torpedoing the case, I could end up patrolling in Staten Island." Jimmy placed a folded piece of paper on the counter and slid it to his right.

"You know me better than that. We have each other's backs." Ethan picked it up and glanced at the fax, a report on official FBI letterhead that contained dates, times, and subject identifier numbers, but no names. He would need a translation. Jimmy obliged.

"Padula met William Castle at the Key Grill around five, went to Arthur's Alley at seven, and was there until midnight."

"And Andrew Castle?"

"He arrived at the club around eight forty-five and left at ten." Jimmy had confirmed what Ethan already knew in his gut—he'd spent the last two-and-a-half days chasing ghosts.

"Thanks, Jimmy." Now out of suspects, Ethan rubbed a hand down his face, dreading having to start over. The only saving grace evidence-wise was the camera. They needed to find that. The server slid a plate and a glass of water over the counter to Jimmy. "They read minds here?"

Jimmy shrugged his shoulders. "Everyone knows it's hot pastrami day." He looked at Ethan's burger and snickered. "Tourist."

"Maybe not for long. I've been thinking about making some changes. You know Erin starts Yale this fall."

Jimmy let out a whistle. "How in the hell can you afford that?"

"Full ride."

Jimmy whistled again. "Obviously, she takes after her mother."

Ethan picked up his soda and raised it in acknowledgment. "You got that right."

Jimmy clinked his glass with Ethan's. "You should know that investigators have been combing through the company financials. They're close to making an embezzlement case against the son."

"What put them on to him?" Ethan saw this coming the moment Alex asked for his help. Every bit of William Castle's personal and business dealings would be under the microscope. He hoped that none of their dealings with Padula, including Alex repaying what Andrew had stolen, would come back to bite her.

"The guy you shot last month. He was tied to Victor Padula, and the son is tied to Victor." Jimmy cocked his smile up on one side and chuckled. "V.P. Construction wasn't much of an imaginative name for a shell company."

Ethan raised his glass again. "I guess not." As much as he disliked Alex's miserable twin, he couldn't let on that he knew all about Andrew's scheme. Doing so would only point the finger at Alex as well as Andrew and hand the DA another motive on a silver platter.

An hour later, Ethan strolled back into the lobby of Castle Resorts Times Square. As he made his way to the bank of elevators, the desk clerk who had delivered his printer the other day caught his attention. "Mr. Falling, a package was messengered over for you." He handed Ethan a small sealed manilla envelope with the return address of Kaplan Jewelers written in the upper left corner.

"Thank you." Ethan's mood perked up when he opened the envelope and read the attached note. The enclosed flash stick, it said, contained the video the jewelry store owner had collected from other businesses surrounding the Castle Resorts headquarters. He hadn't thought Mr. Kaplan would come through. Having more video opened the door for more leads.

Stepping off the elevator, Ethan walked with extra pep. His gut told him two things: the video in his hand could be the key to clearing Alex and that near-kiss earlier in his suite was the sign he was ready to move on. He opened the door to his suite to the cutest sight—Jesse devouring a burger and fries on the comfort of the couch.

She looked up, dabbing each corner of her mouth with a cloth napkin. "Get what you need?"

"And much more. Victor and Andrew are a bust." A smile grew on his lips when he held up the flash stick. "But thank goodness Alex is a kind and valued jewelry customer. I asked the store owner to canvass the other businesses on the block, knowing he'd have better luck than I would, and he came through."

Jesse pushed her plate to the side so Ethan could move his laptop front and center on the coffee table. "This is great news."

Ethan sat close to her on the couch, their thighs nearly touching. He inserted the stick into a side port on his laptop and found four files, each one labeled with the name of one of the neighboring businesses that had views of the streets surrounding the Castle Resorts corner building. If they were lucky, one of these recordings would provide a previously unseen viewpoint.

He opened the first of the four video files, reviewing it at triple speed for the hours leading up to and immediately following William's presumed time of death. An hour of intense focus strained Ethan's eyes once again, but only to the equivalent of the effects of a three-tequila night.

While Jesse took a quick break to call her office, he plowed through the fourth and final video. The footage represented the furthest distance from the Castle Resorts building and provided more of the same—the occasional coming and going of people and cars. When the tape reached a timestamp of nine thirty-five p.m., after Alex had left, Ethan tracked a person dressed in athletic gear, hat, and dark glasses walking across the street away from the building. Once on the sidewalk closest to the camera, the shadowy figure stopped to remove the cap and glasses, stepping under a streetlight and briefly revealing their face before they left the area.

"Holy shit." He wiped spritz of Coke from his shirt. Then, like a bloodhound onto a scent, he paused the video and searched his hard drive for the few viable interior video files from the Castle Resorts building. He opened the elevator recordings and fast-forwarded until he came to the approximate timestamp he was looking for.

Jesse returned to the couch.

"There, there! See? That's the same hat and glasses boarding the elevator with Alex." Ethan jotted down the exact timestamp and then fast-forwarded until he spotted the same person in the elevator again, leaving about fifteen minutes after Alex left. Jesse leaned in to get an up-close view of the video and studied the figure on the screen. "There, again," he said.

"Okay. They got on the elevator in the lobby and exited on the twentieth floor. Aren't they just going to the gym?

"Wearing dark glasses? At night? They wanted to remain hidden. Why didn't I spot this before?" Ethan pulled up the frozen frame of the relatively clear picture of the figure's face from the exterior video and then fished through a collection of hard copy files he'd brought with him from Sacramento. He finally found what he was looking for and tapped his finger on a printout of a photograph. "See?"

Jesse scanned back and forth between the photo and the still frame. "It's the same person."

"Exactly." Ethan smiled, not with pride but relief. He'd found the killer. It had to be. Why else would this person be in the building at that time? "We need to take a field trip tonight."

CHAPTER THIRTY

Ethan had been in the Jackson Heights area of Queens once before. He never thought he'd return, but the video on the Kaplan compilation had brought him here. He was convinced that he'd found the actual killer. Now, he just needed proof.

The idyllic neighborhood was composed of one row after another of uniform, early twentieth-century apartment buildings offset from ample tree-lined sidewalks. On the one-way street in front of the six-story building he was staking out, abundant parking allowed him to blend his rented Ford Taurus into the surroundings. He kept a vigilant eye on a particular second-floor apartment, one he never thought he'd step into again.

Fully expecting this job to be an all-nighter, he had picked up sandwiches, snacks, and water before he settled in—that was three hours ago. Traffic had slowed to virtually nothing, with only the occasional pedestrian passing on the quiet, dark street. Without a partner by his side for company and breaks, he drank sparingly, staving off the need to find a bathroom.

A figure rounded the corner in the near darkness a half block down, walking toward Ethan's rental car on the same side of the street. Recognizing that irresistible face when it passed beneath a streetlight, he flashed his parking lights once, showing his location. She approached and opened the passenger door.

"I know I'm a little early, but I thought you could use a bathroom break." Jesse slid into her seat.

"I appreciate the surprise." His statement was accurate on multiple levels. Besides having a nearly full bladder, he welcomed her company. "There's a 7-Eleven around the corner. I shouldn't be more than fifteen minutes." Ethan pointed toward the apartment building across the street. "We're watching the unit on the second floor that is nearest the fire escape to the left of the entrance. Lights went out several hours ago, so I'm guessing they're bedded down for the night. I'll have to wait until morning to make my move."

"Got it. Do you have binoculars or something?"

Ethan laughed, stepping out of the car. "You've been watching too many TV shows. I'll be right back." Before closing the door, he added, "Don't eat the last of the snickerdoodles. I'm saving those."

Soon Ethan returned with two cups of coffee and extra pep in his step, courtesy of a happy bladder and the company awaiting him. He'd never known a lawyer to get this hands-on during an investigation, and frankly, Jesse was the only one from which he'd welcome such an intrusion. He slid back into the driver's seat and handed a cup to Jesse.

She inspected the drink. "Caffeine? I thought we were supposed to take turns napping and keeping watch?"

"I felt obligated to buy something." Ethan shrugged to camouflage his real motive. "One sugar, one cream, right?"

"You remembered." Jesse's smile meant his attempt to demonstrate his attentiveness had worked. She cupped her hands around the cardboard, soaking in the warmth. "Do you conduct stakeouts often?"

"It comes with the territory, but it depends on the case."

"I find this side of a criminal defense case rather exciting—interrogating possible suspects and tracking down leads. It beats dry legal wrangling with stuffy lawyers and judges."

"We'll see if you think the same way after hours of sitting in a cramped rental car."

They settled into a comfortable silence for the better part of an hour before Jesse said, "Tell me about your girls. I can't wait to meet them tomorrow."

"Erin is my oldest. She's so much like her mother..."

Ethan and Jesse shared stories about their lives, careers, family, and friends for the next hour before taking turns napping. When night turned into day and activity on the street picked up—pedestrians walking their dogs, out for an early morning jog, or hopping in their cars to go off to work—Ethan sensed it was almost showtime. He grabbed his digital camera, a Nikon with a zoom lens, ready to use at a moment's notice.

Jesse had been dozing and stirred when Ethan straightened in his seat. She propped the passenger seat up, blinking away the haze of sleep. "Did I miss anything?"

Ethan remained focused on the building across the street. "Nothing yet, but the neighborhood is waking up. Time to stay alert."

Jesse flipped down the visor in front of her and opened up the mirror. She fluffed her bobbed brown hair and checked her lipstick. A satisfied grin formed, the kind that said, "Not bad after spending the night in a car."

When someone exited the apartment building, Ethan lifted the camera to snap a photograph, lowering it when he realized the person wasn't his target. Soon, another person emerged from the awning-covered building entrance. Ethan lifted his camera again. This time he snapped a dozen pictures. "What an idiot. The same glasses and hat."

His suspect, dressed in athletic gear similar to that in the video from the night William was killed, began a stretching routine in front of the building, suggesting a morning jog was on the agenda. Once the object of his attention took off down the street at the speed of a tortoise out for a morning stroll, he put the camera down and prepared to exit the car. "Time for a look-see."

"As an officer of the court, it's best that I stay here," Jesse said.

"Just let me know if they come back." When Ethan was a police officer, gathering evidence had come with a set of legal and constitutional boundaries he rarely crossed. But he wasn't a cop any longer. He was a private detective, and collecting evidence came with only two limitations—his skill and his willingness to blur the lines.

Ethan crossed the street at a normal pace, fully prepared to blast through several of those lines for Alex and Tyler. He entered the apartment building and ascended the dank but clean stairwell to the second floor. The first door on his left was his target. He gave it a light knock to ensure the apartment was empty. No one had answered following a thirty-count, so he pulled two small tools out of his front pants pocket.

He'd practiced this dozens of times on the garage door leading into his house but had yet to use his newfound skill on a case. After looking left and then right to make sure the hallway was empty, he inserted the tension wrench first and applied subtle pressure. He then inserted the pick at the top of the lock, applied slight torque to the wrench, scrubbed the pick back and forth in the keyhole until all the pins were set in place. *Halle-freaking-lujah!* Within seconds, he had the door open and slipped inside, closing it behind him.

He quickly scanned the living room. Everything looked the same as it had during his previous visit, down to the cheap pressed-wood furniture and withering house plants in dire need of water and attention. Ethan was sure of two things. First, he knew what he was looking for. Second, he was convinced his suspect had a stupid streak. That meant beginning his search in the obvious spots, starting in the bedroom. Wearing latex gloves, he rummaged through the top and bottom of the closet and then moved on to the dresser. After looking through underwear, socks, and various casual T-shirts, he hit the jeans drawer. In the corner, he felt it. He lifted a pair of jeans and revealed an antique camera with the engraved word "Leica."

Allowing himself five seconds of self-satisfaction, he carefully pulled out the camera, making sure to not smudge any fingerprints that might be on it. On close inspection, he discovered a small dark spot that might be blood, but he couldn't be sure. He laid it on top of the dresser and, using his digital mini-camera, snapped pictures of it from every angle before returning it to the drawer. To be thorough, he searched the remaining drawers, under the bed, and the bathroom, but he found no other camera or anything else that might help Alex's case.

He was moving to the living room to search there when the cell phone vibrated in his pocket. Pulling it out, he recognized the number as Jesse's and fast-stepped to the exit, connecting the call on the third buzz. Closing the door behind him, he said. "I'm on my way."

Ethan had been in the apartment for less than fifteen minutes, which meant their suspect had taken the shortest jog in history. Under his breath, he mumbled, "Lazy," before turning in the opposite direction of the stairs he'd come up. He heard the door leading to the stairs open behind him but didn't look behind to avoid being recognized.

Once outside, he went straight to the rental car, where Jesse had done a bang-up job as a lookout. After he settled into the driver's seat and started the engine, Jesse asked, "Did you get what you needed?"

The camera was the key to solving this case, and he'd found it. In seventy-two hours, he'd done his job and tied William's murder to someone he knew who had just as much motive to want him dead as anyone the police had looked at. He was sure now that Alex would be exonerated.

Unable to bottle his excitement, he placed his hands on Jesse's cheeks and pulled her in for the kiss that had been three days in the making. They'd danced around a mutual attraction since they first met in Jesse's office, and it was about time he learned if her lips were as soft as he'd imagined.

The moment their lips touched, he gave into the foreign, yet fantastic sensation. Ever since yesterday's almost-kiss, he'd caught himself staring at Jesse's lips more often than he cared to admit. Those lips were alluringly curved, just as he'd imagined the rest of her trim body was. Moreover, the floral scent of her perfume or shampoo was feminine and quite the turn-on.

Jesse gently grasped Ethan's hands, keeping them in place and prolonging their first kiss. She deepened it, provoking the kind of moan Ethan hadn't emitted during a kiss in years. He'd all but forgotten how satisfying the moistness of lips against his could feel. How a single touch could spark pangs of desire, not merely devotion. But had he taken this too far, too soon? When he pulled back, the sultry look in Jesse's eyes signaled he hadn't.

"I've wanted to do that for a while," he said.

"Me too," she said with a clearly satisfied smile. "Not to ruin the moment, but did you get what you needed?"

Ethan smiled even wider. "I did. Now I go back to Jimmy so he can introduce me to Sterling and Diaz."

"I'll let Alex know you have something in the works. In the meantime, I have a grand jury to wait out today. I'm assuming they're going to fast-track the bail hearing after that."

"I'm counting on you to keep Alex out of jail until I can get Sterling and Diaz focused on the real killer."

CHAPTER THIRTY-ONE

Denny's wasn't the meeting location Destiny had envisioned when she called her regular big tipper, known to her as Pat, on the private number he'd passed to her more than once at the strip club. She would have preferred a less public place but agreed. Insisting on a change of venue would only scare him off. She was vague with him yesterday, making the need to meet sound more like her firm "no" to his advances had finally turned into a "yes."

Destiny arrived ten minutes late, making the point that she was in charge of this meeting. Once through the rain-streaked glass door, she walked past the host station, signaling to the server that her party was already seated. She went past the service counter loaded with single lunch-hour diners and ascended a short set of stairs to the back of the restaurant. Along the street-side wall of floor-to-ceiling windows, she spotted Pat, sitting alone in a booth, sipping on a coffee cup, and reading the morning *Times*.

She took a seat on the restaurant's signature burgundy vinyl bench across from him. "I thought Pat was a pseudonym. It's finally nice to make your acquaintance, Deputy Mayor Patrick Simmons."

He narrowed his eyes. Destiny's bombshell had gotten his attention with a loud bang. "What is this about, Destiny?"

In her sixteen years working the strip clubs, not once had Destiny tried to shake down a customer. She wasn't doing this to line her pockets, though. She owed Alex the same respect she'd been shown. Regardless, what she was about to do today would cement the end of her career as an exotic dancer. "This is about a pompous ass who thinks he can bully everyone into getting what he wants."

"A man in my position is accustomed to such perks." Patrick smugly squared his shoulders, sparking a smile from Destiny. Knocking that arrogant look from his face would be the ultimate pleasure.

"This time you're going to give me what I want."

"And why would I do that?"

Destiny slipped a manila folder onto the table and slid it in front of Patrick. Alex had better be worth the risk, because Destiny had called in every favor owed to her to get her hands on the contents. He opened the folder to an array of photographs that showed him receiving extras from four of her fellow dancers in a private room at the strip club. By the time he reached the last picture, the veins in his neck had popped over his overly snug white collar and his face was flushing redder than the lumpy, cracked vinyl booth he'd chosen to sit on for his own demise.

"There are more where these came from." An overstatement, but Destiny was sure if she had more time to shake the tree, plenty would fall to the ground. "Copies of everything are with my lawyer with instructions to send them to every major media outlet in the city if I send the order or if anything happens to me."

"How much do you want?"

"Typical of you to think this is about money." Destiny stiffened her resolve.

"Then what is this about?"

"Alex Castle."

"What about her?"

"She's a friend, and you're railroading her. I know you've been pressuring the police and the DA about her case."

"She certainly has stooped to a new level, sending a stripper to do her bidding."

"She doesn't know I'm here." Destiny pointed to the folder. "Unless you want to make the front page and the top story on the evening news, you'll back off."

"You expect me to get the DA to drop the charges?"

"That's the difference between those who feel entitled and the rest of us. I expect you to let the justice system take its natural course. If Alex is innocent, which I think she is, she'll beat this rap."

"Things are already in motion. I don't think I could stop them now even if I wanted to."

"Trust me. You want to."

"What exactly do you expect me to do?"

"Keep her out of jail until she has her day in court. That should be easy enough for a man in your position."

"That's it? You're putting yourself on the line just to keep her out of jail? She must be some friend. How much is she paying you?"

"Believe it or not, not everyone does things for money."

"Says the woman who strips for tips."

"Frankly, I don't care what you think of me. I'm doing this because it's the right thing. Alex Castle doesn't deserve to rot in jail, waiting for a court date, because a bully thinks she should. If Alex spends one unnecessary day in jail"—Destiny tapped the folder again—"the entire city will know about your little extracurricular activities. With emphasis on little."

CHAPTER THIRTY-TWO

Tyler tightened her grip on Alex's hand, the click of her heels echoing off a long stretch of the marble floor of the courthouse. She glanced down at Alex's choice of footwear—well-worn tennis shoes—recalling the unnerving explanation Alex had given her in their bedroom as she dressed for court. "They'll make for a better pillow. You have no idea how uncomfortable heels are to sleep on." Alex had also specifically chosen jeans, a long-sleeved shirt, and a light zip-up jacket, explaining, "I don't want any exposed skin. A cell floor is just nasty." Alex may have intended it as a joke, but it was no joking matter to Tyler.

They passed the assistant district attorney, standing near the grand jury room door and appearing confident as he read from a folder. Too confident for Tyler's comfort. Alex tugged on her hand, guiding her toward a bench across the corridor where Jesse was sitting.

Jesse's bobbing knees and stiff posture didn't bode well. She shifted down the bench, gesturing for Tyler and Alex to sit. "You don't have to be here."

"I know"—Alex squeezed Tyler's hand—"but I want to hear my fate firsthand."

Sitting next to Alex, Tyler could feel every twitch of her leg and every shake of the hand she was holding. She studied each finger—long and slender, with slight folds at each knuckle. *When did you have time to get a manicure?* Tyler examined her perfectly shaped nails, each tastefully coated with a faintly opaque pale peach-colored gloss. Alex's ring finger had a slightly elevated curve near the tip. *Why haven't I noticed it before? A childhood injury, maybe? I'll have to ask you about it if you get to come home tonight.* Tyler pushed away the unsettling thought of the alternative.

Jesse retrieved a folder from her leather folio, pulled a stapled, multi-page document from it, and handed it to Alex. She pointed to the printed photograph of Alex in an elevator with two other people. "This is a picture from the elevator in the Castle Resorts building the night your father was killed. Do you recognize the person in the corner with the hat and sunglasses?"

Alex studied the picture. "It's impossible to tell."

Jesse flipped to the next page and pointed at a new picture. "This is a snapshot of security footage the same night, recorded outside the building twenty minutes after you left."

"My God." Visibly shaken, Alex covered her mouth with her free hand.

Tyler had seen this expression, a mixture of heightened fear and regret, once before, when Alex had broken the news to Tyler that Ethan had been shot. Tyler later understood why the information impacted Alex so profoundly—she had felt responsible. Tyler placed a comforting arm around her. "Babe? Who is it?"

Tears filled Alex's eyes. "This is all my fault, T."

Before Alex could explain, Jesse placed a hand atop her knee and gestured toward the grand jury room. Above the door, a blue light flashed.

"What does that mean?" Tyler asked.

"The grand jury has completed its deliberations."

The annoyingly confident ADA disappeared inside, reappearing one minute later. His stoic expression was unreadable. He strode across the corridor toward Alex, Tyler, and Jesse, with a folded piece of paper in his hand. Jesse stood when he approached. He said two words. "True bill."

Jesse's barely perceptible nod meant those words were expected. That the grand jury had indicted Alex for the death of her father. A glance at Alex confirmed what Tyler expected— strength and determination.

"Congratulations on indicting another ham sandwich." Jesse's businesslike tone emphasized the futility of fighting the rigged system at this juncture. "Notify me when the bail hearing is set."

"Already done. I scheduled the Supreme Court arraignment for three p.m. today."

Unprepared for this to happen so fast, Tyler clutched Alex's hand for dear life. She wasn't ready for officers to drag Alex off in handcuffs and be reduced to seeing her through smeared plexiglass for the next six months. Images of Alex dressed in an orange jumpsuit popped into her mind, a premonition that Tyler was about to lose her for a very long time.

"In two hours? You've got to be kidding." Jesse sounded as blindsided as Tyler felt.

"There was an opening on the calendar, so I snatched it up."

"Of course, you did."

CHAPTER THIRTY-THREE

Syd's aggressive, proactive approach to stemming the company's financial bleeding had already paid off. She'd spent the day calling every vendor, business partner, conference host, and VIP regular, reassuring them that Castle Resorts was on sound footing. Offering a twenty percent discount across the board for the rest of the year as a loyalty incentive proved to be a huge enticement. Contract cancelations had stopped, and she had secured an extended agreement with Christie's auction house to host special auctions and exhibitions for the next three years. Piggybacking on Alex's Internet-based marketing scheme, Syd offered additional special perks and discounts and saw an uptick in conference bookings by attracting a broader customer base.

Besides putting out fires, she had also hunted for the person who had leaked information to the media about her father's plans to shake up the company. Having found the leaker through a bit of technological sleuthing, she was relishing the upcoming conversation, one that was more than three decades in the making.

"Send her in, Gretchen," Syd said through the speakerphone atop Alex's sleek executive desk. In her mind, this hunk of glass and metal would always be her Baby Sister's desk. Syd was simply keeping it warm.

Moments later, the person who'd been a thorn in her side since Syd was a young girl entered. Following an insincere "Thank you for coming in," Syd invited her to sit in the guest chair opposite the desk.

"Of course. When the boss wants to see you, it's customary to come running."

"As your boss, I have one question for you, Georgia. Where do your loyalties lie?"

"I'm confused, Mrs. Barnette."

"It's a simple question, really. Are you loyal to this company?"

"I've dedicated the last thirty-seven years of my life to Castle Resorts."

"You didn't answer the question." Syd handed Georgia Cushing a copy of the corporate phone records, four items highlighted in yellow. "Explain to me why you called the *New York Times* on four occasions after Father was killed." Georgia's fidgeting and lack of eye contact meant Syd was on the right track. "I thought so."

Georgia jutted her chin out before replying, "Something needed to be said before the company landed in the hands of Alexandra or, worse, Andrew."

"And how was that any of your concern? Your name isn't on the hotels."

"The last thirty-seven years of my life make it my concern. Your father had a blind spot when it came to his children, even when they didn't deserve his trust. And neither of those two did."

"I don't have time for your smokescreens. I want to know why you leaked confidential company information to the *Times* and implicated my sister in the death of my father."

"Your brother is a thief, and your sister is a liar. Your sister knew all about the theft and covered it up."

"And you would know this, how?"

"Your father suspected before he was killed that Andrew was embezzling money from the company and had me audit his expenditures for the Times Square remodel. A quarter-million dollars were missing. I also unearthed the fact that Alexandra covered it up. William was a fool to think I would let it go after he asked me to back off, saying that only a Castle could correct a Castle mistake."

"You would know all about a Castle correcting his mistake," Syd fired back.

Georgia's face tightened. "I don't know what you're referring to."

Syd had the woman she blamed for having to grow up in two households on the defensive, and she was not going to waste the opportunity to give her a piece of her mind. "Oh, please. I may have only been eight years old at the time, but I suffered the consequences of my father's mistake. Half the company and I knew you were sleeping with my father behind my mother's back. You're the reason they divorced, but he dumped you to marry Rebecca. So much for correcting mistakes. Do you ever wonder why you never made it past Accounting? It's because I vetoed it until the day I left the company and told Father that if he ever promoted you I would never talk to him again.

"By divulging confidential information you have violated company policy and breached the non-disclosure agreement you signed. You have no cause to fight what I'm about to do and if one word of this reaches the media, I'll have your ass in court and take every penny you have. I've wanted to say this for a long time, Georgia. You're fired. Clean out your desk and get your raggedy ass off my property."

Syd picked up her desktop phone with an extra sense of satisfaction. "Gretchen, Georgia Cushing is no longer with the company. Please have Security ensure she cleans out her desk and escort her from the premises."

CHAPTER THIRTY-FOUR

Ethan walked into the Nineteenth Precinct sure that he'd discovered William Castle's actual killer. The only hitch was getting Detectives Sterling and Diaz to listen to him and believe it too. If the roles were reversed and some out-of-state retired cop turned private eye working for the accused waltzed into his station with a story similar to his, Ethan would send him packing. But he hoped that with Jimmy paving the way there was a better chance of them extending him a little professional courtesy.

Thanks to rigorous physical therapy following the shooting, Ethan easily ascended the single flight. Jimmy, however, struggled at the landing, where fading fluorescent lights flickered on his flushed face like they were in a tawdry 1970's disco dance hall. If Ethan had known about Jimmy's bum knee, he would've suggested the elevator and not the stairs.

"Sterling and Diaz are pretty good detectives and don't easily get their noses bent out of shape," Jimmy explained. "They'll listen to what you have to say."

"I appreciate the intro. It's never easy when some outsider blows up your case." Ethan patted Jimmy's back before they zigzagged through the hallways. "When you're ready to hang up the badge, come see me. I've been thinking about expanding the business out here."

"I'll keep that in mind."

Once in the squad room, Jimmy asked Sterling and Diaz for a few minutes of their time to discuss "some important information on a case they were working on." He waved them toward the unoccupied office of their lieutenant.

"What do you have, Lieutenant?" Sterling's posture remained relaxed—a good sign.

"This is my friend Ethan Falling, a retired detective from Sacramento. He does private gigs now and is working for the defense in the Castle murder. I worked with him on a major case a few years back, and he's the real deal. I think you should hear him out."

Sterling and Diaz shifted uncomfortably on their feet but appeared receptive. "We're listening," Sterling replied.

"The last thing I want to do is step on anyone's toes." Ethan pulled out printouts of the pictures he took of the Leica camera he found in the suspect's apartment. "Look familiar?"

Diaz took the photo from Ethan and studied it along with Sterling. "You have our attention. Where did you get this?" she asked.

"Let's just say I came across it when I thought I smelled gas coming from an apartment in Queens, and as a concerned citizen, I conducted a safety check."

Sterling snickered. "Whose apartment is it?"

"Theirs." Ethan slapped down a photograph of the suspect, sans sunglasses, in front of the Castle Resorts headquarters building. "Now, follow me. They rode the elevator up with Alex the night William Castle was killed but got off at the twentieth floor. We all agree that Alex exited the elevator on the twenty-third, after which she met with her father. But two minutes after Alex leaves the elevator, a shadowy figure appears in the stairwell on the twentieth, ascends, is seen on the twenty-second but isn't seen past the twenty-third."

Ethan slapped down several stills from the building surveillance tapes from that night.

"At nine fifteen, Alex rides the elevator from the twenty-third to the lobby and leaves the building. At nine twenty-seven, a shadowy figure appears in the stairwell on the twenty-third, descends, but isn't seen past the twentieth. At nine thirty, the person who rode the elevator up with Alex enters the elevator again on the twentieth, rides it to the lobby, and exits the building at nine thirty-three p.m. When they cross the street at nine thirty-five p.m., they take off their glasses."

Ethan pointed to the revealed face. "This is your killer."

"None of this proves that anyone else was on that floor that night," Diaz said.

"True, but it lends doubt. So does Andrew Castle's confession that he met his father there that night, something which your report doesn't mention. I have a video showing him entering and leaving the building garage on his motorcycle around eight ten. More doubt."

"That little twerp. We confirmed he was at Arthur's Alley until ten, but he never admitted to seeing his father." Sterling pursed his lips. "He even steered us toward his sister."

"My gut tells me Alex didn't do this." Ethan pointed at the clear picture of the suspect. "But I'll bet my last dollar that this piece of work did. They're connected to the family." Ethan explained how he knew the suspect and his theory of how he thought things had gone down the night William was killed.

"Let's say I believe everything you've said." Sterling looked over the pictures again. "This isn't enough for a judge to sign a warrant. And I know the DA. If we brought this to him, asking him to back off until we get that warrant, he'd kick us out on our ear. All he wants is a fast conviction. What we need is a confession."

Ethan considered what it would take to wrap things up with a pretty little bow and get the charges against Alex dropped. And to arrest the real killer. It would be risky, and he'd have to talk it over with Alex, but he was sure she'd agree to his plan. He expected pushback from the detectives, but in his experience, it was their only hope to ferret out the truth. "I have a proposal."

CHAPTER THIRTY-FIVE

Unlike the last time Alex entered a courtroom, handcuffed, alone, and afraid of the unknown, today, she was buoyed by the only thing that made sense in her life: Tyler's warm, soft hand was in hers. She walked confidently through the ornate wooden doors guarding the main entrance, this time unafraid. Not because she was sure she was going home tonight, but because she was convinced that despite how screwed up things had gotten and no matter what happened in the next few minutes, Tyler would be her rock.

Waiting outside the courtroom, Alex took stock of the people in her life. Abby, Harley, and Syd would always remain in her corner beside Tyler. It was a shame she couldn't say as much for her brother. Their father had driven the final wedge between them when he'd announced over lunch that he was picking her to take over the reins of Castle Resorts. *What a bloody awful day that was. Literally.* Andrew had acted like a child, breaking a cocktail glass with his hand and creating a deep gash in his palm. Their father had slammed his hand down in response to the tantrum, cutting his hand on the scattered shards and causing a thin spray of blood to spurt toward her and the beautiful gift Syd had given her for her birthday.

Wait.

"Think, Alex. Think." She concentrated, picturing again the white tablecloth and the bleeding men on either side of her. She remembered moving the camera out of the way, but when? She focused harder. Yes! She'd moved the camera after seeing that her father's blood had leached along the cotton threads and reached it.

"My God!" Alex's pulse raced as she pulled on Jesse's blazer sleeve. "I know how my father's blood got on my camera."

Jesse knitted her brow, looking confused. "What?"

"I remember now. I was at lunch with my father and Andrew the day he announced I'd take over as CEO. I had my camera with me. Andrew broke a drink glass and my father cut his hand on the shards. I distinctly remember blood on the tablecloth reaching my camera."

Jesse's eyes lit up. "This is excellent, Alex."

Tyler placed a hand on her back. "Is there time to reconvene the grand jury to have them hear the new evidence?" Tyler asked.

"Not today, and I doubt the DA would, given the timing of Alex's recollection of the event. Even if he did reconvene, he'd paint the memory as convenient."

"So this doesn't change a thing." The elation Alex felt a moment ago deflated as quickly as it hit her.

"This could change everything. The blood evidence is the one thing tying you to the scene after you'd left. Once I present this in court, it could provide the reasonable doubt we need for an acquittal. Especially if we can get a server to corroborate the incident. Seems like something they'd remember." Jesse glanced at the clock on the wall. "In the meantime, we better get inside for the hearing."

Jesse ushered her and Tyler to the back of the gallery to the only empty space on a bench wide enough to accommodate the three of them. She gave Jesse an inch of space, but crammed tight against Tyler, from calf to shoulder, an arm overlapping Tyler's with their fingers entwined.

As one defendant after another received judgment on their freedom and the clock clicked closer to three, Alex sensed her time with Tyler slipping away. If the proceeding didn't go her way, she'd miss Tyler's intoxicating scent after they'd made love and the comfort of her warm body next to hers in the middle of the night. But mostly, she would miss waking up before Tyler and watching her as sunlight broke through the windows. No matter how many mornings Alex would have to wake behind bars, she'd carry with her an image of Tyler sleeping peacefully, without a worry in the world.

Tyler whispered, her warm breath tickling Alex's ear. "Did you call Syd?"

"No. I didn't want her to worry. She has enough on her plate, righting the ship at Castle Resorts." A lump formed in her throat, thinking that Syd might have to stay on longer than she'd bargained for. "You'll call her if things don't go our way?"

Tyler squeezed tighter and shifted their bodies closer. Her voice was shaky. "Of course."

Jesse stood, urging Alex to do the same. "I have to go, T." She kissed Tyler on the lips, without fear or sorrow but with the promise of tomorrow. When a tear dampened Alex's cheek, she pulled back, dried Tyler's cheek with a thumb, and gave her a confident wink. "I'll be right back."

ADA Marshall took his place at the people's table, slamming his folio atop of it and earning unwanted attention from everyone in the room. He grumbled about something under his breath when the court clerk yelled out, "Docket number eight-six-nine-zero-four, People versus Alexandra Rose Castle, manslaughter in the first degree."

As if everyone was filming a movie and someone had yelled, "Take two," the dialog from her first bail hearing was repeated, almost word for word.

"Your Honor, Jesse Simmons for the defense..."

Alex studied the judge, the man who was about to decide whether tonight she would be behind bars or in the arms of the woman she loved. The thin, white, middle-aged man sat tall behind the bench, dressed in the customary black robe. His dark brown oval glasses and short, conventionally styled salt-

and-pepper hair made him appear more like an academic than a judge. His stern expression made her wonder what kind of mood he was in. Had he had an argument with his significant other this morning? Get stuck in traffic today? Did his lunch give him heartburn? How ironic that her fate could rest on whether the judge had onions on his burger.

"I'm never having onions again if he sends me back to jail," Alex said under her breath.

Jesse glanced at Alex with a confused expression. "What was that about onions?"

"Nothing," Alex replied.

ADA Marshall crumpled a piece of paper in his hand before tossing it to the table. He glared at Alex before redirecting his attention to the judge. "The people request no change in bail, Your Honor."

Jesse's head snapped in his direction, but Alex turned hers to meet Tyler's gaze. She breathed easier knowing that they'd have several months together until this farce of a trial began. Her only hurdle—how to convince Tyler to stay.

After the judge tapped his gavel against its wooden platform, Jesse ushered Alex out of the courtroom, picking up Tyler along the way. They huddled near the windows before Jesse said, "The court will notify me once they set a date and time for the trial. Until then, we prepare your defense."

"Not tonight." Alex pulled Tyler's hand to her lips and kissed the back of it, staring into her eyes. Her heart beat to all the things she wanted to do with this woman until the sun rose again. "Tyler and I are going away for the weekend. We're already packed."

"Yes, we are." Tyler smiled without breaking eye contact, her eyes telling the same story.

"We really should meet up with Ethan," Jesse said. "He's talking to the detectives in your case as we speak."

Tyler kept her gaze on Alex, her eyes suggesting that delaying their departure was out of the question. "Ethan is picking up our girls at the airport tomorrow morning and meeting us at Abby's beach house. You should drive up with him, Jesse."

"Yes." Alex finally broke her stare and turned to Jesse. "We can discuss strategy then. Pack a bag. Abby has plenty of space, so you're welcome to stay the weekend."

"I think I will." Jesse's growing grin hinted that she had more on her mind than strategy.

Alex walked the two blocks from the courthouse as if her feet had wings. The bail hearing had taught her that freedom was precious, and she would not waste one minute of it. She hooked Tyler's arm with hers, with no intention of ever letting it go.

As they approached the Spencer town car, Richard opened the rear passenger door to let Alex and Tyler board. "My apologies, Ms. Castle, but there was an incident at the mouth of the midtown tunnel. I'll have to reroute us over the Williamsburg Bridge."

Given Tyler's phobia, they'd avoided driving over bridges until now. The last thing Alex wanted was to make Tyler a nervous wreck before their getaway. "What about the Carey Tunnel?"

"That would add another forty-five minutes to the trip. We might not make it before sunset as you requested." Richard closed the door and jumped into the driver's seat.

"This is silly. I can suck it up for five minutes. Let's just take the bridge." Tyler waved off the dilemma with confidence, but her shaky voice was less than convincing.

"Are you sure?" Alex asked.

Tyler swallowed hard as if forcing down an ice cube whole when Richard snapped his seatbelt into place. "Yes. Let's go before I change my mind. Take the bridge, Richard."

Richard waited for an affirmative nod from Alex before starting the drive to Southampton. Soon they reached Delancey Street, a signal that the bridge was minutes away. A distraction was in order. Alex unbuckled her seatbelt, scooted closer, turned to face Tyler, and gently placed a hand on her knee, just shy of the hem of her skirt. With a single fingertip, she began an agonizingly slow climb up Tyler's inner thigh, moving underneath the fabric.

With Richard seated a few feet away, Alex expected some resistance, but Tyler was receptive, shuddering at the socially forbidden touch. Her breathing shallowed—the response Alex had hoped for. She leaned in until her lips kissed Tyler's ear, whispering, "What do you want?"

Tyler's loud gulp confirmed that Alex had accomplished her goal of distracting her. Alex was at the doorstep of her desired destination when Tyler pushed on the crook of Alex's bent elbow. "We shouldn't." Everything from Tyler's closed eyes and melting posture, however, screamed that she didn't want to stop.

Alex grazed the silk at the apex of Tyler's legs. She whispered in Tyler's ear, "Richard is well-trained to pay attention only to the road." She licked the patch of skin behind Tyler's ear as her final diversion. "Don't look now, but we just finished crossing the bridge." She kissed Tyler soundly on the lips and moved back to her own seat, buckling her belt back on.

Tyler straightened her skirt and looked out the window of the town car, saying softly but loud enough for Alex to hear, "Fuuuuuck."

CHAPTER THIRTY-SIX

Less than two hours later, driving in Southampton's outskirts, Richard hit the remote to open the understated white metal gate that guarded the final quarter mile to Abby's beach house. While still large, the vacation home was modest compared to the area's sprawling estates. That was what Alex loved about it. Its smaller scale produced a more intimate atmosphere. It was designed for families.

Richard parked the car in his traditional spot at the foot of the walking path leading to the main house and unloaded the few bags Alex and Tyler had brought for their long weekend getaway.

"Shall I bring the bags inside, Ms. Castle?"

"Thank you, but there's no need. We have everything. What time are you bringing the Spencers tomorrow?"

"I should have them safely delivered by eleven. Mrs. Kapoor mentioned something about taking Mrs. Falling's girls boating on her yacht for lunch."

"Yacht? My girls would love that. They've never been on a yacht. Heck, *I've* never been on one." Tyler sounded downright giddy.

Alex gave Tyler a quick peck on the lips. "We'll remedy that tomorrow." She lightly tapped Tyler on her button nose several times after each word. "You…are…going…to…love…it."

After saying goodbye to Richard, Alex and Tyler began their trek to the beach house, bags in tow. The path split into three, but Alex kept them on the main artery.

Tyler asked, "Where do those lead?"

Alex continued to walk toward the house. "The pool."

"And the other?"

"Tennis court and guesthouse, but I don't go there anymore." Alex stopped in midstride, a sadness overwhelming her. She'd never shared the reason for that with anyone but Harley, but the time had come for her to share her every life blemish with Tyler. "I'll tell you why later, okay?"

Tyler rubbed Alex's arm in a reassuring fashion. "Okay."

Alex led Tyler into the beach house, throwing the keys Abby had given her into a ceramic bowl resting on an entry table. She dropped the suitcases at the beginning of the hallway that led to the guest rooms before guiding Tyler to the great room. Unfortunately, they didn't have time to enjoy the large white sectional or floor-to-ceiling stone fireplace. It was six thirty, and Alex wanted to settle themselves on the deck before the sun went down.

"Let's hurry, T. I want to share the sunset with you. I'll grab some wine, and then we can go out on the deck." Alex returned from the wet bar with a deliberately chosen bottle of Bordeaux and two glasses. She led Tyler onto the weather-beaten deck and to her favorite double chaise lounge. Just as she'd hoped, the setting was perfect—calm waves hugging the shore, a faint ocean breeze carrying a briny scent, and a warm orange hue kissing the horizon.

She uncorked the wine and poured some into each glass. "I know I should let this breathe for a bit, but there's not much sunlight left."

"I'm used to Two Buck Chuck, so I'm sure it will be fine."

"Two Buck what?" Alex laughed.

"Two Buck Chuck. It's a cheap but decent wine sold at Trader Joe's in California," Tyler explained with a hint of pride in her frugality. "Don't get me wrong. Syd's wines are much better, but for two dollars, you can't beat the bang for your buck." Alex laughed again, forcing Tyler to defend her choices. "Hey, don't knock it until you try it, Miss Fancy Pants."

"Come here, you." Alex invited Tyler by patting a section of cushion to her left. Tyler sat beside Alex on the lounger, reclining but moving carefully to not spill her wine. Alex wrapped an arm around her, clinked her glass with Tyler's, took a sip, and stared into the waning sunlight, hoping Tyler enjoyed it as much as she did.

Tyler sipped her wine and sighed. "This is beautiful, Alex."

"It never gets old." Alex kissed Tyler on the cheek.

Twilight blissfully faded into darkness while they worked on the Bordeaux. Enough time had passed for the necessary liquid courage to set in, making Alex ready for the truth she was about to tell. She put her glass down on the side table next to the lounger and placed Tyler's next to it. Folding herself into Tyler's arms, she entwined their legs, giving herself the sense that their bodies were one.

Alex took a deep breath before breaking the silence. "The wine we've been drinking is a 1994 Bordeaux. It was bottled the same year I almost killed myself." She felt every muscle in Tyler tense and waited for them to relax before continuing. "I've never talked about this since that awful day because it should've never happened."

"This is about the guesthouse, isn't it?" Tyler kissed the top of her head before resting her chin there.

"Yes." Alex tightened her hold on Tyler. "Kelly and I had been lovers for two months before I had to return home for summer break. Before it was time to go back to Yale, Kelly called. She said something like, 'Oh, Alex, you were a wonderful distraction last spring, but I met Douglas Pruitt over the summer. He's of the Boston Pruitts. Just the kind of man I came to Yale to meet. You'd like him, Alex. He's tall, handsome, and so very rich. We're engaged to be engaged. You'll have to come to the wedding.' I begged her to take me back, but Kelly just laughed and called me naïve for thinking our relationship was anything more than a college fling.

"For weeks, I was depressed and walked around in a daze. I couldn't sleep or do much of anything. Harley was my only confidant, so she kept an eye on me. After a month, she decided I needed to get out of the funk I was in, so she brought me here for the weekend. When we got here..."

* * *

July 1994

Another ball hit an inch inside the line, bounced, and whizzed past Alex's racket in mid-swing. She grunted. For the last forty minutes, she'd been trying to return Harley's power serves and failing miserably more than half the time. "I thought you were supposed to be cheering me up. You know I suck at tennis."

Harley skillfully bounced a ball near her foot several times to prepare for another serve. "You don't suck. Just concentrate and anticipate."

Alex would've prepared for a softer attack if anyone was behind the upcoming serve, but she was up against Harley Spencer. She never let Alex get away with anything.

Alex locked her eyes on Harley's feet as she began her wind up, noticing that she'd angled them for the near sideline on her left. She would have to return a backhand shot. If she angled the return just right, she could send the ball back down the same sideline.

Alex bounced on the balls of her feet, still keeping an eye on Harley's. They didn't change direction. She broke left just as Harley served the ball. At precisely the right moment, she cracked the ball, sailing it down the line for a perfect return: point, Alex.

Alex raised her arms in victory, racket in one hand and a fist formed with the other. "Yes!"

"Nice return. It looks like the old Alex is back." Harley wiped the sweat off her brow. "I'm starved. Let's eat. Mother had the kitchen stocked for the weekend."

"Just as I start winning you get hungry. How convenient."

Harley walked over to Alex, racket in hand, and wrapped her free arm around her shoulder. "Come on, you. I'm sure you're famished. You've hardly eaten all day."

They fixed a dinner that was reminiscent of their long-ago spoiled teenager years—grilled cheese sandwiches, potato chips, and ice cream. After cleaning up or doing something that barely qualified as such, Harley retrieved two glasses and a bottle of scotch from the back of the wet bar's cabinet. She filled both glasses, offering one to Alex. "Join me."

Alex was hesitant. The last time she drank too much, she'd memorialized one of her and Kelly's sexcapades in black and white T-Max 400. "I've never had scotch."

"Just one." Harley handed Alex a glass. "You need to loosen up, my friend."

Following another back-and-forth, Alex relented. "Okay, just one."

Retreating to the couch, they slowly sipped Abby's best scotch. Harley finally broke the silence. "I never liked Kelly, and what she did to you tells me that my instinct was right."

"She broke my heart, Harley." Alex's voice was shaky. "I loved her."

"I know you did, darling. I loved my first, too. You'll eventually get over her. We all do."

Alex's eyes teared up. "But you've never had your heart ripped to shreds. You're the one who does the dumping." Alex downed her drink and held out her glass for a refill.

Harley obliged with a smile. "Just one, huh?"

"Shut up and pour."

"I do not dump. I gently let them go before I fall for them."

"Well, I'm never going to fall for a woman ever again." Alex downed her drink and held out her glass for another.

"Whoa, slow down, tiger," Harley cautioned.

Alex grabbed the bottle and poured it herself. "I'm getting drunk. I think I've earned it."

"That you have. Though I don't think swearing off love solves your heartbreak."

"I'm not swearing off love, just women. I can't go through this again." A man had never treated Alex's heart like a doormat, walking all over it at will. Never ripped her heart in two and then taken joy in telling her why he did. She'd never let a woman do that to her again.

"Oh, please. You're as gay as I am. You just fell for the wrong woman. The trick is to not bare your soul until you're sure she wants you and not your money. Just give it some time. When you're ready, I have the perfect redhead in mind to serve as a palate cleanser. She has an aversion to commitment that rivals Madonna's."

"Madonna, huh?" Alex took another swallow. Who was she kidding? If her time with Kelly had taught her anything, it was that she was as gay as Melissa Ethridge. There would be no going back to men. She downed her drink and readied for another.

By the end of the evening, the alcohol had done its job. Alex had laughed at Harley's cheesy jokes and, despite the spinning room, had danced to Abby's godawful collection of Frankie Valli and the Four Seasons recordings. Kelly Thatcher and her broken heart were behind her. At least for tonight.

She yawned. Twice.

"Someone's finally tired," Harley said.

"I haven't slept in weeks." Another yawn accompanied Alex's slurred words.

"I think Mother's scotch will help in that department."

"I think you're right." Alex rolled off the couch. "I'm heading off to bed."

Harley stepped closer. "Why don't you crash in the main house tonight?"

"But I love the guesthouse now that it's remodeled." Alex wobbled, smacking her shin on the metal and wood coffee table. It should've hurt and likely would leave a mark, but the scotch had done its job. "Plus, my stuff is there."

"You're stubborn." Harley locked arms with her. "But I'm walking you over. I want to make sure you make it in one piece."

Alex let Harley lead her along the well-lit path from the beach house to the tennis courts and guesthouse without complaint. Once inside, Alex raised an index finger at Harley and slurred her following words, "Don't leave yet. We have to close the book on Kelley Thatcher."

Alex dug through her satchel and retrieved twenty-four black and white photos of her and Kelly, pictures she'd once cherished. After Kelly dumped her, however, they'd become a source of self-pity. That would end tonight. After asking Harley to remain a polite distance away so as to not see the contents of the photos, she tossed all but one into the fireplace, lit the final one with the nearby lighter, and tossed it into the pile of sad memories.

"Feel better?" Harley asked.

"I'm not sure yet." When the final photograph burned to ashes, Alex thought she'd feel more relieved. Either the alcohol was holding her back, or it would take a long time to get over her first love.

"Let's get you to bed." Harley helped Alex change into her sleeping shorts and handed her a glass of water and two pills. "Here, take these."

Alex plopped on the bed, willing it to stop spinning. "What are they?"

"Aspirin. Now swallow," Harley ordered. "We have to get an early start tomorrow and head back to the city. Mother needs me to entertain the daughter of an important donor while they talk business."

"How old is she?"

"Nineteen and single."

"Perfect." Alex swallowed the aspirin before handing Harley the glass. She laid her head on the pillow and reached out for Harley's hand. "Thank you for tonight, Harley."

"You're my best friend, Alex. I love you. There's no need to thank me."

"I love you, too," Alex mumbled before nodding off to sleep.

A wave of nausea woke Alex a while later, sending her running for the toilet. The next very unpleasant fifteen minutes convinced her that Scotch was not her drink and that a hangover was in her future. She remembered Harley giving her aspirin before passing out but was unsure if they had been in her stomach long enough to dissolve. *Two more aspirins, to be on the safe side*, she thought.

She rummaged through the medicine cabinet, opened the first bottle she came across, and swallowed two of the pills. She then stumbled back to bed and passed out facedown.

* * *

"I didn't know it," Alex told Tyler, "but I'd taken two sleeping pills. Until I woke up in the hospital, Harley had thought I tried to kill myself. I'll never forgive myself for putting her through that. I can't believe I was so drunk that I couldn't distinguish between aspirin and sleeping pills. I owe my life to her." After Alex finished, she heard only the sound of the waves gently crashing against the shoreline. She tried to move to look Tyler in the eyes, but Tyler was holding her so tightly that she couldn't. "T? Are you all right?"

After several beats, Tyler loosened her vise grip and raised Alex's chin with her hand. Her voice was shaky, slightly above a whisper. "I love you so much."

Alex saw a deep sadness in Tyler's eyes. "I didn't try to kill myself, T. I was so drunk I didn't know what I was doing. Though I won't lie. It was hard getting over her. I even saw a psychologist. She helped me see that not all women were like Kelly and that I needed closure, so I wrote her a letter and got everything off my chest."

"Did it help?"

"I guess so. Kelly never returned to Yale, so I didn't have to see her again. After that, I never let myself get attached to a woman." Alex smiled. "Not until I bumped into you."

Tyler caressed Alex's cheek. "I can't lose you, Alex Castle. Not to sleeping pills. Not to prison. Not to anything."

"You won't lose me, T."

CHAPTER THIRTY-SEVEN

Southampton, New York

Curled against Tyler's warm body like a puzzle piece mated to another one, Alex woke to a cell phone alarm. Tyler shifted toward the nightstand where her phone awaited, but Alex pulled her back. She wasn't ready for their time together alone to end. Lying in bed all morning with Tyler would be the perfect encore to the perfect sunset that had led to the perfect emotional connection.

"Do we have to get up?" Alex snuggled closer.

Tyler stretched to the nightstand, swiped her phone quiet, and read something on the screen. She flipped over to face Alex with the excitement of Christmas morning and the last day of school rolled into one. "Ethan texted. He should be here in an hour with my girls."

"We better start the day then." Alex checked her cell phone for the first time since she'd muted it after texting Syd from the courthouse to tell her that everything was fine and that she and Tyler were heading to the beach house as planned. She had four missed messages from her. "Shoot. My sister's been trying to reach me." She sat up, reclined against the headboard, and dialed. Syd picked up on the first ring.

"It's about damn time." Syd's tone was sharp with irritation.

"You cussed," Alex laughed. Tyler reclined next to her.

"I only cuss when I'm super frustrated."

"I'm sorry, Syd. After the last few days, Tyler and I needed some alone time, so I muted my phone. What's up?"

"I found who leaked information to the press."

Alex popped from the headboard, sitting straighter. "Who was it?"

"Georgia Cushing."

"Georgia? I can't believe that she would leak information to the media about me. Are you sure?" Georgia had been with Castle Resorts since its inception and gave Alex the impression that her loyalty ran deep.

"She admitted it after I confronted her with company phone records, so I fired her." Syd's voice contained a hint of glee. "She also said that Father had her audit Times Square and that she'd told him all about Andrew's embezzlement the day he was killed. She thinks you covered it up."

"She's exaggerating. I repaid the money, but I didn't alter a single transaction."

"But you hid it from Father. No wonder he was so mad at you."

"Don't lecture me, Syd. That's the last thing I need right now." The anger and frustration she had felt that night seemed like a lifetime ago. She'd started that day in San Francisco and in Tyler's arms, still the incoming CEO of Castle Resorts and sure of what she wanted. She had ended it unemployed, disinherited, and more lost than she'd ever been. The only thing that had gotten her through the upheaval was the woman sitting next to her, looking ever so alluring in her shorts and tank top.

"I know you're under a lot of stress right now, but no more secrets when it comes to family or the business." Syd's tone was firm. "Agreed?"

"Agreed. No more secrets." *Maybe I should rethink not telling Tyler about funding Erin's scholarship.*

"In the spirit of no more secrets, I need to tell you something else about Georgia," Syd said.

"Okaaaaay. This doesn't sound good," Alex said.

"She and Father had an affair when he was married to my mother, which led to their divorce. Frankly, I couldn't stand Georgia. So I rather enjoyed giving her the boot yesterday."

Her father's infidelity should've shocked Alex more than it did, but she'd come to expect the worst from the men in her family. Her brother was a conniving, thieving, gambling addict, and her father was a manipulative, judgmental hypocrite. "It figures. Do you have a replacement in mind for Georgia?"

"No, I haven't thought that far out yet."

"Her number two would be an excellent choice. I recently hired a woman named Destiny Scott as an accountant for the Times Square Resort. She'd be perfect to backfill the empty seat. I wouldn't be surprised if she wasn't sitting in Georgia's old office in two or three years."

"Consider it done."

Within an hour, Tyler was standing sentry at the front door, peering out its glass pane. She was so damn cute, rocking side to side and biting a fingernail. Alex slid behind her, wrapping her arms around her torso and resting her chin atop a shoulder. "I haven't seen you this nervous since you came to see me in San Francisco."

"I was a nervous wreck that night until your magical lips kissed me."

"Magical, huh?" Alex squeezed a little tighter.

"I've been under your spell ever since."

Wisps of guilt wormed their way into Alex. Tyler had left her girls for nearly two weeks to help Alex through the most challenging time of her life, and not once had she complained about being away from them. Alex had assumed daily phone calls and text messages were enough, but Tyler's anxious state this morning proved her suppositions wrong.

"I'm sorry," Alex said.

Tyler stiffened her posture but didn't break her stare out the window. "What are you sorry for?"

"I've been so wrapped up in my own troubles that I didn't see how much you missed your daughters."

Tyler leaned back into Alex's embrace. "You have nothing to apologize for. There's no place I'd rather be right now." She pressed Alex's arms firmer into her abdomen. "Though I am anxious for them to arrive."

"I'm excited to meet them."

"Bree should be a pushover, but Erin…"

"I know. She blames me. Don't worry. If I don't win her over today, I'll keep at it." Alex nuzzled Tyler's neck, her heart fluttering at the thought of many more days and years of waking up next to this woman. "I'm in this for the long haul."

Tyler turned around, wrapping her arms around Alex's neck. "I am too. You brought back to life a part of me that was long dead. A side that no one should ever have to learn to live without—the desire to be touched. And that awakening has cascaded. I've never felt more alive, more loved. I feel it in every caress and in every smile meant only for me. I hope my girls can see the change in me and realize you're the reason for it."

The brief kiss they shared sealed their long-haul promise to each other.

Tyler glanced at her phone when it buzzed to an incoming text. "They're here." Her smile stretched to her eyes. It was a level of delight Alex hadn't seen from her before but had witnessed in Abby several times. Alex surmised it had to do with a mother's unconditional love for her child. She wished the same for herself one day. Maybe.

A sleek dark blue Mercedes rolled to a stop at the mouth of the footpath leading to the house. Tyler flew out the door with Alex giggling steps behind. The front passenger door opened, and Ethan exited. He leaned into the rear passenger compartment. "Gather your things up later, girls. Mom is here."

Tyler skidded to a stop several feet shy of the car. The rear doors opened, and her girls jumped out—one the spitting image of her, the other favoring Ethan in every way that counted.

Tyler held out her arms for giant hugs. "There you two are. I've missed you."

"I've missed your cooking, Mom." Bree gave Tyler a hug round the waist that would've choked this morning's breakfast out of anyone.

"Oh, come on, Maddie is a great cook." Tyler released her embrace to inspect Bree from ponytail to sneakers. "I'm sure she fed you well."

"It was all healthy stuff. If I have to eat one more salad, I'm going to scream."

Laughing, Tyler accepted a less substantial hug from Erin, a sign she was either cranky from the red-eye flight or was still coming to terms with her parents' divorce. If the latter, Alex hoped she could find a way to make the journey to acceptance a little easier.

Tyler shifted her attention to Jesse. "Thanks for driving and using your car to pick up my girls."

"It made sense to use my car instead of having Ethan arrange for a rental," Jesse said. "Besides, I know my way around the airport and saved us at least a half hour."

"Well, it's much appreciated." Tyler glanced at Alex to her left. "Girls, I'd like you to meet Alex Castle."

Alex sized up the girls' reactions, assessing Bree was likely the most receptive. She extended her hand. "I'm very pleased to meet you, Bree. Your mother tells me you're quite the speller at school."

Bree shook Alex's hand, her chest puffing out a fraction. "I got a hundred on my last spelling test."

"Wow! That's amazing. I have a feeling you might be an English major in college."

"Yeah, not some wimpy art thing like Erin."

"Oh, art is not wimpy in the least. On the contrary, art is one of the few ways we can experience love, faith, and hope beyond the written word." Bree narrowed her eyes in unmistakable confusion, causing Alex to explain further. "There are so many ways to describe those things, but unless you actually live it, it's hard to fathom. Art, such as paintings and sculptures, and even graphic design like Erin plans to study can transcend the written word and capture the essence of the human experience."

Bree still looked confused, so Alex continued, "Have you heard the saying, 'A picture is worth a thousand words'?"

"Yeah, my mom says it all the time," Bree said.

"Of course, she does. She's an artist. It means just by looking at a picture, we can guess what the person in it was thinking and feeling."

"Wow! That's kinda cool."

"I think so," Alex said before offering her hand to Tyler's oldest daughter. "I'm very pleased to meet you too, Erin. I hope you'll do me the honor of allowing me to guide you around campus tomorrow."

Erin rolled her eyes before shaking Alex's hand. Apparently, the soliloquy on art hadn't won her over. "That would be fine, Alex," she replied with a frosty edge to her tone. Clearly, Alex still had her work cut out for her.

"That's wonderful. I can't wait to show you the campus, the dorms, and the rare book library that is simply amazing. You're going to love it at Yale."

"I still can't believe I received a full scholarship."

"I can." The origin of that scholarship was better left buried, at least for now. She hadn't funded Erin's scholarship to ingratiate herself. She'd done it because she loved Tyler and owed Ethan a debt. Paying for his daughter's education was the least she could do after he found himself in harm's way while working for her. "By all accounts, you're an outstanding scholar and an excellent fit for my alma mater. I have a feeling you're going to excel there and that you'll look back at your time at Yale as the most formative years of your life."

"I hope so," Erin said, dropping her sharp tone. Maybe Alex had made a small dent in her wall of teenage hostility.

"Why don't we get in a quick tour of this place before the others arrive? Then, if you're up for it, our friend, Indra, has arranged for us to go boating on her yacht today." Both girls' mouths gaped. "I'll take that as a yes."

By the time they'd dropped their things, toured the grounds, and gathered in the main house, Richard had brought

Abby, Indra, and Harley in the town car. After another round of introductions, Indra checked her watch. "We should make our way to Sag Harbor. The crew is expecting us soon. I hope you don't mind, but I took the liberty of selecting the menu for lunch."

"Please tell me not another salad." Bree's lament earned snickers from Tyler and Ethan.

Indra smiled. "Only if you want to. I asked for burgers and hot dogs for you girls."

"Finally, an adult with common sense." Bree dramatically flapped her arms in the air, earning hearty laughs from everyone.

Everyone piled into Abby's town car and Jesse's Mercedes for the twenty-minute drive to Sag Harbor. Ethan and Jesse asked Alex and Tyler to ride with them to "discuss an important legal matter."

While Jesse drove, Ethan shifted in the front passenger seat to better see Alex and Tyler in the back. "I met with Sterling and Diaz yesterday and showed them everything I had on our suspect."

"Did they listen?" Alex asked.

"They did. They were leery at first, but I refused to take no for an answer. I don't think Sterling and Diaz have anything personal against you. They're just like every other cop who's been pressured to close a case fast. They're willing to follow up on my leads, so I pitched a proposal to speed things up."

"What's that?" Alex asked.

"That you wear an NYPD wire and get a confession."

"Are you nuts?" Tyler said. The doubt in her eyes clearly ran deep.

"That seems to be a popular question this morning," Ethan said.

"See? I told you." Jesse shook her head, mirroring Tyler's skepticism. She peered into the rearview mirror. "I had the same reaction."

"Is one body not enough?" The fear in Tyler's voice meant she was conjuring up one worst-case scenario after another, each one ending with Alex dead on the floor. Alex had similar images.

"It would be a controlled meet with plenty of police backup," Ethan said. "Alex would wear an audio and video wire, and we'd be right outside."

Despite Tyler's objections and her own fears, the idea of wrapping this up before it went to trial was far more appealing to Alex than having it hanging over her head for months. "When would they be ready to do this?"

Tyler whipped her head toward Alex with the stern look of a boarding school teacher on the verge of corralling an unruly student. It was a look that Alex didn't want to provoke from her ever again. "Are you nuts?" Tyler said again. "So many things could go wrong."

Alex unsnapped her seatbelt and slid closer until their thighs touched. She traced Tyler's jawline with a fingertip. "I know you're scared. You won't lose me. This is how I take back control. For two weeks, I've reacted to everything around me. I need to do more than wait for things to happen. My case could drag out for months, and there is no guarantee the detectives will ever get the evidence needed to get these awful charges dropped before trial. You know there's no one better positioned to get a confession."

"I was a cop's wife for eighteen years. I know that every undercover operation has variables that even the best detectives can't account for. Ethan is the best, but are Sterling and Diaz the best too?"

"Tyler, I've done hundreds of these," Ethan said. "I went over the details with both detectives, and I'm comfortable with their plan. Plus, I'll be there."

Tyler looked Ethan in the eyes, the tension in the car growing thicker than the briny air seeping into the cabin. "Promise that you'll bring her back to me." She held his gaze until he acknowledged her apprehension with a nod.

"I promise."

"I'm holding you to it because I'm going with you." Tyler's firm tone left no room for debate, earning a deep sigh from Ethan, evidence of his unyielding protective nature when it came to Tyler. Alex got the impression it would never change.

"I'm glad you're coming," Alex said, squeezing Tyler's hand.

Jesse pulled into the marina lot and parked.

Alex returned her attention to Ethan. "When?"

"We can go tonight."

"What about the girls?" Tyler asked. "We can't leave them at the beach house alone."

Alex turned to Tyler. "Abby and Indra can take them to Indra's estate in Greenwich for the night. It's only an hour to Yale from there." Then, with Tyler's affirmative nod, Alex pivoted to Ethan. "Set it up."

Everyone boarded Indra's Italian-made Mangusta yacht. Indra explained she hadn't used it since her husband's death the previous year but was glad she'd kept it out of sentimentality so she could accommodate today's excursion. Following a tour of the boat's lavish interior, everyone gathered at the aft exterior deck to gaze at the water and other boats as they motored out of the marina, slogged across the bay, and then picked up speed in the Long Island Sound.

The girls explored the bow, leaving the adults aft and presenting the opportunity to make arrangements for tonight. Alex kept the details vague, simply saying that if things went well tonight, the charges she faced could soon be behind her. Indra was happy to host the Falling girls overnight and have her home serve as a launching point for everyone's big day at Yale.

A server whispered something in Indra's ear. She replied, "Thank you. Can you let our younger guests know?" He nodded before retreating to the interior dining area. Indra announced that lunch was ready whenever everyone cared to grab some food. Once everyone fixed a plate, including the girls, they took seats on the aft deck again, this time forming an irregular circle, facing each other.

"Are you excited to visit campus tomorrow, Erin?" Harley asked.

"Yes, ma'am, especially the dorms."

"Do you know which residential college you've been assigned?" Harley asked.

"Morse."

Alex and Harley looked at each other and grinned from ear to ear. "Alex and I were Morsels." Harley turned her attention to Alex. "I'm sure you'll show her the Crescent."

"If there's time," Alex said. Harley's giggle brought back many not-so-fond memories of the Crescent Underground Theater in the building next to Morse dormitory. Alex cringed at the many make-out sessions she'd had in the backstage area there with her freshman-year boyfriend, who fancied himself an amateur actor. She wished she'd had a stronger backbone then and hadn't ignored her high school crushes on girls and forced herself to live the conforming life of a Castle.

Alex leaned into Tyler after she'd given her a curious look. "I'll tell you later."

Abby juggled her plate on her lap, patting Indra on a leg. "Indra and I were in Silliman. The courtyard, with its large grassy area and beech trees, was a big attraction back then. The boys would start up games of Frisbee or cricket." She turned her attention to her partner. "Indra, remember the beatniks with their hammocks?"

"That's right." Indra tapped her smiling lips as if recalling a fond memory. "What was his name? The poet who always said, 'It's a drag, man'?"

"You mean Billy? The one who left us at Woodstock, only to hitchhike back to White Plains," Abby said.

"You were at Woodstock?" Jesse asked.

"Oh yes. That's where our relationship first sparked," Indra said, giving Abby's hand a loving squeeze.

"It's somewhat of a family tradition, isn't it, Harley?" Oh boy. Abby's accusatory tone and arched eyebrow meant that she still wasn't pleased with the epic road trip Harley and Alex had taken.

Alex snickered, vividly recalling Harley's way of memorializing the adventure. "Harley's the only one of us who came back with a tattoo, though."

"You're as much to blame as I am," Harley retorted.

"Oh, that one was literally on you, my fine-feathered friend."

Bree pointed to Harley's crossed legs and the clamdiggers that exposed the now faded yellow ink drawing on her right ankle. "Is that the tattoo? Woodstock?"

Alex giggled.

"Yes," Harley said, recrossing her legs to better hide one of her less-stellar life decisions.

"It sounds like there's a story behind that tattoo," Erin said.

Alex recalled vividly the wild and crazy fun day she and Harley had spent in Saugerties, New York, in August of 1994. It was filled with lots of music, Melissa Ethridge, a beautiful woman, and plentiful amounts of marijuana. It had cemented her and Harley's relationship as that of sisters as well as friends. The details, however, might not be something Tyler and Ethan would want their children to hear.

"There is, but that's a story best left for another day," Alex said. "Suffice it to say, that there was a failure to communicate. Harley wanted Woodstock the word, not the bird." She shot a glance at her friend, freezing her before Harley could finish giving *her* the bird. Bree didn't catch it, but a stifled snort from Erin indicated she had noted the aborted gesture. A quick glance at her parents revealed a wry grin on Ethan's face and a grateful look on Tyler's.

Friendly banter flowed until the yacht made its way back to the Sag Harbor marina and everyone gathered in the parking lot. Tyler told the girls then that they'd be going with Indra, Abby, and Harley to Greenwich for the night, and she and Ethan would catch up with them as soon as they dealt with a pressing legal matter for Alex.

"You'll make it back in time for my orientation, won't you?" Erin asked.

"We're not sure how long this will take," Tyler said.

Erin glared at Alex. "This is her fault."

Ethan placed his hands on Erin's shoulders in a calming fashion. "This is my idea, not Alex's. We will move heaven and earth to be in Greenwich tonight."

"Fine." Erin's sharp replied signaled more than disappointment. She was angry.

"Then it's settled," Indra said. "If you girls like horses, Abby and I can take you riding."

"First a yacht. Now horseback riding?" Bree squealed. "This is the best day ever."

Indra turned to Alex, Tyler, and Ethan. "Go put an end to this ugly business. Your girls will be in good hands. I'll have rooms prepared for your late arrival."

After seeing the girls off from the beach house, Ethan made a phone call and turned to Alex, Tyler, and Jesse. "We're all set. If we leave now, we can get this done tonight."

CHAPTER THIRTY-EIGHT

Two weeks ago, Alex had learned her father had died. One week ago, she had buried him. Later that same day, police had arrested her for his death, dragged her to the Nineteenth Precinct in handcuffs, and then herded her to the Tombs, where she had had her freedom stripped away in humiliating fashion. It had all failed to break her. Tonight, she was in control as she walked into the Nineteenth. She had one purpose in mind: clearing her name.

It was shortly after six when Alex, Tyler, Jesse, and Ethan entered the second-floor Homicide Division. Detectives Sterling and Diaz introduced them to the other two people there—their boss, Lieutenant Asher, and Sam, their "go-to" gal for all computer, audio, and video needs in the field. Something about the body language between Asher and Jesse left Alex with the impression that they were already well acquainted.

Ethan had clearly picked up on it too. The show he'd made, interrupting a private discussion between Jesse and Asher to bring her a cup of coffee exactly the way she liked it, was no accident. He was marking his territory. And Jesse's broad smile when she accepted his kind gesture signaled unmistakably that Ethan was the clear frontrunner.

Sam installed a wireless micro-camera the size of a dime in Alex's leather designer purse, cutting a half-inch slit in the side below the Coach emblem to accommodate it. Harley would have declared it vandalism of the highest order, but Alex called it a small price to pay if it helped end this nightmare tonight.

Sam then asked Alex to join her in the women's restroom to attach an audio wire to her chest. Tyler, who had remained quiet until now, tightened her hold on Alex's hand, refusing to let go. "I'm coming with you."

Alex returned her concern with a similar squeeze. "I wouldn't have it any other way."

Once in the restroom, Alex lifted her pullover V-neck tunic, allowing Sam to do her work. Tyler had rested a hip against the sink counter, her stance stiff as a board. She wasn't totally happy with Alex's choice to entrap a killer while armed with only a video camera and microphone, but she was keeping her doubts to herself for the moment.

Every wire taped to Alex's torso underscored the danger she'd signed up for, heightening the nerve-racking aspects of what they were doing. Someone needed to ease the tension, so Alex elected herself. When Sam checked the power pack connection, Alex chuckled, "Finally, a use for a nine-volt battery other than in my smoke detectors."

"Actually, one nine-volt stores the same amount of energy as six double-As but takes up a lot less space." Sam pointed to Alex's top. "And it hides well under a shirt."

"This is no joking matter, Alex." Tyler crossed her arms over her chest. Not happy at all.

After giving the door a faint knock, Jesse stuck her head around it. "All set in here? The detectives want to get moving."

"Just finishing up, ma'am," Sam said. "I was just about to do a soundcheck."

"Is it on right now?" Jesse asked.

"Not yet."

"Good. Leave it off and give us a minute." Jesse waited for Sam to leave before she continued. "I know I won't talk you out of this, Alex, but as your lawyer, I need to remind you that the police will be recording everything you say and do tonight. So be careful not to mention any past legally questionable behavior."

Alex understood the cryptic reference to her counter-blackmail; one slip-up could put her back in jail. "I remember, Jesse. You were quite clear about the topics I should avoid." The reminder, while well-intentioned, was unfortunately ill-timed, making Tyler even more upset, if that were possible. Alex turned to her, caressing her arms. "I've got this, T. I'll control the conversation and make sure I say nothing that will get me into more hot water."

"Promise you'll come back to me." Tyler's eyes pleaded along with her voice.

Alex let her lips linger over Tyler's before whispering, "I promise."

She pressed her lips firmly against Tyler's. It didn't matter if Jesse was there. Alex needed this kiss before putting herself in harm's way, and she intended to make the best of it.

Hearing the door closing against its frame, Alex assumed they were alone. She hurried Tyler backward to the sink counter, hoisted her to a sitting position, and stood between her legs. The kiss became desperate as the reality set in that this could be their last. Hands roamed with urgency, not passion. Alex lowered her lips to Tyler's neck, hungry for one last taste of her skin.

Tyler wrapped her legs around Alex's waist, urging Alex to take this to the next level. She slipped a hand under the hem of Tyler's shirt and pushed up a bra cup, teasing a nipple she ached to devour.

A frustrating knock on the door broke her trance, followed by a muffled voice. "Ladies, we need to get going."

Alex stared into Tyler's gray eyes, keeping her hand in place for a few extra beats, not because Tyler was irresistible and Alex was putty whenever she was in her orbit, but because Alex, not some detective out to see her in prison for the next twenty-five years, was in control of what happened tonight. When she was damn good and ready, Alex removed her hand. She straightened Tyler's bra and shirt before giving her one last kiss. "We'll pick this up later tonight."

Tyler gave her what Alex could only describe as a pained smile. "I'm holding you to that."

In the squad room, Lieutenant Asher issued Sterling and Diaz last-minute instructions. "This is a onetime shot. If you don't get it tonight, I'm pulling the plug."

"I understand and appreciate you supporting this op, Lieutenant," Sterling said. "My gut tells me we got this wrong."

"That's for the DA to decide. We just gather evidence," Asher said.

"And that's what I'm about to do." Sterling squared his shoulders, looking like he'd just become Alex's greatest ally. "I'll touch base with you later tonight."

Asher picked up his briefcase and said, "You do that," before walking out.

That brief exchange showed Alex two things: Asher was a jerk and Sterling wasn't. So, while Sam gave Ethan a lesson on the equipment she'd chosen for this op, Alex excused herself from Tyler and pulled Sterling aside. "I just want to say thank you."

Sterling tossed a well-chewed toothpick into the trash. "Contrary to what you might think, I follow the evidence. Arresting you wasn't personal."

"I believe that, and tonight I'll get you the proof you need to arrest the actual killer."

After a few in-house checks of the audio and video equipment, they were set to hit the road. Sterling issued Jesse and Tyler a stern warning to remain at the station house. If Alex correctly read Tyler, though, her cooperation would only last until she felt it was safe to sneak out. That made her crossing the Queensboro Bridge Alex's primary worry. Without a proper distraction, Tyler would be a nervous wreck.

CHAPTER THIRTY-NINE

Diaz drove the precinct's decade-old surveillance van to Jackson Heights with Alex, Ethan, Sam, and Sterling in the back. Five minutes after she parked the van across the street from the apartment building, Alex received an incoming text from Tyler. *Jesse & I are in JH. Which van?*

Alex replied, *Thought u 2 would come. White van.*

Tyler replied, *When?*

Alex's next text read, *5 min. Love you.*

Love you.

Sam placed large noise-canceling headphones over her ears. "Say something, Alex."

"Check one, two, three. Check one, two, three," Alex repeated.

After giving her a thumbs-up, Sam flipped several switches on the console and brought up a crisp, color video feed from the camera hidden in Alex's purse. She removed one earmuff. "We're good here."

Sterling removed a fresh toothpick from his mouth. "All right, Alex, we only get one shot at this. If you feel you're in danger at any time, I want you to get out of there. If you can't leave or feel you're being threatened, I want you to use a duress word. Pick a word that you don't think will come up in conversation tonight, something unique."

The first word that came to mind that made her feel safe was "Napa."

"All right, we'll move into position right after you enter the apartment. If you say the word 'Napa,' we'll bust in the door. Do you have any questions?"

"If I get the confession we're looking for, what then?" Alex asked.

"If you can do so safely, get out of there as quickly as possible. If not, use your duress word, and we'll move in and secure the scene," Sterling said.

Alex looked up at Ethan one last time for reassurance. He winked. "You got this, Alex. I'll be right behind you."

Sam turned on the recorders. Diaz remained ready in the driver's seat. Ethan gave her a pat on the knee, and Sterling slid open the side door. Alex blew out a long, stress-relieving breath before grabbing her purse and exiting the van at a leisurely pace. Each step she took made her more confident that this was the only way to get to the truth. Each step also made her more nervous than she expected. What if she pushed too hard? Would she end up like her father, dead on the floor with her skull bashed in? Out of choices, she pressed forward.

Alex entered the building and took the stairs up to the second floor, her heart pounding harder up each step. In the hallway, she paused to gather her courage, telling herself that this was no time to chicken out. She stiffened her spine before giving the door a firm knock.

A long, excruciating minute later, the door opened. Alex forced a smile. "You are a hard one to track down." She waited for a response, weighing if her unexpected visit was welcomed or considered a threat. The initial response would set the tone and tell Alex how to guide the conversation toward a confession. And there it was. The hint of a smile. "Hello, Kelly."

"Alex? What are you doing here? You're the last one I expected to see at my door." There was a time when Alex could precisely tell what Kelly Thatcher felt from the way she flipped her hair or shifted her eyes. But after thirteen years and the buckets of bad blood between them, her expression was hard to read beyond skepticism.

"May I come in? I really need to talk to you." Alex kept it simple to pique her curiosity.

"Why now?" Kelly narrowed an eye.

During the ride to the precinct earlier, Ethan had instructed Alex on how to work a suspect. His best tip was that a good undercover story was always based on truth. "*Stay as close to the truth as you can without tipping your hand,*" he had said.

"The police and everyone else I know thinks I killed my father. I have no one else to turn to. May I please come in?"

Kelly slowly opened the door wider and stepped aside, offering Alex a pathway into her apartment. The door closed—Sterling, Diaz, and Ethan's predetermined cue to hop out of the surveillance van and position themselves inside the stairwell on the second floor out of the line of sight of the apartment door in the event Kelly opened it.

Alex scanned the living room, but her mother's Leica was nowhere in sight. She hadn't really expected it to be. Ethan had told her he'd found it in the bedroom hidden in the bottom dresser drawer underneath a pair of jeans. She looked for something she could compliment Kelly on, but the room's beige fabrics and bare white walls provided little inspiration. Then she remembered what Ethan had said about staking out the apartment building: "*When she went for a jog, I made my move.*"

Alex defaulted to Kelly's vanity and her carnal instincts. "You're looking good, Kelly. You must run mile after mile to keep those lines of yours so sleek. You look absolutely delicious, in fact."

A second faint grin creased Kelly's cool facade, but as quickly as it appeared, it faded. "What's changed since you threw me out of your office?"

Alex remembered Ethan telling her, "*Get her to trust you. Acknowledge how you left things.*" Remembering Jesse's earlier warning, she knew all mention of blackmail and counter-blackmail was off the table. "I know when we last saw each other last month that we were adversaries."

"That's an understatement," Kelly said the words Alex wanted to say, but she needed to stick to the script.

"When you came back into my life, you threw me for a loop. All the hurt I felt when you broke up with me at Yale came flooding back, and I could barely think straight." Alex reminded herself to be honest, or Kelly would see right through her. "You really hurt me back then. I went into a deep depression and overdosed on sleeping pills."

"You still haven't answered the question, Alex."

"Hear me out. If it wasn't for Harley finding me, I would have died. She helped me put the pieces back together again. Well, almost. After you, I couldn't bring myself to get close to another woman again. One-night stands became my trademark. Then you came back into my life."

"Don't bullshit me, Alex. I saw a picture of you with some blonde last weekend." Kelly's sharp movements bordered on agitation. She went to a table near the kitchen entrance and poured gin into a glass filled with ice. Her need for a drink convinced Alex she had Kelly on the hook.

"*Make her think she's in control. Get her to think she has a hold over you*," Ethan had advised.

Alex walked to the well-worn couch centered in the living room, carefully positioned her purse on an end table so the camera pointed toward her, and took a seat near the far end. "That's what I'm trying to tell you. When I sent you away last month, I realized I had been fooling myself for years. None of the women I'd been with measured up to you. I missed your gentle touch. The pillow-soft feel of your lips and how turned-on I felt every time I wrapped myself around your body. That woman reminded me of you—blonde, runner's body, attractive, and smart. I tried it with her, but it wasn't the same. She wasn't you."

Saying those words to Kelly made Alex's stomach turn even more than it had when she'd had no recourse but to kowtow to her blackmail demands and hire her at Castle Resorts. Happily, that had lasted for only two excruciating weeks. The words she'd just said only rang true when she said them to Tyler. Kelly may have helped shape the foundation of the physical attributes Alex found attractive, but beyond that, those features had no resemblance to what Alex felt in her heart when she was with Tyler. She only felt alive when her body was entwined with Tyler's. The only touches and kisses she craved were from the woman parked down the street somewhere.

Kelly finished fixing two gin and tonics, sat on the couch next to Alex, and handed her a glass. "What are you saying, Alex?"

Alex pretended to sip on the cocktail before putting it on the coffee table in front of the couch and steeling herself for her next nauseating words. "I'm saying I don't want just any woman." She scooted closer to Kelly, resisted the urge to throw up, and said breathily, "I want you."

Kelly downed her cocktail and placed the glass on the table. She turned and kissed Alex, catching her off guard but not surprising her. Kelly had taken the bait. Alex deepened the kiss out of the necessity to sell her cover story, but when Kelly groped her breast, she broke their kiss in an instant.

"*Don't beg,*" Ethan had warned. "*Don't appear weak, or she won't buy it. Assert yourself. You'll need to figure out beforehand exactly how far you're willing to take this.*"

What Alex had to do next made her sick, but it was the only way to sell it. Already mentally begging for Tyler's forgiveness, she grabbed Kelly's straying hand, and in a single, swift motion, she forced Kelly prone on the couch, mounted her, and began devouring her neck.

Alex couldn't bring herself to touch Kelly in the places she ached to touch Tyler, and she took great care, at all costs, to avoid her lips again. She'd have to rely instead on Kelly's appetite for talking dirty during foreplay. She laid it on thick with a low, husky tone. "You're so fucking hot." She worked her lips behind Kelly's ear and reverted to their tried-and-true back-and-forth from thirteen years ago. "Tell me." When Kelly didn't moan, Alex changed to the other side of Kelly's neck and rocked her hips into her again. "Tell me," she repeated.

Kelly let out a loud, familiar moan, signaling that Alex still had her on the hook. "I'm so wet for you," Kelly growled, tossing her head from side to side before moaning again. "I'm so wet. Fuck me, Alex. Fuck me."

"*Don't push it. Let her suggest things,*" Ethan had said earlier.

Alex could only stall for a minute more. If the past was prologue, Kelly expected Alex to fulfill her demand without delay. But Alex had two problems: she needed to get Kelly into the bedroom where Ethan had seen the camera, and she needed the change of location for their tryst to be Kelly's idea.

Alex exaggerated a clumsy shift of her torso and legs and then stopped kissing Kelly and groaned, "Fucking couch. This would've been a lot easier ten years ago."

Without skipping a beat, Kelly said, "Bedroom. Now."

Alex dismounted, pulled Kelly up, grabbed her purse with one hand, and dragged Kelly by the other toward the bedroom. "I thought you'd never ask."

Alex placed her purse on a chair in the corner of the bedroom, positioning it to have an unobstructed view of the bed and dresser. Saying a silent prayer, "Forgive me, Tyler," she leapt onto the bed and fell on top of Kelly.

When Kelly tried again to kiss her, Alex racked her brain to remember what cringeworthy foreplay she and Kelly had engaged in to shift them both into high gear. The only thing that came to mind, unfortunately, was the thing that had led to this situation in the first place: her decision to take pictures of them having sex thirteen years earlier. The photos that Kelly used to blackmail her with. The idea made her want to vomit, but the only way she could think of to get Kelly to admit to having the camera was to reenact that night.

Alex grabbed her by the shoulders. "Wait, wait, wait. I want to watch you, Kelly. Like before. Strip for me."

Kelly took the bait like a shark to chum. She jumped off Alex, turned on the CD player resting on the dresser, and hit PLAY. A slow, sexy song began to play. Alex could guess the reason the perfect striptease song was queued up and at her fingertips, but the thought made her stomach roil.

Kelly winked and began slowly unbuttoning her blouse. Alex focused on her, doing her best not to dry heave at the sight. Alex dug deep to appear convincing, playfully reaching out a few times in a half-hearted attempt to fondle her. When Kelly removed her blouse, Alex dialed up her act. "The last time you stripped for me, I took pictures. Fuck. I wish I could take pictures of you right now."

"*Remember, don't push anything. Let her suggest it,*" Ethan had said.

Kelly added two more hip sways, running her hands down her legging-clad thighs. "I have a camera on my phone."

Alex had to think fast. The only way to get past this stumbling block was to push. She wagged her finger in disapproval. "Digital wouldn't be the same. You deserve to be filmed." Alex reached out again, but to her disgust, Kelly pushed her breasts into her face. Alex nearly hurled. She pushed her back a foot and began caressing a leg covered with spandex. "Damn. I wish I hadn't lost my Leica."

Kelly tossed her head back, mouth agape. "You didn't lose it. I have it."

Alex remembered one more thing Ethan suggested, "*Once you know you have her, take the upper hand.*" When he'd said that, Alex had considered her options. Should she act happy or mad about Kelly having her Leica? Which response would knock Kelly off her game and have her admitting to how she'd come to possess the camera? Before walking into the apartment, she hadn't decided which path to take, but the seething now building in her gut decided for her.

Alex's mood changed on a dime. She stopped her ogling and touching. "What the fuck, Kelly? You've had it all this time?"

"No, baby. It wasn't me." Kelly's scrunched brow confirmed Alex had put her on the defensive.

Ethan had ended his advice with, "*…and then turn the tables on her.*"

Alex recoiled from the bed and straightened her mussed shirt. "Christ, Kelly. You had me thinking I could trust you."

Kelly's extra rounded eyes said she was in a panic. "I swear, baby. It was your fucking father."

"What did that prick have to do with my Leica?"

"That piece of work had it."

"What the fuck?" Alex paced the room. She let her rage over her father enlisting Andrew to do his bidding fuel her response and put Kelly on the defensive. "That camera was the only thing I had of my mother's." She stopped in front of Kelly and stood face-to-face, staring her down. "If you had anything to do with this—"

"I swear." Kelly raised her hands in surrender. "The first time I saw it was in William's office." Kelly was back on her heels, and Alex had to continue firing away. *Don't give her a chance to pause and think.*

"You lie. When were you in Father's office?"

"Two weeks ago. He flaunted it like it was some type of sick trophy."

"I don't believe you," Alex growled.

Kelly cowered. "He said you'd never get your hands on it again. Well, I showed him." Kelly rushed to her dresser, fished the camera from her bottom drawer, and offered it to Alex. "Here. It's only a camera, for fuck's sake. I took it for you. Take it."

That was Alex's golden ticket. Kelly had admitted to taking the camera from William's office. She had to be the one who killed him. Alex snatched the camera and barked, "And I'm sure he just let you walk out of there with this without a fight."

"He didn't put up much of a fight. One shove was all it took."

Bingo! That was it. A full confession. "You killed my father?" Alex crowded Kelly.

"I only shoved him. He fell, but I didn't kill him. I grabbed the camera and got the hell out of there."

"So, you just left him there to die?"

"What was I supposed to do? Help the man who ruined my life? He was breathing, so I left."

"You bitch!" Alex's rage boiled over, and all coherent thought left her.

She tossed the camera on the bed and lunged at Kelly, forcing her to the carpet with a loud thud. She must've knocked the wind out of her because she was gulping for air. But that didn't dampen Alex's fury. She rose to her knees, straddling the gasping woman who had killed her father, and started ripping at her clothing. "You wanted to strip. Here, let me help you." The front door flew open with a bang, which was followed by the sound of a booming, male voice yelling, "NYPD!" Neither slowed her.

From the corner of her eye, Alex saw Sterling and Diaz hit the room and stop dead in their tracks. She had Kelly, naked from the waist up, pinned to the floor. She continued to hold Kelly's hands up over her head with her right hand and stuff her bra into her mouth with her left. If Sterling and Diaz had arrived a minute later, she would have had Kelly's blouse down her throat, too, until she blew buttons out the other end.

Sterling holstered his service weapon and laughed. "All right, Alex. We've got it from here."

Alex released Kelly's hands but pointed an index finger an inch from her face. "The next time you strip, it's going to be for a five-foot-nothing prison guard who will search your vajayjay with a flashlight." Alex rose and hovered over Kelly, menacingly. "You won't last a day."

Shifting her gaze past Sterling and Diaz, she saw Ethan, who was also laughing. He shook his head. "Only one day behind bars, and you're a jailhouse badass."

Diaz threw Kelly a T-shirt she'd grabbed from the dresser and ordered, "Put this on." After Kelly was adequately clothed, Diaz cuffed her. "You have the right to remain silent…"

Alex sagged in relief. Her two-week nightmare was over. She finally had her life back. Her future was hers to build, not the New York State justice system's. She started listing the things she was grateful for, small and large, beginning with Callie and ending with Tyler. Alex swore to herself that she would never take one minute with her for granted, even if it took moving to Sacramento. She wouldn't spend one more night away from her.

Sterling and Diaz perp-walked Kelly toward their van with Ethan and Alex several steps behind. Instead of following, Ethan pulled Alex to a stop and quietly asked, "What the hell happened in there, Alex?"

Taking down Kelly still had Alex amped. She wanted to get back to Tyler, not answer questions. "I got a confession. That's what happened."

"But at what cost? She was practically naked. Exactly how far did you take it?"

"Not as far as you think, but I did what I had to do to sell it."

Ethan was right. Though Alex had drawn the line at what she could stomach, had she gone further than Tyler would understand and accept? Would the kiss, the thigh caress, and the horrifying neck kisses cost her the love of her life?

"Tyler won't like this."

"I want to tell her, but I don't know how."

Ethan lowered his head, raising it a moment later with misty eyes. "Tyler spent thirteen years keeping secrets about the true impact of the rape. They cost me my wife. Secrets will fester until they eat you up inside. I don't want that for either of you. You need to tell her."

"I will, but once things settle down."

"It better be sooner rather than later." He gestured toward Jesse's Mercedes, which was parked near the corner. "Let's tell them it's over."

As Alex and Ethan crossed the street and passed a streetlight, Tyler bolted from the passenger side and shot toward them in a full sprint. Before Alex could take another step, Tyler threw her arms around her neck and pulled her into a tight embrace. Neither said a word. Words would be a waste of time. They stood motionless until the sound of someone clearing his throat broke the silence.

"Ahem." He tried a second time. When neither moved, Ethan interrupted, "I hate to break this up, but we need to meet them at the precinct. They need your statement, Alex."

Alex pulled back. Explaining the fuzzy lines she'd ended up drawing with Kelly would have to wait.

CHAPTER FORTY

The smell of freshly brewed coffee hit Ethan's nose when he opened the glass doors leading to the homicide squad room. That meant one thing: the detectives expected a long night. He held the door for Alex, Tyler, and Jesse and zeroed on Sterling sitting at his desk in the far corner. Sterling waved the group over.

"I'll head down to booking and bring her up after she's processed," Sterling said before directing his next words to Alex. "Meanwhile, Diaz will take your statement."

"Sure thing." Alex followed Diaz to her desk. Jesse sat beside her, with Tyler and Ethan standing close behind. Tyler placed a hand on Alex's shoulder, which Alex acknowledged with a brief squeeze. Those two had a connection that Ethan hadn't come close to replicating in the last thirteen years. The sight of it, though, no longer cut him to the quick. Instead, it made him proud of having pushed them together.

Alex walked Diaz through the happenings inside Kelly's apartment, pausing when she reached a certain point. She shifted in her chair, took Tyler by the hand, and looked her in the eye. "I want you to know that what happened next sickened me, and only thoughts of you got me through it."

Tyler's posture stiffened. Her quiet nod meant she was holding back her anxiety. Ethan whispered into her ear, "Just hear her out and trust that she loves you." Tyler nodded again in silence.

Alex shifted back and directed the rest of her statement to Diaz. "After she kissed me, I knew I had to sell it to get her into the bedroom and produce the camera. So I played along, kissing her in a way I knew would make her want to have sex. I feigned discomfort on the couch, and she suggested the bedroom. When we fell into bed, I asked her to strip for me." She grimaced. "Our foreplay used to include her doing a striptease while I took pictures of her."

"That was great thinking." Diaz jotted down some notes.

Alex acknowledged the comment with a tentative nod. "Before she could take her bra off, I said something about wanting to take pictures and wishing I still had my old camera. That's when Kelly admitted to having it. I pressed her about how she got it. She said my father had it in his office, and she'd taken it after she shoved him. That's when I lost it. I decked her."

Ethan was never so glad to be proved wrong. He should've never assumed Alex had let it go too far. He failed miserably to hold back a snicker. It became contagious. Diaz joined in first, and then Tyler did too. Alex turned around. "You're not mad?"

"Trust me, I'm not happy about the kissing." Tyler drew Alex's chin toward her with a hand. "But that was pretty badass." Their ensuing kiss gave Ethan the impression those two would be all right.

The squad room door opened. Sterling stepped through, pulling Kelly, in handcuffs, into the room by the elbow. Her mascara was running and her long, tangled blond hair looked fit to nest a family of robins. She cast a cold, hard stare in their direction.

"I'm taking her to Interview Room One," Sterling said.

Diaz gave him a thumbs-up.

* * *

An hour later, Detective Greg Sterling greeted ADA Marshall, still dressed in a tuxedo, at the squad room door. "Thank you for coming tonight. My apologies for pulling you away from your evening plans."

"When I'm told I'm about to have egg on my face for indicting an innocent person, I need to be part of the cleanup." Marshall hung his overcoat on the back of a detective's chair as he passed by.

"That's the same reason why I'm here." Sterling should have listened to his gut when he thought the evidence had added up too quickly. Maybe then he wouldn't owe Alex Castle the biggest apology of his life. "We need to fix our mistake. Luckily, we can."

Leading Marshall and Diaz to the interrogation room, Sterling let Marshall step through first. The only light source was a single rectangular ceiling-mounted fluorescent fixture hanging directly over the table. Diaz leaned against the wall closest to the mirror while Sterling and Marshall took seats at the steel table across from Thatcher and her sketchy-looking defense lawyer. Sterling had dealt with this counselor before. He was a step above public defenders, in that he was available around the clock and worked for cheap, but he was notorious for cutting quick deals to keep the clients rolling along like an assembly line.

Following a video presentation of Alex's excellent undercover work, Thatcher and her lawyer privately consulted. Several shakes and nods later, the lawyer asked, "What's your offer?"

"Twenty years with a chance of parole after fifteen," ADA Marshall said. "But she confesses now for the record."

After more consulting and more vigorous head shakes and nods, Thatcher's defense lawyer replied, "We have a deal."

Typical, Sterling thought. The lawyer was in a hurry to keep his ass out of court so he could "defend" more sleazy clients. Everyone involved in this case was in a hurry, and Sterling was guilty of it too. He considered swearing to himself that it wouldn't happen again, but quickly dismissed the notion. The way politics worked in this city guaranteed it would be a promise he couldn't keep.

The lawyer nodded to Thatcher. She then began in a shaky voice, "None of this would have happened if Alex had just paid me for those damn pictures instead of giving me the job I'd demanded as an alternative. Then I would have taken my money and left the city…"

* * *

Two weeks earlier

Kelly Thatcher never thought she'd set foot in Castle Resort headquarters again after Alex's private muscle had escorted her off the premises and repossessed her golden ticket. Those delicious photos of her and Alex were supposed to set her up for life. Now that Papa Castle had summoned her, threatening that he'd tell the police about her blackmail scheme if she didn't show up, she was glad she'd neglected to turn over to Alex's private eye the backup set of copies she had made of the photos. She tapped the envelope she'd tucked inside her warm-up jacket, hoping those pictures would be enough to keep her from sharing a cell for the next several years with a hardened criminal.

She had little choice about attending tonight's meeting, but she could choose when she would arrive, and she decided that showing up fifteen minutes late would make her point. She entered the elevator in the lobby, pressed the button for her desired floor, and moved to the rear, occupying herself with a text message from her new employer, reminding her that it was her turn to do the coffee run tomorrow. Her sunglasses made it harder to read, but she opted to leave them on. Removing them would only reveal to the other occupant of the car how many drinks it had taken to prepare her to face the consequences of her harebrained scheme.

As the door started to slide shut, a voice from the lobby yelled, "Hold the elevator, please." The other occupant pressed a button, reversing the door's movement. A moment later, someone else boarded. "Thank you. Twenty-three, please."

Kelly didn't have to look up for that familiar voice and floor choice to send a sinking feeling to her gut. From behind her dark glasses, she watched as Alex settled against the opposite wall, appearing lost in thought. Even though she was running a few minutes late, the fact that she and Alex were arriving at the same time was no coincidence. Did Papa Castle order her here to humiliate Alex in front of her? To humiliate both of them? Whatever his game was, Kelly decided she needed to play one as well.

The elevator bounced to a stop on the twentieth floor, and when the other occupant exited Kelly did too. Instead of proceeding to the gym as he did, she veered to the east stairwell and jogged up. Climbing the three flights of stairs left her winded and thinking she'd better stop drinking or start jogging more than ten minutes twice a week.

Once inside the Castle office suite, she tiptoed to Alex's office but found it unoccupied. She then continued her sleuthing toward Papa Castle's office, where dim light and angry voices spilled through the wide-open door. She dared not get too close. Ducking under Gretchen's desk allowed her to stay out of sight and to make out most of the conversation. It appeared that Papa was firing his precious cub and that he had also discovered that his other degenerate offspring had been stealing from the others. *Boo-hoo.* How the mighty had fallen.

When Alex said, "I'll pick up my things first thing tomorrow morning," that was Kelly's cue to remain absolutely quiet. She waited until she heard the main suite door close shut, then crawled from her hiding place, baseball cap and sunglasses in hand. The exciting developments of the last few minutes had sobered her enough to construct a plan of her own. She wouldn't take William's threats without a fight. His aversion to gay people and lousy press could finally mark a payday big enough to make a fresh start far away from everything Castle.

She walked through the open door. William was at his wall safe, stowing a legal-sized leather document folio. As he lifted a vintage camera within it to slide the folio beneath it, Kelly announced herself. "That looks like Alex's old camera from Yale."

William fumbled the camera, catching it before it fell to the ground. He turned, his eyes burning with anger and hatred. "You're not as dim-witted as your past would indicate." He returned to his desk, camera in hand.

"Many have underestimated me, and many have paid the price," she said. "I loved that camera. So many wonderful memories."

"That may be so, but this camera has taken its last picture thanks to you." He placed it on top of his desk.

"But why? It captures its subjects so well." Kelly removed the pictures of her and Alex from the envelope in her pocket and tossed them onto William's desk.

"What is this, another one of your feckless threats?" scoffed William.

The battle of wills had begun; Kelly would not walk away empty-handed this time. This was her last chance to profit from these pictures. "That depends on whether you're willing to have these pictures on the front page of *The National Enquirer*."

"I've been one step ahead of you ever since you first slithered your way into my daughter's life." Kelly laughed at William's attempt to deflect, but he continued, "I will never give you the satisfaction of profiting one dime off of this family. I called you here to make sure you knew the risks if you ever tried to squeeze a Castle again, but apparently, you are a slow learner."

"Are you sure of that?" Kelly pointed to the pictures that had given her hours of enjoyment over the years.

"This will end badly for you, as did your engagement to young Mr. Pruitt. You have never been a match for me. I will always make you suffer for bringing your depravity to this family, just as I did thirteen years ago."

Kelly's face heated with a fury she couldn't control as the real reason for her life falling apart after she dumped Alex took shape. "Are you saying you had something to do with Douglas calling off the wedding?"

The pompous ass puffed out his chest. "I had everything to do with it. That and the abrupt end of your scholarship."

"You son of a bitch."

William had engineered everything that had gone wrong in her life and was laughing at her misery. That was all Kelly could take. She lunged at Papa Castle, giving him a forceful shove that sent him toppling toward his desk.

He flailed his arms to regain his balance, but with nothing to grab onto, the speed of his fall made it impossible. His head hit the sharp corner of his executive desk with a loud crack. Before he hit the ground, blood spattered the desk and a good number of its contents. He finally thudded on the floor, remaining motionless as blood pooled around his head on the carpet.

"Shit, shit, shit, shit!" Kelly panicked. She'd been out for a quick buck, not a murder rap. A picture of life behind bars flashed before her eyes. Not in her wildest, most self-conceited dreams did she consider herself cut out for prison.

She started breathing again when she heard him groan, the weight of spending a thirty-year stretch as someone's bitch lifting. She was confident that she could plead assault down to a misdemeanor. But they'd have to catch her first. Her heart beating so fast she thought it might burst, her eyes alit on the camera at the heart of this whole mess. She grabbed it from the edge of the desk and ran out of the office, out the main suite doors, and down the stairs to the twentieth floor. She replaced her cap and sunglasses, slipped the camera under her running jacket, and nervously rode the elevator to the lobby.

* * *

Ethan had leaned against the wall down the hallway leading to the interrogation room while Sterling and the ADA interrogated the suspect he had unearthed. The wait was a glimpse into his future once he settled fully into his life as a retired police officer. Private investigators weren't cops, but they often did the same legwork, investigating cases. He'd have to get used to standing on the sidelines while someone else ran with the ball he'd handed off to them.

At least, Ethan got to do his waiting next to Jesse. She appeared as nervous as he was and likely had the same question: What was Kelly saying in there? She could easily claim to be the innocent victim and spin everything, including the counter-blackmail, to make Alex out to be the villain.

To break the rising tension, Ethan voiced a question that had been gnawing at him since they first stepped into the squad room tonight. "So, I take it you and Lieutenant Asher have a history."

"It's more of a wish than a thing," Jesse said.

"Whose wish?"

"His."

Before Ethan could break a smile following the response he wanted to hear, the interrogation room door opened. Jesse pulled herself from the wall and stood in the center of the hallway. Ethan did the same, forming a roadblock that neither Sterling nor Marshall, who were walking toward them, would get past.

"Well?" Jesse asked.

Sterling cocked up the right corner of his lips before removing the toothpick from his mouth. "We have a full confession and plea agreement for twenty years."

A wave of relief nearly swallowed Ethan. He'd done his job. Besides finding the killer, he'd saved Tyler from years of heartache. Protecting her, he'd decided, would be a lifetime job.

Jesse focused on ADA Marshall. "I believe we have some business to close out. I hope we won't have to wait until Monday for your office to file the paperwork on this."

"Walk with me," Marshall said. Jesse kept up step for step with Ethan one behind. "Don't worry, Ms. Simmons. I'll call my staff tonight and have them file the dismissal motion with the court clerk first thing tomorrow. It should be processed by the afternoon. I'll have a copy of it faxed over to your office."

Steps after entering the squad room, Jesse said, "I appreciate that. My client will be happy to finally put this behind her." She turned to Alex, giving her a thumbs-up, and Alex and Tyler embraced, their bodies quaking. Ethan let a second self-satisfied grin form on his lips. Alex's nightmare was over, and so was Tyler's because he had done his job as a detective and as a husband.

As they parted, Alex ran a fingertip down Tyler's cheek. "Move in with me."

Tyler matched Alex's growing smile. "Yes."

Ethan had a lot to figure out, sooner rather than later.

CHAPTER FORTY-ONE

Greenwich, Connecticut

Diffused sunlight streamed through the windows of the guest room Indra had set aside last night for Alex and Tyler. Alex had been awake for almost an hour, inventorying every inch of Tyler as she peacefully slept on the other side of the bed. She was finally free. The charges would be dropped by the end of the day, and she would be able to start a new life with this unique creature.

She had energy to burn. She considered waking Tyler for another round of lovemaking but discarded the idea as quickly as she birthed it. Tyler needed more than three hours of sleep. Rising carefully, she dressed. After lacing up her running shoes, she hovered over Tyler and kissed her goodbye on the cheek.

Tyler wrapped her arms around Alex's neck and asked in a groggy voice, "Where are you going so early?"

"For a run. I have a lot of extra energy."

Tyler opened her eyes and grinned slyly. "I can think of better ways to burn off that energy."

"Last night wasn't enough?" Alex snorted, considering Tyler's suggestion for a moment, but decided to stick to her plan. "I haven't run in a while, and I miss it."

"I get it, babe. I'd go with you, but— Who am I kidding? I hate running now. Go. Burn off some of that energy."

Alex gave her a quick kiss. "I'll see you in an hour."

Alex descended the broad, sweeping stairs to the main floor and was about to head out the door when she heard someone running down the stairs behind her. Thinking it was Tyler, she asked as she turned around, "Couldn't wait for me to get back?" When she saw it was Erin coming down, her cheeks heated in embarrassment. "Sorry, I thought—"

"You thought I was Mom." Erin, dressed in full running gear, was the spitting image of her mother. How Alex wished she would've met Tyler when she first explored her sexuality and not Kelly Thatcher. Her life would've turned out so differently.

"Are you a runner?" Erin asked Alex.

"Sure am. I ran long distance in high school and Yale. How about you?"

"Long distance too."

"Ah, just like your mom."

"You mean like she used to," Erin snickered.

"I was heading out for three. Would you like to join me?" Alex hoped that last night's announcement that her troubles were behind her and Tyler letting Erin partake in the champagne celebration that followed might have put a tiny crack in Erin's icy facade.

When Erin added a smile to her shrug, Alex got her answer. "Sure, why not?"

Following a good stretch, both started out at a slow warm-up pace. Alex nodded to Erin a quarter-mile in, and they picked up speed, settling at Alex's pace of a nine-minute mile. While they ran, Alex let Erin set the direction and tone of their brief, sporadic conversations, touching on the differences between life in New York and California.

During their post-run stretch, Erin finally ventured out of the safe zone of conversation. "What was your undergrad major?"

Alex stretched out a hamstring, thinking that crack in Erin's facade was expanding. "Humanities."

"Interesting. I thought it would've been economics since you're the CEO of a company. Why that?"

"Excellent question. Let me think." She stretched out her other leg. "Because I thought it would be a good foundation for my MBA, I guess. I knew from a very young age my father expected me to go into the family business."

"Did you want to?"

"Yes. Not because I loved the hotel business, but because I loved this thing my mother and father had had a hand in building. The most important thing about running a business my father said was not to understand the technical aspects but to understand the people who make it all happen—the clientele and employees. Studying humanities helped me understand human behavior, thought, and values. Most importantly, the coursework taught me to think critically, communicate, and problem solve."

"Interesting. I may have to rethink my major."

"You'll have plenty of time to decide on a major, but in your case, if you hope to learn a specific skill such as graphic design, then a specialized degree might be the way to go. My advice is to take your time, take a wide range of classes in your freshman year, and then figure out what you like. Let that be your guide."

"Thanks, Alex. That's good advice."

"We better get a move on. It's an hour's drive to Yale."

Erin stood straighter but shuffled her feet, inspecting the tops of her sneakers. The tone of their talk was about to change. "I'm happy you're my sponsor today."

Alex was grateful for this time with Erin. It was a significant start at getting to know Tyler's family, which she hoped to be part of one day. Alex hesitated at her next question but thought it was time they tackled the proverbial elephant in the room. "So, Erin, about me and your mom."

"I can tell she really loves you."

One step forward, Alex thought. Those words were the first sign that Erin was on the road to accepting her and Tyler's relationship. "And I really love her. She's very special to me, and I hope you know I only want to make her happy."

Erin sighed, perhaps signaling two steps back. "I won't lie, Alex. When I first found out about you and Mom, I didn't like *it* and I didn't like *you*. Because I blamed you for my parents' divorce." Alex opened her mouth to respond, but before she could, Erin added, "But my dad told me you're not to blame for any of it."

"Your dad is an incredible man." But he was more than that. Ethan was a man who never ceased to amaze Alex.

"Of course, I'd like nothing more to see my parents together again, but both of them tell me that's never going to happen. So, the best I can hope for is to see both of them happy. I've never seen my mom smile this much, and I'm sure it's because of you."

"So, would you be okay if your mom and I spent more time together?"

"You've practically been living together and attached at the hips for weeks. I don't think it's mathematically possible to spend more time together," Erin laughed.

Alex joined her. "You are a smart one. Let me rephrase. Would you—"

"I get it, Alex. You're girlfriends." Erin stared her in the eye for the first time and nodded, confirming, at the very least, her acceptance. "Have you two figured out this whole long-distance thing?"

Alex and Tyler had discussed nothing past moving in together. They still had to decide where and how. However, that would change, starting tonight. "We're working on it."

CHAPTER FORTY-TWO

Manhattan, New York, the following day

Knowing the Falling family needed to have what might turn into an emotional discussion, Alex herded her sister from the garden patio into the kitchen. As she helped her clean up the dishes from the delicious dinner Syd had prepared for them when they'd returned after the tour of Yale, she heard her clear her throat and mumble a quiet "Uh-huh."

Alex grinned at her sister's way of getting her attention. "All right, I'll bite. What does uh-huh mean this time?"

"That grin of yours. What have you and Tyler been cooking up?"

Alex turned off the faucet and placed the plate she was holding in the sink. The news she was about to break deserved giving her sister her full attention. "I asked Tyler to move in with me, and she said yes."

Syd couldn't wipe her hands on the dishtowel quick enough and pull Alex into a brief breath-stealing bear hug. "That's wonderful, Baby Sis. I'm so happy for you. Both of you."

"I wanted you to know before we took definitive action." Alex turned toward the sliding door leading to the patio, where the girls were playing with young, fluffy Callie, as Tyler and Ethan looked on. Alex continued, more hesitantly, "Tyler and I plan to sell my townhouse and move into Father's house."

Syd's mouth fell open. "I thought you didn't like that place."

"I don't, but it's large enough to accommodate everyone. I'd like to remodel it and make new memories there."

Syd's eyes softened. "What about Ethan? Is he okay with Bree moving across the country?"

Alex nodded in the affirmative. "Tyler and Ethan discussed it earlier. They're getting ready to talk to the girls right now."

"I love it, but I bet Father is turning in his grave." Syd laughed, nudging Alex on the shoulder. "He always wanted you to have the house, but I bet he never dreamed another woman would be part of the deal."

"We have a lot of redecorating ahead of us to exorcise Father from every room."

The doorbell rang, and Alex excused herself to answer the door. It was Jesse. "Is Syd here? I think she needs to hear this too."

"That doesn't sound good." Alex said as she led her downstairs to the kitchen.

"Hey, Syd. First, the good news." Jesse handed Alex a piece of paper with the official seal of Manhattan on it. "It's official. The DA has dropped the charge against you. They make an announcement later today. You may want to put your PR folks to work on a statement as well. You'll be happy to know that you have the state's apology."

Alex rolled her eyes. "I'll sleep better tonight knowing they're sorry."

"Now the bad news," Jesse continued. "As a courtesy, the ADA told me the police arrested your brother today for embezzlement. The police found documents in William's safe that detailed his larceny. His lawyer is working out a plea deal in exchange for his testimony to put Victor Padula away for a very long time."

Syd gasped, throwing a hand to her chest.

Alex rubbed her temples to stave off a mounting headache. All the effort she and Ethan had gone to to keep Andrew out of jail was wasted—because of their father. It was ironic. William had gone to such great lengths when he was alive to protect the family name. Now, in death, he had precipitated its destruction.

After Erin and Bree played a bit with Callie, Ethan and Tyler asked them to join them at the small outdoor dining table on the patio. Tyler swigged her wine to muster the courage to begin a discussion that would upend all their lives. For the better, she hoped. "So, girls, I have something important to discuss with you."

"You and Alex have finally figured out the long-distance thing?"

Tyler snapped her stare toward Erin, wondering if Alex had spilled the beans during their tour of Yale. "What?"

"When I asked her about you two this morning, all she would say was that you two were working on it. Which I figured was code for, 'ask your mom.'"

Tyler was proud of how mature and perceptive Erin had become. Whatever was behind her transformation, Tyler was grateful it had come when it did. "Yes, Erin, we've figured it out. Your dad and I talked today, and we've come to a decision. Alex asked me to move in with her, and I said yes."

"Here or in Sacramento?" Bree asked.

"Manhattan, but not this house. Alex inherited her father's house close to here. It's much larger than this one, and each of you will have your own room. Plus, there's an entertainment playhouse in the backyard."

Erin listened and waited, but Bree was much younger and couldn't hold back her questions. "What about Dad? I don't want to move away from him."

The alarm in Bree's tone was palpable but unnecessary. Tyler nodded to Ethan. He should be the one to allay her fear. He covered Bree's hand with his and said, "Let me ask you, Bree, do you like it here?"

"Yeah, but not without you."

"What if I told you I'd like to move out here too?" Smiles grew on both girls. "I could get a place in town, and Erin would only be an hour and a half away. You and I would see each other every week, and we could still have our family dinner every Sunday."

Tyler loved Ethan for not making her choose between her family and the woman she loved. While she hadn't been expecting him to offer to move out to New York with the girls, it didn't come as a complete surprise. She was sure Jesse had something to do with Ethan's eagerness to relocate.

"But what about your job, Dad?" Erin asked.

"I'm licensed in New York, so I can move my private detective firm here. And with my new connections"—Ethan winked at Tyler—"I'm sure I can attract a lot of high-end clients."

"What about your job, Mom?" Erin asked.

"I do all of my work electronically. When I need to consult with Maddie or clients, we can call or Skype. I've been doing it for the last two weeks, and it's worked great. Maddie is all for it. My being in New York opens up a whole new market for us. It's a win-win."

Tyler waited as the girls consulted each other among quiet whispers. When both nodded and smiled, she sensed a new beginning on the horizon for the Falling and Castle families. She slapped her hands on the tops of her legs. "It's settled. We're moving to New York City."

Ethan, Tyler, and the girls picked up their glasses and made their way inside. Tyler gave Alex a grin-filled nod, which Alex returned in kind. They had a mountain of details to work out, but soon, they'd blend their families in every way that mattered.

Ethan appeared the most pleased to see Jesse. "Hey, you." Ethan kissed her on the cheek, which caught everyone's attention, especially Tyler's. The way Jesse accepted the kiss and let it linger told her it wasn't the first one they'd shared. Surprisingly, that idea warmed her heart. He deserved a woman who could make him happy in ways Tyler no longer could. And based on Ethan's blushing smile, Jesse already had.

New beginnings indeed.

"Is Alex's case finally dropped?" he asked.

Jesse cleared her throat. She tried to hide it, but Tyler could tell his public show of affection had made her uncomfortable. "Um…yeah…all dropped…she's a free woman."

While the girls continued playing with Callie, Tyler edged her way next to Jesse and whispered in her ear, "I'm happy for you two. He's a good man."

Jesse's shoulders relaxed as if Tyler had lifted a two-ton weight from them. "Thank you," she whispered back. "I think he's great."

"Then you'll be glad to know that we're all moving to New York. Ethan too."

Jesse blushed, smiling at Ethan. "Really?"

Ethan returned her smile. "Really."

"Smile, everybody!" commanded Alex. "Who's up for cupcakes? It's time to celebrate!"

As the girls drizzled chocolate ganache on top of the molten cupcakes Syd pulled from the oven, Ethan drew Jesse out on the patio, away from the clamor.

"Sorry if I embarrassed you in there," he said, holding her hand loosely. "It just sort of…happened."

"It was a bit of a surprise," Jesse replied with a wry smile. "Not an unwelcome one, though. It felt natural, didn't it?"

He raised her hand to his lips and kissed it lightly. "Yes, it did."

Through the patio door the ringing of clinking glasses sounded and Alex's jubilant voice. "Here's to new beginnings! It's over!"

Ethan picked up the half-filled goblet he'd left on the patio table and sipped from it before handing it to Jesse. "To new beginnings."

With a nod, she took a sip of her own. "To new beginnings." Her expression grew serious. "Made possible in large part by you." She took another sip. "I'm looking forward to them. It's not really over, though, is it?"

He nodded. "If details emerge about Alex's counter-blackmail with Kelly, it could get dicey for both of us."

She smiled. "On the upside, thanks to you, Kelly is looking at spending twenty years as a guest of the state of New York."

"There's one thing I still don't get."

Jesse tilted her head to one side. "What's that?"

"The blackmail photos. Kelly said she brought copies of them with her, but she didn't mention taking them when she left. They weren't listed in the police inventory of her apartment. They could make a lot of trouble, legally and for Tyler and Alex emotionally, if they surface. So, where are they?"

"That's for the police to figure out, though I doubt they'll try, since she's signed a confession."

"You know this is going to bug me until I figure it out," Ethan said.

"Which is why you're such a damn good detective. In the meantime, there are a couple of cupcakes in there with our names on them. Let's go find them."

Bella Books, Inc.

Women. Books. Even Better Together.

P.O. Box 10543
Tallahassee, FL 32302

Phone: 800-729-4992
www.bellabooks.com

CPSIA information can be obtained
at www.ICGtesting.com
Printed in the USA
JSHW052044200722
28306JS00001B/1

9 781642 473599